Baseball and Other Lessons

AUBREY GROSS

TABLE OF CONTENTS

*"Baseball is nothing more than
another classroom in the educational process.
Really, baseball is a metaphor for life."*
Augie Garrido

CHAPTER ONE

MATT ROBERTS' CAREER ENDED with a tweet.

@ESPN: Sources confirm @MattRobertsTX career likely over. 35yo pitcher suffered cracked skull, brain bleed. Surgery successful.

Next came the *Deadspin* article.

ESPN Reporting Matt Roberts, Texas' Ace, Out Forever

Followed by the piece from Bleacher Report.

Texas' Matt Roberts' Career Over, Next Steps for Texas to Fill Gap

Sports Illustrated jumped on it next, followed by the *Sporting News*, *Yahoo! Sports*, *The Dallas Morning News* and *SB Nation*. From there, the barrage was endless as social media took one stupid—and highly inaccurate to his knowledge—tweet as gospel.

Matt's head pounded. He wasn't sure if it was because of his stitched up head or if his blood pressure was getting too high. When he noticed his hands were shaking, he figured it was probably his blood pressure.

He sat back on his brother, Chase's couch, closed his eyes and took a few deep breaths, trying to find some internal peace. Instead, all he could find was that damned tweet. Sighing, he opened his eyes and looked back at his open laptop, giving the offending tweet the evil eye, before picking up his cell phone and dialing his agent.

Darrin answered on the first ring. "Hey, Matt. Don't worry, man, we're on it. I don't know who ESPN's sources are, but they're wrong. We haven't heard anything from the front office other than they want you to have a full recovery and that your health comes first."

Matt sighed and pinched the bridge of his nose. "Dammit, Darrin, where the fuck did this shit come from? I've barely been out of the hospital for a week. Nobody knows the future of my career right now, especially not some lowlife who'll give crap information to ESPN."

"I know. Like I said, we're trying to track down the source. I also have a call in to Reed. Hopefully I'll hear something soon and can get this mess cleared up."

Reed Thornhill was the team's president and general manager, and the person who would ultimately decide Matt's professional fate. He and Reed had a pretty good relationship, and Matt couldn't see him making such a definite statement without having all the facts. And the facts were, Matt couldn't even begin rehab until the stitches were out, and after that he had to be cleared by his neurologist. It could take weeks, if not months.

"Thanks, Darrin."

"No problem, man. So how are you doing?"

Matt blew out a breath. How was he doing? He was going fucking stir crazy. That's how he was doing. "Fucking crazy, D. I'm bored out of my mind."

"You know you could have stayed in Dallas, in the comfort of your own condo and all the take out you desire at your fingertips."

Matt snorted. "I know. Mom was worried sick, and I knew she'd be calling me multiple times a day. I also didn't feel like having the media breathing down my neck."

Darrin changed the subject. "How's the ranch doing?"

Matt, along with Chase, Chase's friend Owen, and Darrin were all owners of a managed game ranch just north of Del Rio, on the Devils River. "You know about as much as I do. Chase and Owen do a great job keeping up with it, and Daniel runs the place flawlessly. I'm hoping to get up there some time soon, just have to have clearance to drive."

"Any word on when that'll be?"

"I have an appointment in San Antonio next Monday. Hopefully he'll give me the go-ahead then."

"Keep me up to date. In the meantime, I've gotta go—lunch with Mercer to discuss the contract extension the Cowboys offered him."

Clint Mercer was the Dallas Cowboys' all-pro tight end, Darrin's client, Matt's friend, and all-around good guy. "Getting ready to milk them dry?"

"As dry as I can." Darrin chuckled. "Anyway. Stay off of Twitter and message boards for a while, and I'll call you as soon as I know something."

"Thanks, D." Matt ended the call and tossed the phone back onto the couch beside him. He rested his head against the plush back and stared up at the ceiling. God, he was bored.

Needing to do something—anything—he texted Chase.

> Matt: I've gotta get out and do something. I'm losing my mind.
>
> Chase: Dude, you're supposed to take it easy.
>
> Matt: I know, but if I take it too easy I'm going to jump off a bridge. I just need to get out.
>
> Chase: Whatever. We were planning on going to April's tonight. I guess you can tag along.
>
> Matt: Great. And thanks.

Jenn McDonnell surreptitiously watched Matt as she and Owen played a game of pool in the corner of their usual group's favorite bar, silently cursing her best friend Chase for letting his older brother tag along.

The guy was a jerk, and she so did not want to be around him.

She hadn't always felt that way. Once upon a time they'd been friends. Well, kind of. They'd once gotten along okay, sort of like siblings but not quite. As kids he'd teased her and made her laugh, and she'd almost enjoyed hanging out with him.

Somewhere along the way, though, that had changed. Their family and friends sometimes pried a little too much, curious as to the sudden shift in emotions. She would just shrug her shoulders and say something flippant, or that maybe it was the fact that since he'd made it to the majors eleven years ago he'd rarely come back home to see his family (and Jenn had it on good authority that Sarah Roberts missed her "baby boy"). Sometimes she'd say it was because he came across as an arrogant dick, like being blessed with a ninety-eight mile per hour fastball and a nasty slider somehow made him better than the mere mortals who wore his jersey and cheered his name.

Somewhere along the way, she'd gotten pretty good at evading the truth.

So she would put up with him—when she had to—because Chase was his brother and one of her best friends. Like a brother, really. And tonight she was putting up with Matt more than she wanted to because she was trying to give Chase and Jo—her other best friend since childhood—some time alone together to try and figure out whatever was going on between the two of them (they were obviously meant for each other, but still hadn't come to terms with that fact).

Speaking of…

From the corner of her eye, she saw Chase lead Jo out onto the dance floor, took note of the way they looked at each other and smiled. It may have been the night before the Fourth of July, but Jenn was willing to bet money that there would be fireworks tonight.

She missed her shot, turning the table over to Owen Daniels. As her other best friend—she really was lucky, wasn't she, to have three best friends?—lined up to take his shot, Jenn sipped from her margarita and tried to watch Matt without anyone noticing.

Even with his current crazy haircut, the man was hot. Her gaze kept wanting to skitter up to the stitches on the shaved side of his head—stitches that had happened after he'd been hit by a line drive and suffered a cracked skull and brain bleeding just a few weeks ago.

Looking at the stitches, though, did funny things to her stomach. She'd never been good with blood or injuries; they always made her feel squeamish and jittery inside. Seeing Matt's head—and remembering the moment the injury had happened since she, Chase, Jo and Owen had been watching the game together—made her uncomfortable.

It made her want to care.

Jenn sipped her margarita and focused her gaze on the row of cue sticks on the opposite wall.

"You can look at them, y'know."

Matt's voice, deep and low, a whisper against her ear, startled her. She jolted. Slushy liquid sloshed in the glass in her hand.

She took a half step to the side, away from him. "Look at what?" she asked, not looking at him.

"The stitches. My head."

She shrugged.

"Unless you're one of those women who gets turned on by pain. That shit's too kinky, even for me."

Jenn closed her eyes. Gritted her teeth. "They make me feel squeamish."

She could feel him beside her, hot and big and the epitome of Alpha Male. If he'd been a character in the Regency romances she loved to read, he most definitely would have been a rake.

And she? She would have been a wallflower. Or a governess.

A woman who most definitely did not garner attention from outrageously attractive males with hazel eyes, a lean body sculpted with muscle and lips that would make most women think about hot kisses and raunchy sex.

Jenn, though? She really just wanted to wipe the smirk from those sinful lips and not be aware of that muscled body.

"Stitches make you squeamish?"

Matt's voice was deep and seductive, like the promise of silk sheets, dark chocolate and a bottle of wine. She steeled herself against it, knowing that he was all too aware of his...potency.

"Yes," she ground out.

He sighed. "You're a strange woman, Jenn McDonnell."

She snorted. Owen lined up to pocket the eight ball. "I'm strange? You're the one walking around with half of your head shaved."

"It's different. I like it."

"Or you just haven't gotten to a stylist yet." She somehow doubted he was a Super Cuts sort of guy.

Owen sank the eight ball and asked, "You up for another game?"

"Nah. I'm gonna go grab another drink and make sure Jo and Chase haven't been arrested for public indecency or anything yet."

Jenn made her way through the bar, set her empty glass on a table holding other discarded drinks, and headed for the ladies' room. She sang along as the DJ switched from Josh Abbott Band's "Oh, Tonight" to "Fuzzy" by The Randy Rogers Band. The song's tale of drunken escapades always made her think of *The Hangover*, which never failed to make her smile.

She finished up in the bathroom and walked out to the main bar area, didn't see Jo and Chase and figured they'd stepped out to the back patio to get some air. She stepped up to the bar, ordered another margarita and walked back to the pool tables.

There were three women surrounding Matt, the same three that had fluttered around him when Jenn and Jo had first arrived. They'd scattered for a while, but apparently had decided that Jenn and Jo weren't competition.

Jenn stayed back, sipped her margarita as the fake redhead with fake boobs leaned into Matt and trailed her fingers down his chest and towards the waistband of his jeans. Owen caught her eye and shook his head as he lined up a shot. Jenn stifled a giggle.

The redhead's fingers trailed lower, dipped inside Matt's jeans. He rolled his eyes before removing her hand. Jenn couldn't hear what he said, but apparently Ms. Wandering Fingers wasn't too happy about it, if the mulish expression on her face was any indication.

Jenn was stifling laughter when someone tapped on her shoulder. She turned around and saw Jo, her cheeks flushed, eyes bright and hair slightly mussed. Jenn raised her eyebrows.

"I, uh, feel a migraine coming on. Chase is going to take me home. I'll see you later."

"Migraine, huh?" Jenn teased.

Jo's blush deepened, but Jenn could tell she was trying

not to smile. "Yeah. A migraine."

Jenn laughed and hugged her best friend. "Well, I hope you find a way to get rid of it."

Jo did laugh then, before turning and walking away. Jenn contemplated the sugar crystals on the rim of her glass as a smile tugged at her lips.

She'd so been right about those fireworks tonight.

Matt watched the exchange between Jo and Jenn, vaguely aware of the three women surrounding him. He'd never been a huge fan of jersey chasers to begin with, but having them surround him in his hometown while he was on the disabled list seemed like a little too much even for him to take right now. Jo shook her head at something Jenn said, and Matt noted the tousled hair, swollen lips and beard burn on her neck.

Looked like little brother was finally going to score.

At least someone was.

Disgusted with his self-pitying thoughts, because, really, he was one of the best pitchers in the league with a healthy bank account, wise investments and women at his beck and call if he wanted them, Matt breathed deeply and tuned back in to the jersey chasers currently trying to score with him.

Yeah, that wasn't happening.

Even if he'd been interested, the doctor had specifi-cally told him no sex. Apparently repetitive motions and strenuous activities could still cause complications with the damned head wound.

Fan-fucking-tastic.

"So, Mattie, how 'bout we go back to my place?" The brunette—Kara or Katie or Karma—asked with a pout as she trailed an index finger over his left bicep. "We could play pitcher and catcher, if you know what I mean."

Jesus. Talk about a bad pickup line. "Thanks but, uh, no thanks."

"Oh, come on, Mattie. It'll be fun. Jeanine could join us if you like." The brunette batted her eyelashes at him. Matt couldn't remember which one Jeanine was, nor did he really care.

"Sorry. But I can't. Doctor's orders." He shrugged, adopted an innocent expression and hoped like hell it worked. Despite not liking jersey chasers, he only got tough on them when he had to.

Kara/Katie/Karma lifted up onto her toes and whispered in his ear, "I'll let you do me any way you want, Mattie. My pussy's dripping wet and aching for that cock of yours."

She nipped his ear lobe before lowering herself to her normal height, bit her lower lip and looked up at him with big blue eyes. Matt sighed. Time to play hardball, apparently.

Normally, he would have someone with him he could pawn the girls off on—whether it be Darrin, a teammate, or a friend who was more than willing to take one for the team. Tonight, though, he had Owen—a guy who would be more likely to crack a joke than show any interest in any of the three women—and Jenn, who he was pretty sure would outright refuse to help him, especially after what had happened the last time she'd assisted in a Jersey Chaser Extraction.

Feeling somewhat hopeful, despite the feeling in his gut, he caught Jenn's gaze, mouthed, "Help me" and hoped like hell she'd put that last Extraction behind her.

CHAPTER TWO

Ten Years Earlier, Last Weekend of Spring Training, San Antonio, TX

JENN WALKED INTO HER hotel room, threw her purse onto the bed and then followed with her body. Looking up at the ceiling, she sighed.

What good was it to be in San Antonio on a perfect spring night with no friends around?

Outside her window, she could hear the faint sounds of voices and traffic, a mariachi band playing somewhere down the street. Even after sitting in the AlamoDome for four hours, cheering on the Wranglers in their next to last spring training game against the Astros, she wasn't tired. Instead, she was keyed up and restless.

She bounced up off the bed and grabbed her purse. Screw it. She was in San Antonio on a Friday night, she was sure as hell going to have a prickly pear margarita and maybe take a stroll along the Riverwalk.

Jenn took the elevator down to the hotel's lobby and made a beeline for the bar, the sound of voices and laughter—along with the scent of Mexican food—luring her.

She stepped inside and made her way to the bar, where she waited for a bartender.

"Hey there, pretty lady. Buy you a drink?"

Jenn rolled her eyes and turned towards the low, masculine voice just behind her right shoulder. "No, thanks, I'm—holy crap, Matt?"

Matt smiled, his hazel eyes teasing, and Jenn swatted him on his arm.

"What are you doing here? Shouldn't you be out celebrating the end of spring training with your groupies?"

He snorted. "We have one game left. Besides, groupies are overrated."

She raised an eyebrow. "So you're just chilling out in a hotel bar?"

Matt shrugged. "It's the team hotel. Figured you would have known that. Is Chase or Mom and Dad with you?"

"Unfortunately, no. Your dad came down with the flu, so your mom's taking care of him, and Chase had some last minute thing come up at work, so it's just me."

Disappointment briefly clouded his expression before the smile once again lifted the corners of his mouth. Despite the fact that Jenn had known Matt practically all her life, and as a kid had occasionally thought of him as a bothersome older brother, she wasn't blind. The man was freaking hot.

Unfortunately, her body was sometimes all too aware of that. Like now. She was warm all over and her skin was kind of tingly, like she'd already had a few of the coveted prickly pear margaritas.

Down, girl.

Matt Roberts, Rookie of the Year runner up, was so not for her.

"You want to join us over at our table? That is, unless you have other plans."

"Sure, just let me order a drink."

"Prickly pear margarita?"

How'd he know that?

As if he read her thoughts, he said, "It's what you've ordered every time you've been here since you've been legal."

True. For the past few years, Jenn, Chase, and Matt had met up in San Antonio a handful of times during the off season, and when Jenn had turned twenty-one just over a year ago she'd started ordering them.

"Fine. You know me better than I thought you did."

He winked at her and signaled for the bartender, who almost ran over to them. Jenn sighed. Apparently being semi-famous had its perks. Matt ordered her drink, along with a bottle of Shiner for himself. They stood in companionable silence for the very short amount of time it took the bartender to bring them their drinks.

Matt handed the bartender a twenty and said, "Keep the change" before grabbing their drinks in one big hand and placing his other on the small of her back. Jenn's skin only tingled more at the slight touch. *What in the world is going on?*

Despite the fact that she and Matt had known each other practically all their lives, he'd never really touched her, unless it was to pull her hair, pinch her or tickle her. There had been a few hugs here and there, a peck on the cheek when she and Chase had graduated from high school, but that was about it.

Maybe he's just being nice.

Or maybe he's already drunk.

But he didn't look drunk. In fact, he appeared to be stone cold sober.

The pressure on her lower back increased as they reached a table in the far corner of the hotel's bar. She could see why he and some of the other players had chosen it—the space was slightly blocked off by potted palm trees that were as tall as she was, offering a modicum of privacy from the rest of the bar.

"Hey, guys, look who I found. My old friend, Jenn."

Jenn raised an eyebrow but didn't contradict him, curious to see what kind of game Matt was playing at tonight. She recognized the men at the table, and tried her best not to act like a baseball groupie despite the fact that her inner fan girl was practically *squeeing* with glee.

The three other men at the table introduced themselves as Matt pulled out a chair for her before sitting down beside her. "It's nice to meet y'all. Great game tonight."

Despite the fact that they'd beat the Astros 11-1, the four men all laughed before the shortstop, Andrew Holt, said in his thick Georgia drawl, "Honey that was a spring training beat down. It was like playing in little league."

She snorted, and the catcher, Miguel Rodrigo, elbowed Andrew in the ribs. "Dude, you're not supposed to talk about it like that; it takes away the magic."

Andrew tipped back his Lone Star and smiled around the long neck of his beer bottle, "Might be rude, but it's true."

Miguel rolled his eyes.

"So, Jenn, how do you and Pooh Bear here know each other?" Rick Graves, one of the bullpen guys, asked.

She glanced at Matt. "Pooh Bear?"

Matt snorted but didn't answer.

"Sure, Pooh Bear. It never fails, wherever we are the women just flock to him. Like Winnie the Pooh to his pot of honey."

Jenn opened her mouth, closed it, opened it again and said, "That might be the worst analogy ever."

"Oh, come on, it's not that bad," Rick said.

She shook her head. "No, it's pretty bad. If you were one of my students I would tell you to try harder and give you a B for effort."

Matt laughed. "I forgot to mention that Jenn's a teacher. Seventh grade, right?"

She nodded, surprised Matt knew what she did, much less which grade she taught.

"School teacher, huh?" Rick's gaze flicked over to Matt. "That's a little far off of your usual type, Pooh Bear."

"Oh, it's not like that. We're just friends. Matt's practically like a big brother to me."

Rick raised an eyebrow and scratched at his beard. "Well, if that's the case, Miss Jenn, why don't you come sit over here by me and I can show you how a real man treats a lady?"

Matt tensed slightly beside her and she briefly wondered why before laughing and saying, "Rick, I'm sorry, but I don't think I'm really you're type."

The young pitcher sighed. "I guess you win some, you lose some."

Jenn rubbed her nose. "Absolutely."

Rick brightened again and asked, "Any chance you have a sister?"

Jenn laughed before taking a sip of her margarita. "I do, but I think she might be a little too young for you."

"How young is too young?" Rick asked.

"Five."

Rick cringed. "Ouch, yeah, way too young."

Why Jenn was throwing off Rick's obvious advances? Even if the guy was a bit of a tool sometimes—Pooh Bear? Really?—women usually flocked to him like chickens on a bunch of June bugs. Whatever, though, he was weirdly glad Jenn wasn't falling for Rick's charm.

Between the fronds of the potted trees that sectioned off their table, he could see a group of women looking around the bar. There were five of them, all dressed in sky high heels and skintight clothes with big hair, pouty lips and breasts that defied gravity. He sighed, recognizing their ring leader, Heather Smith (if that was really her last name), immediately.

Heather had been a thorn in his side ever since he got called up. She showed up to every game, always seemed to know which hotel the team was staying in, and somehow had figured out a few times which room was his.

She was like a dog with a fucking bone, and he was *thisclose* to getting a restraining order. Enough was enough.

He knew the moment she found their partially hidden table, because her eyes lit up with a predatory gleam as she licked her lips before tossing her hair over her shoulder and heading their way. Matt leaned in to the table and quietly warned, "Incoming" before sliding his arm around the back of Jenn's chair.

She stiffened beside him slightly before relaxing again, and an idea quickly formed in his mind. He had only a few seconds to spell it out to Jenn, and he prayed she would go along with it.

He leaned over and whispered in her ear, "There's a group of five jersey chasers heading our way. Their ring-leader—Heather Smith—has been stalking me for a year. Can you follow my lead so that maybe we can get them to go away?"

Jenn hesitated and he asked, "Please? For a friend?"

She turned her head towards him and nodded. "Sure. What's a jersey chaser?"

"You'll figure it out once you see them."

The group of women reached their corner, and Heather propped her hip on the edge of the table in a pose he figured she thought was seductive. To him, it just seemed desperate. Completely clueless, the blonde stalker leaned over and ran an index finger up and down his chest before purring,

"Hey, Matt. Great game tonight."

He swatted her hand away. "I didn't pitch."

She leaned in further, giving him a clear view down her shirt, and most likely giving Rick a clear view up her very short denim skirt if the young man's facial expression indicated what he thought it did.

Matt tightened his arm around Jenn's shoulders, turned his head into her and kissed her neck. "Please, just follow my lead," he whispered so that only she could hear him.

She tilted her head to the side, offering him easier access, and Matt breathed a sigh of relief before saying, "Go away, Heather. I'm with my girlfriend and my friends, and we would like some privacy."

Heather snorted, and her voice was laced with scorn when she said, "Girlfriend? Please, Matt. We all know you can do better than *her*."

Jenn stiffened and he fought the urge to turn around. Instead, he nipped at Jenn's earlobe before placing another kiss on her neck—which was really a nice neck, now that he thought about it. Long and graceful and smooth, with soft skin that was perfect for kissing and touching. Or maybe he just hadn't gotten laid recently enough, because thinking about Jenn's neck was simultaneously weirding him out and turning him on. "I would really appreciate it if you wouldn't insult my girlfriend, who by the way has more intelligence, class and sex appeal in her pinky finger than you do in your entire surgically enhanced body."

Jenn's breath caught and he flicked a gaze up to her face, saw she was trying to keep from laughing, and smiled.

"Oh, please. We all know that boobs win any day of the week."

Matt didn't have to look down to know what Heather was inferring. Jenn had never been well-endowed, but at least what she had was real.

Andrew piped up. "Heather, seriously, you're being a

bitch."

"Just being honest, darlin'," she said, mimicking Andrew's drawl.

Matt rolled his eyes. Turning towards Heather, he idly twirled a lock of Jenn's curly red hair around his finger. "Heather, go away before we call security."

She rolled her eyes and flounced off, taking her entourage with her. They didn't go far, though—just to the bar— where Matt could see her flirting with the bartender and giving the rest of the room a view that stopped just short of her ass cheeks.

Heather glanced back over at their table, her mouth in a full-on pout, and Matt sighed. It was going to be a long night.

After Heather and her merry band of skanks left their table, the conversation dimmed a little bit. The guys weren't quite as boisterous, Matt was broody, and Jenn was decidedly uncomfortable.

She got what Matt had been doing. She understood it and didn't blame him for thinking of it. Hell, if she was being honest with herself she had to admit that on the surface it had been a pretty good spur-of-the-moment plan.

Except for the part where her body forgot that it was Matt—Matt!—kissing her neck and nipping her earlobe.

Yeah, that whole part had pretty much sucked.

Well, not the being turned on part. That part was nice. It was more the fact that she was turned on by *Matt*. In all the years they'd known each other—close to twenty—she'd been mostly immune to his looks and charm.

Probably because he'd never directed that charm at you.

True enough, she conceded.

Logically, she knew Matt was attractive. Okay, the man was hot. No two ways about it. Despite being aware of that fact, though, she'd never really felt a smidgen of attraction towards him. Probably because she remembered him as the boy who yanked her pigtails and once put a frog down the back of her bathing suit.

Asshole.

Never mind the fact that he'd been like ten years old at the time.

It had totally been an asshole move.

Well, okay, so looking back it was actually kind of funny. But at the time she'd been really mad at him.

They were a long ways away from childhood antics, though, and Jenn was brought back to the here and now by the light press of his hand on her shoulder.

Oh, who was she kidding? She'd jumped on the Matt Roberts Is a Hot Piece of Eye Candy train back in high school, before he was a semi-famous pitcher and had filled out a once-lanky body with impressive muscles.

She'd once heard a baseball announcer say that pitchers weren't the most athletic guys on the team. Apparently that announcer had never seen Matt shirtless. Because, whoa.

Feeling heat flame across her cheeks, Jenn picked up her margarita and gulped.

But just because she could concede that Matt was hot with a capital H-A-W-T did not mean she was attracted to him. Not really. Mostly because being attracted to Matt would be kind of weird and awkward since for at least part of her childhood he had been like a big brother to her. At some point—okay, in high school when she'd really started to develop an interest in boys—that had changed. For a few weeks her freshman year, she'd allowed herself to daydream about Matt and him being her first kiss.

Until she'd walked in on him kissing Kirsten Marshall

in his kitchen one afternoon before his parents had gotten home. Kirsten was everything Jenn wasn't—petite and curvy with perfectly straight blonde hair, big blue eyes and bigger boobs. If Kirsten wasn't so freaking sweet—genuinely so—Jenn might have hated her.

Instead, she'd just walked on through the kitchen to the backyard, searching for Chase while wishing she looked like Kirsten rather than, well, herself. Jenn couldn't compete with a girl like that, not with her wildly curly red hair, green eyes and flat chest, not to mention the fact that she was taller than some of the boys in her class, and was still a year away from getting her braces removed.

Knowing all of that, though, hadn't made Matt any less attractive—it had just made him impossible to attain.

Jenn sighed and sipped at the remnants of her margarita. Matt's arm was still curved around the back of her chair, and one of his fingers was tracing a pattern on her arm just where skin met sleeve. She suppressed a shiver and pulled her phone out of her purse to check the time and saw she had a text message from Chase.

> Chase: Having fun? Sorry I couldn't make it. This job's going to drive me to drinking.
>
> Jenn: Yeah. It was a great game. Ran into Matt in the hotel bar. Don't drink too much—or by yourself!
>
> Chase: I won't. You still with him?

Jenn debated how much to disclose.

> Jenn: Yes. Him and a few of the guys from the team. They're trying to avoid some skank named Heather.

Chase didn't need to know about her and Matt's method of avoidance, because Jenn had a feeling if Chase did find out he would lay into his big brother.

> Chase: Heather's worse than a skank.

She's been stalking him for a year or so.
Don't get yourself pulled into that one—
that chick does not play around.

Jenn: I'm not. Matt managed to shoo her
off.

Chase: Good. Have fun. Don't drink too
much—those guys can party hard. See
you tomorrow?

Jenn: Yup. I'll bring liquor.

Jenn stuffed her phone back in her purse, yawned and said, "Sorry, guys, but it's been a long day and I'm exhausted. I think I'm going to head on up to my room and get some sleep."

"Awww, come on, Miss Jenn. You can hang out with us a little longer." Rick winked at her.

Jenn smiled. "Sorry, sweetie, but I really am tired, and I have to drive up to Austin tomorrow."

Rick grumbled in protest, but Andrew and Miguel smiled and tipped their heads towards her.

"It was great meeting y'all, though." She flicked a glance towards Heather and the other women at the bar. "Hopefully you'll get to enjoy the rest of your evening in peace."

Rick snorted. "Oh, once Pooh Bear leaves all of their interest in us will be long gone."

Matt sighed. "Only because you're still too young to know how to please a lady."

Jenn's stomach dipped at the thought of Matt knowing how to please a lady. She licked her lips and said, "Except I'm pretty sure 'lady' is not the correct term for Heather."

"Right you are," Matt said as he stood. "Let me walk you up to your room."

Nerves suddenly danced in her belly. This was not typical Matt behavior—at least not in her world. "You don't have to do that, Matt. Stay here with your friends."

He pinned her with that hazel gaze, and the nerves in her belly blossomed from caterpillars into butterflies. "I want to make sure Heather doesn't harass you."

"I can take care of myself, Matt." She stood and put her purse on her shoulder.

"I'm sure you can. But as your friend I want to make sure she doesn't follow you up and give you a hard time. Besides, if I let that happen, Chase would kill me."

His words calmed the butterflies slightly. This was Matt, simply being a friend. Nothing more. Nothing less.

"Fine," she conceded before turning to the other three men and smiling. "'Night, guys. It was great meeting y'all."

CHAPTER THREE

Present Day, Del Rio, Texas

JENN GLARED AT MATT from across the bar and shook her head.

No. Absolutely not. She was not going to come to his rescue again.

Not after what had happened the last (and only) time.

He mouthed, "help me" again from across the pool table and Jenn rolled her eyes before spinning on her heel and walking back out into the main bar area. She found an empty table in a corner, sat down and gazed at her margarita glass.

She pulled her phone out of her pocket, checked her email and Facebook. She supposed she could just go home, except she wasn't sure if Owen had driven or ridden with Chase, whereas Matt. She couldn't just leave them here.

No matter how tempting it was to leave Matt alone with the jersey chasers.

Instead of getting up and going out to her car, though, she opened her Pinterest app and clicked on "humor." Sure, she had a wedding board just like every other single woman between the ages of 18 and 58, but she had a definite soft spot for funny, snarky ecards and internet memes.

And tonight, she needed snarky.

She was giggling over a picture of a lizard wearing Barbie boots when she felt someone staring at her. Jenn looked up and squinted, her eyes adjusting from the bright screen of her phone to the dim lights of the bar.

Matt had somehow managed to extricate himself from the clutches of the Three Whores of the Apocalypse, and was now standing on the other side of her table, muscular arms crossed over his chest and glaring at her. She returned her attention to Pinterest—lizards wearing Barbie boots were *much* better than an apparently pissed off Matt Roberts.

Instead of taking the hint and going away, he sat in the chair next to her, scooted a little too close for her peace of mind, and plucked the phone out of her hands.

"Hey!"

"What the hell are you doing sitting in a corner of a bar all by yourself and looking at," he looked down at the screen of her phone, "is that a lizard wearing Barbie boots?"

"Yes. Now give me back my phone." She reached for it, and he switched it to his other hand and held it away from the other side of his body.

"You want it? Come and get it."

No way was she crawling over him just to get her stupid phone. Hell, she'd buy another one if she had to, if that meant not touching him.

She sat back in her chair. "No. How about you act like a mature adult and just give it back to me?"

"What would be the fun in that?"

She rolled her eyes and glanced away from him. "So what happened to the Skank Brigade?"

"I told them I needed to go to the men's room and that I would be right back."

She turned back towards him and hit him on his shoulder. "You left them there with Owen?!"

Matt smiled, and damn her traitorous body, that smile did funny things to her insides. "Somehow I doubt Owen needs any help fending off those three."

"They're going to come looking for you, y'know."

"I know, that's why we need to get out of here. I'm assuming Jo and Chase left a while ago, correct?"

Jenn nodded. "How'd you know that?"

"I saw her talking to you. Considering she looked like a woman who'd just had the best orgasm of her life, and then she left, it wasn't hard to put two and two together, even with the recent brain injury."

"And what would you know what a woman looks like after having the best orgasm of her life?" Jenn retorted.

Matt leaned closer so that Jenn could feel his breath on her neck, and his voice was like a rough caress over her nerve endings when he said, "Oh, I think I know a thing or two."

Jenn suppressed a shiver, stared straight ahead and worked to calm her beating heart and rapid breaths.

Damn him.

Matt watched, kind of fascinated, as Jenn tried to control her body's reaction to him. He'd felt the little shiver that had passed through her body, noted the way her breath had hitched, and could barely make out her pulse rapidly beating at her neck.

It wasn't fair to mess with her, and he had no intention of hurting her, but dammit if she wasn't a little bit like a hedgehog—all sharp points on the outside, but kind of cute and soft underneath.

At the memory of how soft Jenn could be, his dick

hardened in response.

Shit. That was inconvenient.

Not only could he not do anything about it—at least not with a partner—but he highly doubted that Jenn would be willing to go there even if he could. Logically, he knew sex with Jenn was filed under Very Bad Ideas. Illogically, his body responded to her like a thirteen-year-old looking at his first *Playboy*.

And wasn't that just the hell of it? She wasn't even really his type. His usual flavor of blonde hair, blue eyes and big boobs was a bit clichéd, just as his tendency towards short relationships with women who's IQs weren't on the high side was his way of avoiding any sort of real emotional intimacy. He liked women. He liked sex. And maybe someday—when he could no longer step out onto that mound every five days—he would get serious about meeting The One and settle down.

Until then, he was fine with the status quo.

Which made his attraction to Jenn damned unfortunate and just a little surprising. Sure, at six-four he tended to gravitate towards taller women, and Jenn was definitely that, since the top of her head almost came to his chin. But where he usually preferred blonde hair and well-defined curves, Jenn was all crazy auburn curls and subtle curves. Not to mention the fact that her IQ was most definitely not on the lower side of the scale.

Realizing he'd been staring at her for a while, he smiled and handed her back her phone. "How long ago did they leave?"

Jenn blinked, her green eyes staring back at him, and asked, "Did who leave?"

Yeah, she felt whatever this was, too.

"Jo and Chase? How long ago did they leave?"

She checked the time on her phone. "About thirty minutes ago maybe? Why?"

"I'm ready to get out of here, and you look like you are, too. But I don't want to go back to Chase's place just yet—I have no desire to walk in on my little brother getting it on."

"I did not need that mental image."

"I don't need the actual image."

She sighed. "So then what are you proposing, Matt? I'm sure as hell not letting you walk me to my door again."

"I wasn't offering."

Her eyes flashed with irritation and something else that he couldn't quite name, and he bit back a smile as she said, "Good. Because my answer's no."

"Jesus you're prickly."

"What can I say? You bring out the best in me."

"Oh, I remember."

Even in the dim lights of the bar he could see her blush.

"You're such an ass."

He shrugged, and out of the corner of his eye happened to see the three jersey chasers from earlier making their way towards the dark corner he and Jenn currently occupied. He grabbed Jenn's hand and pulled her out of her seat. "Come on, let's get out of here."

She dug in her heels and pulled back. He wasn't surprised by her action, but he was surprised at her strength. "You can't just drag me around, Matt."

He turned towards her and leaned close, his mouth millimeters from her ear, and said, "Those three jersey chasers are about four feet away from us. I have no desire to cause a scene, and frankly I'm too tired and my head hurts too much to deal with them right now."

"Fine," she grumbled as she walked out with him. She led him to a blue Ford Edge—not the kind of car he'd pictured a single woman in her early thirties driving—the lights flashing as she pressed a button on the key fob in her hand.

They climbed in, and Matt looked back to the entrance of the bar. He breathed a sigh of relief. They hadn't followed him.

Jenn started the small SUV before asking, "Do you know if Owen drove himself, or if he needs a DD?"

"I'm pretty sure he drove himself—he got here after Chase and I did—and he's only had a couple of beers so he should be fine."

Jenn nodded and backed out of the parking space. "So you don't want to go back to Chase's just yet. You're sure as hell not going back to my place. And I don't think we can spend more than ten minutes alone in this car without me wanting to kill you. So what did you have in mind?"

He bit back the response that came to mind first—she would probably kick him out if he didn't—and said instead, "How about Whataburger? I could go for some taquitos right about now."

Without a word, she turned on to Veteran's Boulevard and headed the few short blocks to Whataburger. Silence stretched between them, taut and awkward. Usually, she had no shortage of words and things to say.

So sue her, she liked to talk.

For whatever reason, though, words were totally failing her right now.

Out of the corner of her eye she could see Matt, the glow of passing streetlights accenting his high cheekbones, full lips and the nose that was slightly crooked after having been broken in junior high. His hazel eyes that were usually so full of mischief were currently guarded.

She kind of hated that she'd put that look in them.

Mentally, Jenn shook herself.

This was Matt. Notorious woman-chaser, confirmed bachelor and experienced one-night-stander. What did she care if he was suddenly putting his guard up and acting like someone with, oh, a conscience?

With a sigh, she turned into the Whataburger parking lot.

"Well that was a heavy sigh. I take it you don't like taquitos?"

Jenn snorted as she put the car into PARK. "I love taquitos. I was just thinking, that's all."

They got out of the car and Jenn slammed her door closed before taking off for the entrance. When she realized Matt wasn't behind her, she turned around and asked, "What, Matt? Did you suddenly change your mind and decide you didn't want the thing not minutes before you thought you *had* to have?"

For a brief second, his face clouded with an emotion she was quite frankly scared to analyze.

Hey, at least she was willing to admit it to herself.

And then the emotion was gone, replaced with the same determined expression he usually reserved for the mound.

"Jenn—"

She held up a hand. "Stop, Matt. Before you say something we're both going to regret. I've already said more than I should have. So just drop it, okay?"

He looked like he wanted to argue, so she turned around and resumed walking. She heard his heavy sigh behind her—could almost feel it, even though they were at least fifteen feet away from each other—and then his heavy footsteps, along with grumbling that sounded a lot like, "Baseball isn't the only cruel mistress."

She yanked open the door. *Asshole*.

Matt watched Jenn from across the table as they waited on their order. She was sipping her Diet Coke and looking out the window with a bored expression on her face. Her bouncing knee was the only thing that really tipped him off that she wasn't as unaffected as she was pretending to be.

That, and he could practically feel the tension radiating in waves across the table.

He decided to let her stew and looked around the restaurant instead. Luckily the place was pretty empty— the only other occupants were a teenage couple in a back corner, and they were more interested in eating each other's tongues than the hamburgers in front of them—which helped him relax a little.

He loved his job. Loved baseball. He usually loved meeting fans and signing autographs, especially if those fans were kids. Ever since the accident, though, he'd found himself wanting privacy in a way he never had.

He guessed having a near-death experience would do that to a person.

Matt pulled his phone from his back pocket and pretended to look at the screen while he really took the opportunity to watch Jenn.

Something about her got under his skin. Sometimes she pissed him off. Others she confused him. When she wasn't doing either of those she was making him laugh.

And all of those times he wanted her.

He couldn't wrap his head around it, either. He'd been with some gorgeous women; models, actresses, a former beauty queen. He'd been pursued by no shortage of jersey chasers over the past ten years, most of whom looked (and acted) like they belonged on the set of a porno rather than hanging out at the ballpark.

Matt knew he was attractive in a logical, simple aesthetics sort of way, just like he knew that his fame, athleticism and money were attractive in a different sort of way. If he wanted sex, he could find it. If he needed a date for some swanky fundraiser, he could find one. His contact list wasn't exactly on the small side.

So why Jenn?

He knew himself well enough to realize that part of it was probably the challenge—as a competitive guy, he hated to lose, and she'd definitely thrown down the gauntlet more than once.

It was more than that, though. No, she wasn't his usual type, but she also didn't treat him like his usual type did.

She treated him like a human being.

She wasn't afraid to get snippy with him, or insult him or let him know just what she thought of him. She never had been, and quite frankly, it was refreshing.

An exacerbated sigh met his ears. Jenn was glaring at him.

"What'd I do now?"

"You were staring at me with this faraway look in your eyes."

He shrugged.

"You're not still having concussion symptoms, are you?"

Not at the moment. "No. I was just thinking."

"Don't hurt yourself."

"Original."

"Fuck off, Matt."

"Such a dirty mouth Ms. McDonnell. Do you teach English with that thing?"

She balled a white napkin up in her fist. "You want dirty, I'll show you dirty."

"Oh, I think I have a pretty good idea of how dirty you can get, Jenn." He winked at her, just to piss her off more.

Her skin flushed red from her chest to the tips of her ears, just like he knew she would.

She threw the balled up napkin at him. He was nice and didn't duck out of the way, let it bounce off his nose instead. Really, it was the least he could do, all things considered.

CHAPTER FOUR

"WHY HAVEN'T YOU COME to see me more, young man?"

Matt bent down and hugged his mom. "Sorry, Mama. I still can't drive and haven't wanted to bother Chase too much."

"Bullshit," Chase coughed into his hand.

Sarah swatted Chase before poking Matt in the chest. "You know good and well that Dad or I would gladly come over here, or pick you up if you needed us to." She placed her hands on her ample hips. "So what's going on?"

Matt shrugged and enveloped his dad—Bo—in a hug while trying to formulate a believable answer for his mom.

"It's good to see you, son."

"Good to see you, too, Dad."

The four of them moved from the front entry of Chase's house to the kitchen, where Chase had been in the middle of preparing hamburger patties for the day's Fourth of July festivities. Comfortable in his brother's kitchen, Matt went to the fridge and retrieved a beer for his dad and a bottle of water for his mom.

Sarah leaned against the kitchen island and pinned Matt with her best Mom Glare. "Now why have you been hiding from us?"

How had he forgotten how tough his mom was? "I haven't been hiding, Mom. I've just been relaxing, letting my body heal."

Chase snorted and continued to form hamburger patties.

"I don't need comments from the peanut gallery."

"I wasn't commenting. The inside of my nose itched."

"Whatever. So when is Jo supposed to be back here?"

Chase glared at Matt. Matt fought the urge to let a grin split over his face. Sure enough, when he'd gotten home last night Jo had been there, and hadn't left until about an hour and a half ago. He almost felt sorry for her, knowing she was doing the walk of shame into her grandmother's house, but after hearing what he'd heard at all hours of the night he was having trouble feeling much sympathy.

There were some things you simply did not want to hear your little brother doing. Even when said little brother was over thirty.

"Jo? Back here? What aren't you telling me, Chase Roberts?"

As expected, Sarah had taken the bait hook, line and sinker.

Chase glared at Matt again. Matt somehow managed to not laugh at the faint redness that tinged his brother's face.

It really was too much fun baiting Chase.

"Uh, she came over for a while and had to go check on her grandma, said she'd be back. Did you know that Nellie had a hip replaced a couple of months ago? She's apparently healing well."

Their dad shook his head and chuckled. "Chase, you're a shitty liar."

"In all fairness, Dad, I'm not lying."

"No, just withholding the truth—same difference."

"So when exactly was Jo here?" Sarah asked.

Matt chuckled.

"Fuck you," Chase said and kicked Matt under the island.

"Language!" Sarah admonished.

Matt laughed.

"I don't know why you think this is so funny."

Matt shrugged. "It's nice to see you on the hot seat. Besides, I figure if Mom and Dad know about you and Jo, they won't let you do something stupid to screw it up again."

"I wasn't the one who screwed up, douche canoe."

Of course, Matt kind of knew that; why he was poking this particular hornet's nest, he didn't know. "Are you sure? Because we men are usually the ones to mess up."

Bo snorted. "Matt, you might want to drop it. Don't upset your mama."

Sarah shook her head. "Oh, he's not upsetting me, honey. I trusted you back then and I trust you now. I think poor Jo was the real victim."

"What about me? I'm the one she stopped talking to."

Matt's gaze ping-ponged from Bo to Sarah to Chase. Now this was interesting. Much better than inaccurate tweets about the future of his career.

"Oh, honey, I know you got hurt in that whole mess, too, but Jo lost so much. Her parents. Us. You. All she had were Jenn and her grandma."

"I know, Mom. Jo wasn't the only one who got hurt, though."

Sarah walked around the island and looped an arm around Chase's waist. "Oh, honey. I know that. Try to forgive her, though—for your sake and for hers. She was just a girl, and what her mama did, the way that woman behaved, it wasn't right."

Matt wanted to ask questions. He knew that Jo's mom had been—to be nice—a bit promiscuous. If he were being honest and blunt, from what he'd heard and seen, Chandra Sommers could have given some of the worst jersey chasers a run for their money when it came to slutty behavior. Instead, he stayed quiet, interested in what wasn't being said rather than what was. Had Chandra gone after Chase? Or even weirder, his dad?

"Son, you've been in love with that girl since you were in elementary school, and she's loved you just as long. Don't let her slip away again—you might not get another chance."

Chase shook his head and placed the last hamburger patty on the cookie sheet with the others, and moved to the sink. "I'm not in love with her, Dad. We're friends, still trying to feel each other out."

Matt tried not to laugh—he really did—but just couldn't hold it in. Chase's glare had him laughing even harder. "Sorry, it's just that with the way the two of you look at each other, there's no feeling out involved whatsoever, more like everyone around you is waiting to see how long it'll take for the room to catch on fire."

Chase's shoulders were tense as he washed his hands—a little longer than necessary, Matt thought—and said, "Just stay out of it, Matt."

Their parents were watching their byplay curiously, which made Matt want to laugh again. "I am staying out of it. I just happen to think that you and Jo are good for each other. I don't know all of Jo's story—just what I've managed to pick up here and there—but both of you obviously have trust issues that you need to work out. What I do know is that you make each other smile, and that last night was the happiest I've seen you in a while."

Chase had turned off the water and was in the process of drying off his hands. "What do you know, Matt? You've barely been around for the past ten years."

Matt shrugged. "What I know is that baseball and

life are both games of failure, and it isn't about the failure itself, but how you respond to the failure. So you both screwed up and failed once. You have a second chance. How are you going to respond?"

Chase threw the towel onto the island. "See what I've been dealing with? Baseball Yoda!"

Matt smiled and turned towards the living room. "Speaking of baseball, I do believe there's a game coming on."

As he walked into the living room his smile fell. As much fun as it was to dish out advice to Chase, his little brother wasn't the only one who'd screwed up and failed once upon a time. And just like Chase, he was being given the opportunity to respond to that failure. The problem was, Jenn didn't seem to be remotely interested in letting him atone for his mistakes.

It's not like you've tried all that hard, either. He turned on the game, hoping to shut his conscience up.

Jenn stood on Chase's front porch, her hand hovering just above the doorknob, ready to turn it and walk inside.

Except she couldn't.

Her hand just stayed there, an inch away from the knob. It wouldn't move. Refused, really.

She looked at that hand. Such an ordinary hand. It did things for her all the time. Dialed her phone. Held a knitting needle. Petted her cat. Wrote on the dry erase board in her classroom.

So why couldn't it open a freaking door?

She shook her head. Looked at her hand. Willed it to just turn. the. damned. knob.

Ugh! What the hell was wrong with her?

She could hear voices from inside. Bo and Sarah.

Chase. Matt.

Freaking Matt.

Why was she so freaked out about seeing him, anyway? It wasn't like they hadn't seen each other last night. Hell, they'd spent time *alone* with each other last night. Well, alone in a Whataburger. Whatever. There hadn't been the buffer of Chase, Jo or Owen, or even the distraction of jersey chasers.

It had been weird.

Unsettling.

Somehow, over the past ten years, Matt had grown up a little bit. He'd once been a brash, cocky young pitcher experiencing the kind of success most little boys only dream about. Last night, he'd been a quiet, sort of funny, surprisingly introspective man who seemed a little tired.

He was still a jerk, though.

"Does the door knob have teeth or something?"

Jenn jumped at the sound of Owen's voice, her hand slamming up against her chest.

Hey, her hand finally moved!

"Jesus, Owen, you scared me."

"Sorry. The way you were just standing there, I was wondering if I'd somehow fallen into that scene from Labyrinth."

Jenn fought to get her racing heart under control. "Which scene?"

Owen raised a red eyebrow. "Wow. You must be really out of it today. The scene where she's having to choose which door to open?"

Considering she'd seen Labyrinth, oh, sixty someodd times, the fact that she hadn't immediately picked up on Owen's reference was worrisome to say the least.

Freaking Matt.

"None shall pass," she murmured. That was somehow weirdly appropriate. Or at least it felt weirdly appropriate.

"Well then, may I have your permission, my lady?" Owen bowed, making Jenn laugh.

She gestured towards the door. "By all means."

Owen stepped up onto the wide front porch and stood beside her. "So this door isn't going to bite me or grab me and take me into a crazy world full of goblins and puppets?"

"Goblins, maybe. I don't know about the puppets."

Owen nodded. "Right."

He wrapped his hand around the knob, but paused before turning it. "Are you sure you're okay?"

Jenn smiled. Owen really was a great friend. The best. "I'm fine. Just a little tired."

"Matt keep you up late last night?"

Something that sounded like a fork caught in a garbage disposal rumbled out of Jenn's throat. Owen slapped her on the back a few times, only making it worse.

Oh, God. She couldn't breathe.

She was going to die on Chase's front porch with Owen thinking God knew what.

"Holy shit, Jenn. Did you and Matt…?" Owen asked, his voice a low whisper.

Jenn shook her head, breathed through her nose. Jesus, she needed to calm the fuck down.

Stat.

Otherwise people were going to get the wrong idea about her and Matt.

Or maybe it was the right idea. Hell, she didn't even know anymore.

Owen rubbed her back as she fought to get her breathing under control. "Care to tell me what that was all about?"

Jenn groaned and rested her head on his shoulder. "Sorry. I think a bug flew down my throat."

"Uh huh."

She squeezed her eyes shut and swallowed. *Pull yourself together, woman.*

"I'm fine, really."

"No, you're not."

She sighed. "You're right. I'm really not, but I kind of have to be, or at least I have to try to act like everything's okay and it's totally not okay."

"Am I going to have to drag it out of you?"

Jenn stepped back and tightened her ponytail. "Yes and no."

Owen raised his eyebrows and crossed his arms over his chest, leveling her with that look of his that made her want to confess all of her crazy thoughts and secrets. He really did know her too well. Better than Chase in some ways.

She drew in a deep breath. "I'll be fine, Owen. You know Matt and I don't get along."

"I've always wondered why that was."

She lifted one shoulder in a gesture she hoped came across as casual. Knowing her luck she probably just looked like she had a twitch. "We just don't. Never really have."

"That's not the way I understand it. From what I've heard you were pretty indifferent towards each other growing up, and then one day you suddenly hated each other."

That was so not the truth. It was just easier to let everyone believe that. "Owen, it's not a big deal. Just let it go, okay?"

He looked her over. Shook his head. Sighed. "I can't believe we're even having this conversation. I feel like a fucking girl."

She snorted. "Don't worry. Your secret's safe with me."

As she finally grabbed the door knob and twisted it, Owen dropped his voice to just above a whisper and asked,

"You know your secret's safe with me, too, right?"

The door swung open and she stepped inside. Her gaze immediately went to Matt—damn it—and she flushed from head to toe when he turned his head away from the game on TV and stared back at her, heat and wariness mingling in his hazel eyes. She nodded her head. Managed to look away from all that masculine temptation and step all the way into the foyer.

Beside her, Owen whistled low, chuckled and whispered in her ear, "So how long have you two been sleeping together?"

She elbowed him in the stomach and hightailed it towards the kitchen.

CHAPTER FIVE

MATT RESISTED THE URGE to follow Jenn into the kitchen, and instead stayed where he was in the living room, standing beside the couch and pretending to watch the Nationals beat up on the Cubs. The Wranglers' game was due to start in about thirty minutes.

He was trying not to think about the fact that today would have been his day to start.

Instead of standing in his brother's living room, he should have been standing on the mound, tossing warmup pitches to Miguel, who was back with the Wranglers this season after having been traded to Detroit five years ago. Miguel had made it to the bigs a year before Matt, and for the first five years of Matt's career he had been the starting catcher. When the team had brought Miguel back this year, Matt hadn't hesitated to ask for Miguel as his primary catcher. It was like no time at all had passed, and the two had picked up where they'd left off. There was a lot to be said about having a good relationship with your catcher, and Matt and Miguel's chemistry had led to Matt teasing with a handful of no hitters this season, not to mention the perfect game he'd been throwing before he took a line drive to the head.

Stupid fucking line drive.

He was pulled out of his self-indulgent pity party by Owen stepping next to him. The other man crossed his arms over his chest, pinned his gaze on the television and quietly said, "I know you're not the player the public seems to think you are, and that you're deep down a pretty decent guy, but don't fuck with Jenn."

Matt turned his head and looked at Owen. "I'm not."

Owen met Matt's gaze. "I'm not saying you are, but I'm telling you not to. Jenn's like a sister to me, and she comes across like she's tough as nails, but she's not."

"I think she's tougher than you're giving her credit for." Matt wasn't sure how he knew that, but he did. While he knew just how soft Jenn could be—dammit—he also knew that she was strong and had rock solid core beliefs.

He also suspected what had happened between them ten years ago had been a complete aberration on her part.

Some people just weren't built for casual, and he'd bet his entire savings account that Jenn was one of those people.

Ten Years Ago, San Antonio, Texas

This wasn't a casual thing.

Matt wasn't sure what it was, but he did know it wasn't casual.

It was hard to be casual with someone you'd known for almost twenty years, who'd known you long before you became the guy everyone thought they knew.

He shook his head. Hell, that barely made sense to him, and he was the one who'd thought it.

They'd come back up to Jenn's hotel room--he glanced at the alarm clock on the night stand—God, three hours ago. Three hours of talking and laughing. Curfew had been an hour ago, and he'd completely missed it.

Hopefully no one had figured out he wasn't where he was supposed to be.

Not that he was doing anything wrong. He was just spending some time with an old friend. An old friend who until three hours ago had been someone he could barely call a friend. She'd been more than an acquaintance, obviously, but they'd never really been *friends*. While he'd known surface things about her—like her job, that she had a great sense of humor and that she wasn't partial to having frogs shoved down her bathing suit—he hadn't ever really bothered to scratch below the surface. She'd always been his little brother's best friend, and that had been more than enough to keep him at arm's length.

Somewhere along the way, though, Jenn had grown up and was no longer that gangly little girl he remembered teasing.

Finding an unexpected camaraderie, however, did not explain the pressure in his chest or the erection he'd been sporting for the past three hours. He kept reminding himself that this was Jenn—his little brother's best friend and not a woman he particularly wanted to screw over. Screw, yes. Screw over? Nope.

Determined to ignore the urge to stay all night in this hotel room with her (preferably naked), Matt stood up and yawned. "I need to get back to my room. Curfew's come and went already."

He didn't miss how her eyes traveled up and down the length of his body as he stretched, or how her gaze caught just below his waist and held a few beats longer than neces-sary before her cheeks turned pink and she glanced away.

He'd never expected leaving this room to be so damned hard.

She stood, too, and they awkwardly stared at each

other. Where was this awkwardness coming from? He was never awkward with women.

Disgusted with himself, Matt stepped towards Jenn. "It was great seeing you. I had fun tonight."

Jenn smiled. "I did, too. Shockingly."

He laughed. Awkwardly. "Well, good night."

"Good night, Matt."

He didn't move. She didn't move. Why was this so weird and awkward? Any other woman he would hug her, or kiss her good night, or bend her over the bed.

He wanted to do all of that with Jenn, he just wasn't sure if he should.

Jenn shook her head and sighed. "This is awkward. Why is this so awkward? We've known each other forever, so why the awkward all of a sudden?"

He was so glad he wasn't the only one feeling all the awkward. Instead of saying that, though, he just shrugged and said, "I don't know."

He did know. She knew. They both knew the other knew, considering the tension was so thick you could cut it with a rusted butter knife.

And yet they stood there, staring at each other like they didn't know where all the awkward was coming from or what they wanted to do about all the awkward.

Determined to shut off his brain and not think about what he was doing—or what this awkward thing was between them—he stepped forward and pulled her into a hug. Her body was warm and almost vibrating with all the… awkward…floating in the air between them and fuck it, he was going to kiss her because he couldn't *not* kiss her.

He pressed his lips against hers and she froze.

He froze.

Like ice sculptures in the Arctic, they froze.

Well that's really awkward.

He pulled away slightly, his thoughts a muddled

jumble in his head thanks to beer, the couple of miniature bottles of tequila he'd had earlier, and Jenn. She drew in a shaky breath and then nervously wet her lips with her tongue.

It was like the sun came out, melting away all the ice. Their gazes met and held, and then he was moving and she was moving, their mouths colliding almost violently. Without his usual finesse, he claimed her mouth with his own, a primal need pulsing through his body, demanding that he claim this woman *now*.

She moaned, her hands tugging and pulling his hair. Her body squirmed against his, and he backed her up two steps until her back hit the wall. She wrapped her legs around his waist—who knew Jenn was so flexible?—and he could feel her wet heat through their clothes.

He was harder than he could ever remember being in his life, and all that mattered was getting inside of her. Right. Fucking. Now.

Matt grabbed the hem of Jenn's shirt and quickly pulled it off her body and over her head, threw it somewhere behind him. Her hands were under his shirt, frantically working it up his torso. He grabbed the back of it, drew it off and threw it in the general direction of hers.

She ground against him, and he ground right back. She gasped. He undid the front clasp of her bra with one hand, pushed the cups aside and captured a nipple with his mouth. Her breasts were tiny and perfect, her nipples light pink. He nipped at her breasts, the swell of each and the nipples, making Jenn cry out and moan in that slightly husky voice of hers.

"I have to have you. Now."

She moaned in response and pressed her pelvis against his.

Matt reached down and unbuttoned her pants, slid the zipper down before pushing the denim to her ankles, taking her panties with them. She kicked them off and stood before him, naked and ready.

He'd never seen anything more beautiful in his life.

Her skin was flushed, her fair coloring and freckles like peaches and cream.

He had to taste.

He dropped to his knees, pushed her legs wide open and buried his face between her legs. Jenn automatically tilted her hips for a better angle, and he lifted one of her legs, bracing it on one of his shoulders before spearing her with his tongue. Her hips rolled as he tasted her, her movements and breathy moans picking up their pace.

He found her center with one finger, working her with it and his tongue. She clenched around him and her breath caught as her entire body tightened and then relaxed. He slowed his movements, lapping at her until the last of the tremors had passed through her body.

Matt looked up at Jenn. A secretive smile played with her lips, and she pulled him back up to his feet before kissing him. He knew she would be able to taste herself on his lips and tongue, and the thought had his dick twitching behind his zipper.

Speaking of…he quickly divested himself of his jeans, threw them off to the side and walked Jenn back to the bed. They tumbled onto the sheets together, laughing with the ease of two people who have known each other for forever and who suddenly no longer felt awkward with one another. He moved to hover over her, but before he could roll her underneath him, Jenn pushed up and managed to maneuver him onto his back.

Okay, so he hadn't exactly fought her.

She flashed that secret smile again and kissed him. His hands gripped her hips, and she slid down until he was pressing up and in to her wet heat.

He gripped her hips harder, and held her in place.

"Condom," he gasped out.

He never forgot protection. Ever.

"I'm on the pill."

"I'm clean." He felt like that was something he needed to tell her, something she would find important.

She sent him another one of those secret smiles and said, "Good" before sliding all the way home.

And just liked that, he was wrecked.

Present Day, Del Rio, Texas

Jenn had to escape.

She'd thought she could do this—sit here on the Fourth of July at Chase's house and hang out with Matt and Bo and Sarah. But she couldn't.

It was just all so awkward.

"I'm gonna go grab a drink. Anyone need anything?"

Owen asked for another beer, so Jenn retreated inside to the less awkward environment of Chase's kitchen.

Only to stumble upon Chase and Jo making out next to the island.

Awkward.

Her two best friends jumped apart from each other, Jo blushing mightily, and Jenn smiled. She couldn't help it— Jo and Chase were meant for each other.

"Well then," she said, teasingly.

"Looks like we've been found out," Chase said to Jo.

Jenn's laugh filled the kitchen. "I knew it!"

"Knew what?" Jo asked.

"That y'all had hooked up last night! Headache my right pinky toe." Yeah, she'd totally been right about those fireworks last night.

"Um…"

Jenn walked over and hugged them both. "I'm so happy for you guys." And she really and truly was. If any two people in this world deserved happiness—especially happiness with each other—it was Jo and Chase.

"Thanks," Jo mumbled.

Jenn pulled away, almost bouncing on her toes. "I love you guys, and I'm so glad y'all finally admitted you love each other."

Jo looked anywhere but at Chase and Jenn. The floor. The ceiling. Chase's dog Winchester's dog crate. Chase cleared his throat, and Jenn could feel the awkwardness in the room. She was really getting tired of feeling so freaking awkward today. "Oh hell. I just stuck my big foot in my big mouth, didn't I?"

Jo opened her mouth to respond, but before she could say whatever she'd been about to say Chase said, "It's okay, Jenn. No harm, no foul."

No harm, no foul? Judging by the look on Jo's face, Jenn was so going to have to have a talk with Chase about appropriate responses when one's caught making out with one's…what exactly were Jo and Chase?

Jenn could feel herself blushing anyway. "Sorry, guys. Didn't mean to embarrass you. So. Um. Yay. How 'bout them Cowboys?"

How 'bout them Cowboys? Jesus, Jenn, could you be any weirder?

Jo laughed. "It's okay. We're just…um…yeah."

Chase choked back a laugh and Jo elbowed him in the ribs. "Ow! What was that for?"

"For laughing at me. Isn't this awkward for you, too?"

He shrugged. "Maybe. A little. But not really. I mean, we're all adults here."

Jo turned and faced him. "It doesn't make you feel awkward that we got caught making out like a couple of high school kids, or that the person who caught us happens to be our mutual best friend who mistakenly assumed we're in love with each other?"

Jenn could barely keep the grin off her face as she watched the two of them.

"Well, when you put it that way…" he paused, as if thinking about it. "No, not really. Why do you feel awkward?"

"Because, ah…" she stammered, "we…um…we don't…ah…know what we're doing here?"

Chase wiggled his eyebrows. "Oh, I think we know what we're doing, Jo."

"As fascinating as this is, I think we might be venturing into TMI territory here," Jenn said, beginning to feel slightly uncomfortable. She really didn't want to think about Chase naked. That would just be weird.

"Sorry, Jenn." Chase grinned and didn't look sorry at all.

Jenn's blush had finally faded, at least. "No problem. Normally I would ask Jo for all of the down and dirty details anyway."

Chase raised an eyebrow.

"But I don't think I'll ask her this time. It would be like asking my brother about his sex life. Eww."

"Not that I would tell you anyway. Because, yeah. Awkward. And stuff." Jo said.

The back door opened again, and Owen stepped through this time. "Nobody told me the party had moved in here."

"We were just about to go outside," Jo said.

"After they finished making out," Jenn couldn't resist adding.

Owen wiggled his eyebrows and raised his hand for a high five, which Chase did not return. "Too soon?"

Chase shook his head, Jo snorted, and Jenn grabbed a couple of beers from the fridge. At least things were going well for *someone* today.

Matt barely glanced up from his phone as the patio door opened and Jenn and Owen stepped outside.

Just because he barely glanced up, though, didn't mean he wasn't completely aware of her.

Dammit.

And then Chase was pulling Jo outside. She looked slightly panicked.

This could get interesting.

His parents stood up and greeted Jo like a long lost daughter. Granted, they'd always treated her like a daughter anyway, so their joy at seeing her really wasn't a huge surprise.

They've always treated Jenn like a daughter, too.

One of the many reasons why he never wanted his parents to find out what had happened between him and Jenn all those years ago.

Both of his parents hugged Jo and murmured things he couldn't hear to her. The faint sheen of tears glistened in her eyes, but she held it together. Something told him that wasn't the first time she'd held her shit together.

Water softly splashed behind him. He darted a quick glance towards the pool and barely stifled a groan. Jenn in a bathing suit with all that glorious skin on display? Kill him now.

"Penny for your thoughts," he heard Chase whisper to Jo.

"This is one hell of a view, Chase Roberts."

"It is, isn't it?"

Jesus, his brother was kind of corny.

"You two really need to get a room," Matt muttered under his breath, never once looking up from his iPhone.

Chase kicked him in the leg, causing Matt to look up and glare before rolling his eyes and turning his attention back to his phone. He'd barely managed to get the words of Darrin's text message into focus when Sarah reached out and took the phone from Matt's hands.

"Mom!"

"Matthew Tyler Roberts, you're putting this damned phone away right now and speaking to your friends and family rather than ignoring us."

Matt schooled his features so that his expression was flat, but barely leashed tension that vibrated through his body.

From the pool, Jenn snickered and said, "Matthew Tyler Roberts, huh? Somebody's in trouble."

Matt didn't look at Jenn, just got up and stormed inside. Hopefully his mom wouldn't take it upon herself to go through his texts—he was a grown man, after all, and expected at least a modicum of privacy—and find out that his life was all kinds of sideways.

Stupid fucking line drive.

Stupid reckless incredibly hot night of sex.

Frustrated, he walked to the living room and flopped onto the couch, the ballgame barely registering in his mind. He rubbed his hands over his face, the faint stubble on his cheeks scraping his palms. It felt weirdly good, a reminder that he was at least alive.

But what good was being alive when everything you'd ever worked for and wanted was up in the air?

The back door opened and Jo walked in. He didn't acknowledge her. But then she walked into the living room, holding out a can of Dr. Pepper like it was some sort of peace offering—or maybe an offering to the baseball gods to give him back his career.

"These still your favorite?"

Matt looked up at her, took the can and mumbled,

"Thanks."

It wasn't Jo's fault that his life was falling apart and he desperately wanted the one woman he really shouldn't have ever had to begin with. He just couldn't seem to rein the surliness in.

"No problem." She hesitated.

"Jo, whatever it is you want to say, just say it."

She took a breath, studied the can still in her hand, before saying, "I know I have no point of reference for what you're dealing with right now, Matt, but if you need an ear I'm a pretty damned good listener."

"Thanks, Jo, but I'm fine." He didn't need help. He didn't need an ear. He just needed to get back on the mound and back to his life.

Away from the temptation of an auburn-haired temptress disguised as a human hedge hog.

"Fair enough. The offer stands, though, Matt. And if not me, try to find someone to talk to."

"I'm not a fucking woman, Jo. I don't spend time sitting around talking about my goddamned feelings." Maybe that was a little harsh, but he just wanted to be left alone for a few minutes.

"Somehow that doesn't surprise me. By the way, when the hell are you going to get your hair fixed? You look like you should be coming out of a bar on Sixth Street."

Matt snorted and purposely relaxed his posture. "I don't know. I kinda like it."

Not really, not anymore. But he kept hoping that maybe the crazy hair would keep the jersey chasers away whenever he happened to be in public. So far it hadn't worked.

"Going for the sympathy fuck, hey?"

Matt finally laughed out loud at that. "Honestly? No. My sense of humor's just fucked up enough that I find it funny."

Well, that was kind of true.

"Oh, it's definitely funny. Anyway. I'm going to go back out. Maybe you should join us and apologize to your mom for being a dick."

He was kind of shocked by Jo's language, but admired her ability to just cut to the chase. "When did you get such a potty mouth?"

"Oh, somewhere between my senior year of college and dealing with teenage boys on a daily basis."

He shook his head. "You're braver than I am. You couldn't pay me to deal with teenagers all the time."

"It's definitely challenging. Anyway, I'm gonna go back outside. Enjoy your coke."

Matt looked down at the still unopened Dr. Pepper in his hand, at the TV, up at Jo and then back to the cold can in his hand. "I'll be back out in a few minutes. Just need to cool off a little bit."

The look Jo shot him made worry flow through his body. It was a look that clearly said, "I know something's going on, and I'm going to find out what it is."

God help him if that particular cat ever got out of the bag.

CHAPTER SIX

THE MONDAY AFTER THE Fourth of July party at Chase's, Matt showed up at Jenn's door with a bag with the Rudy's logo on it in one hand and a gallon of sweet tea in the other. She looked over his shoulder, didn't see Chase's pickup or Owen's Mustang, and briefly wondered how Matt had gotten to her house before noticing the shiny new JEEP sitting in her driveway.

"They're letting you drive again?" she asked by way of greeting.

He gave her a devastating grin, and she realized he'd also cut his hair so that it was now even all over his head. The man really was too hot for his own good.

"I was cleared to drive this morning."

Instead of letting herself get caught up by his smile and those hazel eyes, Jenn called on every ounce of bitch she had in her—which really wasn't that much, truth be told— and asked, "What are you doing here, Matt?"

He lifted the bag and the gallon of sweet tea. "Bringing you dinner."

"But I didn't ask you to bring me dinner."

He shrugged. "You have to eat. I have to eat. And Jo and Chase are too busy having wild monkey sex to eat, so I figured I would go someplace where I could watch baseball in peace without the game being interrupted by moaning and a thumping that I can only guess is a headboard hitting the wall."

"What makes you think you can just come over here and take over my TV?"

He glanced behind her and grinned. "I do believe that's a baseball game on your television."

Well, crap. "So? Maybe I want to watch by myself."

Matt's smile began to fall just a little bit. Jenn steeled herself against it. She would not give in, dammit.

He closed his eyes, sighed, and appeared to be praying or maybe contemplating ways to murder her before opening his eyes and leveling her with a gaze that felt more real than anything she'd seen since that night ten years ago.

But no, she reminded herself, that look in his eyes ten years ago had been a lie, too.

"Listen, Jenn, I don't exactly have a lot of places I can go in town and just chill out. If I'm at Chase's, Jo's there and I want to give them privacy. If I go to Mom and Dad's, Mom will just fuss over me. If I go out somewhere people either look at me with pity on their faces, want something from me, or are yet another jersey chaser. This is the only safe place I could think of."

She couldn't help but snort at that. "You seriously think my house is a safe place for you?"

"Sure, as long as I make sure to hide all your knives."

"Good thing you don't know about the gun in the closet, then."

He raised an eyebrow. "That's really not the best place for a single woman to keep a personal defense weapon."

She rolled her eyes. "I was messing with you, Matt."

"Oh, okay."

"It's in my nightstand."

Instead of looking scared, he just smiled at her. "I see

Chase has taught you well."

"Chase hasn't taught me shit. I learned that on my own." And, well, he didn't need to know about her parents constantly urging her to build a safe room, bury guns and ammo in the backyard and invest in firearm concealment furniture. Nobody needed to know about *that* particular brand of crazy she dealt with on a daily basis.

"Noted. Now, can I come in before this food gets any colder?"

She sighed, and against her better judgment stepped aside so he could enter. "Since I have the feeling you won't give up until you've gotten your way, fine."

Jenn closed the door, wary as Matt made his way to the breakfast nook and set the food and tea on top of the small table she'd set up there. He walked into her kitchen, and she pushed away from the front door and followed him.

He was opening up cabinets, presumably looking for plates. She made her way around him and opened up a cabinet on the far end of her galley kitchen, pulled out two plates and handed them to him. Silently, he took them from her, and she opened a drawer right beside him, accidentally grazing his hip with her arm as she did so. She could feel the heat radiating off of him, remembered what all that body heat had felt like wrapped around her and inside of her, and ground her back teeth together.

Get your shit together, McDonnell.

She yanked a handful of silverware out of the drawer, not even noticing what she'd grabbed, and spun around him before hastily walking to the breakfast nook.

"It's kinda hard to eat brisket with spoons, but I'm willing to give it a try."

His breath tickled the back of her neck. Of course her traitorous body responded. This was so not going to work.

But she couldn't give him the satisfaction of knowing he'd rattled her *that* much just by simply standing in her kitchen. "Don't you old, washed-up folks need to eat everything with a spoon?"

Okay, so that sounded kind of mean and a lot lame even to her ears.

She so sucked at this snappy comeback, insult thing.

He chuckled behind her, then she felt him move away seconds before hearing a drawer slide open and then closed behind her. She gripped the back of the chair in front of her so hard her knuckles turned white.

This was stupid. Stupid. Stupid. Stupid. She shouldn't have let him into her house.

But instead of kicking him out, she just stood there like an idiot, waiting for him to come back with what she presumed were forks.

"Here you go. Two forks to the rescue."

"Thanks," she ground out.

"No problem."

He was far too jovial.

Silently, she began to pull cartons and wax paper-wrapped packages from the bag and set them on the table. Matt opened each one after she'd set them down, revealing tubs of barbeque sauce, sliced pickles, creamed corn and new potatoes. There were also a couple of cups of banana pudding, along with what looked like an entire loaf of bread, what had to be three pounds of brisket and a couple of sausage links.

"Good Lord, were you planning on feeding an army?"

She felt more than saw him shrug beside her. "I tend to eat a lot anyway, and the doctors have told me to eat as much protein as possible right now to help this stupid thing in my head to heal."

"I'm not sure any amount of protein is going to help fix stupid, Matt."

"Ouch." He picked up a spoon and scooped up a large helping of cream corn, which he placed on one of the plates. "That one was much better than your last one, though, for what it's worth."

She snorted and pressed her lips together, fighting the smile that teased at her lips. "Every now and then I'm capable of witty repartee."

"And the rest of the time?"

"I'm great at it. Two hours after the conversation's ended and I'm rehashing everything that was and wasn't said in my head."

He chuckled. "Isn't that the case for everyone, though? You think of the perfect insult two days later in the shower while singing along to Mumford and Sons?"

She paused in the middle of placing brisket on a piece of bread, turned to him and asked, "Did you just say you sing in the shower to Mumford and Sons?"

He shrugged. "Sometimes, sure. 'Little Lion Man' is pretty awesome."

"I...I don't know what to say."

"What? Did you think I listened to a bunch of gangsta rap or heavy metal or something?"

"Well...yeah...kind of. I mean, you're this big time, super macho alpha male athlete. Aren't y'all supposed to listen to music about bitches and hos and forties and crazy trains and stuff?"

Matt finished spooning new potatoes onto the second plate before setting the Styrofoam container down, turning towards her and crossing his arms over his chest. "Sounds to me like someone's stereotyping a little bit. If we're gonna go there, where are all of your copies of *Romeo and Juliet*, the litter boxes and sixty-seven cats?"

She swallowed past the uncomfortable lump in her throat. Dammit, he was right. "Fair enough. I shouldn't have stereotyped. I do have to say that I am a bit surprised at Mumford and Sons, though. You really *do* seem more like a heavy metal sort of guy, or hard rock at the very least."

"Eh, I used to love that stuff back in my twenties when I first made it to the majors." He turned back towards the table, grabbed some bread for himself and began to pile the slices high with brisket. "People change. Musical tastes change. When I first got called up, bands like Linkin Park, Chevelle, Velvet Revolver, those were all blowing up and it seemed like everyone had one of their songs as their walk-up music. It was also great party music. I was never much into rap back then, although I did like Eminem and honestly still do. These days I don't party as hard, and I've gravitated towards stuff like the aforementioned Mumford and Sons, Matt Nathanson, The Lumineers. Artists like that, who really seem to have something to say and are great musicians on top of being great songwriters."

Jenn stared down at the brisket sandwich in her hands, not wanting to see this side of Matt. The thoughtful, intelligent, great conversationalist side that she'd tried to tell herself for ten years had been a booze-filled mirage.

Except neither of them had really been drunk. Tipsy, maybe. But drunk? No. She couldn't lie to herself like that, no matter how much she wanted to.

She cleared her throat and reached for unexpected common ground. "I stand corrected. So what's your favorite Matt Nathanson song?"

"'I Saw' off of *Beneath These Fireworks*, but 'Car Crash' from *Some Mad Hope* is right up there."

"Mine's 'Weight of It All'." That song had helped her get through the worst days of her life.

His head snapped towards her. "Seriously?"

She shrugged. "Yeah. What? Were you expecting me to say 'Come on Get Higher?'"

"It's a good song."

"Yeah, it is, and I do love it. But it's also the one most people know."

"So you like Matt Nathanson, too?"

"Maybe if I'm feeling magnanimous one day I'll let you go through my iTunes so you can see for yourself."

"I'm not saying I don't believe you."

"I know." She placed her brisket sandwich on the plate that wasn't in Matt's hand, picked it up and headed towards the living room. She sat on one end of the couch, Matt on the other, so that an entire cushion was between them.

Jenn wasn't sure a measly cushion was enough.

They ate in silence, eyes glued to the TV and the baseball game playing out before them. She stared, not really seeing the action on the screen, too aware of Matt mere feet away from her.

God, she so needed to get over this stupid...*thing*... she apparently still had for him. She wasn't even entirely sure what the *thing* was. Attraction, yes. Jenn was grown up enough to admit that at least to herself. The attraction was as strong today as it had been that night ten years ago, possibly more so, and that in and of itself was frustrating.

Why was she attracted to someone who'd pulled a *wham, bam, thank you, ma'am* on her? That night had been great. The things they'd talked about, the things they'd told each other? She'd never been that open with another human being in her life. And the sex? God, that hadn't just been sex. It had been something so far beyond *just sex* she didn't know what the word was for it. Hell, there might not even be a word for it. Transcendental seemed too artsy, like she was describing an indie film. Making love didn't fit, considering she wasn't delusional enough to think love had been involved at all.

He'd touched her soul. That was really the best she could come up with.

"Are you going to eat that or just keep picking at it?"

Jenn jolted at the sound of Matt's voice. How long had she been off in la-la land? She didn't look at him, afraid he would see her thoughts on her face if she did, and said, "I'm going to eat. I was just giving it a chance to cool down."

"Right."

At least he didn't argue with her.

She took a bite of her sandwich, forcing herself to act normally and like her world hadn't fallen into some crazy, chaotic, jumbled mess with his appearance back in Del Rio.

Not unlike the crazy, chaotic, jumbled mess her life had become after that night a decade ago.

CHAPTER SEVEN

San Antonio, 10 Years Ago

SHE COULDN'T DO IT.

She couldn't drive up to Austin and hang out with Chase after…after…doing what she'd done the night before with Matt.

An ugly mélange of feelings crashed through her, like angry waves on a beach during a hurricane. Raw. Potent. Confusing.

Jenn picked up her phone and texted Chase.

> Something came up at home. Can't make
> it today. Sorry.

She hit SEND and fell back onto the pillows that still somehow smelled like Matt.

Jenn sucked in a breath, the sharp sting of shame careening through her mind and body, reminding her that this was why she'd always shied away from casual sex; the couple of times she'd done it, she'd felt so, so dirty.

Stupid Baptist upbringing.

Except she didn't feel dirty for the reasons she did.

Silent tears leaked out of her closed eyelids as she thought back over the past twelve hours. Seeing Matt downstairs. Matt coming back up to her room. A couple of drinks, good conversation and the hottest, most delicious kiss she'd ever experienced. Images of what they'd done to and with each other flashed through her mind like a soft focus porno flick, carnal and dirty and so, so sexy.

So maybe not quite like a porno flick, because she generally didn't find porn to be all that sexy. But still…her body was sore and stinging, and she totally had a bite mark on her left boob.

Jesus that had been hot.

I can't believe I slept with Matt.

The tears were coming faster now, having moved on from a slow leak to a dam bursting.

She'd slept with Matt—the boy she'd known since she was in elementary school—and she'd woken up this morning to an empty bed, a head full of memories and not so much as a "goodbye" or "it's not you, it's me."

He'd just left.

Sometime in the middle of the night, he'd apparently snuck out (like the cocky asshole she'd always known he was) and couldn't even leave her a note.

Never mind the fact that they'd known each other for almost twenty years.

Never mind the fact that she was best friends with his younger brother.

Never mind the fact that they would have to see each other again at some point in the future.

Never mind the fact that last night had been the best sex she'd ever had.

He'd just left.

Treated her like nothing more than a girl he met in a bar and hooked up with.

And that stung. Even if he had met her in a bar last night and hooked up with her. Shared past experiences made that a completely moot point.

She allowed herself a few more moments of wallowing before sitting up and wiping at her eyes. And okay, a couple more sniffs of the pillow that still smelled like Matt. He really did smell good. Like hot man and leather.

Jesus, she was losing her ever-loving mind.

Would the hotel notice if a pillowcase was missing? She sniffed one more time.

With a frustrated "argh!" she pushed off the bed and began gathering up her things, throwing clothes and toiletries into her overnight bag without folding or sorting anything. Screw it. She didn't give a flying fuck if everything got wrinkled and smelled like toothpaste and deodorant.

Jenn had just tossed her makeup bag in with the rest of her stuff—sans pillowcase, thank you very much—when her phone pinged, letting her know she'd received a text message.

>Chase: Hope everything's okay. Call me later.

Unlike his brother, Chase really was a nice, stand-up guy.

>Jenn: Will do. Later tater.

She looked around the room to make sure she'd gotten everything, made one last trip to the bathroom and then picked up her stuff and left behind the room with its rumpled sheets and pillow that smelled like Matt.

Present Day, Del Rio, Texas

Jenn opened an iTunes playlist, trying not to think about Matt, his unexpected visit last night, or the morning after their little…whatever it was…ten years ago. As she opened her internet browser and began searching teaching forums for lesson plan ideas, she rolled her eyes at the song that began playing.

To be fair, she still loved Jann Arden's "Insensitive," it's just that that was *the* song she'd had on repeat on the way back to Del Rio that morning.

Seriously. Her music wouldn't even let her escape the memories.

"Ugh," she said as she clicked over to iTunes and changed the song. Only to have Ed Sheeran's "Kiss Me" come up next.

"You have got to be kidding me."

She checked the playlist she'd selected. Yup, she had indeed pulled up one of her random playlists that she'd labeled "Work" and sighed before clicking the next arrow.

Which brought up Neon Trees' "Sleeping with a Friend."

"Oh. My. God."

Click. "Going Under" by Evanescence. Slightly better, suitably angry.

Jenn opened her browser back up and started perusing the lesson plan forums in earnest.

Even though classes didn't begin until mid-August, she liked to have her lesson plans finalized by the end of July in order to give herself time to get materials and teaching aides collected and organized. She taught a mix of students, from those whose native language was Spanish to the pre-AP kids who needed more challenging material. Creating lesson plans that suited such a broad spectrum was both challenging and enjoyable.

And, yes, she had a bit of a soft spot for young adult novels.

Most of the schools in Texas recommended the same reading lists for middle school, with some variations between districts and grade levels. This morning she was hoping to nail down her reading lists for the year so she could start working on lesson plans.

As "Going Under" switched to Mumford and Sons' "Little Lion Man," Jenn's mind drifted back to the night before. After finishing supper, they'd sat in silence and watched the ballgame. She'd wanted to ask him questions dozens of times, things like, "Is it weird not being out there every five days?" to "How's your head really doing?" to "Who's your least favorite batter to face?" It was hell having a five-time Cy Young Award winner sitting on her couch and not being able to ask him questions.

But she couldn't.

Self-preservation was a bitch sometimes.

So instead of asking him the questions she wanted to ask him or even making idle chatter, she'd sat there in stony silence, her body rigid and burrowed deep into her corner of the couch. She was vaguely aware of the Wranglers winning, and of the shortstop getting a shaving cream pie in the face, but that was about it. She couldn't even say who the winning pitcher was, mainly because of the pitcher on her couch occupying all of her head space.

Damn him.

She shook her head as if to clear it and went back to researching reading lists. She chuckled at the suggestion of *Curveball: The Year I Lost My Grip* by Jordan Sonnenblick, not familiar with the book but thinking the title was quite timely. Jenn opened up another browser tab and searched for it via Amazon, read the description and laughed out loud.

Seriously? A young pitcher who loses his baseball career due to a freak accident, who's now trying to figure out what his life is after baseball? Hell, she could have her kids read the book and then bring in Matt afterwards for a real-life discussion of freak accidents and life after baseball.

She snorted and muttered, "Yeah, right, like Matt would ever agree to that."

Or like you would want to spend the extra time with him anyway.

Unfortunately, though, the idea had popped into her head and she knew it would be stuck there until she got an answer either way.

Crap.

And the hell of it was, it was a good idea. The book sounded like one her kids would enjoy and that would engage their imaginations, and the idea to bring Matt in would definitely impress at least some of her students. Talk about a great discussion on how fiction often mirrors real life.

Her fingers itched to write down notes and ideas, but Jenn forced herself to take a mental step back. First, there was no guarantee that Matt would remotely agree to this. Second, by the time her classes got around to reading the book he might not be around anymore. She didn't know much about brain injuries, but common sense dictated that they weren't something to mess around with. His head looked like it was healing, but from the little she did know, that didn't mean he wasn't still having concussion symptoms.

Besides, according to Twitter Matt's career was all but over anyway.

Not that she believed that, and she certainly didn't think Matt believed that. The rumors, however, weren't pretty, and if she were a betting woman she would venture that the very public speculation about his future was a big part of the reason why he'd been acting so weird here lately.

And dammit, she really didn't want to empathize with him at all, but she couldn't imagine how difficult it must be to live your life in the spotlight like that, and to have every little thing dissected by people who acted like they knew everything but who really knew nothing. She certainly didn't want to admit that she'd been following the tweets and the speculation, but for some reason she hadn't been able to look away.

Something about Matt simply got under her skin and piqued her curiosity.

She hated every second of it.

Annoyed with herself, she squeezed the bridge of her nose and sighed. Here she was, thirty-two-years old and acting like a twelve-year-old with a crush. It was pathetic.

"Get your shit together, McDonnell, and get back to lesson plans."

Determined, she went back to her lesson plan research and managed to push Matt out of her thoughts and immerse herself for the next hour, until her cell rang, bringing her back to the here and now.

Mom.

"Great."

She closed her eyes, drew a deep breath, prayed for patience and hit the green icon.

"Hi, Mom."

"I didn't interrupt you, did I?"

"Kind of, but I needed a break anyway. What's up?"

"Oh, nothing much. Your dad watched a YouTube video earlier on charging your battery with a chainsaw, so now he's out at the truck with the chainsaw seeing if it works."

"Um, is that safe?"

"Of course it is! You take the blade off and wrap a fan belt or something around it and hook it up to something under the hood and it's supposed to charge the battery."

Images of her father electrocuting himself danced in her head.

"Well, if it works, great, I guess."

"Oh! And we also got our new composting toilet installed."

Fantastic. Just what she wanted to talk about.

"It's great. Your sister complains about having to stir

it, but I keep telling her it's a part of her science project for the next few months."

Only Rebecca McDonnell would consider stirring crap inside a composting toilet to be a suitable homeschooling project. Jenn could only imagine how thrilled her fifteen-year-old sister, Lacey, was about that. Lacey who should be getting her learner's permit and dating boys rather than stuck out in the middle of nowhere with their crazy prepper parents.

"Oh! And I bought you some more MREs. You should get them today or tomorrow. You do have your BOB ready, right?"

Jenn tried to remember where the BOB—or bug out bag—her parents had given her four Christmases ago was. She vaguely remembered shoving it into the back of the closet of her spare bedroom, along with the other dozens of survival supplies her parents had sent her over the years. At this point the closet was beyond full and the buckets of Meals Ready to Eat were lined along one wall and slowly beginning to climb up it.

"Yeah, Mom, I have it ready. But I really don't have any more room for more MREs. Or anything else, really. This house is kind of small, remember?"

"Oh, pshaw. You have plenty of room. What about your spare bedroom? No one's in it, so you might as well use it for your preps."

Jenn closed her eyes and let her head fall to the desk. "Mom, seriously, I know you care about me and that's why you do this stuff, but you know I'm not a prepper nor will I ever be one."

Rebecca sniffed and continued on with her usual blithe attitude. "Oh, for goodness' sake, Jennifer, it's not like it's a big deal. It never hurts to be prepared, and you never know when the shit will hit the fan."

"Mom, the only shit hitting a fan is in the monkey pen

at the zoo."

"Do they have fans in the monkey pen at the zoo?"

Oh, for crying out loud. "I don't know, Mom. Why don't you have Kyle research that for his next paper that's due?"

"Oh! That's a wonderful idea! And I can have him further research primate feces, diseases and how to prepare for them. I'm going to go right now and get him to get right on that one."

Great. Now her youngest brother (and Lacey's twin) was going to want to kill her. Knowing there was no convincing her mom otherwise, though, Jenn followed the advice of the girls from *Frozen* and just let it go. "That's great, Mom. I'll talk to you later. Love you. Bye."

"Love you too, dear."

Jenn quickly tapped "end" before her mother could come up with any other ways to drive her nuts today. Knowing Reece, her other brother, was probably next on Rebecca's to-call list, Jenn picked up her phone and shot him a quick text.

> Jenn: Heads up. Mom alert. Dad's using a chainsaw on the truck battery and she's making Lacey stir shit for a science project.

It took all of five seconds for Reece to text her back.

> Reece: Seriously? If Lacey's stirring shit, what's Kyle doing?
>
> Jenn: Researching monkey shit and diseases.
>
> Reece: I'm so glad I'm getting my MBA.
>
> Jenn: I'm so glad they pulled this crap after we were eighteen.

Reece was eight years her junior, and had just graduated from high school when their parents decided to sell their house in Del Rio, buy some land out in Terrell County close to Sanderson and build the ultimate prepper's paradise. Unfortunately their two younger siblings weren't old enough to be on their own yet, and had been dragged out of Del Rio with Rebecca and Richard McDonnell.

The first year was spent building what Jenn could only describe as a west Texas Doomsday fortress. While the idea of using shipping containers to build a house was a bit weird, she had to admit that they'd actually done a great job and had truly created a home out there. A heavily armed and booby-trapped home, but whatever.

Once the shipping containers had been properly assembled, the next phase had been what Rebecca called their "preps." Jenn had asked as few questions as possible—she'd had a bit of a hard time wrapping her brain around her parents' sudden turn into crazy land—but one Sunday afternoon curiosity had gotten the best of her and she'd found herself watching a marathon of *Doomsday Preppers*.

She was pretty sure her parents hadn't gone that far off the rails, but she wasn't entirely sure so she hadn't asked any questions. Besides, after watching that marathon she'd come to the conclusion that it was kind of silly to prep for something as specific as an EMP, a New Madrid Earthquake or a massive polar shift. If you were going to prep for the end of the world as we know it, shouldn't you play some REM and prepare for just a general collapse of society? That made a lot more sense to her than preparing for something that had a one in a bazillion chance of happening.

So she hadn't asked any questions, and had basically just nodded and smiled as her parents had talked about their preps, their storage container house, and the arsenal they were compiling. Her mom, a former teacher, had chosen to homeschool Lacey and Kyle. Jenn had nothing against home schooling—especially when the person doing the home schooling had been a teacher for almost thirty years—but over the past year or so it seemed as though the lesson plans had gotten stranger and stranger. Seriously? Lacey was stirring human feces for a science project?

Jenn shuddered. Yeah, she was definitely glad they'd pulled this stunt well after she'd turned eighteen. Her life was enough of a hot mess as it was.

CHAPTER EIGHT

@Deadspin: Where's Matt Roberts? Texas ace hasn't been seen in weeks deadsp.in/7mAt9T0

@BleacherReport: TX Ace Reportedly Missing, Hasn't Been Seen in Weeks

@ESPN: Team says haven't heard from @MattRobertsTX in weeks es.pn/0JeE43n

@TheFakeESPN: Matt Roberts missing. So is Taylor Swift. They'll never go out of style.

MATT BARELY RESISTED THE urge to throw his phone across the backyard. He was seconds away from going into the windup when he pulled back. It would do him no good to play pitch and catch with his iPhone and a boulder.

Instead, he set the phone face down on the table, walked away and climbed into the hot tub connected to Chase's pool. Never mind the fact that it was at least a hundred degrees outside; he was just hoping the hot water would help loosen the muscles that had been tense since seeing Jenn the other night.

His phone dinged again and he sighed. Taylor Swift? Really? She was ten years younger than him, for one thing. For another, he'd never even met her. The Fake ESPN Twitter account could have done a much better job with that one. Why not Hannah Davis or Kate Upton? Even if they were both currently taken, at least they both had a track record with baseball players.

The crazy thing was, hot as both of those women were (and if he was being honest with himself, as hot as Taylor Swift was despite the age gap), neither of them turned him on like Jenn did. Jenn with her crazy curly red hair, green eyes, perky breasts and constant hatred of him. If the attraction hadn't been simmering under the surface for the past ten years, Matt would have to wonder if that hit to the head he'd taken had been much worse than the doctors had thought.

He sighed and closed his eyes. Showing up at her place the other night probably hadn't been his best idea ever, but he hadn't been able to stay away. Chase and Jo were in that newly in love phase and he had no desire to horn in on that. He and Owen were friends, but not the type that hung out together by themselves. His parents were great, but Mom hovered and babied him, which just made him feel itchy and angry.

So that had left Jenn, since public places were pretty much out these days. In all honesty, the decision to unexpectedly show up at her place had been an easy one. He'd wanted to see her, simple as that. Even though she was constantly sniping at him and definitely threw up a "don't touch me" vibe, he was finding it harder and harder to *not* touch her.

Memories of their night together in San Antonio had filtered through his head more often than he cared to admit over the past ten years. He wasn't sure if it was the memory, the way he'd left things, or the fact that his life had become a clusterfuck with one horribly placed line drive, but he wanted to see her, be with her and make her smile and relax with him like she had that night.

God, he wanted to be with her again.

Even with her hedgehog vibe, he wanted her. He wanted sex, yes, but more so he simply wanted *her*. He wanted to get to know her, to talk with her again the way they had that night. He wanted to feel the way he had again that night, even if that feeling had scared the crap out of him then and still scared the crap out of him now.

Matt groaned and lightly thunked the back of his head against the limestone rocks lining the edge of the hot tub. If anyone knew he was sitting here in his brother's hot tub, going all *True Confessions* in his head about a woman he'd once had a one-night stand with, they'd think he was certifiably crazy.

To be fair, Matt sometimes wondered himself. This constant need to be around Jenn had to be madness, right?

"You okay? That was a pretty heavy sigh."

Matt opened his eyes at Chase's voice and turned his head to see his younger brother standing a few feet away from the edge of the hot tub.

"Just thinking too much about stuff."

"Anything you want to talk about?"

Matt shrugged. "Go take a look at my phone and the latest tweets."

Chase didn't move. "Haven't we all told you to ignore Twitter?"

"Yeah. But even if I turn it off I still get text messages and emails about what other people are seeing on Twitter. It's easier to keep up with it myself rather than getting them second and third-hand."

Chase shook his head. "So what you're saying is Baseball Yoda is more than willing to dish out advice, but not so willing to take it?"

Matt pinched the bridge of his nose. "I'm not going to argue with you."

"There's a first."

Matt barely refrained from rolling his eyes. "So where's Jo?"

"She's having a girls' night out with Jenn. They've barely spent any time together over the past few weeks, and apparently margaritas and then dancing were called for."

"Dancing, huh?"

Chase glanced at him. "Since when are you into dancing?"

"I'm not. Was just asking a question." He could totally be into dancing if Jenn were involved, but he wasn't about to share that information with his brother who also happened to be pretty protective of the woman in question.

"Actually, I was kind of thinking about crashing their girls' night a little bit later. Jo hinted it would be okay, so if you want to get out and maybe have some fun, you're welcome to come with Owen and me."

"Sure. I have nothing better to do."

Chase grinned. "I figured you would say that. And hey, turn off the fucking tweets for the night."

"Don't look now, but the boys just walked in," Jo yelled in Jenn's ear over the strains of "Uptown Funk."

Jenn kept dancing and didn't bother to look towards the front door of April's, the small bar she, Owen and Chase had been frequenting for the past few years. "I thought this was supposed to be a girls' night out?" she yelled back, a smile on her face.

Jo's guilty look pretty much said it all. "Sorry!"

"No worries! Let's go say hi so you can make out with your man."

Jo's skin flushed even pinker than it had been and Jenn laughed. They wound their way through dozens of dancing bodies towards the table the boys had co-opted. It wasn't until they reached the table that Jenn realized Matt was with Chase and Owen. Their gazes met, and Jenn barely resisted the urge to smooth her hair and fidget with her tank top. Instead, she glared at him briefly before smiling at Owen and leaning in to hug him.

"I wasn't expecting to see you tonight," she shouted in his ear.

"Chase didn't want to crash y'all's party alone. Where the hell have you been?"

Jenn tried not to feel guilty about not seeing or really even talking to Owen all week. "Busy. I've been working on a bunch of lesson plans and dodging calls from my mom."

Owen was the only person who was privy to all the details about her parents' new lifestyle, and only then by accident; he'd happened to be at her place one day when a shipment of MREs had arrived on her doorstep. Being ex-Army and a current member of the Army Reserve, he'd taken one look at the packages and asked her what the hell was going on. Really, she'd had no choice but to break down and tell him. He'd laughed and shook his head at most of it, and hadn't judged her for her parents' actions. Not that she'd thought he would but, well, her parents had kind of gone off the deep-end.

"What crazy stuff are they up to now?"

She grimaced. "She's making Lacey stir shit as a science project."

"Do I even want to know what kind of shit?"

"Human."

"That's disgusting."

"I know, right!"

"Why's Matt glaring at me?"

Jenn glanced over at Matt, who was looking down at his phone. "Um, he's not."

Owen grinned before leaning back in and lowering his

voice just slightly to say, "No, but he's been watching you the entire time."

A tingle ran down Jenn's back from her head to her toes, and she silently beat down the butterflies that suddenly erupted in her stomach. "You're seeing things, Owen."

"No, I'm not. I don't know what happened or what's going on between the two of you, but that man can barely keep his eyes off of you."

Jenn snorted. "Now I know you're full of it. He's Matt freaking Roberts. He can have any woman he wants!"

"I can't believe I'm about to say this because you're like a sister to me, but Jenn, I'm pretty sure he wants you."

"You might want to go get your eyes checked, dude. In the meantime, I'm going to go get another drink."

She spun away from Owen and the supposedly hot stares from Matt and marched up to the bar. She caught Shae, the bartender's eye, and signaled to the younger woman that she would like another margarita. She briefly thought about switching drinks since she, Matt and margaritas didn't seem to be the greatest of combinations. Oh hell, she was willing to risk it. Mostly because she wasn't about to allow herself to be alone with Matt tonight.

Or ever.

Maybe.

Disgusted with herself she closed her eyes and rubbed her temples. This was getting beyond ridiculous. If she wasn't mad at him she was pretending to be mad at him just so she wouldn't jump his bones again.

And *that* pissed her off. The man had walked out on her without so much as a goodbye and yet she still wanted him.

Maybe her family's crazy had rubbed off on her.

Shae set a margarita in front of Jenn, leaned across the bar and asked, "Is that Matt Roberts over at your table?"

Jenn nodded and sipped the icy, fruity concoction.

"Yup. The one and only."

"Jesus, he really is hotter in person than on TV, isn't he?"

Oh, you have no idea. "I guess, if you like assholes."

Shae glanced at Jenn, a confused expression on her face, but before she could say anything else Jenn brightly said, "Anyway. I better get back over there. Thanks for the refill!"

She took her sweet time walking back to the table, steeling herself for being close to Matt again. She sidled up and between Jo and Owen, which put her across from Matt, and smiled before drawing another drink through her straw.

His eyes narrowed and his Adam's apple bobbed up and down. Jenn smiled even wider. Jo and Chase had eyes only for each other, and Owen had been drawn into conversation with some guy she didn't recognize. Jenn licked margarita sugar off her lips before taking another sip. Across from her, Matt shifted in his seat.

She dared to glance at him through her lashes. He was watching her like a hawk watches a rabbit, and warmth that had nothing to do with tequila sluiced through her body. Suddenly nervous, Jenn pushed her glass a couple of inches away, turned and walked back to the dance floor. Maroon 5's "Sugar" gave way to Kelly Clarkson's "Heartbeat Song" and Jenn closed her eyes and tried to make her mind go blank so she could lose herself in dancing and the music.

She was moving with the song, unselfconsciously, singing along quietly with the words when suddenly there was a warm body behind her seconds before there was a pair of big hands on her hips. She didn't bother to open her eyes—her stupid body recognized Matt—and continued to dance. He pulled her closer so that their bodies brushed against each other with every movement.

Aware that their friends were just tables away, Jenn pulled away slightly, even though she wanted to move in closer. His fingers tightened on her hips and she couldn't help but smile. Some little demon must have inhabited her body tonight, because she allowed herself to briefly press against him before pulling away again and spinning to face him.

His hands dropped from her hips and she leaned in, put her mouth to his ear and asked, "What the hell do you think you're doing?"

"Dancing."

"I didn't see you as the dancing type."

"I didn't see you as the dancing type," he threw back at her.

She shrugged, closed her eyes again and continued to dance along to the music without paying too much attention to the lyrics. Because, yeah, Matt had definitely turned her heartbeat up.

The final notes of "Heartbeat Song" faded into Sam Smith's "Stay with Me," and Jenn abruptly opened her eyes and walked off the dance floor. There was no way in hell she was staying out there with Matt for *that* particular song.

She grabbed her margarita as soon as she reached the table, and promptly downed the rest of it. The tequila hit quick and hard, blurring the hard edges enough that she could breathe again.

She hadn't planned on getting drunk tonight, but it was beginning to sound like a damned good plan. Matt sat back down on his barstool across from her, and she turned her back to head towards the bar again.

She had to get that man out of her head, and in her slightly buzzed state more tequila seemed like the best way to go about doing that.

Since Matt had stepped out on the dance floor with

Jenn, she'd successfully avoided their table—and him. Instead, she'd danced almost every dance, with small margarita breaks. She danced and laughed, drank, and did a pretty damned good job of ignoring him.

The pop tunes from earlier had switched over to country, and he watched as she chatted with some cowboy as Mike Ryan's "Dancing All Around It" poured through the bar's speakers. She'd definitely been dancing all around the tension between them all night, seemingly preferring to get drunk and ignore it rather than be an adult and talk about it.

Matt rubbed his hand over his face. What the hell was wrong with him? Since when did he want to talk about his feelings?

Christ, the woman had him all kinds of mixed up.

The cowboy leaned closer and then looked down her shirt. Jenn didn't seem to notice, or if she did notice she didn't mind. He shouldn't mind, but he did. Dammit.

She finally clued in to the creep staring down her shirt, grabbed her margarita, smiled politely and turned away from the cowboy. As she walked back towards their table, Wade Bowen's "Trouble" began playing.

Jesus, did the DJ have some sort of super mind-reading powers or something?

Jenn set her half-full glass on the table opposite him, hopped up on to her seat and grinned. "I love this song. It's just...sweet."

Matt raised an eyebrow. "Wait a second. Are you actually starting a conversation with me?"

Jenn frowned and started to slide off her barstool. "If you're gonna be an ass, Matt Roberts, I'll go somewhere else."

He reached across the table and grabbed her hand. "I wasn't trying to be an ass, promise."

Her forehead puckered just above her nose, but at least she slid back on to her seat.

"So you're a Wade Bowen fan, huh?" *Scintillating conversation topic there, Roberts.*

"Yup. Where is everyone?"

Matt tilted his head to the left. "Playing pool."

"Oh, I guess I should maybe join them."

"Running away?"

Her green eyes met his and he felt her sadness all the way to his toes. "It's called self-preservation, Matt."

Apparently Jenn was an honest drunk.

"Why self-preservation?" He knew why, but he needed to hear her say it.

She looked away. "You know why."

"I'm not sure I do." He was pretty sure he did.

She blew a curl out of her face. "Yes, you do."

Like the soundtrack of a movie, "Trouble" faded into The Civil Wars' "The One That Got Away," and Jenn thunked her head on the table before looking back up at him and saying, "Okay, is it just me or does this DJ have some really weird, screwed up sense of humor?"

Matt laughed. "I've been thinking the same thing all night."

"I mean, seriously. There are times when I really wish I'd never, ever seen your face."

Matt considered her words. "I get that. There are times when I wish I'd never, ever seen your face, too."

Green eyes narrowed. "You're a dick."

"No, I'm being honest. Seeing each other's faces and being the ones that got away sure as hell didn't make life simpler, did it?"

She shook her head. "No. It didn't."

She slid off her barstool and grabbed her glass. "In the meantime, *Pooh Bear*, I'm going to take my face over to the pool table so that you don't have to see it."

"Jenn, wait!" Dammit, how had that conversation gotten so far out in left field?

She waved at him over her shoulder and he closed his eyes. Jesus, why couldn't he seem to find the right words around her?

Jenn walked away from Matt, her heart pounding and tears stinging behind her eyes. She wasn't sure why she was so upset, considering she'd been the one to say she wished she'd never seen his face.

She just hadn't expected him to agree.

The hell of it was that when she said it, she wasn't trying to be mean for once, just honest. If she was honest with herself, she did wish she hadn't seen him that night, because that night had knocked her world right off its axis. Sometimes she regretted her decision to sleep with him that night. Other times, she pulled the good parts out and savored the memory of what was still, hands-down, the most intimate experience of her life.

She reached the pool table. Jo looked over and her best friend's smile turned to a concerned frown. Jo sidled up next to Jenn and wrapped an arm around her waist. "You okay? You look like someone just kicked your puppy."

Jenn's laugh was humorless. "Just another conversation with Matt."

Jo pulled Jenn into a corner and turned them so that they were facing each other. "Okay, Jennifer McDonnell, what the hell is going on between you two?"

Jenn stared at a painting on the opposite wall. "Nothing's going on, Jo. Like I've told you before, we just don't get along."

"Nothing my ass! Have you seen the way that man looks at you?"

"Shh! Quiet down!"

Jo dropped her voice to something more closely resembling a stage whisper. "Seriously, Jenn. Matt looks at you like he wants to throw you over his shoulder, take you home and tie you up."

Warmth flooded through Jenn's body at the image that popped into her head. "Jesus, Jo! No, he doesn't!"

"Yes, he does. Trust me on this one. And if Matt's anywhere near as good in bed as his brother, what the hell are you waiting for?"

"Oh my God. Jo. Too much information."

She wasn't about to tell Jo that Matt was probably better than Chase because, well, that would be both hard to explain and kind of weird because she honestly didn't want to think about Chase naked.

"Fine. Whatever. I know there's something going on, though. I know you, and I can see it on Matt's face. Something's happened between you two at some point, and it's eating y'all alive."

Jenn took a steadying sip of margarita. "It's in the past, Jo. Him being here is just making things difficult, that's all."

Jo poked Jenn's arm. "Aha! So I was right?"

Jenn rolled her eyes. "It was a long time ago, Jo. Just let it go."

"Nope. Not gonna happen."

Jenn sighed. "Are you sure you can't go back to Austin sooner?"

Jo snorted. "Not a chance."

CHAPTER NINE

JENN WOKE UP THE next morning with fuzzy teeth, a roiling stomach and a construction crew swinging sledge hammers in her head.

"Ugh." She rolled over in bed and buried her head in her pillow, willing the nausea and pounding to go away.

After a few minutes, the nausea subsided but the pounding didn't, and she belatedly realized someone was knocking on her door. She glanced at her alarm clock. 9:48 a.m. Ugh.

The knocking continued and she muttered, "Hold on to your horses. I'm coming, I'm coming."

She unlocked the door and opened it without thinking to look through the peephole at first, and reflexively slammed the door shut when she saw who was standing on her porch. The only problem was the door didn't slam shut, it just quietly opened back up seconds before a certain six foot two pitcher stepped inside.

Not even bothering to speak, she headed towards the kitchen and her Keurig. Going through the motions, she grabbed a mug from a cabinet, popped a pod of Columbia's finest into the machine and pressed the button to make it brew. Seconds later, the smell of coffee wafted through the kitchen. Before the Keurig was done, Matt joined her in the kitchen and set an orange and white striped bag on the counter top in front of her.

"If those are Whataburger taquitos I might just have to kiss you."

"Guess it's my lucky day, then."

Jenn heard rather than saw the grin on his face and suppressed a smile as she grabbed her now full coffee mug. She quickly added sugar and creamer before taking her first, fortifying sip of caffeine.

Leaning against the countertop, she said, "Okay, I hate to sound like a broken record, but what are you doing here, Matt?"

"I thought that was obvious—bringing you hangover food."

She took another sip of coffee. "But why?"

"Consider it an apology."

She didn't even have to ask him what he was apologizing for. "You don't have to apologize. I know what you meant. I was just slightly drunk and took things a little too personally."

He settled against the counter next to her, close enough that their arms brushed ever so often, causing little tingles to shoot up and down her arm and straight to her core.

"It was a personal conversation, how else were you supposed to take things?"

She looked down into her coffee mug and asked, "Why are you being so nice to me, Matt? I've been nothing but a bitch to you since you came home, and yet here you are. You keep showing up, bringing me food. I don't get it."

"Maybe it's my way of trying to make things up to you. Maybe I just need a friend. Maybe I'm in to self-torture."

She smiled and took another sip of coffee. "I'm going with door number three."

"You would." She could hear the smile in his voice. "Nice PJs, by the way."

Belatedly, it dawned on Jenn that she was wearing a skimpy pair of sleeping shorts and a thin-strapped, light yellow camisole that hid absolutely nothing. As smoothly as possible, she crossed her arms over her chest and took another sip of coffee.

They stood side by side in silence for long moments, Jenn now painfully aware of her lack of clothing and the sudden absence of her animosity. Heat came off of Matt in waves, along with the subtle scent of him, the scent that made her think of tangled sheets, leather, warmth and man. She didn't know what that scent was, but she kind of wished she could bottle it up and take it out to sniff every now and then.

"Your taquitos are getting cold."

"They'll heat back up. I need to finish this coffee first before I can do anything else."

"Are you one of those people who needs a gallon of coffee in the morning in order to not go homicidal on everyone?"

"Not a gallon. I usually just need a cup. But get between me and that cup of coffee and I might get stabby."

"Thanks for the heads up."

"No problem. What about you?"

"Me? I rarely get stabby."

She snorted. "You know what I mean. Are you a coffee drinker?"

"Not really. I like a cup every now and then, usually in the winter time, especially when I'm sitting in a deer blind freezing my ass off."

She smiled, used to hunting talk considering Chase, Owen, Matt and Matt's friend and agent Darrin all owned the Devils Ranch just north of Del Rio. It was a huge place with fantastic views of the Devils River, and butted up to a big ranch owned by Texas Parks and Wildlife. The four men had bought it at auction some years back, and had turned it into a private hunting ranch that catered to businessmen and wealthy folks wanting a bit of privacy along with their venison.

"Do you get to hunt often? I would imagine you're pretty busy, even in the winter time."

"I try to make sure to get in a few hunts a year, including one out at our ranch. Honestly, I wish I could get in more, and spend more time out there. Chase and Owen do a great job with it, and God knows Daniel's an amazing manager, but it feels more like an investment than something I'm actively involved with."

She didn't know the ins and outs of how ranch tasks were handled, but with Chase and Owen being the two owners in Del Rio and therefore close by, they were definitely more hands-on than Matt and Darrin were. Come to think of it, she couldn't remember ever even meeting Darrin. And Daniel, the ranch manager, was a super nice, very bright guy who ran the place as if it were his own. "Has Darrin ever been out here? I was just thinking about it and realized I can't remember ever meeting him."

"Not that I'm aware of. I was talking about it with him back before we bought it at auction, he mentioned he'd been looking for some good investments and figured land was a great one since they're not making any more of it. That was that. I don't think he's ever hunted a day in his life." Matt chuckled. "Actually, it would be hilarious to see him out of his designer suits and in a camo jumpsuit."

"I take it he's a bit of a city boy?"

"Oh, absolutely. But he's great at his job and a good friend, so I put up with him."

Jenn smiled. "Do you miss Dallas?"

Matt looked down and picked at his thumb nail. "I miss playing ball."

She asked the question she'd been wanting to ask him for weeks. "What are you going to do if they don't clear you to play again?"

"That's not going to happen."

"Matt…"

"That's not going to happen, Jenn. I'll be cleared to play again."

"Are you still having concussion symptoms?"

"Not really. I've had a couple of headaches, but nothing excruciating and that could specifically be blamed on the head injury."

"Fair enough. But what if your skull doesn't fully heal before the end of this season? Or what if the doctors think it would be too great a risk for you to pitch again?"

"Is it just me or do you maybe care just a little what happens to me?"

Jenn snorted. "I'm curious and practical. That's all."

"I think you care."

"Whatever." She turned and set her empty coffee cup in the sink. Matt reached out and grabbed her hand with his own. She glanced down at their entwined fingers and raised her eyebrows as she looked up at him. He was gazing at the refrigerator across from them.

"I don't know what I'm going to do after baseball. I figured I had a couple more years to make plans for the future."

"Matt, you're thirty-five. You have to know you can't pitch for forever."

"I know. I'm not stupid, Jenn."

"I never said you were."

"I know. I'm just…I thought I had time. I still have a couple of years left on my contract. I figured I would let it play out, retire gracefully and find something else to do. Maybe get more involved with the ranch. Maybe do some charity work. I've thought about coaching, but I don't even know if I would enjoy it."

"So you have thought about your future after baseball."

He shrugged. "I guess I have, a little. Nothing serious, though."

"Well, those all sound like good options."

"Yeah. I'm just not ready for those to be my only options."

They stood in silence, her hand clasped in his, and for the first time in ten years Jenn allowed herself to feel something other than anger and antipathy towards Matt. She looked at him and saw a proud, confused man who needed guidance and, yes, a friend. If someone had told her a month ago that she would be standing in her kitchen with Matt Roberts, contemplating being his *friend*, she would have told them they were crazy.

His hand tightened around hers, and Jenn did something even crazier than thinking of him as a friend—she wrapped her arms around his waist and settled her head against his chest.

Matt stood frozen for a few seconds, and then tentatively hugged her back. It was kind of awkward, a little sweet and a lot confusing.

Jenn wasn't sure what this meant going forward, but she did know that they couldn't go back to the anger-filled place they'd been in for the past ten years. Could she be friends with Matt, or was that playing with fire?

The feel of his thumbs brushing against the small of her back in a slow, relaxing pattern pushed through the swirl of thoughts in her head. Like the first flowers of spring, her body slowly woke up nerve ending by nerve ending.

This stupid attraction was so inconvenient.

She pulled away, tugged her camisole down and grabbed the Whataburger bag on the countertop. Before she could move away completely, Matt reached out and cupped her face with his hand. She wanted to arch into his palm like a cat.

Instead, she stood there, still, watching him watching her. His Adam's apple bobbed up and down and he inhaled a quick, shaky breath. Her heart pounded in her chest and dammit, she *wanted* this man.

He hadn't even kissed her, and she wanted to climb inside of him.

Matt stepped closer, crowding her body with his own, and Jenn's pulse thickened in her veins like some crazy voodoo drumbeat. Her fingers itched. Her skin tingled. Her lips wanted nothing more than to press against his.

That Matt Roberts scent wrapped around her nose and her brain, making her thoughts fuzzy at the edges.

She was having a hard time remembering why kissing him would be a bad idea.

His thumb stroked her cheek while his other hand rested on her hip. His fingers flexed against the cotton of her boxers and she kind of wished his fingers were flexing against nothing but bare skin.

Matt's eyes darkened to that mossy green color she remembered from all those years ago, and she licked her lips. He moved closer, nuzzled his nose against her temple and then her cheek.

Her eyelids fluttered shut, anticipating what was next no matter how wrong it was. Matt's lips were soft and he kissed her cheek, the tip of her nose and then her other cheek, taking his time. Jenn's breath caught at the unexpected affection, and the slow heat building in her belly.

He kissed the corner of her mouth, her chin, the curve of her jaw.

How was it that big, masculine Matt Roberts could be so gentle?

Jenn sighed as Matt pulled away from her. Her body swayed forward of its own volition, and his grip on her hip tightened.

"I think someone's at the door." His voice was hoarse, like he'd just run a marathon through the Sahara.

"Hmmm?"

He chuckled. "Someone just rang your doorbell."

Oh, did you ever.

Wait, what? Jenn's eyes blinked open and Matt slowly came into focus. His beautiful mouth was twisted into a wry grin, his hazel eyes burned with something that looked a lot like lust and his breathing was just the slightest bit uneven.

Oh. Shit.

What the hell had she just done?

Matt knew the moment Jenn returned to the present. Her green eyes sharpened, the flush on her cheeks deepened and her body tensed. Not two seconds later she'd taken two steps away from him and couldn't seem to look him in the eye.

One step forward, two steps back. Wasn't that just the way of it?

She set the Whataburger bag back on the counter and cleared her throat. "I, uh, should probably get that."

She walked around him—making sure not to touch him—and towards the front door. Matt closed his eyes, sighed and ran his hands over his head.

What the hell had he just done?

He turned and followed her into the living room, only to see her wrestling a box half her size through the front door.

"Need some help with that?"

She shook her head and continued to try to pull the box through the doorway.

It didn't move.

She made a cute frustrated sound before letting the box drop to the floor and turning towards him. "Screw it. Can you help me with this?"

Matt moved towards the front door and then bent and picked up one end. The damned thing had to weigh at least eighty pounds and was probably the size of a mini fridge.

"What the hell is it?"

"I have no idea."

He managed to wrestle the entire box into the living room enough so that they could shut the front door. He pulled out a pocket knife and Jenn held up a hand.

"Wait."

"Okay."

She checked the label on the box and sighed. "I'll open it later. Can you just move it to a corner or something?"

Matt put the knife back in his pocket and shrugged. "Okay. But are you sure you don't want to just go ahead and open it? I can break down the box so you don't have to worry about it."

"No, it's really okay. I can get it myself later."

Jenn clearly did not want to open that box with him around, that much was obvious. Curiosity piqued, Matt glanced at the shipping label as he moved the box to a far corner of the living room.

"Rebecca McDonnell. Isn't that your mom?"

Jenn sighed. "Yes. How'd you know?"

Matt set the box down. "She was my ninth grade chemistry teacher."

"Right. I forgot she was still teaching while you were in high school."

"She's retired now?" It didn't seem like Mrs. McDonnell was old enough to be retired, but what did he know about being a teacher?

Jenn shrugged. "More or less."

A phone rang from down the hall and Jenn held up a finger. "Hold on a second. Let me go get that."

She headed down the hall to what Matt assumed was her bedroom—best not to go there right now—and waited as she took the call. Jenn's house was small, and he could hear her side of the conversation with no problem.

"Yes, Mom, it just got here."

Pause.

"No, I haven't opened it yet."

Pause.

"Because I have company and I'm kind of busy."

Pause.

"No, not that kind of company. Just a friend. I'll open the box later."

Pause.

"Mom, I'm not opening it right now."

"No."

"I told you, I'll do it later."

"Seriously? Ugh. What's the hurry?"

Jenn marched into the living room, a disgruntled expression on her face. She held out her hand and mouthed to him, "Pocket knife."

Matt dug it out and handed it to her, amused and way too curious about what was in the box. Jenn dropped to her knees before she sliced through the packing tape, pulled the edges of the box and then wadded up newspapers up and out. She tossed the paper over her head, sat back and groaned.

"Seriously, Mom?"

Matt was beyond curious as Jenn began pulling items from the box. First was a camouflage military-grade backpack followed by a gallon-sized container labeled "Heirloom Seeds."

"Jesus, Mom. Really?" Jenn muttered.

Matt raised his eyebrows but remained silent. This was

utterly fascinating.

She reached back into the box and pulled out two ammo cans. Matt squinted and could make out .223 written on one and 9mm written on the other.

Well, that explained what had weighed so much, although none of this was stacking up against the person he thought Jenn was.

Everyone has secrets, Roberts.

His attention was drawn back to Jenn as she pulled another item out of the box and made what could only be described as a low, keening sound like that of a cat about to attack. "You have got to be shitting me."

He was totally enthralled as Jenn lifted up what could only be a gas mask.

"Wait a second. Are you a closet prepper?"

Jenn's head snapped around towards him and she shot him a panicked glare. "Mom, I've gotta go now that you've ruined my life. Love you, bye."

She ended the call and tossed her phone onto the couch, then dropped her head to her knees.

Matt wanted to laugh—really, the urge was quite overwhelming—but he had a feeling that laughing right now would go over like a fart in church. Instead he walked over to Jenn, sat down on the floor beside her and picked up the gas mask.

"I've always wondered what one of these would look like up close and personal. And yup, still a little like an alien."

Jenn snorted and muttered into her knees. "I'm going to kill my mom. This shit has got to stop."

"So you didn't have 'gas mask' and 'bug out bag' on your Amazon wish list?"

"God, no. She just randomly sends me this crap. Yesterday I got four buckets of MREs from her. Two weeks ago it was a homemade Faraday cage, which I had to Google in order to even know what the hell it was used for."

"What is it used for?"

She shook her head. "To protect electronics in case of an electromagnetic pulse, or EMP."

"Like in the book *One Second After.*"

"Yeah, she's sent me that one, too."

Matt laughed. "I guess I know what you meant when you said your mom was 'more or less' retired."

Jenn looked up and rolled her eyes. "You don't know the half of it. Long story short, Mom and Dad quit their jobs some time ago, bought some land out near Sanderson, sold their house here and have been building a prepper's paradise ever since."

"And apparently embarrassing you in the process."

She shrugged. "I don't know about embarrassing, at least not until today. I've managed to hide their lifestyle from most people. Chase and Jo know a little, but Owen happened to see the MRE stash one day and grilled me about it. Until today he was the only person who knew about all of the crazy."

He inclined his head towards the backpack. "So what's in the bag?"

"I'm not sure I even want to know."

"Want me to open it for you?"

She picked it up and handed it to him. "Sure. You've already seen the crazy, might as well let you have fun with it, too."

He unzipped the bag and said, "It's like Christmas or my birthday or something."

"I wouldn't go that far."

"Easter?"

She snorted, leaned over and peered into the bag. "Only if the Easter Bunny was in the habit of leaving you Lifestraws and trauma kits."

Matt pulled said Lifestraw and trauma kit out of the

bag and set them on the floor. Next was a bundle of para-cord, a military-style compass, two rolled elastic bandages, a pink canister of pepper spray, a Bear Grylls multi-tool, a large flashlight that could double as a club, a small sewing kit, a slingshot, a sixty-count bottle of toothpaste tablets, a package of no-rinse bathing wipes, a bottle of no-rinse body wash and some square package with "Urinelle" written on it in a script font.

"What the hell are these?"

Jenn took the package from him, flipped it over and back and laughed. "Apparently you missed the lovely illustration right here," she said as she pointed to something that looked suspiciously like a drawing of a semi-naked woman standing up with a paper party hat in front of her goody bits.

"Wait. Is this what I think it is?"

Jenn opened the package and pulled out a triangular-shaped, thick piece of paper. She unfolded it along the seams to reveal that it was actually a cone. "Yup. Now we women can stand up and pee like you guys."

Matt eyed the paper cone suspiciously. "Somehow I doubt that thing's going to work as well as, well, being a dude and having a penis."

"You're probably right. I've talked to some women who have used something similar called a Go Girl. Some of them love it, and some of them hate it. Me? I think I'll just hand these out as party hats. Throw some glitter and tassels on them and we should be good to go." She set the cone aside. "What else is in there?"

Matt turned his attention back to the bag and resumed pulling out items. "There's a poncho. A package of carabiners. A roll of Duct Tape. Oh, here's a weather radio, for all those hurricanes we get here on the Rio Grande. And your mom apparently knows you well enough to send you an old school percolator."

"Let me see that thing," Jenn said before grabbing it and looking at the metal contraption. "I don't think I've seen one of these since I was a kid. How do you even use it?"

"You put the grounds in the part with the holes and then pour hot water over them, I think."

"You think?"

Matt shrugged. "I haven't used one of these since I was about ten years old and we went camping with Dad. Been a while."

Jenn sighed and set the percolator aside. "Anything else in there?"

Matt peered into the bag and pulled out the next item. "Yup. Apparently there's a blanket."

It was gray and scratchy.

"Well, at least that's somewhat useful. At the very least I can put it in my car."

"I think some of this stuff is somewhat useful. Plus, you got free party hats."

Jenn tucked a curl behind her ear. "Fair enough. Anything else in there? It seems like we should be getting to the end. That bag couldn't have held that much."

Matt reached into the bag without looking, wrapped his hand around a box and pulled out the final item.

"I'm going to kill my mom."

He looked at the box in his hands and couldn't help but laugh. "Well, at least she got the right size."

"Argh!" Jenn growled before leaning over and grabbing the box of Trojan Magnums out of his hand. "I. Am. Going. To. Kill. Her."

Matt held the box above his head, playing keep away. Jenn briefly thought about lunging for them, but then decided plastering herself all over him probably wouldn't be her smoothest move.

Besides, there'd already been that almost kiss in the kitchen. She wasn't sure she needed to play with fire anymore today.

Rolling her eyes and trying to act unaffected, she sat back on the floor and looked at the stuff strewn around them.

"Oh, come on, you don't want them?"

She played dumb. "Want what?"

Matt shook the box of condoms and Jenn shrugged a shoulder. "I don't even know why she sent them. You can keep them, hand them out to all those jersey chasers always skulking about."

"Please. And when was the last time you saw any jersey chasers hanging out anyway?"

She glanced sharply at Matt, trying to figure out if he was teasing or being serious. "Um, last night at the bar. They were everywhere."

"I don't remember any of them."

"So they're just faceless bimbos with boobs to you?"

"Making assumptions today, are we?"

"Oh, please. I've seen those girls, and I've heard enough from you and Chase to know that to most athletes they *are* nothing but faceless bimbos with boobs."

"And *you* know I don't mess around with jersey chasers."

"How would I know that, Matt? We've barely spoken to each other in ten years, and when we have it's been to do nothing more than trade insults and be mean to each other."

He set the box down on the floor beside him and leaned forward. "No, Jenn, the only time we've talked to each other is so you could insult me and be mean to me."

"Oh, and you've just been Mr. Nice Guy?" she shot back as she threw her hands in the air.

"Not exactly. But I've let you insult me and get your digs in because I felt like I deserved it."

She poked him in the chest. "What the hell? So now you're a freaking martyr?"

He grabbed her finger and gently squeezed it. "No. I'm just a guy who did a shitty thing and figured if insulting me made you feel better I'd deal with it."

Jenn swallowed the lump in her throat and looked down at her hand, which was now cradled in Matt's hand against the soft cotton of his t-shirt. She could feel his heart thumping behind his chest, so steady and sure. She slowly spread her fingers until her entire hand was flat against that solid wall of muscle. She let it linger there for just a second before slowly pulling back and looking away.

"I'm sorry. I really wasn't meaning to be a bitch just then."

The corner of his mouth twitched. "Old habits die hard?"

"Something like that." She cleared her throat. "Anyway. Let me put all this crap back in the bag so I can throw it in the spare bedroom with the rest of the stuff Mom's sent me."

He started handing her items, and asked, "Why do you keep it if you don't see a use for it?"

Jenn shrugged. "They spend a lot of time and money on this stuff, and I know they do it because they care. Well, it's mostly Mom who does it—Dad's usually too busy building booby traps or charging his truck battery with a chainsaw—but I know it comes from a place of love, so it's hard to just toss it."

"Wait. Did you just say charging his truck battery with a chainsaw?"

"Yeah, long story. Don't ask. Apparently there's a YouTube video if you're really curious."

Matt shook his head as she zipped up the backpack. "I

guess your folks definitely keep life interesting, huh?"

She stood up and slung the backpack over one shoulder. "Don't judge. I know it's tempting and honestly easy to do, but just don't, okay?"

Matt stood, too, and grabbed the two ammo cans. What she was going to do with all that .223 was beyond her—she didn't even own an AR-15.

"I wasn't judging, just commenting. If living that lifestyle is what your parents want to do, more power to them. And it's nice that you don't just toss the stuff they send you—makes me realize there is a soft, gooey center under that prickly exterior."

Jenn snorted. "Really? 'Soft, gooey center'?"

"I seem to recall a pretty soft, gooey center once upon a time." He winked at her. Actually winked.

Jenn face heated. She had to be crimson by now. Embarrassed—and so not on his flirting level—she made a sound that she could only liken to a strangling fish before whirling around and heading to the spare bedroom. She could feel him behind her, considering the man radiated heat like a freaking furnace, and that Matt scent was invading her nostrils making her tongue-tied and muddle brained.

Still, though, she couldn't lie to herself—Matt was proving to be even more dangerous now than he had ten years ago.

CHAPTER TEN

"Well, Matt, I have to say that your CT scan came back good. Your head's healing quite nicely."

Matt breathed a silent sigh as relief crashed through him. "So when do you think I can play ball again?"

Dr. Cushon glanced at Matt and then back at the CT scan. "When was the last time you had a headache?"

He shrugged. "A couple days ago, but it went away with a couple of regular strength ibuprofen."

"And before that?"

"A week or so."

"You know I can't clear you to play until your headaches have gone away."

Matt rubbed a hand over his head. "But you and I both know I haven't had any other concussion symptoms, and that a couple of headaches could be nothing more than just that—a couple of headaches."

"Yes, but rules are rules. Besides, even though your head's healing well, it's not completely healed."

"How long until you think it is completely healed?"

Dr. Cushon turned and looked at him rather than the stupid CT scan result. "It's hard to say. Head injuries are tricky, Matt. I've seen people recover from trauma such as yours quite quickly, and I've seen others take years. It wasn't just your skull that was affected, as you know, and while your skull is looking good, I'm not going to take chances with your brain."

Matt gripped the edges of the exam table until his knuckles turned white and the tips of his fingers tingled. "Doc, I have to play ball again."

The older man pulled out a chair and sat, an expression of patience mingled with pity etched across his grizzled face. "Matt, you're thirty-five. Even though you're in excellent physical condition, your body takes longer to heal as it ages. Plus, there's the added complication of a brain injury thrown into the mix. You have to be realistic here and start thinking about your future beyond baseball, because you might not get to play again."

He refused to accept that. "You don't understand, though. We have a chance to go to the World Series and win this year. This is the best team I've ever been a member of, and I'm not going to let them down."

There was more of that pity from Dr. Cushon. "Matt, I know you think you're letting your team down, but you have to take care of yourself first. If you took another blow to the head right now, it could kill you. You're lucky you're not dead right now, or at the very least in a vegetative state. The fact that you left the hospital within a week and that a month and a half out you're doing much better than anyone would have guessed is something you need to consider. You've basically been given a second chance at life."

"So you're saying there's a chance?"

Dr. Cushon sighed. "I'm saying you need to seriously evaluate your priorities and think about what means more to you—playing baseball or being alive and sound of body and mind forty years down the road so you can be around to see your grandchildren."

"Oh, for crying out loud! I'm not even married, and

I sure don't have any kids running around. Who's talking about grandchildren?"

Dr. Cushon sent him a sharp look. "That's exactly what I'm talking about, Matt. Priorities. I can't clear you to play baseball right now. I might be able to in a few weeks or a few months, it could be a few years or it could be never. You need to consider all of the possibilities."

Matt sighed. "How long do I need to go without headaches to meet concussion protocol?"

"At least a week. But concussion symptoms are only a small part of everything we have to consider in your situation."

"I know, but it's something I can at least focus on, a goal to work towards."

"Matt, you can't finesse your brain the way you can a breaking ball. These things are huge unknowns, and every person is different. Every brain is different. My advice would be to take it easy—nothing more than light workouts for at least another couple of weeks—and really sit down and think about your future after baseball. I would love to see you pitch again and win the World Series, but as your neurologist I have to warn you that the odds of that happening are slim to none right now."

Matt closed his eyes and focused on his breathing, counting backwards from ten in an attempt to find some small amount of calm amidst the storm of emotions. "Fair enough."

Dr. Cushon stood and slid the chair under a desk. "I'll see you again in a week. In the meantime, if you have any questions or if anything comes up, you have my number."

"Right. Thanks, doc," Matt said as he shook the neurologist's hand.

He slid off the exam table and followed the doctor to the checkout desk, where he scheduled his next appointment and ignored the flirtatious glances from the receptionist. Calmly, he exited the building and walked towards his JEEP, hit the unlock button on the key fob and climbed inside. He slid the key into the ignition, turned the engine over and closed his eyes against the blast of hot air followed by cold.

Then he hit the dashboard with his fist. "Godmother-fuckingdammit!"

"So how's your summer been so far?"

Jenn scooped up queso with a chip and pondered how to answer Rene's question. "Interesting, I guess."

The other woman leaned forward, a dimple flashing in her cheek. "Really? Please say there's been some good gossip. I desperately need some good gossip."

"Hubby and kids driving you nuts?"

"God, yes! I mean, I love them, don't get me wrong, but when I'm looking forward to the school year starting and spending time with other people's kids more than I am spending time with my own kids, you know it's been a rough summer."

Jenn's grin turned into a frown. "That doesn't sound good. What's been going on?"

Rene waved a hand through the air. "Nothing major, really. The boys are teething, Brad's been traveling a lot for work and Mama still hasn't forgiven me for marrying a gringo and has been passively aggressively bitching about it to my sisters."

Rene had shocked her very traditional Mexican-immigrant Catholic mother two years prior when she'd not only gotten pregnant out of wedlock, but had married a blond-haired, blue-eyed white man rather than the black-haired, dark-eyed Mexican man Mama had chosen for her. Mama had come around slightly and at least showered her grandchildren with love and affection, but she would passively aggressively make Rene's life a living hell at times by stirring up non-existent drama, seeing the boys but not acknowledging Brad, giving everyone but Brad gifts at Christmas, and even going so far as to not invite Rene's husband to family events.

Rene had learned to live with it, but Jenn—very open-ly—thought that Rene needed to set her foot down and tell Mama that either she could accept Brad as her son-in-law, or she was no longer a part of the boys' lives. Rene obvi-ously hadn't had the guts to draw that line in the sand, even though she'd thought about doing it for at least the past six months.

Jenn reiterated her thoughts on the situation. "Rene, you really need to tell your mom to either accept Brad or go jump off a cliff—figuratively speaking, of course. I mean, this is ridiculous."

"Oh, I know. It's just that Caden and Logan love her, and I know she adores them."

"But what good does that do as they get older and they realize their grandmother wants nothing to do with their father? That's going to confuse them and send a pretty bad message."

Rene nibbled on the corner of a tortilla chip. "Right. Brad and I actually got into a bit of an argument about it the other day, and I'm getting pretty fed up. Thus, the wanting school to start back now."

Rene taught seventh grade math, which was partially how she and Jenn had become friends; the real bonding had come over their mutual love of regency romance novels.

"So what about you? Why's your summer been 'inter-esting' so far?"

Jenn stuffed a queso-topped chip into her mouth and shrugged.

"Nope, you're not getting out of sharing and giving me

some small amount of joy."

She swallowed. "Fine. Well, Jo's back in town—her grandma had hip surgery about a month and a half ago, and Jo came back to help out over the summer."

"Jo's your best friend who lives in Austin, right?"

"Right. Well, ends up Jo being back in town has made things quite interesting."

Rene leaned forward, her brown eyes shining with interest "Ooh. How so?"

"Have I ever told you about her and Chase back in the day?"

Rene shook her head.

"Well, long story short, the three of us were best friends since like Kindergarten. There was always a bit of a thing between Jo and Chase, something that was always a bit different than what was between Chase and me, especially once we hit our teens. It was pretty obvious they were totally into each other, but then one day Jo just stopped talking to Chase. She never explained why, and I learned after a while that asking her got me no answers, so I stopped. It ends up she'd stopped talking to him because she'd overheard her mom hitting on his dad one day, and Jo thought it was somehow her fault and that if she stopped talking to Chase her mom wouldn't be tempted anymore."

"That's kind of dumb."

"I agree, and so does Jo now. But at fourteen? We all do dumb stuff at fourteen, you know."

"So true."

"Exactly. Anyway, she came back to town and I may or may not have decided it would be a good idea to throw the two of them together and essentially force them to either continue ignoring each other or finally get around to talking it out. Ends up they're now doing a lot more than talking it out."

Rene gasped. "No! Chase and Jo are together now?"

"More or less. They're certainly having lots of wild monkey sex from what I understand. Honestly, I've been scared to ask for details considering Chase is kind of like a brother to me."

"I can see how that would be a bit weird."

"Yeah. The only problem is that Jo has to go back to Austin in a few weeks for work since she's a high school guidance counselor. I don't know what they're going to do then, and I haven't wanted to ask for fear of popping their little happy bubble."

That, and you've been a little preoccupied thinking about the other Roberts brother.

"Wow. That's got to be tough. Does it seem serious or like they're just getting teenage lust out of their systems?"

"Oh, it's serious. They've been in love with each other since we were kids. I just hope they get stuff figured out, because I don't want to see either of them get hurt again. It was hard enough to watch the first time around; I can't imagine how difficult that would be now."

Their waiter appeared and set their plates on the table and refilled their drinks before rushing off to the next table. Both teachers ate in silence for a moment before Rene said, "So I heard a rumor that Matt Roberts is in town."

Jenn almost dropped her fork.

"And that the two of you may or may not have been doing some pretty close, pretty sexy dancing at April's a few nights ago."

Jenn's appetite vanished. "I don't know why you would have heard something like that."

Rene pulled out her phone, tapped on the screen a few times and then turned it so Jenn could see. And there, in all her sweaty, tank top-wearing glory, she was, dancing with Matt to "Heartbeat Song."

"Oh fuck me."

"Well, it kind of looks like that might have gone on a

little later."

Jenn set her fork down and dropped her head into her hands. "Where did you get that?"

"Betsy and her boyfriend of the week were there that night. She took the video and sent it to me."

Betsy was the middle school drama teacher, which was fitting considering how much drama the woman liked to stir up.

"Do you know if she sent it to anyone else?"

Rene shook her head. "It looked like it was just sent to me, but who knows with her? I just thought you should know about it, just in case you get some flack for it."

Jenn shook her head. "I was just dancing with him. It's not like we were having sex in public or something."

"But you want to have sex in public with him," Rene stated, pointing at Jenn with her fork.

"Absolutely not."

"In private, then?" Rene's voice was hopeful.

Jenn groaned. "There's nothing going on between Matt and me. We're just…acquaintances? Kind of friends? I really don't know."

"I didn't even know you knew him. I mean, seriously, Jenn, why'd you hold out on me?"

"Rene, I'm best friends with his brother. Of course I know him."

She absently waved her fork in the air. "Details, details. You've never once mentioned him, so I just assumed you didn't really know him *despite* being best friends with his brother. So now I find out you do know *the* Matt Roberts, and I find that out by seeing a video of you grinding your ass against his crotch and yeah, I have some questions."

She hadn't been grinding her ass against his crotch, had she? She didn't think so, but she had drank a lot of margaritas that night. "Let me see that video again."

Rene handed her the phone and Jenn pulled up the video. Watched it. Again. And again. Her body and face grew warm and her stomach dipped. Crap. Her secret was out.

She wanted Matt Roberts, and the video evidence was probably already uploaded to YouTube.

Shit.

She sent the video to herself before handing the phone back to Rene, who was watching her with an expectant look on her face.

"So, friend of mine, want to tell me how your summer's really going?"

Jenn motioned towards Rene's phone. "I think that video pretty much sums it up."

"Lots of bumping and grinding with no heavy duty action?"

"Something like that." *Unfortunately.*

She was prepared that evening when Matt knocked on her door. Not that he'd let her know he was coming over—as far as she knew he didn't even have her phone number—but Chase had mentioned earlier that Matt had had a doctor's appointment in San Antonio that morning, and Jenn had had a feeling he would show up on her doorstep that evening.

Why she'd had that feeling, she didn't know. But she had, and she'd been right. So there. Or something.

She closed the door behind him and didn't bother with niceties before saying, "So, there's kinda sorta a video of us dancing together on YouTube."

Matt sunk onto the couch and sighed. "Seriously?"

"Seriously." She sat down on the other end of the couch, curled her feet underneath her and launched into the story about her conversation over lunch with Rene earlier, and then how she'd sure enough found the video uploaded to YouTube when she'd searched after getting home.

"It's not a big deal, Jenn. We were just dancing."

"Yeah, but how's the team going to take that? You're on the disabled list right now for a really traumatic brain injury, and there's video of you dancing at a bar with bright lights and loud music."

"I've been cleared to do those things, just not to play ball."

She looked at him—really looked at him—and saw the lines of worry etched across his face. Even worse, his voice was almost despondent. She uncurled her legs and nudged his thigh with a foot. "What's eating you?"

He rolled his head on the back of the couch and looked at her, his hazel eyes dull, and she felt a swift ache in the vicinity of her heart. No, not allowed. She could not start feeling sorry for him.

He shrugged. "Doc says my skull's healing nicely."

"That's good, right?"

"Yeah."

"Then why the woe is me vibe?"

Matt closed his eyes. "He still can't clear me to play."

"Matt, you just took a line drive to the head a month ago and had brain surgery. You're smarter than that. You know you're not going to be cleared so soon."

"You think I'm smart, huh?"

Jenn scoffed. "You and I both know there's a lot more going on upstairs than you like to let on. That's beside the point, though. You've got to be realistic here."

"I'm so fucking tired of everyone telling me to be realistic."

"What do you want us to say? Do you want us to tell you, 'Yeah, Matt, go get back out on that mound before your head's had a chance to heal. Another line drive won't kill you.' Because it could, Matt. You're lucky this one didn't."

"You don't think I know that?"

"I know you do. So why the rush?"

He stared at the wall across from them and slumped into the couch, body language that was completely uncharacteristic of him. "Baseball's all I have."

His quietly uttered statement filled her with sadness. *Shit. I cannot feel sorry for him.*

But she did. She was naturally empathetic, but she'd long ago turned that off around Matt, because to be that way near him was to ask for heartache. Somehow, though, over the past few days, the walls she'd built had slowly begun to crumble. They were still there, but missing a few bricks here and there.

She wasn't sure she liked it.

"Matt, you have so much more than baseball."

"Logically, I know that. I have unfinished business, though. We were so close to winning the World Series last year, and after we lost in Game Seven I vowed to make it back this year and win it all."

"You have no control over that."

His head snapped towards hers. "Yes, I do. I'm the ace. I go out there and I pitch lights out every time I'm on the mound. I go as deep into games as I can, throw as many pitches as I can without hurting myself. I was throwing a fucking perfect game the night that ball hit me, Jenn. A perfect game, and that was the third I'd flirted with this season so far. We have all the pieces, and we've been firing on all cylinders all season long, starting back to spring training. So yes, I do have control over us going to the World Series and winning."

"There are eight other guys on the field with you," she said quietly.

"But I'm the leader of the team."

"Yes. Matt, though, don't you see? You're putting

unrealistic expectations on yourself. Baseball is as much an individual sport as it is a team sport. Each individual has to play well, and those individuals have to play well together as a team. If one guy's in a hitting slump, you don't just shun him, right? No, you don't. You pick him up. Other guys in the lineup produce hits and runs and know that he'll eventually come out of it. Every pitcher has a bad night where he just gets shelled. Do the guys lay into you for that? Or do they pat you on the butt and say you'll get them next time?"

"You know they don't lay into a pitcher for having an off night. It happens to everyone."

"Exactly. So this isn't on you. The entire season isn't riding on your shoulders. So stop forcing it and just focus on healing your head."

"That's easy for you to say; you're not a major league pitcher."

"Thank God. If I were as whiny as you are I might have to shoot myself."

He glared at her before shaking his head and smiling. "I knew coming over here would make me feel better."

Jenn rolled her eyes and tried her damnedest to ignore the warmth sluicing through her body at the sight of that grin lighting up his eyes. "See? That's how I know you're still fucked in the head—you thought coming over here would make you feel better."

He barked out a laugh. "One day, I'll get you to admit that you like me showing up over here unannounced."

"Not gonna happen."

He shrugged off her denial. "Whatever. So about this YouTube video, care to show it to me?"

Jenn retrieved her phone from the coffee table and

pulled something up on it before handing it to him. He took the phone from her and hit the "play" arrow, watching as the two of them danced like no one was watching and they had a private room.

Matt chanced a glance at Jenn. Her cheeks were tinged a faint shade of pink, and he wondered what embarrassed her more—the fact that she was now a YouTube star or the fact that she was now a YouTube star with him.

The video came to an end and he handed the phone back to Jenn. Their fingers brushed and briefly tangled in the exchange (he may or may not have done that on purpose), and Jenn's blush deepened. She snagged the phone out of his hands and curled her fingers around it in a death grip.

"It's pretty bad, huh?" she asked.

He wasn't sure if she was referring to the fact that the video existed or the fact that for a few minutes on a Friday night in a crowded bar, they'd been unable to hide their attraction to one another.

"I don't know, I think we're both pretty good dancers."

"Be serious here. You know what I mean. Couldn't this get you into trouble with the team?"

The video *was* a bit of an inconvenience, but nothing he didn't think he couldn't explain to the team's powers that be. "They might have a few questions for me once it reaches the team office, but I don't think it's that big of a deal in the grand scheme of things."

"I'd hate to think that they would question you over this, but I also know how these things work. All it takes is one tweet, one person questioning if you're taking your injury seriously enough, for all hell to break loose."

He pinched the bridge of his nose. "There's already a ton of Twitter speculation. Might as well add fuel to the fire, right? That being said, I'm sorry."

"For what?"

"Getting dragged into the mess that is my life."

Jenn raised an eyebrow. "Um, didn't you pretty much drag me kicking and screaming in that mess the first time you showed up over here unannounced?"

"Yeah, but I didn't mean to drag you into the public mess." And he really hadn't.

"Whatever happens, happens. There's not much we can do about it now. I mean, if you asked to have it taken off of YouTube that would just add fuel to the fire."

"Exactly. I suggest we don't even acknowledge it. If it gets picked up and goes viral, that's one thing, but for right now we're better off acting like it doesn't exist."

Jenn turned the phone over in her hands. "You know that if Chase, Jo or Owen sees it they're going to have questions. Or—oh shit—your mom."

Jenn was close to his parents—hell, they'd considered her the daughter they'd never had since they were kids—and his mom could be like a dog with a bone when she got hold of something involving one of her children. He wasn't sure how his parents, his brother or their friends would react if they thought something was going on between him and Jenn. In all honestly, he wasn't sure he wanted to find out.

"I think Owen's put two and two together, at least a little bit," he finally said after long, silent moments.

Jenn removed a ponytail holder from her wrist, gathered her hair behind her head and secured it into a messy spray of curls on top of her head. It should have looked ridiculous, but instead he wanted to run his fingers through all that wild red and bury his face in her neck.

"Yeah, I think so, too. He hasn't said anything to me about us since the Fourth, but that's just how he works; he knows I'll spill when and if I'm ready and won't push me."

"He warned me not to hurt you."

Jenn glanced away, her features pinched. "Little too

late for that, isn't it?"

He wanted to reach over and touch her, slide closer and pull her tight against his body. Instead, he stayed where he was. "Are we ever going to address the elephant in the room?"

"What elephant?" She'd rounded her eyes into what he figured was supposed to be an innocent expression. It looked anything but that.

"Jenn…"

"Listen, Matt, there's no point in rehashing past mistakes, right?"

Wait. Mistake? She thought that night had been a mistake?

Logically he understood how she could feel that way. Illogically, he resented the fact that she thought the most earth-shattering sex he'd ever experienced had been a mistake.

"Right," he ground out, willing to let this woman see his pain and frustration regarding his career, but somehow unwilling to let her know she'd just cut him off at the knees with a simple, offhand remark.

He stood suddenly, needing to get out of her house and away from her before he did something stupid or said something he couldn't take back. "Anyway. Thanks for listening to me whine. And don't worry about the video. I'll…" he reached into his pocket and grabbed his keys, feeling out of sorts, "I'll see you later."

He walked out of her house and to his JEEP, feeling even more conflicted than he had when he'd arrived on her doorstep earlier.

Jenn sat rooted to the couch for long moments after Matt left, feeling relieved and yet a lot like crying. She'd seen the look of hurt that had flashed over his face after her "mistake" comment. Sure, he'd hidden it quickly, but it had been there, and he hadn't been able to completely hide it from his eyes. Those beautiful hazel eyes that had haunted her dreams and waking thoughts far more than she cared to admit over the past ten years.

She drew in a shaky breath, opened the video file and watched it for the hundredth time that day. Betsy had managed to capture that moment when she'd given in just a little and allowed herself to relax against Matt for far too brief a time. His hands were on her waist, his front to her back, and while her eyes were closed—reveling in the feel of his body against hers, she remembered all too clearly— his were watching her. Focused. The expression his face was clear, his emotions undeniable.

He was looking at her like a man looks at a woman he wants with a burning passion, like a man who cares.

The song and video came to an end and Jenn hit play again. Over and over she watched it until her phone battery was almost dead and she could no longer deny the obvious truth—they were playing with fire and it was only a matter of time before they got burned.

CHAPTER ELEVEN

MATT DIDN'T COME BACK over for four days. Jenn tried to convince herself she wasn't disappointed, but she kind of was.

Hey, the man was gorgeous and it was nice having all that hotness to look at.

Or, rather, she tried to tell herself it was only his face and his body she missed. If she were being honest with herself, though, she had to admit that she kind of missed him. Even though it seemed like they always ended up arguing, in a very short period of time she'd started to enjoy watching baseball with him and occasionally picking his brain regarding strategy. She liked the way he relentlessly tried to make her laugh, and that he respected her personal space and stayed on his end of the couch (even if she did kind of wish he would move a little closer sometimes).

Unfortunately, she was finding out that Matt Roberts was actually a decent guy and possibly a good friend to have in her corner.

This whole kind of sort of friends thing they had going on was making things really, really complicated in her head.

So Friday—in an effort to clear her head of Matt Roberts and all of his sexiness—she booted up her laptop and set about making lesson plans for the upcoming school year. Hours later she was startled out of her planning by the ringing of her doorbell. She glanced at the clock in the bottom right hand corner of her laptop screen. It was past six in the evening. How had it gotten so late? As she walked to the door she rolled her shoulders to ease some of the knots that had taken hold.

She looked through the peephole. Matt was on the other side looking slightly disgruntled. She fought back a smile.

You're supposed to act like you hate him, remember?

Yeah, except that wasn't working out very well at all.

She opened the door and tried to affix her snarkiest expression to her face. "What do you want?"

"Well, hello to you, too."

She wasn't sure how she felt about the fact that he wasn't exactly phased by her snottiness. Resigned—and, yes, weirdly happy to see him—Jenn stepped aside and let him walk past her.

He glanced towards her open laptop and back towards her. "Am I interrupting your work?"

She shut the door behind him and rolled her shoulders. "Kind of, but I needed a break anyway. I'd been at it for three hours without even realizing it. Besides, I need to take the towels out of the dryer and get them folded and put away."

She hated having laundry lying about.

Matt shrugged and followed her to the laundry room off the kitchen. "Need help with those?"

"I've got it. Besides, I'm kind of weird about how I like to fold my towels."

He raised an eyebrow. "Do you fold them into swans and stuff like they do on cruise ships?"

"Please. Ain't nobody got time for that."

He laughed and she pulled the towels out of the dryer

and piled them into a laundry basket, which she then took back to the living room. She sat on the couch and began folding them.

"So what's up? I thought maybe my bitchiness had finally gotten to you and you'd given up."

He sat down beside her. "Nope. I've just been busy."

"Doing what? You're on the DL and you're kind of limited on what you can do right now."

"Visiting my parents, talking to my agent and the team."

Her heart almost stopped. "Everything okay?"

"They still haven't seen the video, if that's what you're wondering about."

She exhaled the breath she hadn't realized she'd been holding. "Okay. That's good."

He watched her as she folded towels, and her skin was hot and itchy under his gaze. She finished as quickly as she could, uncomfortable with his gaze upon her, and got up to put them in the linen closet in the bathroom.

He followed her.

Why did he follow her?

The hot, itchy feeling spread, making her feel prickly and edgy. Jenn shoved the stack of just-folded towels into the linen closet, using the mundane chore to gather her emotions.

"Matt, really, why do you keep showing up here? We don't really know each other. We're not friends. Don't you have better things to do with your time than harass a seventh grade teacher?" She asked as she stuffed the towels into the closet, her words harsher than she'd intended them to be, but dammit, he was making her feel too much, too many things she didn't want to.

Behind her, she could feel his body heat and briefly closed her eyes against the sheer potency of him.

"I caught Jo and Chase having sex on the kitchen island tonight. Figured I would give them some privacy."

Jenn raised an eyebrow and murmured, "Go Jolene."

Matt chuckled. "Believe me when I say Jolene is definitely going."

She ran out of towels to straighten and reluctantly backed away from the linen closet, closed the door and turned around to face Matt. "I'm not sure I want to know."

Matt held his hands up, palms out, and shook his head. "Believe me, I don't either. I'm glad Chase is happy, but there are things I just don't need to know about my little brother. Or Jo, for that matter."

Jenn snorted and brushed past him to make her way back to the living room. Matt's hand on her elbow brought her up short. She looked down at his hand and up at his face and asked, "Do you mind?"

He couldn't touch her. If he touched her she might just lose it.

Matt removed his hand and lifted it to rub over his buzzed head. She'd never admit it, but she kind of missed the crazy do he'd sported after the surgery. It had made him oddly approachable. The buzz cut only accentuated his strong facial features and penetrating hazel eyes.

In other words, Matt was most definitely bringing sexy back.

"Sorry."

"For what?"

He shrugged. Glanced away. Brought his gaze back to hers. "Everything."

Jenn was suddenly all too aware of the fact that she was wearing nothing more than yoga pants and a thin tank top and no bra. Defensively, she crossed her arms over her chest (okay, so she was also trying to hide the fact that her nipples were hard enough to cut glass—no reason to give the man false signals). "I'm afraid you're going to have to be clearer, Matt. Everything could mean a lot of things. Are you apologizing for putting a frog down my bikini when we were kids? For grabbing my arm just now? For inviting yourself to my house constantly despite the fact that I keep telling you to go away?"

"You're not going to make this easy, are you?"

She didn't respond, just gave him her best teacher stare and waited for him to continue.

It was the hardest teacher stare she'd ever given.

Matt sighed. "Fine. I'm sorry for grabbing you just now. I'm sorry for coming over when you clearly want nothing to do with me. And I'm sorry for walking out ten years ago without so much as a note or a phone call. Happy now?"

A heavy weight settled somewhere in between her throat and her stomach. She'd waited ten years to hear those words, but now that she had, she wasn't sure what she wanted to do with them. What she should do with them.

She swallowed, opened her mouth to accept his apology and instead said, "It wasn't so much the fact that you snuck out like I was the worst one-night stand of your life, it was the fact that you didn't even seem to care that I wasn't just another jersey chaser."

Matt turned and began to pace in the small confines of the bathroom. "I shouldn't have treated you like that, Jenn. I know we're not exactly friends and never have been. But I shouldn't have walked out. I knew that then and I certainly know that now."

"Then why did you?" Her voice was surprisingly level, despite the emotions that were swirling inside.

He hesitated, looked over at her, and began pacing again. Shook his head. Wiped his hand over his face. "Truth?"

"Truth."

"I was scared shitless."

Jenn barked out a laugh. "Somehow I doubt that,

Matt."

He stopped in front of her and placed his hands on the countertop behind her, caging her in. His expression was reminiscent of the one she'd seen on his face dozens of times just before burning an opponent with a nasty slider for the last out of an inning.

"If you don't want to believe me that I was scared, fine. But believe me, Jenn, when I tell you that that night was the most intense of my life. You came out of nowhere and blindsided me. I'd never felt that way before, and haven't since. So yes, Jenn, I was scared shitless and ran rather than trying to figure out what was going on between us."

Jenn stared at his ear rather than looking him in the eye, afraid that if she did he would see the truth reflected in her own gaze.

Matt lifted a hand and gently caressed her jaw. "Jenn."

Her name, spoken so softly, caused heat to pool low in her belly. Resolutely, she locked her liquefied knees and without looking at his face said, "I think you need to go."

Matt sighed and pushed away from the sink. "If you want me to go, I'll go. But ignoring this doesn't make it go away."

Jenn shook her head. "There is no 'this,' Matt. You're just bored and looking for a distraction."

"Is that really all you think of me?"

She had to believe he was just bored, for her own sake.

She shrugged a shoulder and kept her gaze focused on the photo on the wall across from her. At least she thought it was a photo. Her vision was a bit blurry.

"You know what? Fine. Whatever." Matt made his way down the hall and into the living room.

Jenn stood in the bathroom, still as a statue and her back against the countertop, trying to push down the pain and longing and simple want that she felt any time Matt was near. The photo on the wall blurred even more, its lines wavering and moving as she dimly heard her front door open.

She closed her eyes. Heard it slam closed. Exhaled. Took long moments to try to steady herself.

"I changed my mind. Fuck this."

At the sound of Matt's voice her eyes flew open. She barely had time to register that he hadn't actually left before his hands were cupping either side of her face and his mouth was crashing down on hers.

His lips were soft, despite the fact that she could feel the anger humming through him. Jenn brought her hands up to his chest to push him away, but then his tongue slipped between her lips and somehow her hands ended up clutching his shirt as if it were a lifeline.

Her eyelids fluttered closed, tears still burning her eyes, as his kiss turned gentle. Instead of taking, he gave, his hands never leaving her face. Her grip on his shirt relaxed as she gave herself over to his gentle, unexpected onslaught.

Slowly, Matt backed away, kissing her lightly on the nose before withdrawing completely.

"Goodnight, Jenn."

It wasn't until he'd closed the door behind him that she was able to whisper, "Goodnight, Matt."

Matt sat in his JEEP in silence, barely resisting the urge to bang his head against the steering wheel. Instead, he stared at Jenn's front door, wondering what the hell had just gotten into him.

Sure, the apology was long overdue, and he may have been a guy, but he wasn't stupid enough to think that that particular conversation was over and done with. He'd acted like an ass that night in San Antonio, and his actions had never sat well with him.

Unfortunately, he didn't know where to begin when it came to explaining to Jenn why he'd high-tailed it out of her room like his ass was on fire. He honestly wasn't sure she would believe him—hell, she obviously thought the only reason he was coming around was because he was bored and not because he simply enjoyed her company and wanted to get to know her better. He also had a hard time believing his reasons himself.

Matt rubbed a hand over his face and tilted his head back. Jesus, this was such a freaking mess, and that kiss just then hadn't helped matters at all.

Oh, it had helped him to at least prove a point—that their chemistry was still red fucking hot—but that was about it. The only other thing that kiss had accomplished was leaving him with a hard-on for a woman who some-times acted like she would be fine if he jumped off a bridge.

Knowing that going back to Chase's right now prob-ably wasn't a good idea considering he had no desire to catch Jo and his brother having sex yet again, Matt started his vehicle and pulled out of Jenn's driveway, driving aim-lessly with his head lost in thoughts and memories.

Ten Years Ago, San Antonio, Texas

Matt waited until Jenn had fallen asleep to make his escape.

The only problem was, he didn't want to escape. In-stead of sneaking back to his hotel room he wanted to stay right there with Jenn, watching her sleep before waking her up so they could go for round three.

That way madness lies.

He figured she would appreciate the Shakespeare reference, even if it wasn't exactly appropriate. That being said, it did feel like madness to want to simply watch her sleep.

It made him feel a little bit like a pansy.

But she was so pretty with her red hair wild around her shoulders, a lock curling over one naked breast. He'd never been into chicks with small breasts, but he was thinking hers were just about perfect.

And her skin. God, it was so soft and lightly dusted with freckles, making him think of cinnamon and sugar, which made him think of that stupid nursery rhyme about what little girls are made of.

He traced the curve of her hip with his gaze, burning the image of her like this into his brain.

Something told him he'd want to take that image out later, to remember fondly.

He'd never realized how beautiful Jenn was. Sure, he'd thought she was kind of cute, but she'd suddenly gone from the cute girl next door type to a beautiful, sexy woman. He wasn't sure if it was because they'd both grown up, because of a little bit of alcohol or the fact that this was the first time they'd been around one another without Chase or his parents around, but he'd been struck senseless from the moment he'd watched her walk into the hotel bar.

Gone was the little girl he used to tease when he bothered to give her the time of day at all, and here was a beautiful, intelligent, funny woman capable of great conversation and who kissed like every guy's wet dream.

No wonder he was smitten.

Smitten? What the fuck kind of word is that, Roberts?

Disgusted with himself, Matt gently eased himself out of the bed. He waited, made sure he hadn't woken her up before finding his scattered clothes and putting them on piece by piece. And then he stood there, watching her some more.

His fingers itched to pull his shirt back over his head,

to unbutton his jeans and climb back under the covers with her. Instead, he clenched his hands into fists and fought back the panicky feeling that had begun to beat at his chest. He should leave considering he needed to get back to his room before he was caught, and before he climbed back into bed with her and gave in to the fanciful thoughts and emotions roaring through him.

What if she's The One?

What. The. Fuck.

Shaking his head, Matt clenched his fists harder and forced his feet to move.

Panic beat at his chest, harder, like a prisoner in a cage.

You can't just walk out without saying goodbye or leaving a note.

Except what would he say? "Hey, Jenn, thanks for the mind-blowing sex. Wanna do that for the rest of our lives?"

Jesus Christ what the fuck was wrong with him?

The panicky feeling in his chest grew, spread until it churned in his gut. He turned away from the bed, tried to swallow the panic down, but it beat harder and harder, like a bird's wings flapping fruitlessly against the jet stream.

Oh, God, he was going all poetic all of a sudden.

He *had* to get out of this room, before he did something he would never be able to take back.

As quietly as possible, he hurried to the door, turned the knob and slipped out. He looked one last time at Jenn, still sleeping peacefully in the middle of the king size bed, and shut the door behind him with barely a sound.

Present Day, Del Rio, Texas

Jenn's hand shook as she lifted her fingers to her mouth. She could still taste Matt on her lips, feel his skin on hers. She closed her eyes and drew in a shaky breath. Her cheeks were hot, so she turned and opened the tap on the sink and splashed some cold water on her face.

As she patted her face dry with a towel she chanced a peek in the mirror and saw that her cheeks were flushed, her eyes were bright and her nipples were so hard they were almost cutting through her tank top.

Great, just what I need—blade-sharp nipples.

Frustrated with herself—and, yes, with Matt—she hung the towel back up and hurried into her bedroom. Feeling almost frantic, she searched through her drawers for public-appropriate clothes. Skinny jeans. Loose, flowing tank top. Lacy, racer back bra. Matching boy shorts.

She threw them onto the bed and made her way back to the bathroom where she took a quick shower. Threw on her clothes, slathered on some lotion and swiped on some mascara before pulling her hair up into a messy bun. A pair of strappy sandals completed the look. Jenn snagged her purse and headed out the door, lesson plans and laundry forgotten.

What she needed now was dancing, loud music, and maybe a couple of drinks to help her temporarily forget about a hazel-eyed pitcher who was once again turning her world upside down. As she backed out of her driveway she hit the voice button on her steering wheel, said, "Call Owen" and waited for him to answer.

"Hey, what's up?"

"Wanna meet me at April's? I'm in the mood to get out of the house and listen to music."

"Sure. I was just heading there now actually."

Jenn smiled. "Sweet! I'll see you in a few minutes, then. Later, tater!"

"See you in a few."

She disconnected the call and turned up the volume on the radio. "Demi Lovato? Really? *Really?*"

To be fair, she actually kind of liked "Heart Attack," but right now was so not the time for her to hear that song. Because, yeah, she was totally putting her defenses up because a particular man made her glow. She turned the volume back down, and moments later pulled into the bar's parking lot.

She parked her car, got out and made her way inside. She looked around, didn't see Owen yet, and made her way to the bar.

She was strictly on a three-drink limit tonight; last weekend's hangover had been her first in years and she wasn't looking to repeat that particular experience.

Like most Friday nights at April's it was a mixed crowd of younger and older patrons. Since it was still early in the evening, the place wasn't too packed, and the DJ was playing something other than country.

Not that she didn't like country—she actually loved country music—but right now she needed pop and rock with maybe a little bit of R&B thrown in. Lucky for her, it sounded like she was going to get her wish, if the current choice of Live's "I Alone" was any indication.

At the very least, it was an interesting song choice for a Friday night.

With a mental shrug, Jenn waited for the bartender to make his way over to her.

"What's up with the song choice?"

Jenn turned at the sound of Owen's voice and threw her arms around his neck. He hugged her back before unwrapping his arms and stepping away. "You okay there?"

Maybe a little too brightly, she said, "Yes! I was just happy to see you. It seems like it's been weeks."

He raised a reddish gold eyebrow. "We saw each other last Friday, when you got drunk in this very bar."

"Yeah, don't remind me."

"What was up with that, anyway? I haven't seen you

like that in years."

She shrugged, uncomfortable now under his too-know-ing gaze and turned back to the bar. "Nothing, really. It wasn't intentional—I just had one too many margaritas and they went to my head."

He stepped up to the bar beside her. "Are you sure it didn't have something to do with a certain Roberts brother who may or may not have a head injury?"

Saved by the bartender, Jenn opted to not answer Owen's question and instead ordered a Jack and Coke.

"What the hell? I've never seen you drink whiskey before. Ever. You okay?"

She shrugged, trying to act like everything was normal and like she ordered Jack Daniels every day rather than admitting the truth and correcting her drink order.

Dammit, she was flustered. First, Matt with his confusing apology and bone-melting kiss, and now Owen with his too-knowing gaze and slight smirk.

"What? Can't a girl switch things up every now and then?"

The DJ switched from "I Alone" to Lady Gaga's "Poker Face"—admittedly, not the best musical transition ever—and Jenn handed Owen her purse. "Watch this for me, will you? I'm gonna go dance."

"Are you sure you're okay?"

"Absolutely! I just need to dance and let loose a little bit. Lots of lesson plans today." And hot kisses from an even hotter man.

Jenn joined a group of people she didn't know on the dance floor, not caring that they were total strangers. They didn't seem to care, either, and widened their circle to include her. She allowed herself to get lost in the music, moving her body to the beat and pushing thoughts of Matt out of her head. She closed her eyes, allowing her body to take over for a couple of blessed minutes until the song changed over to Liz Phair's "Why Can't I?"

What the hell is wrong with this DJ tonight?

He was seriously musically schizophrenic or something.

She chatted with one of the women she'd been dancing with—a girl in her second year of college, home for the summer. Jenn had taught her eight years prior.

Holy crap, she'd just been dancing to Lady Gaga with a former student who was now old enough to be in a bar, if not old enough to drink. She wrapped up the conversation quickly and turned to head back to Owen and the drink she'd mistakenly ordered, and stopped short.

What the hell was Matt doing here?

"Fuck. I can't get away from him."

"Did you say something, Miss McDonnell?"

She was being called "Miss McDonnell" in a bar. Her life was officially nuttier than a tree full of squirrels.

"Sorry, I was just thinking out loud."

Her former student—Katelynn, Jenn remembered now—gave her a smile that clearly said, "Step away from the crazy lady" and half-waved before walking away. Jenn breathed deeply before heading towards the two men. Might as well face the issue head-on.

Or, rather, as head-on as she could with Owen standing right there. Which meant not at all.

"Thanks for watching my purse for me," she said to Owen, ignoring Matt completely.

Owen snorted. "Like you gave me a choice. You shoved it at me and ran out to the dance floor."

She leaned over and kissed him on the cheek, watching Matt out of the corner of her eye. Owen was surprised— she really didn't kiss him. Ever. But the corners of Matt's mouth tightened, and she felt a sick sense of satisfaction.

What the hell are you doing?

She had no freaking clue.

The only thing she did know was that only about an hour ago Matt had been standing in her bathroom, his hands on her face and his tongue in her mouth and she'd felt things she hadn't felt in ten years.

Desperate, she reached for the full glass of dark liquid on the bar, snagged it and brought it to her lips. Avoiding the straw all together, she gulped it down, set the glass back on the bar and promptly clutched her hand to her fist. "Jesus. What was that?"

Owen chuckled. "The Jack and Coke you ordered."

Jenn gasped for air past the burning in her throat and chest. "Oh, fuck me. Never let me order that again. Ever."

Behind her, Matt said something to the bartender, and seconds later a big hand holding a glass of water appeared in front of her. "Here. Drink this. Slowly. It'll help."

She wanted to glare at him. Elbow him in the ribs. Grab his head and kiss him like her life depended on it. Instead, she took the glass of water and slowly sipped until the burning sensation subsided and left a warm glow in its place.

Oh, that was nice.

Except the warm glow combined with Matt's unexpected nearness was causing that warm glow to spread to her lady parts, which were most definitely not thinking about elbowing him in the ribs.

"So I have a question," Owen said.

Jenn glanced at the man who was like a brother to her and didn't like the mischief twinkling in his clear blue eyes. She sipped her water, knowing he would continue whether she said anything or not.

"Go on," Matt said. Apparently he didn't know that Owen would continue whether he said anything or not.

"Why did you," he pointed at Matt, "call me asking me if I wanted to meet you at a bar just ten minutes before you," he pointed at Jenn, "called me asking me if I wanted to meet you at the same bar? Now, I realize that you," he pointed at Jenn again, "calling and asking me to meet you here isn't such an odd occurrence. But you," he pointed again at Matt, "calling me and asking me to meet you here *is* an odd occurrence. So I have to wonder just what is going on here."

Jenn shifted on her feet and sipped at her water. She knew Owen had pretty much already figured out the truth— he'd done that a couple of weeks earlier on the Fourth of July—but she wasn't willing or ready to say that truth out loud.

Matt shifted behind her. His hand grazed the small of her back for the briefest of moments before slipping away, and he said, "Nothing's going on, Owen. It's just a coincidence."

Owen looked between the two of them. "Bullshit."

Neither of them said anything, and Jenn felt like a kid caught with her hand in the cookie jar.

"Here's the thing. You're both adults and you can do whatever—and whomever—you like. Yes, Jenn, you're like a sister to me and I will beat to a bloody pulp anyone who treats you like shit, but you're still a grown ass woman who's capable of making her own decisions. And Matt, yes, you're a friend and a business partner and I like you, and I could care less who you date or screw. But you're both standing here lying to me, and I'm not sure why. Yes, you're entitled to your privacy, and the minute you tell me to butt out that this is private, I'll butt out. But right now you've both dragged me into whatever this is between the two of you, so I'm making it my business. Now, which one of you is going to tell me what the hell is going on?"

Jenn swallowed, her throat dry. She didn't *want* to tell Owen. She didn't want to tell anyone. The events of ten years ago had been her secret for so long she wasn't sure how to go about divulging it.

Matt was silent behind her, so Jenn cleared her throat. "Well, you see…"

"I'm sorry we dragged you into this, Owen. I didn't mean to, just needed a friend to hang out with while my brother and his woman have wild monkey sex all over his house."

Owen raised an eyebrow but didn't say anything.

Jenn fought the urge to squirm.

Matt, however, was apparently unaffected.

Jenn sighed. "Owen, it's really not a big deal. Matt and I had a bit of an argument earlier, that's all."

"Is that what you call it?" Matt murmured in Jenn's ear.

She elbowed him in the ribs and got a satisfying, "oof!" in return.

"And I've got some ocean front property in Arizona. Seriously, y'all, I have no desire to play relationship counselor or Dr. Ruth or whatever, but I've watched you two dance around each other for the past few weeks and it's getting ridiculous. And now you've dragged me into the dance with you, and I don't like to dance. I'm not sure when y'all slept together—and don't even try to deny it, because I'm not an idiot—but it obviously didn't end well and you're clearly avoiding the subject, but either you need to just screw each other again, talk it out or both because this is crazy."

Nerves danced in her belly at the thought of Owen knowing and the thought of sleeping with Matt again. The nerves turned into a quick, clawing panic that threatened to cut off her airway. Hastily, she grabbed the purse Owen had been holding the entire time, spun on her heel and ran from the bar as if the hounds of hell were nipping at her heels.

CHAPTER TWELVE

Matt watched as Jenn ran out of the bar, torn between going after her, giving her space, and smoothing things over with Owen. In the end, he chose smoothing things over with Owen.

The decision was two-fold—one, his gut told him that pushing Jenn right now would be a bad idea, and two, he figured that in talking to Owen about what was going on he could maybe get some insight as to how to handle the situation going forward.

Matt gestured towards the pool tables. "You up for a game?"

Owen shrugged. "Sure."

Owen grabbed his beer and Matt grabbed his water and they headed towards the relative privacy of the pool tables. Matt waited until Owen racked and broke before saying, "She's driving me crazy, has been for years."

Owen leaned over the table and lined up a shot. "How many years?"

"Ten."

Owen looked up at Matt. "Seriously? Ten fucking years?"

Matt nodded and took a drink of water before saying,

"Yup. Ten fucking years."

Owen shook his head and leaned back over to line up his shot. "Now how'd that come to happen, and how the hell has no one ever picked up on this?"

"See, that's the sticky part." Matt watched as Owen moved around the pool table after making his last shot, and continued, "Long story short, ten years ago at a spring training game in San Antonio, we ran into each other in the hotel bar. I walked her back to her room because this holy terror of a jersey chaser who'd been stalking me was there that night. She invited me in for a drink and a game of cards. I don't think either of us thought it would go beyond that, all things considered. But then a game of cards turned into a few hours of talking and when I went to leave, well, that's when things went beyond a drink and a game of cards."

Owen stood still on the other side of the table, watching Matt with an indecipherable expression. He had no idea what Owen had done while in the Army, but damn if he didn't want to confess everything right fucking now before he lost a couple of fingers.

"So you slept together." It was a statement, not a question.

Matt nodded once. "The next part is where things get a bit tricky."

"Because sleeping with your little brother's best friend isn't tricky enough?"

"Well, there is that. Where things get tricky, though, is that I didn't expect to feel the way I did and I freaked out. I waited until she fell asleep and snuck out."

"I should punch you for that." There was mild heat behind Owen's words.

"I wouldn't blame you."

"So you were, what, twenty-five at the time? And you apparently had amazing sex—the details of which I don't want to know all things considered—and freaked out because it wasn't just physical. Then you pulled a total dick move and left without a note or a phone number or anything. Did I get the story straight?"

"Pretty much." Jesus, when you laid it out like that it sounded even worse.

"What you're saying is that you acted like almost every other dude has acted at least once in his life."

"Well, when you put it that way…yeah, kind of. But it was Jenn that I acted that way towards, not some random chick I'd picked up in a bar. I mean, we've known each other since we were kids."

"Right, that does complicate things. And knowing Jenn, her feelings were probably hurt when she woke up and realized you'd skipped without so much as a 'it's not you, it's me.' The thing that I don't understand is why she's still mad at you. Ten years is a long time, and in the nine or so years she and I have been friends I've never known her to hold a grudge."

Matt rubbed a hand over his head. "That's kind of been my thought, but she's stayed pissed at me this entire time. I can't blame her—I was a total d-bag for doing that—but it's like I keep taking one step forward and two steps back with her."

Owen pinched the bridge of his nose. "I can't believe I'm about to say this, because this heart to heart stuff is so not my thing, but don't give up on her. I've never seen Jenn as flustered as she was tonight, not even when her parents moved out of town and threw her for a loop. Anyone with eyes can see the way she looks at you—that's how I pieced things together in the first place. A woman doesn't look at a man like that unless she wants to get naked with him. Something had to have happened, though, for her to still be pissed about what happened. I can understand irritated, but she's been flat out mean to you at times, which isn't the

Jenn I know."

Matt leaned a hip against the pool table, the game all but forgotten at this point. "She was flustered tonight because I'd kissed her earlier. And in defense of Jenn, she's dropped the knives for the most part. I've, uh, been randomly showing up at her place in the evening, telling her I'm giving Jo and Chase some privacy. At first she wasn't happy about that, but she's started dropping her guard and letting me in a little bit. I know about her parents, too."

"Wait. Jenn told you about her parents?"

"Well, I happened to be there when the delivery guy showed up with the latest shipment from her mom. She wasn't going to open the box, but then her mom called and apparently goaded her into opening it. Those were some fascinating items."

"More MREs?"

Matt chuckled. "Nope. Random survivalist stuff and a huge box of condoms."

"I'm sure that went over like a lead balloon."

"Jenn may have mentioned wanting to commit matricide."

"I couldn't blame her at this point; it's gotten pretty kooky." Owen shook his head. "Here's the thing. I've said it before, but I really do love Jenn like a sister. But like I've told you before, I know you're not the guy everyone thinks you are. If she slept with you before, that's saying a lot since I can think of two men she's had sex with in the past seven years, and then I'm only assuming since our sex lives have been topic non grata. The key is figuring out what really set her off and made her so upset and mad at you."

"Yeah, but how the hell do I do that without pissing her off so badly she pushes me away for good?"

Owen shrugged. "Beats me. You're the ladies' man here. I do know, though, that Jenn's a good woman, and I want nothing but happiness for her. Hell, I wish I could find a woman like her…but not. If that makes any sense."

"Not a damn bit, but that's okay considering we've been sitting here talking about feelings like a bunch of chicks."

"Right. So how do you think the Wranglers are going to do now that the All Star Break's over?"

Matt willingly followed the topic change, even if talking about his team was almost as frustrating as thinking about the red-haired woman who was driving him crazy.

Two hours later Matt pulled into Jenn's driveway. He'd left April's almost thirty minutes ago and had driven around a bit, trying to figure out what he should do next, struggling with the sense his life was spinning out of control.

His career was in the hands of other people.

His brain and skull weren't healing as fast as he would like.

He had no idea what the future held.

He was tired of being a verbal punching bag when he wasn't sure he deserved to be one in the first place.

The only one of those things he had any sort of control over was the last one, and even then the idea of control was specious at best. Considering he'd never been one to give up, though, Matt decided to grab the bull by the horns and get to the bottom of Jenn's attitude once and for all.

This is either going to go really well, or you're going to end up with another head injury.

Matt turned off the JEEP and got out, locking it behind him as he walked to Jenn's door. He knocked twice and waited. After long moments, the door finally swung open, revealing Jenn with a frown on her face, her red curls piled high on her head, and those mile-long legs in a teeny tiny pair of boxers. She crossed her arms over her chest, making him realize she was wearing a tank top and no bra. His body tightened with the same response he always had around her.

Shit. This could be harder than he'd thought.

No pun intended.

Feeling slightly off-kilter but determined to regain some semblance of control over his life, Matt allowed his gaze to travel the length of her body—making sure to pause at the interesting spots—before saying, "Mind if I come in?"

"As a matter of fact, yes, Matt, I do."

He adopted an air of calmness and hooked his thumbs inside the back pockets of his jeans. "Well, if you want to have this conversation in the front yard so all of your neighbors can hear, that's fine with me. What's one more YouTube video?"

Jenn narrowed her eyes but stepped aside. "Fine, asshole."

Matt stepped inside, wondering when he'd become such a masochist that he was turned on by someone who sometimes seemed to hate his guts. Jenn closed the door behind her and walked back over to the couch, where she picked up a remote and turned off the TV.

"I would say I'm sorry to interrupt, but I'm not."

She heaved a sigh and flopped back onto the cushions. "Just get it out, Matt. What do you want?"

He stalked over to the couch and sat on the coffee table in front of her, took a quiet, steadying breath and said, "Well, after you left, Owen and I got to talking and it occurred to me that in the entire time you and I have been around one another I've never known you to hold a grudge. Sure, you can have a bit of a temper at times, but you generally seem to be able to forgive and forget. Yes, I realize what I did was a dick move and that you had every right to be mad at me—hell, I was pissed at myself. What

I don't understand, though, is why you've held a grudge for ten fucking years, and why you at turns seem to like me and hate my guts while wanting to get me naked. So what gives, Jenn? What's really going on in that head of yours?"

She rolled her eyes. "I so do not want to get you naked."

"Bullshit, but that's also not the point here." Matt leaned closer, lightly placing his hands on her knees. "I'm sorry for what I did ten years ago—I regretted it that night and I regret it now—but something tells me no matter how much I apologize you're still going to hold this unexplainable anger towards me. Why is that, Jenn?"

She looked away and pressed her lips together. Matt stood up and headed towards what he assumed was her bedroom. He got halfway down the hall before she yelled, "Where the hell do you think you're going?"

"Fact-finding," he tossed over his shoulder.

"The hell you are," she muttered. Seconds later she slapped his arm. "I swear to God, if you go into my bedroom I will castrate you."

He winced internally. "That's a little harsh, don't you think?"

"Not at all."

"Threaten me all you want, but I'm going to get some answers. I'm tired of being your verbal punching bag." He turned and began walking again, just steps away from her bedroom.

"Then why the fuck do you keep coming around, Matt?" Jenn shouted.

Finally, some honest emotion.

He turned around and walked back towards her, crowded her against the wall. "Because I like you, Jenn. Despite the fact that you're almost always a bitch to me, and despite the fact that sometimes you act like you wish I didn't even exist, I fucking like you."

"For the love of God, *why*? I treat you like shit."

"Honestly? Sometimes I wonder. But then I remember that night in San Antonio and how easy it was to make you laugh, and how much we had in common, and how it felt to be inside of you and I want nothing more than to go back to that night and do things differently. Then I think about now, and the times when you let down your guard and you let me in, and I see this amazing, smart, fun, loyal and absolutely beautiful woman and I wonder what it'll take for you to let me in all the way, because, dammit, Jenn, I want in all the way."

And there went any sense of control he'd had over the situation.

"You're insane."

Matt pushed away from the wall. "Seriously? That's all you have to say? I'm insane? For the love of God woman, I'm standing here basically cutting myself open and bleeding for you and all you can say is I'm insane? Just let me in, Jenn, let someone in because something has obviously been hurting you for a long, long time and all signs are pointing towards me being the culprit. So please, just tell me something, anything. Tell me your truth."

Matt was pacing like a caged animal, and Jenn could feel his frustration pulsing in the air around them. Her hands pressed into the wall behind her. She had to restrain herself from clawing, trying to escape into the drywall and insulation.

She didn't want to have this conversation. Didn't want to tell Matt her truth.

Because it wasn't pretty.

It was awful and beautiful and painful. Oh, so, painful.

She closed her eyes against the sting of tears and the

frantic pounding of her heart that almost always accompanied her memories. She drew in a shaky breath, and moments later Matt's body was against hers. She wanted to sink into it and lose herself in him.

God, she wanted to lose herself. Her memories. Her truth.

His hand gently cupped her face, and his voice was just above a whisper when he asked, "What is it, Jenn? What happened?"

She shook her head. She couldn't do this. She couldn't tell him.

His lips gently landed on her forehead, her nose, her cheeks. Feather light, like a blessing. Or maybe a curse. She didn't know anymore.

She felt like she didn't know much anymore, other than that ever since Matt had been injured she felt like she'd been losing herself. Some days it seemed like the very fabric of who she was and the life she'd built was being torn apart, the stitches slowly, painfully ripped out one by one, to the point where she couldn't hide and hold all of her pieces inside anymore. They were spilling out, one by one, messily leaving behind emotions she'd thought she'd long buried.

"Jenn," he whispered. Just her name. But it sounded like a plea and a prayer, an invitation she'd never intended to accept.

She opened her eyes and held Matt's gaze with her own, the stinging in her eyes now a river, a flood that threatened to sweep them both away. "You want my truth, Matt? You want to know why I'm angry and bitter and why I try to keep you at a distance despite—yes—wanting you?"

She gulped in a huge breath of air, made sure she had his full and undivided attention, and told him her truth.

Del Rio, Texas, Ten Years Ago

Jenn mentally counted back the days. Once. Twice. Three times.

Fought to stuff down the panic that threatened to take over.

Six weeks.

She glanced at the stick resting on the counter of the bathroom sink, afraid to fully focus and actually see it.

Just do it. Just get it over with.

Slowly, she reached out a shaking hand and gingerly picked up the white plastic.

Two pink lines.

She swallowed down the panic-laced bile that burned the back of her throat, checked the instructions one more time and barely managed to lean over the toilet in time.

Once her stomach was turned inside out and the heaving had finally stopped, she curled into the fetal position on the floor, the pregnancy test still clutched in one hand and the instructions in the other.

Minutes or hours later, she wasn't sure, Jenn pulled herself up off the floor, gently set the pregnancy test and instructions in the trashcan and walked into the living room of her tiny one-bedroom apartment. She'd been scrimping and saving since she was in college for the down payment on a house (thank you, full-ride scholarship and dual credit courses), and she was realistically a couple of months away from being where she wanted to be for that, especially considering she was just about to wrap up her first full year of teaching.

I can't raise a baby, a child, in this tiny apartment.

She sat on her couch, more exhausted than she could ever remember being. Mentally and emotionally she felt wrung out, confused, scared shitless and yet filled with wonder. She rested the palm of one hand on her stomach, rubbed her still-flat belly.

There's a life in there.

It wasn't how she'd planned it. She wanted children, but they hadn't been in the plan for right now. Not yet.

And there was that little fact of not being in a relationship with the baby's father.

Yeah, that made things slightly more difficult.

She didn't know how she was going to tell Matt. She expected him to be pissed, and she couldn't blame him. After all, she wasn't exactly happy about the current situation, either.

But still, there was a life under her hand.

Her thoughts swirling in her head and her eyelids heavy, Jenn lay down on the couch and pulled a throw over her body. With her palm still pressed against her belly, she fell into a hard, dreamless sleep.

The next morning she woke up mentally refreshed but with a hell of a crick in her neck. Slightly more at peace with her current situation, Jenn spent her Sunday making plans, looking over her finances and finally getting in touch with a mortgage broker her family had known since she was a kid. If she was going to have this baby, she was damned sure going to do so in a house with a yard in a good part of town, even if she had to pinch a few more pennies.

The following weeks were a whirlwind of activity, but a month later she'd found the perfect house—a small, two-bedroom, one bath with a fenced-in yard in a good neighborhood. Even better had been the price. A fellow teacher's mother had recently passed away, and she had decided to sell the house rather than try to maintain the upkeep on it since she and her husband owned a home already. She'd approached Jenn before even looking for a

Realtor to list it, and had offered Jenn the house at a price well below appraisal. It needed a little bit of work, but she could handle having new floors put in, repainting the walls and bringing in a plumber.

A few weeks later she was a homeowner.

As contractors came in and out of her new house, replacing the 1970s shag carpet, painting the walls and fixing the plumbing, Jenn wrapped up the school year and enjoyed her little secret while packing up her apartment in her spare time. So far, the only person who knew about the baby was her OBGYN, and she was content to keep it that way.

She still hadn't figured out how to tell Matt, but she'd watched every Wranglers game she could, especially if he was the starting pitcher. Even though it was early in the season, he was already on pace to have an All Star year. Every time he stood on the mound Jenn would rub her stomach and whisper, "That's your daddy up there."

Sometimes, her stomach would bubble in response, but she knew enough to know that the feeling was probably just gas since it was still too early to feel the baby moving.

Her OBGYN had set her due date at December 20. A winter baby. Possibly a Christmas baby.

Matt wouldn't be playing baseball then. In fact, he might even be home.

The thought would slip through her mind, unbidden, and she knew she needed to tell him. She just didn't know how.

"Oh, by the way, remember how I told you I was on the pill and it was perfectly fine to not use a condom that night? Yeah, so, apparently your little swimmers are just as competitive as you are and decided hormonal birth control was no big deal."

Somehow she didn't think that would go over too well.

So instead of asking Chase for Matt's phone number (which was going to be awkward as hell), she kept putting it off, secretly growing her baby and telling people who asked that she'd simply thought it was time to buy a house and she'd been presented with an offer she couldn't refuse. It wasn't really lying if it was telling part of the truth, right?

She couldn't imagine how Matt would react. Anger. Disbelief. She couldn't blame him for feeling any of those things and more, considering she'd been the one to tell him it was okay to have sex without a condom. In all fairness it should have been okay—she'd been on the pill since she was a teenager to regulate her periods, and the failure rate was something like less than one percent.

In other words, she shouldn't have gotten pregnant that night.

But she had.

She would often think back to the days before that night, trying to remember if she'd accidentally forgotten to take a pill or had taken one late. She couldn't remember that happening—she took it like clockwork every morning as soon as she woke up. She hadn't been sick or on antibiotics, either, so that excuse had to be thrown out the window.

No, this had been a fluke of Mother Nature. A fluke she was quickly falling more and more in love with. She'd cried at her twelve week checkup when the doctor had listened for the baby's heartbeat the first time. She could hear it lightly whooshing through the machine. It was the most miraculous, wondrous thing in the world.

Sometimes it was hard to believe that for those first few disbelieving hours, she'd wanted to rail against the world and fate. Once she'd woken up to the dawn of a new day, she'd done so with an overwhelming feeling of love and protectiveness towards the life growing inside of her. No, none of this was ideal, but she was pregnant and would soon be responsible for another human being, and she was damned sure going to be the best mother she could be.

Which meant she should probably tell the father.

A few times over the next week, she picked up her phone to call Chase and ask him for Matt's number. She always chickened out right before the first ring.

In a matter of weeks the floors had been replaced, the paint had dried, the plumbing had been repaired and Jenn was ready to move into her new house. Seventeen weeks after that wonderful, heart breaking night with Matt, Jenn moved out of her apartment and into her new house, effectively closing the door on her past and opening the door to her future.

She still hadn't told anyone but her OBGYN about the baby. The fact that she hadn't started to show yet definitely helped her to keep the secret a little longer. She'd remembered her mom showing pretty early with all three of her younger siblings, so she'd asked her doctor, worried that something was wrong with the baby. The doctor had smiled her kind smile and reassured Jenn that her baby was doing just fine.

Over the summer break she discreetly bought a couple of items for the baby's room—a crib and a car seat on a trip to San Antonio, unisex baby clothes that she told people were for a friend if they asked.

A part of her wanted to shout from the rooftops and share her news. The other part enjoyed knowing something no one else was privy to and feeling fascination as her baby began to move and become more active.

There was still that pesky little fact that she still hadn't managed to tell Matt.

At twenty weeks she went in for a full ultrasound, and gripped the edges of the exam table as the sonographer took picture after picture of her growing baby. Finally, towards the end of the exam, the baby moved and they got a fairly clear look at the sex.

She was having a boy.

Somehow that only seemed fitting, and already she could form a picture in her mind of what he would look like. He would have her red hair and Matt's hazel eyes. He would be athletic like his uncle and father, and share her love of books (not that Matt was a mental slouch).

He was probably going to be a handful. She was definitely going to love every minute of it.

She also mentioned to her doctor that she'd been having some mild back pain and abdominal cramps. Her OBGYN assured her that was normal—her body was going through a lot of changes, after all—and that they only needed to worry if the pain and cramps were accompanied by vaginal bleeding.

She left feeling reassured and excited, yet determined to finally tell Matt. She went home and tried to muster the courage to call Chase and get Matt's number.

Three times she picked up her phone.

Three times she set it back down.

Instead of calling Chase, she sat on the couch and looked at the black and white picture the sonographer had printed out for her. Her baby.

Every time she thought to call Chase to get Matt's number, she allowed herself to get distracted by something else. Lesson plans. Baby names. Making the two and a half hour drive into San Antonio for maternity clothes, since her normal clothes had finally gotten too snug and the school year would be starting in a week. The back pain and cramps would come and go, but they never stuck around long and she hadn't experienced any bleeding, so she didn't worry too much about anything other than how to tell Matt.

She also needed to tell her principal and human resources, considering she would be going on maternity leave over Christmas break. Somehow, telling them during the in-service week made her baby feel more real, more concrete.

She was going to be a mother.

The first couple of weeks of school flew by. She still hadn't told her family, Chase, Jo, or most importantly Matt. She went home at the end of the second week of classes, determined that tonight would be the night that she would call Chase and get Matt's number. She couldn't keep putting it off.

But first, she needed some music and a bite to eat, maybe a bubble bath since her lower back had been cramping on her all day long. Sure, she was used to being on her feet for a good portion of the day, but she'd never taught while pregnant and she guessed her body was telling her to take it easy.

She thought about eating something first, but a bubble bath sounded better. Her lower back cramped again as she bent to turn on the taps, and she stood up and massaged the offending tissue with her fingertips. Jenn walked into her bedroom, disrobed and looked at herself in the mirror. The curve of her stomach was more prominent now, but still somewhat hideable with loose shirts and dresses. A few people had asked questions, but for some reason she'd just brushed it off as weight gain.

She ran her hands over her belly and smiled.

"I love you, little man," she whispered.

She needed to remember to buy a camera so that she could take photos, since she figured years from now she'd probably wish for them.

Absently, she pressed play on the CD player on top of her dresser, not remembering what she had in there.

The opening strains of Evanescence's "My Immortal" powered through the bedroom. Mix CD it was.

Jenn walked back into the bathroom, added some bubble bath to the nearly half-full tub then massaged her lower back as another cramp hit her. She mentally reminded herself to drink more water. Maybe she was a little dehydrated, considering how much she was peeing these days.

She stepped into the tub, sank down into the warm water and vanilla-scented bubbles and closed her eyes. Oh, this was heaven.

Until it wasn't.

As she lay in the tub the pain in her lower back got worse and worse, and she started experiencing abdominal and pelvic cramps that at first felt like she was getting her period, but then began to feel like her uterus was ripping itself apart.

She struggled into a sitting position, looked down. The water in the bathtub had turned pink.

Oh, God, what was happening?

She pressed her legs together and clutched her stomach, fighting against what her intuition told her was going on but that her brain refused to accept. She was at twenty-three weeks. There was no way this could be happening.

Maybe she'd cut herself and hadn't realized it, and the scab had come off in the hot water.

Except the pink had gotten darker, despite how tightly she pressed her legs together. Beyond the pain in her back and abdomen was a pain even deeper, one that stole her breath and made her vision go black at the edges.

She watched, blurrily, as the water turned from pink to red, and then she could look no more, could no longer focus on the red in the bottom of her bathtub.

Another wave of pain tore at her, tore her apart, and through the haze of blood and tears she could only think one thing.

I wasn't supposed to have met you yet.

CHAPTER THIRTEEN

As Jenn tearily spoke, Matt's world dropped from underneath him. Everything he'd ever known tilted on its axis, throwing him off-balance.

Jenn had been pregnant? With his baby?

There were so many questions, thoughts and emotions running through him he didn't even know where to begin.

Then he looked at the woman in front of him, at her tear-streaked face and the pain that seemed like it was as fresh today as it had been ten years ago, and he knew where to begin.

Without a word he bent at the knees, put an arm behind Jenn's legs and another around her waist and picked her up.

"Matt! What are you doing? Should you be carrying me considering your head injury?"

"Shh. Just give me a minute."

He carried her back to the living room, where he sat on the couch with Jenn draped across his lap. He tucked her head so that it was against his chest. He rested his chin on top of her curls and tightened his arms around her. She sniffled.

"I shouldn't have sprung all that on you like that. It was unfair."

He could argue that not telling him about the baby in the first place was unfair, but he wasn't going to pile on to her misery. Instead, he rubbed her back and asked, "Did you ever tell anyone about the baby?"

She shook her head. "You're the first person other than my doctor, the principal and the HR director."

Ten years later, and he was finally the first person she'd told. The irony was not lost upon him.

"I'm sorry you went through that alone."

"It's my fault, Matt. I had a million chances to tell you, or Chase, or my parents. Someone, anyone. I just never did." She glanced up at him. "I should have told you. I'm so, so sorry I never did. I just didn't know how you would react. And then in my head it became not telling you because I didn't want to throw you off your game and jinx the rest of the season, or I didn't want you to think I'd lied that night about being on the pill and was trying to cuckhold you."

"You were scared." He understood scared. He'd been scared back then, too, and probably would have been even more scared had she told him about the baby. Hell, he hated to admit it but there was a good chance he would have wondered if she'd lied to him in order to trap him, or blamed her if he'd suddenly tanked that season.

The fact that she'd known him that well, even back then, kind of floored him.

"I was plenty scared, but that doesn't excuse me keeping your baby from you. I knew I shouldn't, that it was wrong, but like I said, I just kept making up excuses."

"Don't beat yourself up, Jenn. We were both young and in a situation that definitely complicated matters."

She glanced at him. "You're being much more level-headed about this than I thought you would be."

"What did you expect?"

"Yelling. Cussing. Disbelief. Wanting to run away

from me as fast as you could because I'm obviously off my fucking rocker."

He snorted. "You're not off your rocker. If anything, I'm just glad I finally got it out of you."

She rested her head on his shoulder again, her fingers tracing the letters on his t-shirt. "How is it you know exactly which buttons to push?"

"Why do I get the feeling no one's ever tried before?"

Her fingers stilled briefly before resuming their path. "It's hard for people to try when you don't let them get close enough to do so."

Her quiet admission made his gut clench with recognition and a little bit of guilt, wondering if he'd been the one to make her that way, if it had been the baby, or something else altogether.

Matt swallowed before asking his next question, not sure if he should but curious nonetheless. "So after the... bathtub...what happened?"

Jenn drew in a shaky breath and exhaled on a ragged sigh. "Luckily, I'd taken my phone into the bathroom with me, so I grabbed it and called my OBGYN. She told me to get to the hospital as soon as possible, to call an ambulance if I needed to. I made myself get out of the tub and towel off, put on some sweats and a t-shirt. I couldn't look at the tub, and every movement was just awful. I was having contractions, which made it hard to drive."

Matt closed his eyes, pain for their baby and the woman in his arms ricocheting through his body.

"I got in my car and drove to the hospital. They got me checked in, took me up to labor and delivery." She laughed, the sound tinged with a hint of disbelief and anger. "It was hell, being up there and hearing the sounds of other women having babies, the cries, the joy and laughter while knowing that the odds of my baby surviving were slim to none. They told me the actual delivery didn't take long, but it felt like forever."

She pushed back a sob. "He didn't cry. They tried, but in the end he was stillborn."

Jenn's body shook with sobs, and Matt wrapped his arms around her tighter, horrified at the thought of Jenn going through that alone. He kissed the top of her head.

After a few minutes the sobs quieted and Jenn continued. "I knew he wasn't alive, but I needed to hold him, to know that the past five and a half months hadn't been a dream. I needed to know he was real. He was perfect, Matt, fucking perfect. They ran some tests on him and me. I think the most horrible part was that there wasn't anything really wrong with him, he was just too little to survive and they said the shock of premature labor had caused him not to live. Most of the time when you miscarry it's because there's something wrong with the baby, a chromosomal abnormality and the mother's body realizes that and miscarries. In this case, it was because I have what's called an incompetent cervix. I mean, no shit, obviously it's incompetent—the stupid thing couldn't even hold a baby for forty-one weeks."

"Forgive my ignorance, but what does that mean?"

"How much do you know about babies, women's bodies and childbirth?"

"Nothing much beyond the fact that childbirth seems extremely painful."

Jenn's smile was wobbly. "Well, time for a brief biology lesson, then. When you're full term, the cervix basically does this thing called dilating and effacing which is a fancy way of saying it gets soft and the opening gets bigger, which allows the baby to come out. With an incompetent cervix, it dilates and effaces much sooner than it should. Sometimes, if it's caught soon enough, you can get stitches to strengthen it and keep the baby in utero until it's full term. We never had any reason to think mine was weak, and I hadn't had really any symptoms that would cause my OB to worry, so by the time we knew it was too late."

"So, uh, I have no idea how to ask this without sounding incredibly morbid, but…"

Jenn answered without him having to finish the question. "I had a ceremony with just me and the preacher from our church. Luckily, he respected my privacy and didn't ask a lot of questions, just offered counseling if I needed it."

Matt swallowed. "Would you…would you mind taking me one day?"

Jenn nodded. "If you want to, yes. It's probably well beyond time that you met him."

"Did you name him?"

Jenn pushed herself out of his lap and stood before him. She pulled up the hem of her shirt, eventually revealing a small tattoo on her rib cage, just below the curve of her left breast.

Tyler.

One word, so simple and yet…Matt swallowed the lump in his throat and fought the stinging sensation in his nose and eyes. Moved and saddened and a little angry, he leaned forward and pressed a gentle kiss on the simple script before pulling away.

Jenn's skin was covered with goosebumps and he couldn't help but notice that her nipples were hard. His dick twitched in response and he forced himself to ignore the physical reaction.

Now was so not the time.

"You gave him my middle name." His voice was rough even to his own ears.

Jenn nodded and pulled her shirt back down, covering up her breasts and their baby's name. "I had to. He was half of you and half of me, and considering I'd been a chicken-shit, I think it was my way of acknowledging you without drawing too much attention."

Looking up at her with her eyes rimmed with red and still brimming with tears, Matt made a snap decision on what he told himself was gut instinct alone. He lay down on the couch and patted the cushion beside him. "Join me?"

He could see the war in her head playing out all over her face. Usually Jenn was much better at hiding her emotions, but he guessed that the emotional upheaval tonight had weakened her usually strong defenses.

While he had no plans on taking advantage of those lowered defenses, he also wasn't one to look a gift horse in the mouth. Tonight could be a turning point in whatever this thing was going on between them.

He knew the moment she caved, could tell by her slumped shoulders and the way she nervously played with the hem of her shirt. Slowly, as if he was a feral animal that might bite, she lowered herself to the couch and then finally lay down beside him, her back pressed to his front. He immediately wrapped his arms around her, unwilling to let her go now that she was here.

Jenn sighed and began to relax against him.

"So what were you watching when I barged in?"

"*Pitch Perfect.*"

"You can keep watching it if you want to."

"You do know what this movie's about, right?"

All he knew about it was that the pretty hot Anna Kendrick was in it and there was singing. "Doesn't really matter. If you want to finish watching it, watch it. If you want to talk, talk. If you want to sleep, sleep. I'm up for whatever."

Unfortunately, he was most definitely getting up for whatever with her backside pressed against his crotch.

Down, boy. Think about nuns. Old nuns.

That did it. Kind of.

"I'd just started it. Are you okay just starting over from the beginning?"

Chick flick it was. Which was totally okay as long as he had Jenn pressed up against him with her armor down. He would watch a thousand chick flicks with singing if it meant she was his.

Now where the hell had that thought come from?

Matt mentally shook himself. "Sure. It's whatever you want."

She glanced over her shoulder at him, and he could tell she was trying to figure out if there was an angle. There wasn't.

She didn't say anything, though, just leaned forward, grabbed the remote off the coffee table and started the movie over from the beginning. When it began with a bunch of dudes wearing red velvet jackets on stage dancing and singing "Please Don't Stop the Music," he knew he was a sucker.

⟡

"So let me get this straight—chicks actually enjoy and laugh at vomit humor?"

Jenn hit STOP and snuggled back up against Matt on the couch. "Of course we do. We also laugh at fart jokes."

"Seriously?"

She turned so that she was on her back, looking up at him. "Wait. You mean to tell me the biggest ladies' man I've ever known doesn't realize we women laugh at bodily functions and base humor?"

"I'm not that big of a ladies' man."

"Whatever. Don't change the subject."

He shrugged. "I don't exactly have a lot of female friends. Make that any."

"That's kind of sad."

"It's just the truth. It's hard to become friends with a woman when I never know if she actually wants to get to know me or just wants to get to know my dick, bank account, or both."

"Not that that's cynical or anything."

"It is, but it's also just a product of who I am. Hell, you've seen the jersey chasers."

"Speaking of jersey chasers, whatever happened to our good friend Heather?"

Matt grimaced. "I finally filed a restraining order against her a few weeks after that night in San Antonio, when I caught her in my hotel room. Believe it or not, she'd managed to get a key card from the teenage clerk at the desk."

Jenn could only guess at just how Heather had gotten that key card, and almost all of those guesses involved sexual favors. "Did she stay away?"

He shook his head. "Nope. She waited a few weeks then showed up at a game. Security tossed her out. Next thing I know she's making a scene in the hotel lobby, crying and carrying on about how much she loved me and how she couldn't believe I would leave her after finding out she was pregnant with my kid."

Jenn sucked in a breath. "She didn't!"

"She did. I called hotel security and the cops. They arrested her. Ends up she was trying to extort a couple of other ballplayers so she got to spend a little bit of time behind bars. Never bothered me after that."

"What a...dumbass."

"Okay, I have to know what you really wanted to call her."

Jenn cheeks grew warm. "What makes you think I wanted to call her something else?"

"Please. You just stumbled over your words. Tell me what you wanted to call her. I promise I won't tell."

She rolled her eyes. "How are you still such a little kid at the ripe old age of thirty-five?"

"You're not that far behind me. And if you don't spill, I'm going to tickle you until you do."

Jenn had a sudden flashback to when they were kids, still in elementary school, and Matt would hang out with her, Jo and Chase more often than not. Chase knew Jenn was extremely ticklish, and had let Matt in on that little secret. Matt being Matt, he'd waited to cash in on his knowledge and had waited until they'd been telling ghost stories under a sheet fort one summer night to quietly pounce and scare the bejeezus out of her.

He'd tickled her for forever, 'til she was laughing so hard she'd thought she was going to pee her pants. Which would have been super embarrassing, all things considered.

The fact that he still remembered how ticklish she was filled her with a hot rush of pleasure.

Whoa, what's going on here? Down, girl.

This was Matt. The same Matt who'd made—her brain skittered around the phrase—who'd had sex with her and then left without a word. The same Matt who'd avoided her and barely talked to her for the past ten years (okay, so maybe she'd been the one doing the avoiding, but he hadn't exactly sought her out, either).

The same Matt who still lights up your body like it's the freaking Fourth of July and who just held you while you totally lost your shit in front of him while telling him all about his stillborn baby and then watched Pitch Perfect *with you and didn't complain once.*

Go away, voice of reason.

"I guess I'm going to have to tickle you, then."

Matt's voice jerked her out of her thoughts so quickly she didn't even think, just blurted out the answer to his original question. "Cunt. I was going to call her a cunt. But I generally hate that word so I didn't."

"Y'know, with that dirty mouth you sometimes have you could fit in in a baseball clubhouse."

"I don't think that would be a good idea."

"Why not?"

"All those hot baseball players barely clothed and really sweaty after a hard-won game? Nope, that wouldn't be a good idea at all."

He drew his eyebrows together. "What do you mean by 'all'?"

"Just what it sounds like. All."

"Well, there goes my ego."

She laughed and nudged his chest with her shoulder. "As if. You've got enough ego for both of us."

His expression turned serious. "You know I'm not actually some crazed egomaniac, right?"

The worry in his voice caused Jenn to reach up and smooth his brow. How her hand ended up running itself over his buzzed hair and cupping the back of his neck she had no idea. "I know you're not a 'crazed egomaniac,' Matt. But I also know that it does take a certain amount of ego to be a team's ace and to carry that kind of pressure and *like* it."

"Ego or craziness, one or the other."

Her fingers slipped under the edge of his t-shirt's collar without her telling them it was okay to do so. "Probably a little bit of both, truth be told." Her voice was low and husky, almost unrecognizable to her own ears.

Matt closed his eyes and inhaled a sharp breath. "What are you doing, Jenn?"

Her hand slipped further under the collar of his t-shirt. Her whispered response was shaky. "I don't know."

His hazel eyes darkened to that lovely green shade that told her he felt whatever this was, too, but he didn't move. "You're vulnerable right now, sweetheart, and your hand on my neck and those green eyes looking at me like that are making it really hard not to kiss you."

She licked suddenly dry lips while her insides went all

warm and gooey at being called "sweetheart." Jesus, she was the easiest woman on earth right now, willing to drop her panties at the slightest endearment.

Yeah, keep fooling yourself there, sister.

Shut. Up.

"So then kiss me."

"I don't want you to regret this in the morning, and I don't want us to go back to circling each other like wary cats, either."

"Dammit, Matt!" She rose up while bringing his head down to hers at the same time. Fine. If he wasn't going to make the move she sure as hell would.

She moved her lips against his, finesse flying out the window. All she knew was this sudden—okay, not so sudden—aching *want* that clawed at her gut and pulsed through her veins. He responded, capturing her mouth with his and she almost sighed in relief.

Instead of letting her continue to take the lead, though, Matt slowed the kiss way down. Jenn relaxed against the arm of the couch, her hand still inside the collar of his shirt. Their tongues caressed each other, a slow dance building to a slow burn. Sparks shimmered behind her eyelids. Why hadn't she been kissing him all along?

Matt was a great kisser.

Sure, he'd been a pretty damned good kisser ten years ago, but like a barrel of whiskey he'd only gotten better with age and had gone from pretty damned good to phenomenal.

He curled his tongue around hers, stroking and gliding before pulling away and nibbling on her bottom lip. She chased, but he continued to pull away.

Jenn whimpered—actually whimpered—when he pulled away completely. A part of her brain realized she *was* emotionally vulnerable right now and simply needed to feel a connection with someone. The vast majority of her brain, however, was stuck on the look in his eyes, the heat of his neck under her hand and the fact that his bottom lip was slightly plumper than the top.

Oh, sweet baby Jesus, she had it bad.

Matt's smile was rueful as he tucked a curl behind her ear. "I'm not going to take advantage of you, sweetheart, and if I let this go any further that's what I'd be doing."

"Is it taking advantage if it's what I want, though?"

"In this case, yes, and you and I both know I don't need to spell out all the reasons for you."

Jenn's hand under his collar drifted up to rub at the nape of his neck. Matt briefly closed his eyes and drew in a hard breath. "We both want this, though. You can't lie to me and tell me you don't."

He shifted and his erection brushed against her hip. "If circumstances were different, I would have you naked right now and would be buried so deep inside of you you saw stars."

Jenn squirmed as desire pooled low in her belly.

Insta-wet. Right there.

"But you're hurting and vulnerable right now, and despite what you might have thought about me for the past ten years, I'm not that man. I want you, Jenn, but not like this, not when you might regret it in the morning and I would feel like a dick."

His expression was so earnest, his gaze so determined, that she was helpless against the tumbling of her heart inside of her chest. "Why can't you be the person I thought you were?"

"Who's that?"

A corner of her mouth quirked up. "An asshole."

Matt snorted more than laughed, but she was rewarded with a grin playing at his lips. "Well, to be fair, once upon a time I was an asshole, and if you ask certain American League batters, they'd probably tell you I'm still an asshole." His expression grew serious again. "I really am sorry, Jenn. I've always regretted the way I left things back then."

She looked away, unable to meet his gaze as her fingers continued to play at the nape of his neck. Apparently it was time to address the remaining elephant in the room.

Might as well just rip all the bandages off at once, right?

"I'm not going to say 'it's okay,' because it's obviously not okay." She brought her gaze back to his. "I wasn't looking for forever, wasn't under some misguided assumption that you were, either. I wasn't looking for fancy words or lies. But I had expected respect—not only for me, but for us and our history. I can't say friendship, because I don't know that we were really all that great of friends. We had known each other for forever, though, which kind of makes the whole one-night stand thing a bit awkward. And I knew it was one night, Matt."

"I never meant to make you feel like I didn't respect you—it was honestly the complete opposite. Still is."

She chewed on the inside of her cheek, memories of emotions flooding through her mind. "The funny thing is, Matt, up until the point when I woke up and you were gone without a single word, I had felt respected. Even knowing it was a one-time thing, and even with the fact that I'd never had sex like that with anyone, I knew you respected me and that I wasn't a faceless warm body. But then you left, and I felt so, so used. It's not a fun feeling, believe me."

His fingers brushed her cheek as he met her gaze—unflinching—and said, "I left without saying anything because you scared the shit out of me."

Jenn raised an eyebrow. "Me? I scared the big, bad Matt Roberts?"

Yeah, right.

The corner of his mouth ticked up in a crooked grin.

"Yes, you. That night was…special. It was crazy and unrestrained and I felt freer with you than I ever had with anyone else. I had no clue where the sudden attraction had come from. I knew you were smart and funny and could be a bit of a smartass, but I hadn't known that you tasted like heaven or that there was so much passion inside that small body."

Jenn's cheeks warmed slightly at his words, and she had to fight the urge to look away. "I am not small."

He shrugged. "You're tall for a woman, sure." He smiled again. "But compared to me, you're small."

And wasn't that just the hell of it? In normal situations, she felt like a bit of a giant. With Matt, though, she did feel a bit like a dainty woman.

It was kind of nice.

"After you fell asleep, I lay there and watched you for what felt like hours. I didn't want to leave, which was a first for me. A part of me wanted to wake you up and make love to you all over again, and another part wanted to wake you up and just talk. As much as I wanted to be inside of you again, I wanted to get to know you, too. That scared me. I was young, was just starting my second year in the majors, and falling in love was not in the plan for that time in my life. I'd had it all worked out in my head, ever since I was a teen—make it to the bigs by twenty-five, start the All-Star game by age twenty-seven, win my first Cy Young by twenty-eight. Love, marriage and babies didn't come into the picture until I was in my late thirties, after I'd re-tired with a guaranteed spot in Cooperstown."

"I…" she didn't know where to begin. "But I wasn't thinking love, marriage and babies. That wasn't even on the table."

"You weren't, but I was."

And suddenly, things made some sort of sense to her. His running out was still not the nicest thing he could have done, nor was it the most mature, but she understood it now. Hell, if he'd told her he was thinking love, marriage and babies she probably would have been the one to sneak out in the middle of the night.

Or run away screaming. Whichever.

Because at twenty-two? Yeah, she hadn't been ready for forever. At all.

The fact that Matt had been, though, threw her for a freaking loop. The fact that Matt had been thinking about those things with her threw her right off the tracks.

The fact that she hadn't been ready and he had and she'd accidentally gotten pregnant and then lost the baby? Yeah, her world hadn't just been knocked off its axis, but had been grand-slammed outside of the Milky Way.

"Matt—"

"You don't have to say anything, Jenn. It was way past time I explained to you what was going through my head back then. I owed you that."

"Why didn't you tell me all this before, Matt? We've seen each other plenty over the past ten years, but instead of just telling me the truth, you've let me be an angry bitch towards you—which has been kind of difficult, considering all the questions that have been asked about it."

He shrugged. Looked away. Looked back at her. "Because it was easier to let you be angry. As long as you were pissed at me and keeping me at a distance, it was easy to tell myself that I'd imagined everything I'd felt that night, that I'd just been drunk or feeling some sort of home sickness."

She'd tried to tell herself the same thing. "But you weren't drunk that night."

"It was self-preservation. Don't you get that?"

Of course she got that—what did he think she'd been doing for the past month? Hell, for the past ten years?

She moved her hand back to the inside of his collar,

needing to feel his solid strength. "I'm tired of fighting, Matt. I'm tired of manufacturing reasons to stay angry with you."

"In all fairness, you've done a pretty good job at that."

A choked laugh escaped. "Truce?"

"Truce."

Even though there were still hundreds of things they needed to talk about—like the fact that he'd been thinking love, marriage and babies with her—she pushed all of those thoughts to the back of her mind and asked him the craziest, possibly the most destructive question she could ask.

"Can you stay here tonight? I really don't want to be alone."

CHAPTER FOURTEEN

MATT WALKED INTO CHASE'S house just after nine the next morning to find Chase in the kitchen by himself, spooning scrambled eggs onto a plate. His younger brother looked up and raised an eyebrow before returning to his task.

"You sure don't look very happy for a dude who's doing the walk of shame."

This was one of those rare mornings that called for coffee. Matt ambled to the Keurig, grabbed a coffee mug, popped in a pod and hit BREW. "Do men even do the walk of shame? I thought that was solely in the domain of women."

Chase shrugged. "I honestly don't know."

The coffee finished brewing and Matt picked up his now full cup. "I mean, seriously, it's more like the walk of high fives."

"The stride of pride?"

"Complete with the theme from *Rocky* playing in the background." Matt sipped his coffee.

Chase shook his head. "You're a piece of work, you know that?"

"You're the one who accused me of doing the walk of shame."

Chase took a seat at the island and dragged his plate in front of him. "Fair enough. So if you weren't out having wild sex—and I'm still not sure if I believe that or not, by the way—where were you all night?"

Matt leaned against the kitchen counter, adopting a relaxed pose despite being anything but relaxed. There was no way in Hell he was telling Chase where he'd been all night; he was pretty sure his little brother would kick his ass five ways to Sunday if he did know.

"I met up with Owen at April's last night. It got late. I wanted to give you and Jo some privacy so I stayed somewhere else. End of story."

His brother pushed his eggs around his plate. "'Somewhere else' sure does sound vague."

"Why the twenty questions?"

"Just curious. You haven't exactly been yourself here lately."

Matt looked down into his coffee cup. "Yeah, well, getting hit in the head by a line drive and having your entire future on hold tends to throw you a bit off-kilter."

Chase scooped up some eggs on his fork, but paused before eating them. "How is your head healing? It seems like we've barely talked the past week or so."

"In your defense, you've been kind of busy with Jo and I've tried to give you two some privacy."

"Thanks for that." Chase set his fork back down.

Matt drew his eyebrows together. "Are you gonna eat those?"

Chase glanced at his plate and shook his head, sighed before saying, "I don't know what's going on. I was hungry, but as soon as I took a bite the texture was just off. I'll find something else in a bit."

Matt peered at his brother, couldn't see anything that stood out to him as being out of place, and asked, "That been happening often?"

"Off and on, but it's happened a few times in the past week. I guess I'm just going through a weird food phase. We all have them."

Except not everyone had the health issues Chase had. "When's the last time you saw your nephrologist?"

Chase glanced sharply at Matt. "I go in for a check up on Monday. Why?"

"I did some reading years ago when you first got your diagnosis. Apparently some people start having issues with food textures as their kidneys get worse, but it seems to be related more to the folks who are constantly puking."

"Huh. I haven't heard that one, but I guess it makes sense; if you're throwing up all the time you probably don't want to eat." He got up and walked over to Winchester's bowl, which he scraped his eggs into. "Why were you reading about kidney failure?"

"I was curious, but I was reading more about Vesico-ureteral Reflux than kidney failure—that just happened to be a related subject that I decided to read up on while I was at it."

Chase had been diagnosed with the disease as a child, but the doctors hadn't figured out what was wrong until after they'd already performed six other surgeries looking for cysts and other issues. Once they'd finally gotten a proper diagnosis, they'd operated in an effort to reverse the reflux. Unfortunately, the first procedure hadn't held and they'd had to perform a second one. Because of the multiple surgeries and the time spent undiagnosed, his kidneys had endured a lot of scarring.

When he was in his teens his doctor had warned them all that Chase would probably one day end up in kidney failure, which would require a transplant and possibly dialysis. Just after he'd graduated from college, Chase had found out he was in Stage 2 Chronic Kidney Disease, which meant his kidney function was definitely declining. A couple of years ago he'd been diagnosed as having Stage 3 Chronic Kidney Disease. Stage 4 basically meant he didn't have much time before hitting End Stage Renal Failure, which meant a transplant, dialysis, or death.

Because his kidneys would most likely fail at some point in his thirties or forties and that the stress of high-level athletics could do more harm than good, Chase had chosen not to pursue a career in baseball, even though he'd been one of the best collegiate closers Matt had ever seen.

And he wasn't just saying that because Chase was his little brother.

"So how have you been feeling here lately?"

Chase closed the door of the dishwasher. "I've been fine. A little tired, but I'm not getting enough sleep between work and Jo, and I'm not complaining about either."

Matt wasn't getting much sleep either these days, between worrying about his career and thinking about a certain redhead he'd left curled up in bed this morning.

"Speaking of, you've been looking pretty tired here lately yourself. Who's got you tied up in knots?"

He allowed the change in subject. "What makes you think someone's gotten me tied up in knots?"

Chase snorted. "Please. I know that look—I was seeing it in the mirror every day just a few weeks ago."

Matt shrugged, hoping he looked casual rather than guilty. Why he felt guilty he didn't know, but the feeling was definitely one he'd gotten to know a little too well here lately. Hell, if he were totally honest with himself, he'd been feeling guilty regarding Jenn for the past ten years. "No one's got me tied up in knots. I just have a lot on my mind."

"You any closer to an answer regarding your career after baseball?"

"Not a fucking clue."

Chase shook his head. "How have you not thought

about this before?"

Matt casually sipped his coffee. "Have you thought about what you're going to do once Jo goes back to Austin?"

"Not a fucking clue."

Matt tried to fight the smirk that stole across his lips, but couldn't. "It appears I'm not the only one who's been living in the moment."

"Shut it, asshole."

"Hey, now!" Matt held up his free hand. "I'm just your big brother who cares and wants to see you happy."

"Since when have you cared about how happy I am, Matt?"

He set his mug down on the counter. "Do you really believe that?"

Chase shrugged. "You've always cared more about yourself and your career, and I get that to an extent. I could have been in a similar position and I'm not, but I have at least an idea of what the pressure cooker's like. You've just always seemed to care more about Matt than anyone else."

"Once upon a time I did care more about myself than anyone else. People change."

Chase peered at him. "I don't know that you've changed all that much, bro."

"Believe what you want, but I have," he placed his coffee mug in the dishwasher and started to walk out of the kitchen, tired and confused and feeling too many emotions to name.

"Seriously, dude? You're gonna start this conversation and then walk out on it without even participating? Whatever. You keep talking about changing and being different but we both know it's just bullshit."

Matt whirled and stormed back to his brother, poked Chase in the chest as he said, "You don't know what you're talking about, Chase. Everyone sees what they want to see, and that's my fault—I only let people see what I want them to see, so what else should I expect. I'm not good at expressing emotions or letting people in. You of all people should get that at least."

Chase grabbed his finger and scoffed. "You? Not good at expressing emotions? You're like one big emotion factory you dipshit. All you do is emote here lately, but no one has any clue why. You emote and then you spout weird philosophical stuff that would make Augie Garrido proud, and then you disappear for hours on end and come back once again emoting all over the fucking place. You're right though about one thing, Matt—you don't let people see you, to the point I'm not even sure who you are anymore and I'm you're fucking brother!"

Matt snatched his finger away and glowered. "I do not emote all over the place."

"Yes, you do. That's not the point, though, Matt."

"Well what is the point, then?" He barely refrained from yelling, the tension with Chase, the tension with Jenn, and the news of Tyler that he was still processing creating a pressure cooker inside of his heart.

"Who are you, Matt? Are you Matt Roberts, the Wranglers' Ace and future Hall of Famer? Are you Matthew Roberts, son of Bo and Sarah Roberts and my brother? Are you Matt, the guy whose future is completely up in the air right now? Or are you someone else altogether?"

Weren't those just the million dollar questions?

He took a step back, and kept taking steps back until he bumped into the island. "I honestly don't know. It's probably easier to list who I'm not."

"Well then, start there."

He blew out a stream of air, looked out the window over the sink and stared at everything and nothing. "I'm not the jerk you think I am, that's for sure."

"Fine. Fair enough. You're not a jerk. I call you that

mostly to razz you anyway."

"I know. And I let you. But…I don't know who I am right now, Chase. I don't know if I'll ever be able to pitch again, and baseball's been my life for the past twenty years at least. Sometimes I feel like I don't know who I am without a baseball in my hand, which is kind of sad and pathetic when you think about it."

"Give yourself a break, Matt. Like you said, baseball's been your life for the past twenty years. That's a long time, and an old dog like you doesn't learn tricks quite as easily as he once did."

"Dude, you're two years younger than me, therefore you're in no position to talk about me being an old dog unless you're willing to call yourself an old dog, too."

Chase chuckled. "Sometimes I swear you should be an English teacher."

Everything inside of him went still, got hot then cold in an instant. "Why would you say that?"

"Have you never heard yourself speak? Your grammar is sometimes better than Jenn's, and if the two of you could ever get along you could probably team up and kick everyone's asses at Scrabble and Boggle."

He wasn't about to tell Chase that he often played Boggle online and on his phone. He also wasn't going to tell Chase that he and Jenn were getting along; that was something he currently wanted to keep to himself considering how new their truce was.

"I don't think I would have the patience to teach English."

"Maybe not English, but have you ever thought about coaching? I've seen you at summer camps with kids—you're a natural and surprisingly a great teacher."

Thoughts of Tyler suddenly flooded his brain. What would he have been like? Would he have been athletic and a baseball lover like him and Chase or would he have been bookish like Jenn? Would he have had Jenn's red hair or his dark brown hair? Her green eyes or his hazel ones? Would he have gotten all the best parts of both of them, or all the worst parts?

In his mind's eye he could see a ginger-haired boy, tall and gangly, switching out a baseball glove for a paperback—or these days, a Kindle—his hazel eyes laughing as he did so.

Invisible bands tightened around his chest, making it impossible to breathe. Last night when Jenn had told him about the baby he'd felt her emotions; all of her sadness, anger and despair. He'd pushed aside his own because she'd needed his strength to lean on.

Apparently all those emotions he'd pushed down last night had decided to appear right fucking now.

White lights danced at the edges of his vision, and Matt gulped in a harsh breath of air as the bands tried to tighten. He should be a father right now. Would have been someone's dad, someone's world. He and Jenn had created a fucking life that night.

And then just like that, that life had been lost.

The unfairness of it—the pain and bewilderment—hit him like that stupid freaking line drive had hit his head: suddenly, sharply and painfully with no warning.

The bands tightened and the white lights danced brighter.

Vaguely, he realized he was having a panic attack, but had no frame of reference to really help get him out of it. He didn't *do* panic attacks. He was a guy—men weren't supposed to feel like this. He was supposed to have his shit together—not lose it entirely.

"Matt, are you okay?"

Chase's voice sounded far away. He tried to nod. His movements were jerky, not at all like his usual self. He tried to speak, but the only thing that came out was a wheeze.

"Are you having a panic attack?"

He jerked his head from side to side. Chase moved towards him and put a hand on his back.

"Here, head between your legs. And no, I'm not being a smartass. Head between your legs." He guided Matt until he was bent at the waist, his head between his legs.

"Now, breathe in slowly. Hold it just a second. Okay. Let it out slowly." Matt did as he was told.

"Okay, let's try that again, but a little slower this time. Breathe in."

Matt inhaled.

"Okay, now breathe out slowly."

Matt exhaled slower than he had the previous time.

"Better. Now let's do that a few more times."

After a couple more rounds of inhale/exhale Matt realized Chase was breathing with him, like they were in some psychiatric Lamaze class or something.

The thought of a Lamaze class made the bands around his chest tighten again. Shit.

He forced thoughts from his head—which was not an easy thing to do—and focused on breathing slowly in and out. After long moments—minutes?—the band around his chest loosened and the white dots no longer danced at the edges of his vision. He repeated the exercise a few more times—come to think of it, the breathing technique was a little like the one he practiced in yoga—and finally stood back up.

"Better now?" Chase asked.

Matt nodded. "How'd you know what was going on?"

Chase's shrug was casual. "I've been having panic attacks since we were teens. They started after Jo stopped talking to me."

"You started having anxiety attacks because a girl stopped talking to you?" Okay, he no longer felt like such a pussy.

Chase ran a hand through his hair. "It's more that Jo ignoring me was the straw that broke the camel's back. After all the surgeries and then finding out I would probably experience kidney failure at some point, Jo not talking to me was kind of like the cherry on top of the shit sundae, y'know. I didn't really realize back then that I was in love with her, all I knew was that it felt like my world had ended."

Okay, so maybe Matt could empathize—he'd felt a little like his world had ended the morning he walked out on Jenn.

Slightly different situation there, asshole. You chose to walk out on Jenn—Chase didn't choose to have Jo drop out of his life.

Chase's voice broke through Matt's thoughts. "Mom figured out what was going on and took me to the doctor, who referred me to a therapist. Ends up I had Generalized Anxiety Disorder and PTSD. Who knew?"

Apparently not him. "How did I not know that?"

Chase shifted uncomfortably. "I asked Mom not to tell you. I was afraid you would make fun of me, which was probably stupid but we were also in high school."

"I want to say I wouldn't have made fun of you, but at that age I probably would have."

"Exactly. But hey, at least you can admit it."

"Small consolation, right?"

His brother's grin faded. "So, you wanna talk about what happened just now?"

Matt shook his head and Chase's face fell briefly before he managed to school his features. Still, though, it was enough for Matt to know he'd unintentionally hurt his brother. "It's not that I don't want to, it's that I can't."

"Well that's a bit cryptic."

"I know, and I'm sorry. It's not my story to tell, and I'm honestly still processing that story."

"Sounds intriguing."

"More like heartbreaking," he said, his voice quiet.

"You gonna be okay?"

Matt nodded his head once. "I have to be. The owner of the story needs me to be."

"Okay, so it's obvious you've met a woman, she has a pretty devastating story and it's hitting you hard. Do I have my bases covered?"

"Everything but home plate."

"And we are officially baseball nerds," Chase teased. "Seriously, though, if and when you need to talk, I'm willing to listen. Isn't that what brothers are for?"

Matt smiled, but he could tell it didn't reach his eyes. "Something like that."

Later that afternoon, Jenn sat on her couch, staring at the baseball game on TV, not seeing a thing.

Matt had stayed the night last night.

Wait. Scratch that. Matt had stayed the night last night after she'd asked him to.

Oh, holy shitbeans Batman, what had she been thinking?

That you didn't need to be alone and he's the only person who knows the story.

Shut. Up. Brain.

Unfortunately, her voice of reason was correct. She'd been lonely and emotional and knew herself well enough to know that being alone last night was the last thing she needed. Matt was there, being all comforting and smelling all manly and stuff, and she hadn't been able to push him away.

She wasn't sure she'd ever be able to push him away again after last night.

He'd been a perfect gentlemen the entire night, had held her on the couch as they'd watched another movie (*The Hangover* this time, to reward Matt for watching *Pitch Perfect*), and then had held her later on her bed. They'd both remained fully clothed and had mostly kept their hands to themselves.

It had been sweet and had kind of sucked at the same time.

Feeling confused and frustrated, Jenn threw a pillow across the room. Dammit. He was making her lose her ever loving mind.

She dropped her head into her hands and began to laugh. Oh, God, she really was going crazy. She'd told him the most emotionally devastating secret of her life last night and today she was frustrated that he'd ended that kiss and hadn't made any moves on her.

Ugh. She was the very definition of a hot mess right now.

She was antsy and full of nervous energy, like she could dance up and down her street while singing at the top of her lungs.

Is this what a mental breakdown feels like?

She closed her eyes and shook her head, opened her eyes and picked up her phone. She shot a group text to Jo, Chase and Owen.

> Jenn: Y'all up for an impromptu trip out to the lake or anything? I have some energy I need to burn off.

A few seconds later Jo responded.

> I don't know. Let me see if Chase had plans for us this evening.
>
> Chase: No plans. I'm up for whatever.
>
> Owen: Sure. Give me an hour. I'll bring beer.
>
> Jenn: Meet at Chase's since he has the

boat?

Chase: Sounds like a plan to me.

Jo: I was about to head over there anyway.

Owen: Sure.

Jenn set her phone down and smiled, feeling slightly more centered. A day out on the water with her best friends was exactly what she needed to help get her mind off of Matt.

CHAPTER FIFTEEN

SWEET BABY JESUS HE was going to die. Right here. On Chase's boat in the middle of Lake Amistad.

He was going to die a tortured, tortured man.

It was everything Matt could do to rip his gaze off of Jenn in what had to be the hottest bathing suit he'd ever seen.

Or maybe he was just going freaking loony tunes, because it wasn't like her bikini was even close to being the most revealing he'd ever seen. Still, though, viewing all that cinnamon and sugar skin was making him feel well beyond hot and bothered.

She'd shown up at Chase's about an hour ago, tote bag on her shoulder and sunglasses perched on top of her head, and had actually smiled at him when he'd opened the door. He'd been both relieved and scared—relieved that their truce was apparently still intact, scared because of all the things that simple smile had made him feel. Then she'd tilted her face up, kissed him on the cheek and whispered, "Thank you" before brushing past him and into the living room.

He'd stood there like an idiot for a good thirty seconds before remembering to close the door before Winchester escaped.

Jenn had further surprised him by inviting him to go out to the lake with them. Sure, Chase had already invited him and he'd already accepted, but the fact that Jenn had openly extended an olive branch had made him feel as good as his first professional strike out.

Right now, though, he was kicking himself for coming; seeing Jenn in that little blue bikini was driving him freaking nuts.

Yeah, but if you hadn't come, you wouldn't have gotten to see her in that little blue bikini.

Sometimes his inner voice was too smart for his own good.

Matt had to concede the fact that, yes, he was getting to see Jenn in her little blue bikini. And yes, it was an awesome sight.

Unfortunately his dick agreed, which was a little embarrassing considering his brother and Owen—not to mention Jo and Jenn—would be able to see his erection if they happened to glance at his crotch.

Think about pregnant nuns. Tommy Lee. Old people with sagging tattoos.

Slightly better.

Even though he didn't want to, he tore his gaze off of Jenn in the clear water of Lake Amistad and stood up. He walked across the boat to stand beside Chase, who was currently bass fishing.

"Why don't you join them?" he asked.

Chase slowly reeled the line back in. "I do sometimes. Mostly, though, I like the fishing. It's relaxing in a way playing chicken isn't."

"Aren't we all a little old to be playing chicken?"

Chase snorted before casting the line back out. "With this group? Never. We have to blow off steam somehow."

Matt thought about that statement, the realization that

he wasn't the only one constantly under pressure coming to him suddenly. Why that had just occurred to him, he didn't know.

Probably because you've been locked up in your own little world.

The fact was, though, they all faced different types of pressure. People thought playing a game wasn't exactly a high-stakes job, but it was; not only for himself, but for his team and the fans. If he tanked, the team wouldn't do as well, the fans would be unhappy and attendance and merchandise sales would decrease which would negatively affect the bottom line in the front office. That meant player cuts, trades and contracts worth less money. Plus, there was the pressure he put on himself as a competitor.

He'd thought he had a good grasp on the outside world, but he hadn't. Chase, Owen, Jenn and Jo all had just as much pressure on themselves as he did, probably more so considering his nest egg. Chase and Owen weren't hurting financially, but with both of them being small business owners in fields that were dependent upon the economy there was always pressure to make sure accounts balanced and that they could pay their employees. He'd seen first-hand this summer how much work Jenn put into teaching, and he didn't envy her at all the stress of being responsible for so many young minds. And Jo…good Lord he couldn't imagine the pressure that went along with being a high school guidance counselor.

He closed his eyes, the sunlight suddenly too bright. God, he really had been living in a bubble.

"You okay over there? Sure got quiet all of a sudden."

Matt blinked. "Yeah. Just thinking."

"Anything you want to talk about?"

He shrugged. "What's up with you wanting to talk about shit all of a sudden?"

Chase cast his line back out. "Dude, we're brothers.

I know talking about things isn't exactly the manly thing to do, and that we've drifted apart a little over the past ten years or so, but I still know you well enough to know when something's bothering you."

Had it really been ten years since he and Chase had truly had a conversation with some substance? He thought back, tried to recall the times they'd seen each other over the past decade, and couldn't come up with anything substantive after him sleeping with Jenn.

He swallowed the lump that had suddenly formed in his throat.

Jenn. How was it that so much in his life right now kept circling back to that long-ago night with her?

He'd been scared at the time. Scared of his emotions that night. Scared of how *right* being with her had felt. Scared of how he hadn't wanted to leave and instead had wanted to throw it all away and just stay there with her. So he'd run from her.

Apparently he'd run from everyone attached to her, too.

And wasn't that just a kick in the balls?

He rubbed his hand over his face, realized he was shaking, and let it drop again to his side. Not wanting Chase to see his physical reaction he stuffed his hands into the pockets of his board shorts.

"I know this may seem like too little too late, but until this summer I didn't realize how much I'd distanced myself from home."

Chase snorted, but didn't say anything. Matt swallowed and continued. "I think it was a little too easy. I made a lot of excuses in my twenties—I needed to train, I needed to prepare for a game, I had film to study, I had a fundraiser I needed to attend. There's always one thing after another, and instead of pushing some things aside or shuffling my schedule in order to make time, I just rolled with it because going with the flow was easier."

Chase slowly reeled in his line, but Matt could see the stiffness in his brother's shoulders. "What happened to make you change? Your rookie year it wasn't like that. When you were in the minors it wasn't like that. You always made time for us. Hell, you came to more games my senior year than Mom and Dad did."

"That wasn't exactly difficult, considering I was playing double-A ball not thirty minutes away from the Disch."

The Disch—also known as Disch-Falk Field—was the home of the Longhorns' baseball team.

"True. But you know what I'm talking about, Matt. Something happened right around the start of your second year in the bigs. At first we brushed it off as you being busy with all the things you mentioned. You'd had such a great rookie year we all understood the pressure you would be under that second season. But after that year you continued to stay distant. In the past ten years you've come home for Christmas and maybe five times for Thanksgiving. You've come to the ranch, sure, but even then you've been pretty hands-off—which I'm not complaining about, by the way, since Owen and I are here and it makes sense for us to be more hands-on with it. I'm just saying, I'm not stupid, Matt, and seeing you take that line drive to the head made me realize that life is really, really fucking short and I would kind of like to have my brother back."

Matt nodded and blinked rapidly as he stared out at the craggy limestone formations along the shoreline. "I shouldn't have pushed y'all away, I know that, and I have missed y'all. It's just…" he shrugged and sighed, "…some stuff did happen right before that year and I kind of freaked out and didn't know how to handle it. I insulated myself, tried to numb myself and just focus on what I could control. At the time that was baseball."

Chase abandoned all pretense of fishing. "Wha—I—

you didn't start doing drugs, did you?"

"Jesus Christ, Chase! No I wasn't doing drugs. I've never even so much as smoked a joint. I wouldn't jeopardize my career like that."

"Well, you said you tried to numb yourself. What else was I supposed to think?"

"Fair enough. But no, I didn't turn to drugs. I may have drank a little more than I should have, but even then I controlled it, would only let myself get to the point of relaxation. I can count on one hand the number of times I've been drunk in the past ten years."

"Sex, then?"

Matt choked out a laugh. After that night with Jenn he hadn't had sex for eight months, two weeks and five days. Not that he'd been keeping track or anything. "Not sex, either. I just…I guess I kind of turned off my emotions. The only time I allowed myself to feel anything was when I was on the mound. When I wasn't pitching, it was like I flipped a switch and just turned it all off."

Chase shook his head and laughed. "Holy shit. I can't believe I'm just now figuring this out." Panic slid through Matt's belly. "You got your heart broken."

The panic receded slightly at the realization that Chase hadn't put all the puzzle pieces together. Yet. "I wouldn't say I got it broken. But yes, there was a woman," he conceded.

"So if you didn't get your heart broken, what the hell happened man?"

Matt squinted and looked off in the distance, seeing Jenn asleep in her hotel bed rather than the lake in front of him. "I met a woman. There was a very sudden, unexpected attraction and camaraderie. It was one of those things that just hits you, that you can't explain, but you know deep down that she could be The One. We had what most people would call a one-night stand, but in my head I was thinking she was a woman I could marry, love forever and have babies with. I figured telling her that would scare her shitless, considering I was scared shitless as it was, so I left while she was asleep. I tried to forget about her, but I couldn't. No matter who I've slept with or who I've dated, she's always been there."

"Why didn't you ever try to find her and explain things to her?"

"Because I figured she hated me."

"Why?"

Matt drew in a deep breath, knowing he had to tread lightly so that he didn't give anything away. "Because when I left I didn't even so much as leave a note or my number. I just left. And yes, I'm aware that it was a total dick move."

"No shit, dude. Have you seen her since that night?"

"Off and on at social events. We mostly avoid each other." Until the past month. Being around Jenn had turned into his favorite drug. He simply craved her.

"You're an idiot. You're obviously still hung up on this chick. If she's still single you need to tell her what you just told me, get on your knees and grovel if you need to." He glanced towards the water where Jo, Jenn and Owen were splashing each other and laughing. "Believe me when I say that second chances are incredibly rare and special."

"What did happen between you and Jo all those years ago?" he asked, turning the subject off of him and onto Chase.

His brother smiled and winked. "That, my friend, is a story for a different day and time; I think we've far exceeded our quota for heavy, non-manly conversation for the day."

Matt was sure Chase heard the relief in his laugh. "Thank God. So are you gonna catch any fish or just keep throwing that line out?"

Chase scoffed and handed him a pole. "If you think

you can do any better, here. Let's see if you're still any good."

"Loser cooks dinner later?"

"You're on, sucker."

As Matt took the fishing pole from Chase he felt something he hadn't in years—relaxed.

Later that evening Jenn, Jo, Chase and Owen settled around Chase's patio table while Matt tended to the fish on the grill. Luckily Jenn had chosen a seat that was directly across from the grill, making it easier to covertly watch Matt.

She licked her lips over her glass of wine. God, the man was sexy, even in flip flops, board shorts and a faded t-shirt.

He laughed at something Chase said—something about losing a competition—and Jenn's womb clenched.

"Judging by the look on your face right now, I'm guessing you two still haven't done the deed but you desperately want to."

Jenn's cheeks warmed at Owen's whispered statement.

"Shh! Someone might hear you!"

Owen leaned closer. "Jo and Chase are totally into each other right now and Matt's way over there. No one's going to hear."

"So you think. Jo has like super hearing or something. She can sniff out emotional distress from a mile away."

"I'm not sure she can do that while her tongue's down Chase's throat."

Jenn glanced over and sure enough, Jo and Chase were having a pretty hot and heavy make out session. Watching two of her best friends kiss like teenagers should have embarrassed her, but instead all she felt was warm and slightly aroused, which kind of weirded her out.

She snapped her gaze away, and unfortunately caught Matt's in the process. He glanced over to Jo and Chase and smirked before looking at her again, his eyes heating before he turned his attention back to the grill.

"I can't believe I'm about to say this, but Jesus, Jenn, put yourselves out of misery already and jump his bones."

Jenn tore her gaze from Matt and looked at Owen. "Did you seriously just tell me to 'jump his bones'?"

Owen shrugged. "I figured I would use your language rather than mine."

"I'm not sure I should, but I'm going to ask anyway—what would your language be?"

"Fuck his brains out."

Jenn choked on air, and Owen slapped her on the back. Jo and Chase broke up their make out session long enough for Chase and Jo to simultaneously ask, "Are you okay?"

Jenn nodded yes while trying to get her breathing under control. "I'm fine. Just went down the wrong way."

Owen snort-chuckled beside her and she elbowed him in the ribs. She knew exactly where his dirty mind had gone.

Not that hers wasn't right there in the gutter with him. She was no stranger to strong language—obviously—but something about the phrase "fuck his brains out" had caused wild, hot, *carnal* images to pop into her mind.

She set her wine down and fanned herself as her coughs turned into sputters. Matt was watching her again, and she swore she could actually feel her skin glowing from his attention.

"I can't believe how much fun this is to watch," Owen whispered.

"Better watch it, Owe—you're starting to sound like a chick."

He laughed. "I guess I've spent too much time with

you."

"Whatever. I think we need some music." She pulled her phone out of the pocket of her shorts, tapped on "Music" and started up one of her playlists.

Chase groaned. "Oh, God, it's going to be one of your random playlists with pop crap on it, isn't it?"

Jenn smiled. "Deal with it, Mister. We listen to y'all's Texas country all the time with no complaints, so you can listen to something different every now and then. I promise it won't kill you."

Mumford and Sons started playing, and Jenn smiled. "See? This isn't that bad, is it?"

"I'm not really a fan, but it's better than Lady Gaga I guess," Chase said.

"I like it," Matt piped in from the grill, where he was moving the fish onto a platter.

Chase grinned. "First it was True Confessions with Matt this afternoon and now you're admitting you like some British dudes playing banjos? This has really been quite an enlightening day."

Jenn noticed that Matt faltered just slightly while setting a filet onto the platter. He steadied himself quickly, but she didn't miss the quick glance he shot her way, either.

It made her worry slightly, and wonder just what he'd told Chase this afternoon.

Calm down. If he'd told Chase about the two of you odds are Chase would have either given him a black eye or confronted you about it. He sure as hell wouldn't be teasing Matt about it right now.

"Well, there's a lot you don't know about me. And yes, I'm aware that's my fault."

Jenn's breath caught at Matt's words, and her gaze hopped from one brother to the other. For the first time that evening she realized the tension that was usually between the two men was gone. She'd seen them talking to each other out on the lake, but hadn't thought much about it. Apparently it had been one hell of a conversation, though.

"I Will Wait" came to an end and the song switched over to Taylor Swift's "Style." She laughed—couldn't help it, really—at both the look on Chase and Owen's faces (tortured pain would be the best description) and the fact that once again iTunes had proven itself to have a sense of timing and humor.

"I can't believe you're making us listen to this crap," Owen said.

She rolled her eyes. "Guys, stop being such music snobs and just relax."

"Hard to relax with this crap playing," Owen mumbled.

"Here. Maybe you'll like this playlist better," Matt said as he pulled his phone out of his shorts pocket. Jenn put Taylor on pause and watched as Matt tapped on his screen a few times. He set his phone beside hers as "Run" by Matt Nathanson and Sugarland began playing. Their gazes met and held, and both of them started laughing.

Oh, it really was just too, too perfect of a song all things considered.

They kept laughing, until Jenn was doubled over and clutching her stomach, her breaths coming fast and hard but not deep enough. Great, big belly laughs like she hadn't had in a really, really long time.

As she gulped in air and began to calm down, she noticed that there were four sets of eyes on her. Matt's were still dancing with laughter, as were Owen's. Jo and Chase, however, both had quizzical expressions on their faces.

Oh crap.

"Sorry about that. Something just struck me as being funny. Long story." She waved a hand in the air as if to dismiss the entire incident. Jo's brow was furrowed and Chase's eyes were narrowed, swinging back and forth between Matt and Jenn. She purposely didn't glance at Matt, afraid that if she did the jig would be up.

What the jig was, she didn't really know. All she did know was that she still wasn't ready for everyone else to know her business. Granted, not knowing what was going on between her and Matt probably played a part in that.

She was saved from having to make up something completely off-the-wall by the sudden ringing of Matt's phone, cutting off the song. He reached in, picked it up and glanced at the screen.

"Sorry, guys, I've gotta take this." He stepped away towards the pool and Jo got up to grab the platter of now cooling fish.

As they piled their plates with grilled, freshly caught bass, salad and roasted potatoes, Jenn kept one ear tuned to Matt. Just minutes ago he'd been more relaxed than she'd seen him in…well…ten years. Now, though, his body was tense, his jaw clenched. He rubbed a hand over his face and then his head—a sure sign he was frustrated about something—before stepping further away from the group.

Apparently whatever was going on, he didn't want anyone else to know about it.

The realization caused a tiny pang of disappointed hurt to course through her. She fought to shake it off.

It's not like you're dating. Hell, you're not even sleeping together.

Yet.

Shut. Up. The point is, you're not sleeping together and you're not dating, so you have no right to know what's going on in his life.

But I want to.

Jenn almost dropped her plate.

Instead, she tightened her grip and sat back down. She smiled as she dug in, making appropriate noises and comments when necessary while watching Matt under her lashes. He rubbed a hand over his face again, and Jenn fought the urge to go to him and offer him comfort the way he'd offered her comfort last night.

Staying in her seat was harder than she'd expected.

"You have got to be shitting me."

"Nope. I emailed you earlier but when you didn't respond I figured I should maybe call before things blow up in the media."

Matt rubbed a hand over his face and then his hair, feeling tension seep through every muscle in his body. "I've had a restraining order against that woman for years, Darrin, and we haven't heard a peep out of her. Why now all of a sudden?"

"Who knows? Apparently she saw the video on You-Tube and decided to concoct one hell of a lie about the two of you."

"Fuck."

Apparently his dear old stalker Heather had seen the YouTube video of him and Jenn dancing and had decided to start circulating lies on social media that the woman in the video was her rather than Jenn.

Never mind the fact that Heather had straight blonde hair and artificial breasts the last time he'd seen her, which was pretty much the opposite of Jenn.

"So does this mean the media's figured out where I am?"

"It looks like Heather's claiming the video was filmed here in Dallas, so for right now you're still safe. That being said, it probably won't take long until people start to figure out where that bar actually is." Matt could tell from Darrin's sudden silence that he was trying to figure out the best way to say something.

"Just spill it, Darrin."

His agent sighed on the other end of the line. "What the hell were you doing dancing with some chick at a bar? You and I both know you've been cleared for social activities, but to anyone who doesn't have access to your health record it looks like you're living it up rather than healing."

Matt tried to remember what all the video had captured. It had been taken from some distance away, so it hadn't been an incredibly clear shot of him and Jenn. It had been taken from his left side, and he'd been hit on the right side of his head, so the video hadn't captured the scar from where they'd stitched him back up.

"Any way we can spin this as an old video that someone just recently uploaded to YouTube?"

Darrin snorted. "I'm not sure if we could, especially considering the fact that it was just recently uploaded."

"Seriously, D, hear me out. The video was taken from far away and the quality was kind of shaky. It was fairly dark in the bar that night, except for the lights on the dance floor, and those were colored. Everyone knows dance floor lights in bars distort things. There's also the fact that the video was taken from my left side, and my scar's on the right. Instead of just laying low and ignoring it, why don't we get out ahead of this thing, be aggressive about it and make this story follow the narrative we want it to."

"Did you really just say 'follow the narrative'?"

Matt sighed. "Yes, I did. I find it hilarious everyone seems to forget I was an English major."

"I wasn't aware many people knew that."

He shrugged. "They don't. But that's beside the point. My point is, we need to get ahead of the count here and spin this our way rather than letting Heather take the lead. We also need to show proof of the restraining order."

Darrin fell silent again, but Matt could hear the tap tap tap of fingers against a hard surface. "Your idea has merit, I'll give you that. I also agree that getting ahead of the count would serve us well in this situation, not only for your reputation but also for your privacy. That being said, I don't know how far back we could go with this story, considering the song you were dancing to is a fairly new one."

He hadn't even paid attention to the song, had just been fascinated by Jenn and had needed to get close to her in whatever way possible. "How new?"

"Hold on, let me Google it."

Matt waited as Darrin worked his search engine magic.

"Okay, I'm back. It's not quite as new as I thought. Looks like it was released back in January so I think we should be able to spin this."

Matt breathed a sigh of relief and his muscles began to relax. "Thank God."

"I have to ask, though, who is she?"

And just like that, Matt tensed back up. "Who's who?"

"The cute redhead you're dancing with in the video."

"Are you asking as my agent or as my friend?"

"Both. As your agent I want to know about any possible problems that might pop up. As your friend I'm curious about the woman you're trying to protect."

Considering Darrin was probably the only person in the world who really knew him, Matt didn't even try to hide the truth. "She's someone I've owed an apology to for a very, very long time."

Darrin's sharp inhalation was unmistakable. "Wait a second. Is that San Antonio girl?"

Darrin was also the only person Matt had ever told about that night, mostly because he'd been drunk off his ass one night about five years ago and had been feeling maudlin and nostalgic. "Yes, it is."

"Holy shit, man. Okay. I'm going to run with your idea and see what we can do legally regarding Heather. I'm also going to see about pulling that video. In the meantime, try to stay out of bars, alright?"

Matt relaxed again. "I'll try."

"And don't fuck this up with San Antonio girl again."

Matt turned, caught Jenn watching him and smiled. "I don't plan on it, D."

He ended the call and walked back over to the patio.

"Everything alright?" Chase asked.

Matt smiled as he sat across from Jenn. "Fine. Darrin just had some stuff he needed to talk to me about."

"On a Saturday night?" Jo asked.

He shrugged and met Jenn's worried gaze. "You know how it is, no rest for the weary and all that."

She gave him a little half smile, but he could tell she was still worried. "Everything's good. No worries. Anyway. How's the fish?" he asked as he reached for the platter of what was probably now-cold fish.

Everyone murmured sounds of appreciation, but his gaze remained fixed on Jenn. He gave her a reassuring smile, waited until everyone's attention was elsewhere and mouthed to her, "Later."

She nodded her head, smiled and went back to her salad as Matt thought about the fact that in just twenty-four hours they'd gone from Jenn hurling insults at him to worrying about him. The obvious concern on her face—for him—caused a slight pang somewhere in the vicinity of his heart. Idly, he rubbed his chest, wondering if she would ever stop making him feel like he was on the craziest roller-coaster ride of his life.

CHAPTER SIXTEEN

"So do you want the good news or the bad news first?" Rene asked as soon as Jenn answered the phone.

Jenn closed her eyes and sighed. "Lay it on me, Rene. Give me the bad news first."

She sensed her friend's hesitation before the other woman finally said, "Well, the bad news is that the You-Tube video went viral yesterday."

"Seriously?" Why hadn't Matt told her? Unless he didn't know, but he was constantly on Facebook and Twitter—he would know if it had gone viral. Then again, he'd barely touched his phone yesterday and last night, except for that one call from Darrin.

"Seriously."

"So what's the good news?"

"The good news is that it was mysteriously taken down this morning and there's some chick on Twitter bitching about it. Apparently she'd started bragging yesterday about the video, sending the link to media outlets and telling them the woman in the video was her and that she could give them an exclusive as to how Matt Roberts is doing and where he's been hiding."

Is this real life, or is this just fantasy?

Jenn groaned. "Do you know what the chick's name was?"

Rene made a dismissive sound. "Heather something or other. She sounds like a total flake."

Jenn collapsed back onto her bed and threw an arm over her eyes. "I cannot believe that bitch just popped back up."

"Wait. You know this woman?"

"I wouldn't say I know her. I know of her, and I've had a run-in with her in the past. Long story short, she's not a nice person and Matt's had a restraining order against her for like the past nine years or so."

Rene whistled low. "Girl. I don't know what you've gotten yourself involved with, but this is almost as good as *Grey's Anatomy* re-runs."

"I don't know if there's a TV show on the planet that could compare to the weird mess that is my life right now." *Or, y'know, the weird mess your life has been for the past ten years.*

"So I have to ask…"

"No."

"You didn't even let me ask!"

"Because I totally knew where you were going with that."

"Where'd you think I was going?"

Jenn sighed. "You were going to ask me if I've slept with him."

"I was just going to ask if you'd kissed him."

"Bullshit," Jenn laughed.

Rene tried to feign hurt, but then dissolved into laughs of her own. "Damn, you do know me too well. I take that as a no, you haven't slept with him or a no, you're not talking about it?"

"How about 'it's a really complicated situation'?"

"Girl, I told you, this is better than a *Grey's* re-run."

"You're just bored is all."

"Damn straight I am. I have to live vicariously through someone these days."

Jenn rolled her eyes. "I'm not sure I'm the one you should be living vicariously through."

"Girl, you're sleeping with a super hot baseball star. I am so living vicariously through you."

"I am not sleeping with him!" she exclaimed—loudly—just seconds before hearing her doorbell.

"Ooh. Booty call?"

"Are you for real?" she asked Rene as she climbed out of bed and padded towards the living room.

"I am so for real. Please tell me it's McBaseball at your door, looking all hot and like he wants to ravish you."

Jenn stopped in the middle of her living room and whispered into her phone, "McBaseball? Really? How many *Grey's Anatomy* re-runs have you watched this summer?"

"All of them. Every. Single. One."

"My God you need a life."

"Like I said, I'm totally living vicariously through you."

Jenn reached the door, looked through the peephole. It was indeed McBaseball—erm, Matt—at her door. She smiled and opened the door. Matt stood there, smiling back at her and Jenn said, "Hey, Rene? I'm gonna let you go."

She could hear her friend yelling something about ravishing and baseball as she pulled the phone away from her ear. She tapped on "end," and stepped aside to let Matt in.

"Sorry, didn't mean to interrupt your call."

She closed the door behind him. "It's okay. Besides, you had no way of knowing I was on the phone anyway."

Said phone dinged in her hands. Jenn glanced down at the screen. There was a text message from Rene telling her to "Jump all over that and get you some." Jenn shut down her phone. The last thing she needed was more suggestive text messages from her very married, suddenly inappropriate friend.

"So what's up?" she asked once her phone had shut down.

Matt shrugged, his hands tucked into the back pockets of his jeans, causing his faded Wranglers' Championship tee to stretch across his chest. Her mouth watered.

"Nothing, really. The sex bunnies were going at it again this morning—loudly, I might add—so I decided to get out of there and stop torturing myself."

"Sex bunnies?"

A corner of his mouth twitched upwards. "I figure they're going at it like rabbits these days, might as well give them a cute nickname."

Jenn shook her head. "Sex bunnies. Well, I have to say I'm glad they're doing so well. They've been in love with each other since we were kids, so it's about time."

He rocked back on his heels. "I'm going to have to get that entire story at some point."

"I would tell you, except it's not my story to tell. Let's just say we all do dumb things when we're young and hurting."

"Fair enough. I can't say I haven't done some stupid stuff, so I'm the last one to cast stones."

"Like I said, we've all done something stupid at one point or another."

He moved towards her, closing the gap between them. He removed his hands from his back pockets and brought one up so he could tuck an errant curl behind her ear. "I don't know if I can say 'I'm sorry' enough."

He cupped her cheek with his palm and Jenn closed her eyes. "You don't have to keep apologizing, Matt. We both did dumb things."

"Yeah, but you're the one who bore the brunt of the

hurt."

Jenn opened her eyes and mimicked him, cupping his cheek with her hand. Despite the fact that it was ten in the morning stubble already scraped against the sensitive skin of her palm, causing heat to pool in her belly. "I'm strong, Matt. I got through it okay."

"I know." He closed his eyes and nodded his head once before opening them again. "I know that. I just wish I'd done things differently is all."

"Woulda, coulda, shoulda. I wish I'd handled things differently, too. Friday night, though? I feel like I finally put the past behind me, Matt, so let's not go there again, okay?"

He nodded and gave her a small, uncertain smile. "Okay. The past is in the past. Kind of. I have something I need to tell you first."

"Is it about the YouTube video and Heather?"

He dropped his hand. "How'd you know?"

Jenn waved her phone in the air. "That was my friend Rene, the one who told me about the video in the first place. She'd called to let me in on the latest gossip, and I put two and two together and figured that's what Darrin had called you about last night."

"Are you okay?"

"Why wouldn't I be okay? You're the one who's apparently still being stalked by Psycho Barbie."

Matt threw back his head and laughed. "I think I'm going to have to share that one with Darrin."

"Feel free. At any rate, she told me the video went viral yesterday, that Heather's claiming she was the woman in the video and that as of this morning it had suddenly disappeared."

"That's the condensed version, yes. I needed to tell you about the statement Darrin's sending to media outlets, though."

Jenn grabbed his hand and led him to the couch, where they sat and she snuggled up to him. Matt slung an arm around her shoulders and she rested her head on his chest. It was everything she could do to not turn her head and breathe him in. The man smelled so freaking good.

She must have made some sort of sound, because Matt shifted slightly and said, "Okay, let's talk about this statement before you completely distract me."

She could feel herself blush, but couldn't hide the pleased smile that curved her lips. "Sorry. Didn't mean to distract you."

"You always distract me," he practically growled. Her ovaries quivered.

She looked up at him, and the look on his face was intent, like he'd zeroed in on her and had pushed everything else out of his brain. She'd somehow forgotten about his single-minded focus.

It had served him well on the mound and in bed. The thought made her nipples tighten and wetness to pool between her thighs.

A strangled sound escaped her throat and she pushed up onto her knees, swung around so she straddled him and claimed his mouth with hers. Matt's arms tightened around her briefly before his hands began to roam over and claim her body.

Oh, God, she so wanted to be claimed by him.

She moaned and pressed against him, could feel the hard length of him behind the zipper of his jeans surging and pressing against her core, and she wiggled her hips. Delicious friction arched through her body, and she rotated her hips again and his fingers dug into her ass. Their tongues tangled and dueled, caressed and seduced as she ground against him, no longer in control of her body's movements.

The lace of her panties scraped against her clit with

every movement. Jenn wiggled closer, wanting nothing more than to climb inside of Matt. Anything to release this wanting, needing ache.

He tore his mouth away from hers and groaned. "Jenn. If you don't stop…"

She rested her forehead against his. "Can't. Stop."

Jenn sought his mouth again, swallowed another groan from him as the pressure gathered, coiled tight and built higher, higher, higher. Matt's fingers dug into her flesh, and the thought that she was going to have handprints on her ass tomorrow briefly flew through her mind until that thought spiraled down, low, low, low where it coiled and tightened before exploding.

She moaned against his mouth as her muscles continued to spasm, feeling satisfied but empty. The thought left her suddenly sad. As much as she wanted to crawl inside of Matt, she probably wanted him inside of her more.

As her movements stilled his grip on her ass loosened and their kiss turned more languorous and exploratory rather than explosive. Jenn's hands drifted down his chest, and when they reached the button of his jeans she scooted back enough to work it free.

"Jenn…"

"Shh." She placed a quick kiss on his lips. "I got mine. Fair's fair."

He kept his hands on her hips as she unbuttoned and then unzipped the denim. She looked down. His blue boxer briefs were wet and the fabric darkened against the head of his dick. She smiled and looked back up at him as she slid the cotton over and down until he sprang free, and smiled at his hard swallow when she grasped him in her hand.

He was bigger than she remembered. Hard, thick and hot as she caressed his cock. He flexed his hips. "I don't know how long I'm going to last."

"That's okay."

She continued to pump her fist up and down his length as he flexed his hips. Their harsh breaths were the only sounds in the house. Her muscles clenched again at the thought.

This man is going to be the death of me.

His fingers tightened on her hips as his dick stiffened and surged in her hand. She watched his face as he came all over her hand, the sensation weirdly erotic.

After long moments Matt's body relaxed beneath hers, and he opened his eyes. Their gazes met, and she detected a brief glint of embarrassment in his before he covered it up. She looked down at her hand, his cock still hard and slowly pulsing, and back up at him. "Don't you dare be embarrassed about this."

Pink tinged his cheeks. "It's been a long time since I came from a hand job."

"Well, then, that just means I'm awesome."

He smiled and shook his head. "I don't know what to do with you sometimes."

She looked down and back up again. "I think you've got some of it down." She then swung around so that she was no longer straddling him, got up and walked to the bathroom where she washed off her hand and grabbed a washcloth to help Matt clean up.

She looked up. He was standing in the doorway of the bathroom, his pants still unbuttoned and his boxer briefs pulled down. She handed him the washcloth, which he took, dampened and cleaned up with.

Even though watching him felt uncomfortably intimate she couldn't look away.

He finished, tossed the washcloth into the hamper in the corner and pulled up his boxer briefs before zipping and buttoning his jeans. He looked up and met her gaze with his own. She blushed, knowing she'd been caught watching him.

Instead of saying anything, though, he simply leaned in and softly kissed her before pulling away, looking more like a shy, unsure man than the most intimidating pitcher in baseball.

Something in her chest tightened then loosened, spiraled down down down and settled deep and unmovable.

She didn't have long to consider the sensation, though, because Matt grabbed her hand and led her back into the living room.

Later, she told herself, *I'll think about that later.*

"So about this statement," Matt said once they'd settled back onto the couch.

Jenn tucked her legs underneath her as she snuggled back under his arm. "Yes, about this statement."

"Darrin's sending it to media outlets and telling them it's an older video that was just recently uploaded to YouTube for some reason. He's also releasing the terms of the restraining order I have against Heather to prove it's not her."

"That makes sense."

He wound a curl around his index finger. "You're not upset?"

She looked up at him. "Why would I be mad?"

"One, that Heather's trying to claim I was dancing with her rather than you and two, that I'm trying to disassociate myself from being in Del Rio and in April's that night."

"I'm not going to be mad about you trying to disassociate yourself from being in Del Rio. You've gotten lucky so far that the media hasn't tracked you down. As for Heather? That bitch doesn't even deserve a thought much less my anger."

He kissed her on the top of her head, grateful she'd

been so understanding. "So what do you have planned for today?"

Her stomach rumbled and she laughed. "Apparently my stomach wants me to feed it. After that I figured I would work on finalizing some lesson plans since this is my last free week before my summer break is over."

"Sounds exciting."

She picked at her thumb nail. "Actually, I was going to ask you something I've been thinking about for a couple of weeks, but haven't known how."

He stilled briefly before continuing to wrap her hair around his finger. *Kind of like how she has you wrapped around hers.* "Shoot."

"So there's this book I'm teaching this year to my students, called *Curveball: The Year I Lost My Grip*. It's a young adult novel about an all-star pitcher who injures his arm just before his freshman year of high school and he finds himself trying to figure out who he is without baseball. I was wondering—if you're still around when I have the kids read the book—if you would be willing to come in and talk to one or two of my classes about baseball and other lessons and stuff," she said in a rush.

Matt shook his head. "What makes you think I would be a good person to talk to a bunch of seventh graders?"

She shot him a look that clearly said *please*. "Because you're a great speaker. You're engaging, you don't lay on the bullshit and it would be great for my kids to hear from someone they look up to as a role model."

"I'm nobody's role model."

Jenn sat up and turned so she was facing him. "Like it or not, Matt, you are. Kids look up to you. Boys want to be you when they grow up. You're our hometown boy done good, and you've mostly done it the right way."

"Mostly?"

Her mouth quirked up. "Well, there was that one-night

stand in San Antonio."

He laced his fingers through hers. "You know you were more than that, right?"

"I know." She squeezed his hand. "But that's not the subject at hand. I understand if you don't want to do it, and I understand if you can't. It was just an idea I had that I thought would be a really cool bonus for one or two of my classes."

"Can I think about it?"

She nodded. "Absolutely. And I mean it, Matt, no pressure. Don't feel like you have to out of some misguided sense of honor or because of whatever this is going on between us right now."

Apparently now that they'd addressed the elephant in the past Jenn wasn't holding back on addressing the elephants in the present. "Fair enough. I'll think about it. As to the rest of your statement…"

She rolled her eyes. "That's okay, too, Matt. I'm good with just going with the flow right now. To be honest, I'm enjoying this truce and not feeling any pressure. Besides, with so much in the air what good does it do us to try to define anything?"

Her statement left him feeling slightly unsettled because, in a weird sort of twist, he did want to define whatever this was between them. If Jenn was okay with going with the flow, though, he could try to do the same for her sake.

Definitions could always come later.

Jenn's stomach growled again, and Matt pushed aside his unease and uncertainty and smiled at her. "Come on, pretty lady, let's go get some lunch."

She smiled back at him. "Sounds good to me. Let me throw on some clothes first, though."

"Don't get dressed on my account." He really did like seeing her in these tiny tank tops and even tinier boxer shorts she seemed to enjoy wearing.

She unfolded her long legs and got up from the couch. "More like on account of public decency. Be right back."

She disappeared down the hall and into her bedroom, and Matt rested his head against the back of the couch cushions. He blew out a long, slow breath and closed his eyes against the swirling, falling sensation in his gut.

This woman. This woman was either going to be the life or death of him, he wasn't sure which just yet.

CHAPTER SEVENTEEN

"WELL THERE YOU ARE, stranger," Sarah said as Matt stepped into his parents' kitchen later that afternoon. His mom quickly came to him and wrapped flour-covered arms around him, enveloping him with the scent of vanilla and sugar.

He glanced hopefully towards the mixer on the countertop. "Chocolate chip?"

"With walnuts."

He squeezed his mom and bussed her on the cheek. "Best. Mom. Ever."

She swatted him once he let her go, and then turned back to her cookie dough. "What's got you in such a good mood?"

He shrugged and fought the smile that wanted to spread across his face. "Just been a good day is all."

She looked over her shoulder at him, her salt and pepper hair held back by a thin silver headband. "Even with the rumors that girl tried to get started about the YouTube video?"

Matt's happiness faltered and stumbled just a little bit. "Even with the rumors."

Sarah spooned dough onto a baking sheet and Matt

leaned against the kitchen island, his mouth watering. His mom made the best chocolate chip cookies.

"You and Jenn sure did look cozy in that video."

Matt choked on air and coughed to cover it up. And this was what he'd been afraid of. Sarah didn't look back at him, but he could only imagine the expression on her face. She was probably ready to kill him, or at least leave the walnuts out of his cookies. His parents loved Jenn like the daughter they'd never had, and he could only imagine what they would think—or do—if they found out about him and a certain sexy seventh grade teacher.

He schooled his features and tried to make sure his voice was calm and even. "We're friends who were just dancing with each other."

"Oh, please. Don't try to B.S. me Matthew Roberts. I saw the way you were looking at each other in that video. You don't dance together like that if you're just friends."

She didn't sound angry. Instead, she sounded weirdly pleased. Thrown for a loop yet a little curious, Matt cautiously said, "Would you have a problem if we were more than friends?"

"I love that girl like a daughter. I obviously love you like a son. I've been waiting for both of you—and Chase— to settle down and give me babies to cuddle. It looks like Chase and Jo are finally getting their acts together, so I was hoping either you or Jenn would be next. If you and Jenn get your acts together, well, together, that's even better as far as I'm concerned. Just don't break her heart—that girl's got some secret pain, and try as I might I've never been able to get it out of her."

Matt swallowed the lump of guilt lodged in his throat. Before he could say anything, though, Sarah continued. "And she better not break your heart, either. I know you think you've got this tough guy image but I know you—I did give birth to you, after all—and you've always been a bit sensitive."

Matt rubbed at his chest as Sarah opened the oven and slid the cookie sheet onto a rack. "I'm not sensitive."

Sarah wiped off her hands with a dish towel and stepped towards him. She cupped his cheek with her palm—a sign of affection he hadn't realized until now he'd picked up from her—and smiled. "Oh, my sweet boy, yes you are. You may have the arm and body of a serious athlete, but inside you have a poet's soul." She turned away and pulled another cookie sheet out of a cupboard. "Do you remember when you were a boy, before the first time you picked up a baseball? You used to sit with me and have me read fairy tales to you. As you got older your favorite books were always escapist tales of adventure and romance. Do you not remember how many times you watched *The Princess Bride*?"

It was probably well over a hundred at this point. The movie was a classic, for crying out loud. "All those stories had danger and intrigue, too, and there's humor and sword fighting in *The Princess Bride*, not to mention Andre the freaking Giant."

Sarah swatted him with the end of a cup towel. "Oh, please. Don't try to pull the wool over my eyes young man."

He held up his hands in surrender. "Fine. I have a thing for fairy tales and *The Princess Bride*. There's nothing wrong with that."

It sure didn't make him less of a man. Right? Right?

"No, there's nothing wrong with that." Sarah turned towards the oven, opened the door and pulled out a sheet full of perfectly baked walnut chocolate chip cookies.

Matt's mouth began to water, so he walked over to the refrigerator, grabbed a gallon of milk and poured himself a glass. Before Sarah could catch him he grabbed a still-hot cookie off the sheet, bounced it between his hands briefly before setting it down on a saucer his mom handed him. He bit in, closing his eyes as the flavors danced over his tongue, savoring the semi-sweet chocolate mingled with walnuts and vanilla. He chased his bite of cookie with a drink of his milk.

"You're using protection, right?"

He spit milk everywhere. Sarah simply handed him her cup towel.

"Jesus, Mom. What the hell kind of question is that? And with whom?"

"With Jenn, obviously. And it's an important one."

He mopped up the milk and prayed for patience. "Jenn and I aren't...we're not...we're just friends, Mom."

Friends who make out and have really hot fooling around sessions.

He set the towel aside and pinched the bridge of his nose.

"But you want to be more than friends."

"What am I, in high school?"

Sarah laughed. "No. You're definitely not in high school. I just like to know what's going on with my boys."

Matt broke another piece off his cookie, popped it into his mouth and chewed thoughtfully. It was kind of weirding him out that his mom seemed to be encouraging him and Jenn dating, not to mention her sudden interest in his love life. On the flipside, the fact that his mom wasn't freaking out at the thought of him and Jenn dating made him feel slightly less nervous about the situation. If he had Mom in his corner, that would go a long way towards getting Chase in his corner, and if he were being completely honest with himself his brother's reaction was the one he worried about the most.

He took a sip of milk and swallowed before choosing his next words carefully. "That secret hurt you mentioned

Jenn having? Part of that is my fault."

Sarah continued to calmly spoon cookie dough onto the baking sheet on the counter, her back towards Matt. "I don't know that I want details, but I'm willing to listen if you need to talk."

He contemplated the final piece of his cookie, the lumps and bumps of disparate ingredients that combined to form something so good, and said, "I'm sorry I haven't been around much the past ten years. I always thought I was living without regrets, but being home this summer and, well, almost dying have kind of shown me that that was bullshit."

"I always knew you would come back to us completely, Matthew. You had to go your own way and live your own life, and Dad and I understood that."

His mom's words, spoken with affection rather than anger, soothed a place in his soul he hadn't realized was hurting. "It's just…I hurt Jenn and I was embarrassed and honestly a little scared to be around her, and I knew that if I came home too often, spent too much time with y'all or Chase that odds are Jenn and I would bump into each other. It was just easier to avoid everyone rather than confront my own mistakes."

Sarah moved to the oven and removed the second cookie sheet, setting it on top of a trivet before placing the next one in the oven. Once that was done, she propped her elbows on the island across from him, her eyes filled with understanding. "Oh, honey, we've all made mistakes. Some of us never own up to them, while others simply take time to find their way. While a part of me wants to ground you for hurting Jenn, the other part of me is proud you're facing those things now—whatever those things may be."

A small smile played at his lips. "Mom, you can't ground me anymore. I'm thirty-five."

"No, but I can take away all of the cookies."

He held a hand to his heart. "Ouch. Way to hit a man where it hurts."

"Judging from that video I saw last night, you're doing a good job making up for whatever it is you did."

Matt shook his head. "Believe it or not, at that point she still wanted to rip my head off."

Sarah arched an eyebrow. "Matthew, honey, who ever said love has to make any sense?"

"Love? Who said anything about love? She just decided she likes me two days ago."

She threw her head back and laughed. "Oh, sweetie, you have so much to learn about women—and yourself, still."

Love? That's just crazy talk. Jenn doesn't love me. I don't love Jenn.

Or does she?

Do I?

Oh fuck this. I'm just gonna have another cookie.

Later that night, Matt lay in the bed in Chase's guest room and replayed the conversation with his mom in his mind.

What if Jenn was in love with him?

He dismissed the thought almost as soon as it entered his head.

There was no way Jenn was in love with him. Like he'd told Sarah, Jenn had just decided two nights ago that she could get along with him.

Now, if they were talking about lust, Matt had no doubt that Jenn wanted him. But wanting someone physically and wanting someone emotionally were two completely different things. Jenn seemed to finally be getting comfortable with the attraction that burned hot between them—if this morning was any indication—but he seriously doubted she was in love with him.

His phone dinged beside him. He picked it up. Another freaking Twitter alert. He set the phone back face down on the bed.

He was so fucking tired of Twitter.

Sighing, he returned to his conundrum.

He was pretty sure there was no way Jenn felt anything beyond lust and a budding friendship towards him. He tried not to let that thought hurt, but it kind of did. Dammit.

Was Mom kind of right? Is love involved here?

Honestly, he didn't know. He'd never been in love before, had always managed to stay emotionally detached from the women he'd casually dated. The only woman he'd ever been with who'd made him feel anything was Jenn.

And it scared you so bad you ran from her hotel room like a fucking pussy.

But had it been love that night, or just an unexpected attraction that he blew up to something bigger in his mind because of their shared history? Besides, who fell in love after one night of sex?

No one. That's who.

So, no, he couldn't be in love with Jenn.

But if he wasn't, what *was* this feeling, this burning need to be near her, to see her smile and hear her voice? Why did he crave her touch and her scent?

Why the hell couldn't he get her out of his head?

His phone dinged again. He picked it back up, read the latest tweet and barely resisted throwing the phone across the room.

CHAPTER EIGHTEEN

@Deadspin: Throw hard. Party hard. Matt Roberts livin' it up while on DL deadsp.in/lO1VeRs

@ESPN: Where's Matt Roberts? Club says pitcher in DFW. Mystery video says elsewhere. es.pn/0danC1E

@BR_MLB: Per sources, @MattRoberts not in Dallas but Del Rio, dancing it up ble.ac/2LIgit2

JENN SIGHED AS SHE read the latest tweets coming in tonight. Trepidation slogging through her veins she clicked on the link to open up the *Deadspin* article, half afraid of what she would see. Considering the source, she never knew if she was going to get a legitimate sports news story or pictures of some random athlete's dick.

As much as she'd enjoyed seeing Matt's penis earlier, she wasn't sure she wanted to see photos of it plastered all over the internet.

The article loaded and she found herself staring a gif of her and Matt dancing at April's that night. Shit.

"The internet really is forever," she murmured to herself.

Jenn scrolled past the gif to the story. Or, rather, the one paragraph and couple of lines of text that passed for an article.

That right there is a gif of a man loving being on the DL, folks. Just a month after taking a line drive to the head that almost killed him, Wranglers' ace Matt Roberts was seen living it up at a bar. Somewhere. Professional athlete stalker Heather Smith claims the woman in the video is her, but Smith is a blonde with artificial breasts, which this woman obviously is not.

So, folks, who's the mystery lady? And where's Waldo—erm, Matt Roberts?

Ugh. Apparently *Deadspin* hadn't received Darrin's statement yet, or they were ignoring it for the sake of celebrity gossip.

Which she was suddenly a part of.

Her life had taken a really strange turn over the past few weeks, that was for sure.

Jenn closed out the tab with the *Deadspin* article and clicked on the ESPN article next.

As Matt Roberts was carted off the field on a stretcher a month ago, baseball fans around the country held their collective breaths. It was the image of baseball nightmares—a quick comebacker straight to the mound, and the pitcher's head.

Over the course of any given season close to a million pitches are thrown. 99.9% of those pitches will not result in a line drive that comes back to the mound—and the pitcher's head. Roberts, unfortunately, became a part of that less than .10% of a chance and suffered a fractured skull and brain bleed. Fans sighed in relief when the Wranglers' released a statement about Roberts' health just a few days later. Their ace would be okay and was recovering in a local hospital which he would be released from most likely within the week.

No one has seen or heard from Roberts since that final hand wave as he was rolled off the field.

Until this past weekend.

Yesterday a video surfaced of Roberts dancing with a woman in a bar. A woman named Heather Smith claims the woman is her, but court records show Roberts has had a restraining order against Smith for nine years. So who is the mystery woman, and why is the Wranglers' injured number one hurler dancing in a bar when he should be healing?

"The video that went viral on Saturday is not a current video, but rather one taken several months ago prior to Matt's injury," said Darrin Mann, Roberts' agent and business partner in a media statement. "Matt is currently focusing on healing his body so he can get back out on the mound and help lead the Wranglers to a World Series championship."

When asked for comment, Wranglers' Manager Toby Prince said he'd been in touch with Roberts and he was "resting comfortably" at his Dallas condo. Wranglers' General Manager Reed Thornhill could not be reached for comment at press time.

Despite Mann and Prince's comments, though, the mystery remains—where is Roberts and is he taking his injury seriously? An online search of the username associated with the YouTube video found that the owner of the account lives in Del Rio, TX, which is Roberts' hometown.

Many injured athletes—especially those on the DL for an undetermined amount of time—often return to their homes to recuperate and to enjoy a certain amount of privacy while doing so.

This could be an old video, or it could be a new one and Roberts and the Wranglers are simply trying to spin this in order to keep fan confidence high. Whatever it may be, we here at ESPN hope one of baseball's brightest stars is not jeopardizing his future and more importantly his health for the sake of a pretty woman.

Well, that certainly didn't sound too promising, but at

least the ESPN writer had included part of Darrin's state-ment in his article.

With a sigh, Jenn clicked on the link in the *Bleacher Report* tweet and loaded what she was sure would be yet another scintillating article speculating on Matt's where-abouts and post-injury behavior.

The Texas Wranglers have a problem on their hands. No, not the fact that they're in a very tough division in a tight pennant race but the fact that their ace Matt Roberts was recently videoed partying in his hometown of Del Rio, Texas rather than rehabbing in Dallas like the team claims.

Roberts' agent and business partner, Darrin Mann, released a statement earlier today claiming the video is an old one, taken earlier this year rather than recently. We reached out to several sources who refuted Mann's com-ments and have informed us that the video is in fact recent.

"Oh, yeah, he's in here all the time," said one source who wished to remain anonymous. "I've seen him dancing with several women and have seen him leave with women, too. Sometimes more than one."

Jenn rolled her eyes. She would bet hard-earned money that this supposed anonymous source was either Heather or one of the numerous jersey chasers who'd unsuccessfully tried to pick him up over the past few weeks.

While speculation about Roberts' activities runs ram-pant, another source has identified the mystery woman in the video as seventh-grade teacher Jennifer McDonnell.

"That's my seventh grade English teacher, Ms. Mc-Donnell," said former student Lucas Oakenfeld. "She was really cool, for a teacher. I think she's best friends with Matt's brother or something."

McDonnell is indeed friends with the Wranglers' ace's brother, Chase Roberts. The younger Roberts was the closer for the Texas Longhorns during their decade-ago dominance of collegiate baseball that included two Col-

*lege World Series Championships and seven College World
Series appearances in a ten-year span. Sources tell us that
McDonnell is a long-time family friend.*

*"Oh, she and those Roberts boys have been friends for
ages," said Betty Harris, a family friend. "They've known
each other since they were children, which is probably why
they were dancing together."*

Jenn snorted. Family friend her ass. Betty Harris was a
gossiping old biddy who probably had a pair of binoculars
trained on the entire neighborhood at all times.

*As for what Roberts was doing in a bar just a month
after a horrific injury is anyone's guess. All that is known is
that the Wranglers have a problem and need to get it fixed
before the pennant race begins in earnest.*

Oh, for the love of all things chocolate, Matt was not a
problem the Wranglers needed to worry about. It appeared,
though, that she *did* have a problem on her hands—her
name was now out there in the media, and it wouldn't take
long before other outlets picked it up and showed up at her
doorstep.

Fantastic.

She picked up her phone—thankful she and Matt had
actually exchanged phone numbers this morning—and texted a certain too-sexy pitcher.

> Jenn: Did you see the Bleacher Report
> article that just hit Twitter?
> Matt: No. I think I'm taking a Twitter
> break.
> Jenn: Bad timing for that.
> Matt: Why? What's up?
> Jenn: Just go read it. Please?

She waited a few minutes for Matt to
respond.

> Matt: Fuck me. I am so sorry. I don't
> know how they got your name.

Jenn: It was bound to happen sooner or
later.
Matt: Calling you.

Jenn's phone rang seconds later, Matt's name popping up on the screen. "Seriously, don't stress yourself out about it. This was bound to happen sooner or later."

"It shouldn't have happened, though." She could almost feel Matt's anger through her phone.

"Matt, it's okay. I've always known this was a possibility considering I'm so close to Chase. I've been through this media mess with him before, too. This ain't my first rodeo."

Matt sighed. "I know it's not. I just hate that you got dragged into this and now people are going to be hounding you and speculating."

"Frankly, I'm more ticked about the fact that people are even considering your loyalty to the Wranglers and your dedication to rehab."

"I haven't even gotten to start rehabbing yet."

She waved a hand in the air, despite the fact that he couldn't see it. "Whatever. You know what I meant. You're taking this injury seriously, and for anyone to doubt that pisses me off. It's killing you to not be playing, and you certainly haven't been out partying or 'living it up'."

He chuckled. "I kind of love the fact that you're defending me now."

She shrugged one shoulder. "Well, that's what friends do."

"Is that what we are? Friends?"

She swallowed past the lump in her throat. "I think so."

"What if I told you I think we should be more than friends?" Jenn was glad she was sitting down considering how weak his low, husky voice made her knees.

"I'd say you were crazy."

"That's not what your body said this morning."

"Yeah, well, my body's a whore."

Matt laughed. "You did not just call your body a whore."

"Sure I did. I mean, come on, it has a mind of its own. I sure as hell didn't give it permission to do what it did this morning."

"Now I know you're lying. You enjoyed every minute of what happened this morning."

She resisted the urge to bang her head against the desk.

"I'm pushing too hard, aren't I?" The quiet concern in his voice nearly made her melt.

Nearly.

She stared at her computer screen, not really seeing it, and slowly said, "Yes and no. I can't lie to you and say I'm not attracted to you, but us being more than friends? That's just crazy talk, Matt."

"Why?"

"You know why."

"No, I really don't. Spell it out for me."

She sighed. "You're you and I'm me, for one. For another, it would just be a really bad idea."

Epically bad, even.

"What does that even mean? I'm Matt and you're Jenn. We've known each other since we were kids. We slept together ten years ago, I reacted badly and hurt you. Now we're actually somewhat friends. I like you. You like me. End of story."

"It's not that simple."

"Yes, it is."

"God, you're stubborn."

"I prefer determined."

"Semantics."

He chuckled. "Okay, I'll stop pushing. For now."

A part of her was relieved. The other part kind of wanted him to keep pushing her. How messed up was that?

"Anyway, back to the original subject. I'll call Darrin and let him know about the *Bleacher Report* article. If anyone shows up at your house let me know, please?"

"Okay."

"And Jenn?"

"Yeah?"

"I still think we should be more than friends."

Matt ended the call before Jenn could respond, his grin quickly dying. He was telling the truth—he really did think they should be more than friends—but more than that he was worried about Jenn.

He knew better than anyone how the media beast could chew you up and spit you out without so much as a "thank you." The media was ruthless, especially in today's social media-driven twenty-four hour news cycle. Now that one major sporting news outlet had gotten a hold of Jenn's name it was only a matter of time before they all did and reporters started camping out in her front yard.

He texted Darrin, knowing it was late and not wanting to disturb him with a phone call.

>Matt: We have a problem.
>Darrin: The Bleacher Report article?
>Matt: Yes. How'd you know?
>Darrin: As soon as I saw Jenn's name I knew we were in trouble. I'm guessing Jenn and San Antonio girl are one and the same?
>Matt: Yes.
>Darrin: She's your brother's best friend.
>Matt: How the hell do you even know that?
>Darrin: It's called putting two and two

together.

Matt: You've never even met her.

Darrin: Nope. But I know you and Chase, and Chase has mentioned Jenn several times. Not too difficult.

Matt: Anyway. I don't want this causing problems for her.

Darrin: Should have thought about that before dancing with her in a bar.

Matt: Fuck off.

Darrin: Don't get your panties in a twist. I'm on it.

Matt: Good. I don't want people hounding her or this affecting her job.

Darrin: What about your job?

Matt: I'll get that worked out. Right now I'm worried about Jenn.

Darrin: You've got it bad. Okay. Like I said, I'm on it.

Matt: Thanks, D. And I don't have it bad.

Darrin: Yes, you do.

Matt tried to figure out a response and couldn't because, dammit, he did have it bad. He sighed as he noted the time. Eleven thirteen. Tired and weary he set his phone on the nightstand before walking into the adjoining bathroom and taking a long, cold shower.

CHAPTER NINETEEN

"MOM, YOU CANNOT BE serious."

"As a heart attack."

Jenn groaned. And here she'd been having a pretty good Friday. "You're really going to be on that *Doomsday Preppers* show?"

"Yes! Isn't it exciting?"

About as exciting as a pap smear. "Not really. But to each their own."

"You're such a buzzkill. This will be great. I can't wait to find out what our score is."

Oh, sweet baby Jesus, save me now. "I have no idea what that means, Mom. But I'm happy you're happy. Anyway, I need to get back to work on these lesson plans. In-service starts soon."

"Have fun, dear. I'll let you know when they're going to be out taping in case you want to be here, too."

Not a snowball's chance in hell. "Sounds great, Mom. Love you. Bye."

Jenn ended the call and collapsed onto her couch. Her parents were going to drive her crazy.

Going to? They already had.

This was ridiculous. She didn't get the whole serious

prepper thing. Sure, there was nothing wrong with having some extra food and water on-hand, or having a first-aid kit and knowing how to use it, or even thinking about what you would do in the event of a wildfire or tornado or something. Her parents, however, were taking it way beyond the extreme. If Pluto was extreme, her parents were like fifty galaxies away from that, in places scientists hadn't even discovered yet.

They were that extreme.

A headache began pulsing behind her eyes. She'd been on pins and needles since her name had been linked to Matt's Sunday night. Having him come over all week hadn't helped matters. Sure, he was nice to look at and she could no longer lie to herself about enjoying his company. Hell, she'd been enjoying his company since he'd come back to town last month.

Being around him so much, though, was wreaking havoc on her system. As soon as she caught a whiff of him it was like her body went on high alert and her ovaries started partying hard. Just his voice made her wet, and his casual touches literally made her weak in the knees.

And okay, so his touches seemed casual but she knew what he was doing. He was seducing her one touch, one look, one baseball game at a time. Watching Wranglers games with him was both heaven and hell; on one hand she loved being able to pick his brain and get insights into the game she'd never had, on the other, the intensity with which he gave those insights seriously turned her on.

Then there was his intelligence. Sure, she'd always known Matt was no dummy, and that night ten years ago had proven that even further. Since that night, though, he'd matured, become more comfortable in his own skin and more comfortable letting his intellect shine through. Yes, they talked a lot of baseball, but he'd surprised her by initiating conversations about books he'd recently read, current events and even one time engaging her in a heated debate on the best modern-retelling of one of Shakespeare's plays (she'd said *Romeo + Juliet*, he'd said *Sons of Anarchy*).

He hadn't kissed her again, though. The not kissing was driving her nuts, but in all fairness she was the one who'd insisted on being "just friends."

She was beginning to think being "just friends" was for the birds.

Her phone dinged, drawing her out of her own head.

> Jo: Apparently Chase and Owen are go-
> ing up to the ranch for a couple of days.
> Girls' night?
> Jenn: Sure. Miguel's then drinks some-
> where not public?

She really didn't want to court temptation by being out in public too much. So far she'd been lucky, but she knew it was only a matter of time before her privacy was further invaded.

> Jo: No problem. You wanna come over
> to Gran's? We can figure out something
> from there.
> Jenn: Or we could just party with Gran.
> ;-) Be there in a few.

Jenn got up from the couch and went into the bedroom to change out of her battered pair of denim shorts and tank top into a maxi dress and cute pair of sandals. She checked her hair in the bathroom mirror and deemed it presentable before heading into the living room where she grabbed her phone, purse and keys and left to go meet Jo.

About an hour later, they found themselves seated at a corner table at Miguel's.

"Alright, so why don't you want to have drinks some-where public?" Jo asked without preamble. Leave it to Jo to just cut right to the chase.

Jenn sighed and blew a curl out of her eyes, reluctant

to tell Jo the real reason why. As far as she knew the article with her name in it hadn't spread like wildfire, and if someone in her inner circle had read it they would have said something by now. "Because people are driving me freaking crazy."

"Like who?"

Jenn dropped her head into her hands briefly before looking back up. "Everybody."

Jo lifted an eyebrow. "Everybody?"

Jenn groaned. That, at least, was completely honest. "Okay, not everybody. Mostly my parents and Matt."

That, however, was only partially honest.

"What's up with your parents?"

Before Jenn could respond, their waiter arrived to take their drink order. They both asked for sweet tea. Jenn waited for the teenager to leave.

"I think I taught him a few years ago. That makes me feel old."

Jo laughed. "Nuh uh. You're not getting away with changing the subject."

Jenn rolled her eyes. "Fine. My parents are just…" Jenn's hands fluttered in the air. "They're crazy. Mom called me this morning to tell me they'd been contacted by that *Doomsday Preppers* show and they're thinking about filming an episode. What would my principal think if he found out my family's a bunch of nut job preppers?"

"Wait." Jo held up a hand. "They're that far into it?"

Jenn nodded. "Unfortunately, yes. It's gotten steadily worse over the past year. They're at the point where they have weekly drills and play renegade soldier."

Their waiter returned, set their teas down and took their order. Neither of them bothered to look at the menu— Jenn wanted enchiladas, and she was pretty sure Jo would order the same thing. As soon as the teenager was gone, Jo asked, "Weekly drills?"

Jenn groaned. "Yes. They get out their guns, dress up in desert camo and act as if their compound is under siege."

"Compound as in Branch Dividian or compound as in Kennedy?"

"Compound as in off the grid shipping container fortress. They have a landline and satellite cable and internet. That's it."

"Wow. I didn't realize they'd gone that far off the deep end."

"Yeah. It's ridiculous. Mom keeps ordering emergency food kits and other survival stuff and sending them to my house. I've just been stashing it all in the spare bedroom, figuring I'll ship them to Mom and Dad eventually, or use them as a science experiment or something. Matt happened to be there one day for the latest shipment, and it was embarrassing to say the least."

"Wait. Matt knows your family's a bunch of preppers? What was Matt doing at your place? I thought you guys hated each other."

Before Jenn could concoct an answer, their waiter returned with their food. Instead of answering Jo's question once he left, Jenn dove into her enchiladas.

"Seriously? You're going to drop that on me and then not answer my question?" Jo asked.

Jenn swallowed before saying. "Sorry, I'm hungry, and don't know where to begin."

"How about, I don't know, at the beginning?"

Jenn took a deep breath and tried to gather her thoughts, mentally weighing how much to tell and not to tell Jo right now. "I don't know that Matt and I hate each other. There was just some...animosity there."

Animosity's one way of putting it.

"At any rate, he's been coming over to my place in the evenings here lately, so you and Chase can have some privacy. He was there that day and he kind of teased me a little bit about it." *That's not completely true and you know it. Yes, he teased you a bit, but he never made you feel bad about it.*

"So that's where he's been going," Jo murmured.

"Yeah. He says he wants to give you guys some alone time, and that he doesn't want to hear all the wild monkey sex going on when he's not getting any."

"That's oddly sweet."

"Matt, sweet? Yeah, right." She didn't know why she was trying to hold up the charade with Jo, especially since she knew that Matt could indeed be sweet.

"So you and Matt have managed to hang out together—alone—and not kill each other? I'm impressed."

"Oh, I almost stabbed him with a fork the other night."

Jo laughed. "What'd he do to deserve that?"

Jenn looked away before saying, "Nothing, really. He was just being a jerk."

Not really, he hadn't. She'd almost stabbed him with a fork out of sheer sexual frustration, which really was no excuse.

Jenn changed the subject off of Matt before Jo began putting two and two together. "So what's up with Chase? I've called him a couple of times this week and he hasn't answered. He's barely responded to text messages. That's not like him."

Now it was Jo's turn to dive into her enchiladas.

"Uh oh. What's going on? Y'all didn't break up, did you?" Not possible. Jo and Chase totally belonged together.

"Not that I know of. We had a pretty serious talk the other night, and he seemed like he had a lot on his mind, really worried about something. I tried to get it out of him, but all he would do is ask me what our plan was once I go back to Austin."

"And what is the plan? I love you guys, and obviously y'all are meant for each other, but even soul mates can't survive distance for too incredibly long." Not that she'd thought about long distance relationships or anything recently.

Jo shrugged, misery settling around her like an old cardigan. "I know that. He knows that. Part of it's my fault—I haven't exactly wanted to talk about it, even though I know we need to."

"Uh, yeah." Jenn took a sip of her tea before continuing. "What I don't understand is why you've been avoiding the inevitable. Just rip the damned bandage off already."

Why don't you take your own advice, oh wise one?
Shut. Up.

Jo pushed her enchiladas around her plate. "I know, I know. I'm just so scared of the what-ifs, and the thought of losing him. I think by avoiding having that particular conversation, it's been easier for me to keep reality at bay."

Jenn shook her head, even though a part of her understood all too well. "You counselors really can be some screwed up people."

"Tell me about it."

"Oh, I can if you really want me to."

Jo snorted. "No, thanks. I'm well aware of just how messed up I am. But seriously, I get the feeling that there's something else bothering Chase, that it's not only the distance thing. I just can't come up with any ideas."

Jenn shrugged. "I really don't know. I mean, the distance thing is kind of a big one, y'know. And knowing Chase, he's probably scared to death to let you in all the way, because even though he's one of my best friends and one of the nicest men on the planet, he also has some issues and has a really hard time letting people in."

"Yeah, thanks to me," Jo said bitterly.

"Partially, maybe. But I don't think it's just you. Chase tells me most everything, but I know there are things he keeps pretty close to the vest." Jenn dragged her fork through the remaining enchilada sauce on her plate, making swirly patterns with the tines. "I know he tells Owen more than he does me, and Owen would never divulge state secrets, so to speak."

"How exactly did Owen and Chase and you become friends to begin with? I don't remember him from high school."

"Really? He moved here like our junior year, I think, but he was pretty quiet. Junior ROTC. Graduated a year ahead of us. After he graduated he joined the National Guard and moved to Houston for a while. Came back to Del Rio oh…nine years ago maybe? At any rate, he came back here and opened up a construction business. Chase moved back not long after that, and with him being in commercial real estate they ended up working together a lot, and then ended up doing a lot of the same community events. They just became friends really quickly."

"So you became friends with Owen by proxy then?"

Jenn shrugged. "Kind of. More like, Chase started inviting Owen to go to the lake with us or come over to his place or to April's, and before I knew it I suddenly had two hot guy friends who unfortunately both treated me like I was a sister."

Jo snorted. "About that…was there seriously never anything between you and Owen?"

Jenn laughed. Loudly. "Oh, God, no. I mean, did I think he was hot? Obviously. Even a blind woman could see that. But there simply wasn't any chemistry, and at the time I honestly wasn't looking for a boyfriend or even sex. It was a very easy slide into friendship. Anyway, though, enough about me. How about we get the check and head back to Gran's for some ice cream and alcohol?"

"Ice cream and alcohol, huh?"

Jenn signaled for the waiter and said, "Just feels like that kind of a night."

"Chase wants to have dinner tonight," Jo said as she sat down on the edge of Jenn's bed. Instead of going to Gran's last night they'd come back to Jenn's and indulged in Mudslides made with ice cream, which really was the best of both worlds.

Jenn yawned and stretched. "So? That's a good thing, considering y'all are together and all."

"I've got a bad feeling about this."

Jenn sat and pushed her hair out of her eyes. "Okay. Why do you have a bad feeling?"

Jo shrugged and slid down on to the floor, her back against the mattress. "I don't know. I can't quite explain it. But he's basically ignored me all week, and then when he texted me a few minutes ago he was pretty short about it."

Jenn slid off the bed and sat on the floor beside Jo. "I can see how that would make you nervous. But didn't he also say he was going to spend a couple of days up at the ranch? Sounds to me like he's coming home early because he wants to see you."

"Or maybe he's planning on breaking up with me and just wants to get it done and over with."

"Way to think positive there, counselor."

Jo sighed. "I know, I know. I just can't shake the bad feeling."

"Well, then, we need to make sure you change his mind if he's planning on making the dumbest move in the history of the universe."

"And how do we do that?"

Jenn wiggled her eyebrows in an effort to make Jo smile. "We make sure he knows exactly what he would be missing. How about you wear what you wore on the Fourth? That sundress with those cowboy boots was kind of hot, and Chase definitely seemed to think so."

Jo's cheeks pinkened, but she smiled and said, "You do have a point."

CHAPTER TWENTY

"YOU'RE SURE YOU HAVEN'T seen anyone weird hanging around outside? No strange men with cameras or anything?" Matt asked.

Jenn sighed, acting like she was put out by his questioning, but Matt had a sneaking suspicion she liked his concern. "None. I haven't seen a single strange person hanging around here. Except for you. You're kind of weird."

He flopped down onto her couch and pulled her down with him. "Admit it, you like my weird."

"Kind of. It's growing on me a little bit."

Instead of sitting in the middle of the couch or on the other end, she surprised him by sitting right beside him, close enough that their thighs were touching. Speaking of thighs…he glanced down at her legs that were bared thanks to the pair of shorts she was wearing, and immediately grew hard.

Matt shifted, brought his gaze up from her legs and tried to focus on her face, the smattering of Spanish he knew, anything to help him keep his hands off of her. As much as he wanted to make a move, he was leaving the ball firmly in her court.

His fingers twitched and his dick swelled inside his pants.

Very firmly. In her court.

"Oh, hell," Jenn whispered.

Matt swallowed. "You can't tell me you don't feel this, too, Jenn."

She shook her head.

"Please don't lie to me."

"I'm not. I don't want to feel this."

Her desperately muttered statement hurt more than he cared to admit. "And yet you do. I do. We do."

"Yeah, we do."

"So what are you going to do about it?"

She continued to unflinchingly meet his gaze. "What I want to do and what I should do are currently battling inside my head."

He crooked up a corner of his mouth. "Which one's winning?"

Her gaze dropped to his mouth and her tongue darted out to wet her lips. His cock surged again. "It's a draw."

"Bullshit."

Her gaze flew back up to his. "Sometimes I hate you."

"No, you don't."

She looked at his mouth again. "No, I don't."

"It's up to you, Jenn. I told you I wouldn't push, so I'm not."

"And yet here you are. Every single night."

"Ever stop to think I simply like you?"

She swallowed. "I like you, too."

"Jenn, look at me."

She looked back up at him, and he could see her fears shining clearly in her eyes. His fears probably didn't come close to hers, considering everything she'd been through ten years ago thanks to him, but she wasn't alone in the scared department.

"This is unfamiliar territory for me, too, and I'm a little scared, too, but this feels too right not to see where it goes."

She turned her body into his. "I doubt you're scared of anything."

He tentatively pushed a curl behind her ear. "This feeling I get whenever I'm near you? This all-consuming need to be with you? The fact that I can't stop thinking about you and the fact that I will rip someone apart if they try to go after you because of your association with me? Yeah, those feelings scare me."

She grabbed his hand with her own and held tight. "What about after? After you've healed? After you've gone back to baseball? The aftermath from ten years ago nearly crushed me. I don't think I can go through that again."

"You slay me, you know that?"

"Ditto."

"I'm not that guy anymore, Jenn."

"I know that, Matt. That doesn't make me any less scared of the aftermath, though."

Fuck, he was scared of the aftermath, too, not to mention the fact that for the first time in his life he was beginning to seriously wonder if maybe he should hang up his cleats and walk away from the game he loved. Some of that was because of his head injury, some of it because of his age. He'd be lying, though, if he said Jenn wasn't a part of that wondering.

God, the woman had him thinking crazy thoughts.

The doorbell rang before he could respond, causing Jenn to jump away from him like she'd just been burned.

"I should get that."

She almost ran to the front door, and Matt tried to adopt a casual pose on the couch. Jenn opened the door, and he caught a brief glimpse of Jo bursting into tears. Oh, hell. His brother better not have done something stupid.

Jenn ushered Jo inside and closed the door behind her.

"Did you know?" Jo choked out.

A look of confusion passed over Jenn's face, and Matt tried his damnedest to hide his own confusion.

"Know what?" Jenn asked.

"That he's sick?" Jo sniffled.

"Who's sick?" Jenn asked, still clearly confused.

Matt, however, was no longer confused and instead had the sudden urge to find his brother and pummel some sense into him. Apparently he'd finally gotten around to telling Jo about his Chronic Kidney Disease and apparently had botched the entire thing.

"Chase," Jo choked out.

Jenn guided her to the couch, and Matt watched Jo warily, not sure what to say or do considering his relationship to the man in question.

Jo turned to Matt and pointed her finger at him. "You. You knew, didn't you?"

He swallowed. Nodded.

Jo lunged for him, but before she could inflict any real damage he wrapped an arm around her, pinning her arms to her sides, and used his free hand to rub her back. In a soft, soothing voice, he said, "Just calm down, Jo. Breathe. That's it. Breathe."

Jo stopped fighting and buried her head on Matt's chest, sobs wracking her body.

Jenn sat down beside them, and Matt kept rubbing her back, ignoring the moisture that had his shirt clinging to his skin.

"You're kind of good at this whole comforting thing, y'know," she mumbled against his chest.

Matt snorted. "It's one of my secret talents."

"I'm afraid I got snot all over your shirt."

He shrugged. "That's okay. I have plenty."

She pulled back and looked. "It's your World Series t-shirt!"

He was wearing a 2012 World Series t-shirt. The year the Wranglers' won. He smiled at her. "Jo, it's okay. I literally have a dozen of these. At least."

She grabbed a tissue out of the box on the coffee table and blew her nose, somewhat calmer now but obviously embarrassed. "I'm sorry I attacked you."

Jo managed to wedge her body in between him and Jenn.

"It's no biggie. I have to admit, I was kind of impressed—I don't think I've seen you that worked up since the time I stuck frogs in the back of y'all's bathing suits," he teased, trying to lighten the mood and coax out a smile.

It didn't work.

"Still, though, I shouldn't have done that."

"It's okay. So what got you so worked up to begin with?" He asked, even though he figured he already knew the answer, or at least part of it.

She looked from Matt to Jenn, and he saw it in her eyes the moment she put two and two together. "Was I interrupting something?"

"Nope. We were just watching the game."

The TV wasn't on. Oops.

Jo looked from it to Jenn, who blushed.

"We were about to watch the game. I just got here," Matt said, trying to throw Jo off the scent. Now was not the time to delve into that particular subject.

Jo's face fell, her chin trembled and her shoulders slumped.

"So what did you mean, Chase is sick?" Jenn asked, worry in her voice.

Jo rolled her head towards Jenn. "So I take it you don't know?"

"Know what?" Jenn asked, sounding a bit bewildered.

He was going to kill Chase for not telling Jenn anything about the CKD.

Jo sighed. Rolled her head to look at Matt. "What about you?"

He nodded, afraid his answer would effectively put a complete stop on his and Jenn's budding…whatever it was…but knowing he couldn't not be honest. "The family's known since he was a teen, and then he found out in his early twenties, I think, that he had Chronic Kidney Disease."

Jenn gasped and her face drained of all color. "He's been sick that long and never told me?"

"Don't get mad at him, Jenn. He probably kept it from you to protect you," Matt said. Yup, he was so going to kill his brother when he got home later.

"Kind of how he just broke up with me to protect me, you mean?" Jo asked, her voice bitter.

"My brother's a fucking idiot."

"On this, I wholeheartedly agree with you."

Jo sniffled, and Matt handed her the box of tissues while watching Jenn out of the corner of his eye. She was too pale, but he was afraid to reach out and touch her, to try to comfort her right now. Afraid she would push him away for unknowingly hiding something so important from her. "So I take it the CKD's gotten worse?"

Jo nodded her head. "From what he just explained to me, yes. His doctor thinks he'll probably need a transplant within a year."

Jenn asked, "Hold on. He's sick enough that he needs a fucking transplant? And he never told me? I'm his best friend!"

Jo closed her eyes as if she was in physical pain. "I'm his girlfriend. Was his girlfriend. Fuck if I even know what I am anymore. And he just now told me. So join the club."

The three of them fell silent, each lost in their own thoughts. Matt finally broke the silence by asking, "So what are you going to do?"

Jo sighed. "I don't know. I have to be back in Austin early next week for work, when what I want to do is stay here and show him I'm not that easy to push away."

Matt met Jenn's gaze over the top of Jo's head, saw the confusion and hurt etched all over her face and quietly swore.

He was definitely beating the shit out of his brother.

As soon as Matt left about thirty minutes later, Jo turned to Jenn and demanded, "Okay, spill."

Jenn got up from the couch and walked into the kitchen. "You want some wine?"

Jo got up and joined her. "God, yes. And then I want you to spill."

Jenn grabbed a bottle from the fridge then concentrated on pulling the cork, using that as an excuse to not look at her best friend. "Spill what?"

"You know what."

"No, I really don't," she said as the cork finally popped out of the bottle.

"What's going on with you and Matt? And don't you dare tell me 'nothing,' because I saw the way y'all were looking at each other."

Jenn rolled her eyes and grabbed two wineglasses out of the cabinet. "How could you see how we were looking at each other when you were bawling your eyes out almost the entire time he was here?"

She poured both of them a healthy serving of the chilled Moscato before handing a glass to Jo.

"'Almost' being the key word here." Jo took a healthy sip of her wine. "Looks like you and Matt are doing more than simply hanging out."

Jenn took a healthy sip of her own before asking,

"Why the sudden fascination with Matt and me? How about we figure out what you're going to do about Chase and Jo?"

Jo grimaced before taking another large sip—and by large sip Jenn meant gulp—of wine. "Honestly? Right now focusing on something other than Chase and me seems like a really good idea, otherwise I'm going to get really mad and possibly do something I would regret. I need a distraction, and whatever's going on between you and Matt seems like a pretty damned good one right about now."

Jenn sighed and rested her back against the edge of the kitchen counter. "It's…we're friends, I guess. Complicated friends."

"You mean friends with benefits?"

Jo sounded way too excited by that. "Not exactly, no."

"I'm sensing a story here. A really epic, possibly long and most likely juicy story. Please don't deny me that in my time of need."

Jenn chuckled before finishing off her glass of wine with one long drink. She refilled her now empty glass and stuck another bottle in the freezer to chill. Jo lifted an eyebrow in a silent question. Jenn said, "If I'm telling you this story, we're going to need more than one bottle of wine"

"Sounds good to me. I think I'm definitely in the mood to get rip-roaring drunk."

Jo held out her now empty wine glass and Jenn poured the rest of the first bottle of wine into it. They both quietly sipped for a few minutes before Jenn inhaled a shaky breath. *Am I really going to do this?*

"I slept with Matt."

Jo almost spit a mouthful of Moscato all over Jenn's kitchen. She turned and grabbed a paper towel, wiped her mouth and the front of her dress before setting her wine glass on the counter top and asking, "What? When? And why the hell did I not know this?"

Jenn grimaced. "To be honest, no one really knows

except Matt and me. Well, Owen figured it out a few weeks ago even though I never confirmed his guess. I think Matt might have, though." She waved a hand in the air. "Anyway. To answer your other question, it was ten years ago."

"Jennifer Anne McDonnell. How have you held out on me for ten. freaking. years. and not told me that you slept with Matt?"

"Like I said, it's complicated."

"Well obviously. But seriously. You never told anyone?"

Jenn shook her head. "Nope."

Jo narrowed her eyes. "Was he a dick to you?"

She snorted. "Are we talking before, during or after?"

"I'm going to kill him."

"No, you're not. We've talked about it and things are okay now. Kind of. It's hard to just let go of ten years' worth of hurt."

Jo opened the freezer and pulled out the other bottle. "I don't care if this is cold yet or not; we clearly need more."

Jenn sipped on her wine, feeling such an odd mix of emotions churning through her head and heart she didn't know where to begin to untangle them all. Desire and frustration where Matt was concerned. Relief to finally be getting this off her chest. A lot of anger towards Chase for not telling her about being sick in the first place, topped with even more anger for breaking up with Jo.

With the second bottle open, they went back into the living room and sat side by side on the couch. Jo set the bottle of wine on the table in front of them, propped her feet up and said, "Okay, spill. All of it."

Jenn swallowed down her anxiety, rolled her wine glass between her hands and told the story from the beginning. She told Jo the entire crazy, emotional, complicated, heart-breaking mess, from her initial surprising attraction to Matt and her surprise that the attraction was mutual to the incredible sex and the dejected feeling she'd had the next morning to her panic, excitement and eventual heartbreak in losing Tyler. Jo remained silent through it all, sipping on her wine with one hand and rubbing Jenn's back with the other.

All the things she'd kept bottled up, all the emotions and thoughts spilled out like water from a dam. Jenn was crying, but she didn't really care; it was cleansing. Necessary.

"God, Jenn, I'm so sorry. I should have been here for you through all of that."

Jenn shook her head. "No. You were in grad school and dealing with your own stuff. I didn't tell anyone. I was hurt and felt like a fool. I mean, I knew how Matt was. We saw him growing up, and I knew he wasn't the relationship type. But then, that night…God, Jo…he looked at me and touched me and kissed me and it just felt *right*, like he was supposed to be touching me and kissing me. It was…I still don't have words to describe what that was between us, but I do know I've never experienced that with another person. It wasn't just physical, it was like we were trying to crawl inside of each other's souls. Jesus, I've been reading too many romance novels."

Jo sniffled. "No, you haven't. I understand exactly what you're saying since that's the way it is with Chase and me."

Jenn tilted her head and rested it on top of Jo's, staring silently at the blank television screen.

"So you had amazing sex with Matt, he pulled a typical guy move and freaked out and left without saying a word. You ended up pregnant and never told him then had a stillborn baby and never told anyone. That explains why you've been a bit of a bitch to him over the past ten years, but what about now?"

Jenn sighed. "That's even more confusing. We've

talked about that night, and I told him about Tyler. He was devastated, Jo. I've never seen him like that."

"So are you two dating? Just friends? What, exactly?"

"Hell if I know. And with that stupid YouTube video and then the press figuring out he's in Del Rio and then dragging my name into things, it's gotten even more complicated."

Jo sat up and turned towards Jenn. "Hold on here. Have I been in that big of a sex bubble that I've totally missed all of this?"

"Sex bubble. I like it."

"Not the point."

"I know. And yes, you and Chase have been in your own little world. Owen has seen some things on the periphery, but that's it. Anyway. There was a YouTube video of Matt and me dancing together at April's one night. The press got hold of it and started questioning where he was and what he was doing. Darrin released a statement last weekend when the video went viral and tried to mitigate any damage. It didn't work and the press tracked him down to here. Bleacher Report did some digging and found one of my former students who blabbed about it being me in the video dancing with Matt. Luckily it hasn't picked up a whole lot of traction and so far I haven't been harassed, but Matt seems to be worried that I will be."

"Holy shit, Jenn. I feel like an awful friend. I've just been off having crazy monkey sex with my boyfriend—well, I guess ex-boyfriend, hell if I know—and had no clue."

"It's been an eventful summer."

"I'll say. But that still doesn't answer my question—what's the Matt and Jenn status?"

Jenn rolled her eyes. "You're like a dog with a bone. And I honestly don't know. I think we're friends. Maybe. But we're friends who want to get each other naked, which is still kind of mind-blowing for me. I mean, this is Matt freaking Roberts we're talking about here."

"You mean the Matt freaking Roberts who put frogs down our bikinis when we were kids?"

"Yeah, that one. Also the same guy who dates super-models and hot female athletes and who's been on *People's Sexiest Man Alive* list. Multiple times. Not to mention the fact that he's a future Hall of Famer and collects Cy Young awards like I collect books. I'm pretty sure I've read this story before."

Jo lightly punched Jenn in the arm. "So because he's a famous athlete and you're a school teacher he shouldn't be attracted to you?"

"I didn't say that. It's just surreal. I've never really seen Matt as super famous considering I've known him since we were losing our baby teeth, but it does kind of give one pause."

"You think he's just bored and looking for a distraction."

Jo knew her far too well. "Correct."

"I don't think that's the case."

"Why not?"

Jo shrugged. "I've seen the way he looks at you. He doesn't look at you like he's bored and just wants a distraction. He looks at you like…like you're a really interesting puzzle and he's trying to solve you."

"I'm not sure if I should be flattered or not."

"Matt's a cerebral guy, that's not a bad thing."

"You have no idea just how cerebral he is. That's honestly been one of the things that's shocked me the most. He's definitely not a mental slouch."

"So what are you going to do?"

Jenn groaned. "I don't know. I want him, Jo. Bad. And not just physically. I want him so bad it hurts and scares me at the same time. What I felt ten years ago is nothing compared to what I feel now, and considering I ended up with my heart smashed to smithereens then I'm scared to death to find out what would happen this time around if he walked away again."

Jo sighed and sank into the couch cushions. "Sounds like we're both in love with wonderful men who are fucking idiots."

Jenn gulped down the rest of her wine and poured herself another glass. In love with Matt? No, she couldn't be.

Ah, fuck. Who am I kidding? I've been in love with him for ten years.

"Stupid freaking Roberts brothers."

Jo clinked her wine glass against Jenn's. "Amen, sister, amen."

CHAPTER TWENTY-ONE

"ARE YOU OUT OF your fucking mind?"

Chase looked up from the bottle of beer in his hand, took one glance at Matt's face and looked away.

Chickenshit.

Chase shrugged. "Probably."

Matt sat down in the patio chair across from him, somehow managing to not wrap his hands around his brother's throat. "You're seriously just going to let her walk away? No, screw that. You're seriously just going to push Jo out of your life when now and the next few years are when you're going to need her most?"

Chase stared blankly at something over Matt's shoulder. His voice was wooden when he said, "You don't understand, Matt."

"No, I really don't. First, you don't tell anyone how bad it's gotten, and then when you do you break up with your girlfriend and shut everyone out. Then you throw a pity party—population one—and sulk like a sixteen-year-old who had his car keys taken away. And now you're sitting there looking like the poster child for a Prozac commercial. That's not like you, Chase, so no, I don't understand."

Out of the two of them Matt had always been the more emotional of the two, even if he'd done a better job of hiding that from the world. Chase was usually the logical one, unfazed by the ups and downs of life. Hell, he'd had to learn to be at too early of an age.

"What would you know, Matt? You've barely been around the past ten years," Chase's words were meant to goad.

Instead of getting angry, Matt simply shook his head. "No, you don't get to use that card right now, because you and I both know it's bullshit. What's up with the poor pitiful me act anyway?"

Chase's shoulders sagged as if a giant weight had suddenly settled upon them. "Fuck if I know, Matt."

"I think you do." Matt paused before continuing, trying to find a calm center or something considering he wanted to both hug and hit his brother. "So you're going to need a transplant?"

Chase nodded. "Not immediately, but sooner rather than later. The doctor thinks it's only a matter of a year or two."

He processed that information. The finality of it settled in his gut. It was an uncomfortable feeling, knowing your only sibling was inching closer to possibly dying. "When are you going to tell Mom and Dad?"

"Soon. I don't know why I haven't yet. How'd you even find out?"

Matt waved his hand as if to indicate his answer didn't matter and said nonchalantly, "I was at Jenn's when Jo came in earlier bawling her eyes out. She hit me then got snot all over my shirt."

Chase finally looked at Matt and narrowed his eyes. "What were you doing at Jenn's?"

Matt shrugged. "I sometimes go over there and hang out to give you and Jo some privacy."

"At Jenn's?" Chase sounded skeptical. Matt couldn't blame him, considering Jenn's previous animosity towards him.

"Yeah. So?" *That didn't sound defensive, right?*

"So I thought you two hated each other for some reason."

"I wouldn't say we've ever hated each other," Matt evaded. He wasn't about to get into that story right now. Besides, it wasn't his alone to tell.

Chase raised an eyebrow.

"There was just a bit of a misunderstanding years ago. It's been cleared up now."

"I swear to God, Matt, if you hurt Jenn…" Chase let the implied threat hang in the air between them.

Matt raised his hands, palms out. "Not my intent. She's just nice to hang out with sometimes, that's all. We're friends."

Yeah, friends who want to rip each other's clothes off.

"I've never known you to be friends with a woman."

"I'm friends with Jo. But I'm not the subject at hand here—you are. You and your idiocy." Matt turned the conversation away from him and back to Chase.

"It's not idiocy."

Matt shot him a look that he hoped said, "You're an even bigger idiot than I thought you were."

Chase's Adam's apple bobbed up and down before he asked, "Since when are you in to heart to hearts? This is starting to feel like some Lifetime movie."

Matt snorted. "Hardly. As far as I know of neither of us has slept with a fifty-year-old woman who's twenty-year-old son slash lover wants to murder us."

"You know far too much about Lifetime movies."

"I had a lot of time to sit and watch cable TV in the hospital."

One corner of Chase's mouth tilted up in a half smile.

"The truth is," he picked at the label on his beer bottle, "I'm scared shitless, Matt. I've always been a bit of a loner, mostly because I've been in love with Jo since I was a kid, along with having the possibility of renal failure looming over my head. Finding out I was going to need a kidney transplant so soon…it's not fair to her. She's gone through so much, man. She's already lost both her parents. I can't do that to her."

"I don't think you're giving her enough credit."

"Probably not."

"That woman loves you, bro, and when you find something like that you don't just throw it away like last night's leftovers. You hold on to that and don't let go."

Like you should have done with Jenn ten years ago, right?

Shut. Up.

Chase glanced up at his brother. "Where'd this philosophical side come from?"

Matt shrugged. "It's always been there. Everyone's always seen what they wanted to see is all."

"So there's more to you than womanizing and a ninety-eight mile per hour fastball is what you're saying?"

Matt snorted derisively. "To the public and my adoring fans? No."

"How is it I've never seen this side of you until the past month?"

"I guess I never wanted you to. Facing your own mortality kind of gives you a new perspective on life, though."

Chase rubbed his chest and Matt had a feeling his comment had hit home. "Point taken. Were you this scared when you came-to on the mound?"

He nodded, once. He'd never forget the way he'd felt that night on the mound. "Absolutely. I couldn't move for a few minutes. My ears were ringing and I could feel blood trickling down my face and neck. My head hurt like nothing I've ever felt before. Luckily I didn't know how bad it was at the time—just that the situation wasn't good. And when I woke up later, in the hospital," Matt shook his head, "I remember feeling lost and worried, mostly about Mom and Dad. It wasn't until a couple days later that the uncertainty of my baseball future really hit me, and that scared me, too."

"That's why you really came back home, isn't it? Because you were scared," Chase said.

"Yeah." Matt sat back and sighed. "I was scared. I still am. Sure, my head seems to be healing fine, but baseball? I don't know if I'll ever be able to play again. I'm thirty-five and I'd already been thinking about retiring in another year or two, but I'd wanted to go out on my terms, y'know?"

"I had no idea you'd even thought about retirement. You've seemed so oblivious to the fact that you're kind of old for a pitcher."

Matt glanced at Chase and shook his head. "Again, everyone sees what they want to see. I'm not an idiot—I did graduate summa cum laude from Texas, y'know."

"Wait. What? But you were taken in the first round after your junior year. When did you go back and get your degree?"

"In the off-season and through online courses. I finished it in 2008." He could have sworn he'd mentioned it offhand to Chase, or at the very least their Mom would have said something. Apparently not, though.

"Jesus, man. What other secrets do you have hiding out in there? I don't know if I can take much more."

Matt avoided answering Chase's question and instead rubbed a hand over his jaw, looking over his brother's shoulder for long moments before turning his gaze back to him. "You know when you need a transplant I'll be the first one to offer a kidney, right?"

Chase sucked in a deep breath and blinked. "You don't

have to do that."

"I know I don't, but you're my brother. We're the same blood type and siblings tend to be the best matches. My kidneys are in great shape, I'm healthy, and if I can do something to keep you alive as long as possible I'm going to."

Chase nodded, but didn't speak.

"In the meantime, I suggest you figure out how you're going to apologize to Jo and grovel appropriately. You need her now, and you're going to need her in the future. Don't be a dick and make decisions for her—it's her choice to make, whether she wants to stick with you through this or not."

Chase sighed. "Do you know what the statistics are like for kidney transplant recipients? How long donor kidneys last? The complications, not to mention the cost involved?"

Matt crossed his arms over his chest, knowing what he was about to say would be yet one more surprise for his brother. "Most donor kidneys will last on average fifteen years, with some lasting for twenty, possibly more if it's a really good match and the recipient takes their meds and takes care of themselves. That means you'd probably need another kidney in your fifties, and another in your sixties or seventies. Obviously, they're hard to come by the older you get, but it's not impossible. As for cost, the anti-rejection meds are incredibly expensive for most people, but good insurance plans will usually cover at least a portion of the cost, and once you hit your out of pocket you pay nothing for the rest of your plan year. And yes, there's a risk involved with being on anti-rejection medications, including cancer, but most cases are skin cancer that's easily treated. You just have to be careful—wash your hands, use hand sanitizer, clean regularly, stay away from anyone who has the flu, that sort of thing. In other words, it's nothing insurmountable."

"I feel like I owe you an apology."

Matt shrugged. "Nah. Like I said, people see what they want to see, and I don't do anything to dispel that image. It's more comfortable that way, honestly. But don't think for a minute I don't care, or that I haven't done research. You're my brother."

Chase was silent for a few minutes before saying, "I don't want to tell Mom and Dad."

Matt nodded. "I would imagine not. They can handle it, though. We've all known it was going to happen sooner or later." He grinned. "But wait until Mom finds out you broke up with Jo. You might wish you were dead then."

Chase rolled his eyes and flicked his bottle cap at Matt. "Shut it, asshole. I already know I screwed up big time in that regard."

"So what are you going to do to fix it?"

He cocked his head to the side. "You think you could help me with something?"

"If it ends this pity party and wraps up the Prozac commercial, absolutely."

"You're such an ass."

"An ass with a healthy kidney, so shut it," Matt shot back. "Anyway, what's the plan?"

"I think I might need to grovel."

Matt: You okay?
Jenn: I think I'm a little drunk.
Matt: I'll take that as a no.
Jenn: No, I'm not ok. Chase is a dumbass and I'm mad at him.
Matt: I agree. He's a dumbass.
Jenn: Glad you concur. But I probably

shouldn't text you anymore tonight.

Matt: Why's that?

Jenn: Might say something I shouldn't.

Matt: Like what?

Jenn: Bad, not friendly things.

Matt: That covers a lot of territory.

Jenn: Yes. It does. I'm leaving it at that.
Night.

Matt: Night.

When Jo left the next morning, Jenn said goodbye with a heavy heart and a long hug. There may have been some tears. She knew Jo needed to go pick up her stuff, load up her car and head back to Austin, but dammit, she didn't want her to go.

"It's been so good having you home again," Jenn said as she hugged her best friend. Hard.

Jo hugged her back, just as hard. "It's been good being back home. I'm going to miss you."

"You know you're welcome here any time, right? I'll even try to make room around all of the MREs for you."

Jo's chuckle was watery. "That's sweet of you, but I can always stay with Gran when I come back to town."

"Please don't be a stranger again."

Jo pulled away and swiped at the tears rolling down her cheeks. "I promise I won't be. No matter what happens with Chase and me I'm not going to stay away again."

"Good. And just so you know, as soon as you're out of town I'm going over to Chase's house to kick his ass."

Jo snorted and pulled Jenn in for another hug. "I love you."

"Love you, too."

They separated and Jo walked to her car in Jenn's

driveway, opened the door and climbed in. She waved as she drove away, and Jenn waved back, tears freely streaming down her face.

She was so going to miss Jo.

An hour later Jenn had managed to pull herself together enough to climb into her own car and head towards Chase's house. As Ed Sheeran's "Thinking Out Loud" played over the radio, she thought about everything that had happened over the past twenty-four hours.

Hell, not even twenty-four hours. More like twelve.

One minute she'd been sitting beside Matt on her couch, pretty sure he was about to kiss her, and the next she'd found out one of her best friends was seriously sick and hadn't bothered to tell her. Oh, and let's not forget everything she'd ended up telling Jo last night.

Ugh.

Honestly, she felt a little guilty for unloading all of that last night considering Chase's little bombshell and his subsequent breaking up with Jo. But she knew her other best friend and understood that she'd needed the distraction. And hell, Jenn had needed to get it off of her chest.

It was a win-win for everyone, right?

Right.

She mentally shook herself as she pulled into Chase's driveway and parked behind Matt's JEEP. Nerves danced in her stomach at the thought of seeing Matt after her admission to Jo last night. Would her feelings be written all over her face? Would he somehow know her walls had come crashing down and she was too tired of fighting to keep them up to put them back together?

You are the very definition of 'hot mess' right now.

Yeah, no shit.

Jenn cut off the engine and got out of her car, stepping into the sweltering August heat. She quickly made her way up to Chase's front porch and rang the doorbell once before turning the knob and letting herself in like she usually did.

It struck her then that since Matt had been back in town she'd only come over here a handful of times. She was usually here a few times a week.

Like you said last night, it's been an eventful summer.

Not to mention the fact that for most of it she'd been actively avoiding Matt.

She stepped into blessed air conditioning and shut the door behind her before walking into the living room. Matt walked in from the direction of the kitchen. He drew up as soon as he saw her, their gazes colliding briefly before his traveled down and then back up the length of her body. Jenn's her skin warmed as if he'd touched her.

When his gaze met hers again, she swore she could feel heat radiating off of him. His pupils dilated slightly and his tongue darted out to wet his lips. Jenn's nipples tightened behind the thin cotton of her tank top. He started towards her, his gaze intent. Her belly danced with butter-flies and her womb tightened, moisture pooling between her thighs.

They really needed to do something about this crazy attraction.

Stat.

Like, right now.

On the living room floor.

The couch.

The stairs.

Didn't matter.

Matt stopped just inches away from her, and she gripped the strap of her purse until her fingers started to go numb. She wanted to touch him. Needed to touch him. But as soon as she did it would all be over.

He would know. And he would break her heart all over again.

Jenn cleared her throat and took a tiny step backward.

Matt's brows drew together in confusion, but the heat didn't leave his eyes.

Jenn swallowed and opened her mouth to speak, but before she could say anything Chase's voice rang out from the kitchen.

"Matt, who is it?"

Without turning his head, Matt responded. "It's Jenn."

"Don't get blood on my floor you two."

Unable to break Matt's gaze, Jenn said, "Ha ha. Very funny. I haven't spilled anyone's blood in at least three days I'll have you know."

"Wow. A whole three days. I'm so proud of you," Chase shot back.

Matt's mouth twitched. She wanted to lick it.

"Jenn," Matt whispered.

"What, Matt?" she whispered back.

"I have to do something real quick."

"What's that?"

Before she knew what was happening he'd moved in for the kill, capturing her mouth with his.

Oh, thank God.

No! No! This isn't supposed to happen!

Oh, fuck it. This is so happening.

She let go of her purse strap and wrapped her hands around his neck, holding on for dear life as Matt's tongue caressed hers. It felt like an invitation. Like a promise. Like all her wants and desires and heartache wrapped up in one big, muscular package.

His hands settled on her hips, his fingers curling and digging into her flesh. She stepped towards him, closing the distance between their bodies. His chest against hers and the thick ridge of his erection against her belly felt like heaven and hell and home.

This kiss wasn't like the one last Sunday on her couch. It wasn't full of fire, burning them to embers. This one was slow and heady, luxurious like expensive dark chocolate melting on her tongue.

"You guys aren't silently murdering each other in here are—what the fuck?"

Too late Jenn heard Chase's voice and pulled her mouth away from Matt's. His fingers flexed against her hips and she glanced up at his face. Instead of looking worried, he looked amused.

Of course he did.

She unwound her arms and took a step back. Matt's arms fell to his sides before he casually put his hands in his pockets, drawing her gaze to the fly of his khaki shorts. She pressed her lips together but couldn't quite hold in her snort of laughter.

What was one more thing on top of everything else that had happened this weekend?

Matt watched as Jenn tried to contain her laughter, and had a hard time containing his own.

The situation really was kind of ridiculous.

"Seriously, guys. What the hell did I just see?"

Jenn surprised him by stepping to the side and facing Chase head-on. "You just saw two adults kissing each other. I realize it might be a lot for your pre-pubescent brain to comprehend right now, but I promise you you'll understand it one day."

Matt really wanted to turn around and see Chase's face at that, but considering the raging hard-on he had right now he didn't think that would be the best idea. And then Jenn stepped between him and Chase, close enough so he could still feel her. Matt turned, effectively shielding the situation in his shorts from his brother's view for the time-being.

"I know what I just saw, smartass." Chase's brown

eyes had gone almost black—a sure sign he was pissed off. "What I don't understand is why you were kissing each other. Y'all hate each other."

Matt sighed. "I thought we'd cleared that one up?"

Chase waved a hand in the air, and for the first time Matt noticed the butcher knife.

Well, that escalated quickly.

Matt glanced at Chase's hand. His brother turned his head, saw the butcher knife and lowered his hand. "I'm gonna go set this down in the kitchen real quick."

"That might be a good idea," Matt said.

Jenn's body shook with silent laughter as Chase walked back into the kitchen.

Matt whispered to Jenn, "Sorry. I'm not sure what happened. I just saw you and couldn't not kiss you."

She looked up at him, a small smile playing at her lips. "It's okay. We were gonna get busted sooner or later."

"You're not upset?"

She shrugged. "I told Jo everything last night. It was time."

"Everything?" he asked, wondering if that meant everything now or everything *everything*.

"Everything. The whole sordid ten-year mess."

He dropped a kiss on the top of her head. "You okay after that?"

She reached back, grabbed his hand and squeezed before letting it go again. "I'm okay."

"How's Jo?" he asked somewhat belatedly.

"Hurt but determined. Slightly hungover. She's on her way back to Austin now."

Chase finally walked back into the living room, gave them a cautious glance and leaned against the back of the couch. He crossed his arms and pinned them with a stare Matt had seen numerous times during Chase's pitching days.

He almost laughed again. Almost.

"So does anyone care to explain what the hell is going on?"

"Well, see, when two people like each other they sometimes express that by kissing and touching each other. Sometimes they even have sex," Jenn said.

"You are such a smartass," Chase muttered.

Matt laughed, causing Chase to narrow his eyes.

"And you. What the hell, man? I told you not to hurt her."

Matt held his hands up in the air. "Did it look like I was hurting her?"

"You know what I mean."

"No, I don't. Why don't you spell it out for me?" He did know what Chase meant, but he wanted his brother to spell it out. Some masochistic part of himself needed to know just how little his brother thought of him at times.

"You don't stick, Matt. You go from woman to woman. Find 'em, fuck 'em and forget 'em, right?"

Jenn tensed in front of him and he wanted to punch Chase in the face. "You don't know what you're talking about."

Chase snorted. "Bullshit. How many times have I heard you say that in the past? Too many. If this were anyone other than Jenn I wouldn't give a shit—you're a grown man and make your own decisions. But that's my best friend you were just kissing. My best friend who's like a sister to me, which, by the way, makes what I just saw even weirder."

"Chase, seriously. I know you love me and I love you, too, but what's going on between Matt and me is our business alone. Besides, you're kind of the last person I would go to for relationship advice right now all things considered."

Go, Jenn.

Chase dragged a hand through his hair and blew out a long breath. "I know I fucked up with Jo, and I have a plan to fix it. Right now, though, I'm trying not to throat punch my brother."

Jenn stepped away from Matt and stepped towards Chase until they were virtually nose to nose. She poked him in the chest as she spoke. "You are not going to throat punch him. He just had brain surgery for crying out loud!"

Jenn protecting him made him feel weirdly warm and gooey. Matt rubbed a hand over his chest at the sensation, not knowing what to do with it.

"Jenn, seriously, what are you thinking here? You hate Matt."

Jenn took a step back and stuck her hands in the back pockets of the denim skirt she was wearing. The same denim skirt that showed off her long legs and had made his tongue nearly stick to the roof of his mouth.

"I don't hate Matt. I've never really hated Matt. There was a misunderstanding once, a long time ago, but we've talked about it and we're fine."

Chase narrowed his eyes. "That's the second time in less than twenty-four hours I've been told there was some sort of 'misunderstanding' between you two."

"Dude, let it go," Matt said in the same tone of voice he often used with rookies.

Chase threw his hands up in the air. "Whatever. Everyone around me is clearly going effing nuts these days."

"Yeah, including yourself."

Chase grimaced at Jenn's words. "Yes, including me."

"Speaking of," Jenn shoved Chase in the chest, pushing him back a couple of inches. "What. The. Fuck. You've been sick all this time—for freaking *years*—and never said one single god damned word to me about it. So imagine my surprise when I find out last night you're sick—like really sick—and are going to need a *fucking kidney transplant*!

And then, to top it off, you broke up with Jo? Seriously, Chase? What the fucking fuck?"

Matt walked the few steps it took to reach Jenn and calmly touched her shoulder. She wheeled around and looked up at him, and he could see all of her hurt and confusion and anger written all over her face. He wanted to make it better, but this wasn't his to fix. This one belonged to Chase.

For some reason that thought rubbed him the wrong way.

Almost like he was jealous. Of his brother.

And isn't that just messed up?

"And you knew all this time and didn't say anything to me, either."

"It's not my story to tell."

She nodded once, understanding what had remained unspoken—that she of all people should get that. She turned back to Chase, but leaned slightly in to Matt, almost as if she needed the support or simply wanted to be near him.

Whichever it was, he was more than happy to oblige, and he wrapped a hand around her hip.

Chase looked down and then back up, shaking his head. "This is way too weird for me."

"Stop changing the subject," Jenn's tone brooked no argument.

Matt would bet hard-earned money she'd just used her teacher voice on his brother.

Chase grimaced. "I should have said something, I know that. I just didn't know how, especially considering we didn't know when or if it would even get to this point. I didn't want to worry you, and I think by not telling people what was going on it was my way of avoiding reality."

"I get that. Believe me, I completely understand keeping secrets as a way of avoiding reality."

Chase once again flicked his gaze between the two of them, curiosity in his eyes. "Something tells me there's a whole lot to this story y'all aren't telling me."

Jenn shrugged. "Maybe, maybe not. We're not the subject at hand here."

Chase sighed and Matt almost laughed. "Fine. I'll get to the bottom of this eventually, though."

"Probably. But until I'm willing to tell you the entire story, back off, okay?"

"Fair enough."

Jenn relaxed under his hand. "At any rate, I kinda sorta told Jo I was going to kick your ass for her."

A pained expression crossed his face. "I figured you probably had. How is she?"

"A little hungover and probably on her way back to Austin by now. She was going to Gran's to pack up her stuff and was leaving right after that since she has to be back at work in a few days anyway. She figured she could get settled in this afternoon, clean up and go grocery shopping tomorrow before the work week started."

Chase tunneled his hands through his hair before rubbing them over his face. "I fucked up bad."

"Hello, Captain Obvious."

Matt snorted at Jenn's comment.

Chase just looked like he wanted to cry, which was kind of disturbing considering his brother was a grown ass man, but then determination etched his features instead and Chase said, "Okay, I have a plan, but I could really use your help, too, if you think you can forgive me."

Jenn stepped forward and wrapped her arms around Chase's neck. "Of course I can forgive you. I'll even forgive you enough to give you a kidney."

Matt swallowed the lump that had suddenly lodged itself in his throat. NO way was he going to cry like his brother, though.

"You don't have to do that."

"I know. But I love you, and that's what friends are for, right?"

"Right."

Jenn stepped back towards Matt. "So what's this plan of yours?"

CHAPTER TWENTY-TWO

Matt: Chilling out with Chase today. He's beating himself up pretty bad.
Jenn: As he should be. He's an idiot. ;-)
Matt: He knows he's an idiot.
Jenn: I know. And have fun with mopey pants.
Matt: Mopey pants?
Jenn: It's a Jennism. Don't question it.
Matt: Jennism? Is that a thing?
Jenn: It is now.
Matt: Fair enough. I have a DR appointment tomorrow. OK if I come by when I get back into town?
Jenn: I guess. ;-) Good luck.

"So I HAVE SOME good news and some bad news. Which do you want first?"

Matt resisted the urge to glare at Dr. Cushon as he walked into the exam room, and instead said, "I guess good news first. I could use some."

Dr. Cushon sat on the stool and smiled. "The good news is that I can clear you for all activities."

A mixture of emotions pinged through him. Relief. Elation. Brief panic. "That's great. So what's the bad news?"

"Well, the bad news is that while I can clear you for all activities, the team doctor's still nervous about you getting back out on the mound."

"I can deal with Andrews."

Dr. Cushon raised an eyebrow. "If you say so. I don't doubt you can. At any rate, you're free to go. Just be careful with your head, listen to your body, yada yada yada."

The neurologist stood and held out his hand for Matt to shake. He stood and took the doctor's hand, his thoughts spinning in his head. "What, no lectures about how I should step away from baseball?" he teased.

"You already know how I feel about that. You're a grown man, and it does no good to lecture you."

"Could you try telling that to my mom?"

Dr. Cushon laughed at Matt's joke. "I'll see if I can write out a prescription for that. In the meantime, though, it's been a pleasure working with you, Matt, and I really do wish you nothing but the best."

Matt nodded. "Thanks. I appreciate that. And thanks for dealing with me. I know I can't have been the easiest patient in the world."

"Easier than some, more stubborn than some, but that's partially why you're such a great athlete." He turned towards the door. "Anyway, it's been great working with you. Good luck."

And with that, Matt was left alone in the exam room, the weight of future decisions weighing heavily on his healed brain.

"The team wants me at the Triple-A club tomorrow."

Jenn stepped back and opened the door completely, her head spinning with a million different questions with Matt's sudden announcement. He stepped inside and she closed the door behind him, turning the lock for good measure.

They stood there, staring at each other, and instead of elation she saw cautious happiness tinged with doubt etched across his features. She reached up and touched his cheek with her fingertips. "I'm happy for you. I really am."

He wrapped his arms around her waist and pulled her in close, resting his chin on her head. He breathed deeply, and she wrapped her arms around his back.

"Are you really happy for me?" he asked, his words slightly muffled by her hair.

She nodded. "Of course I am. This is what you wanted, right?"

His hold on her tightened. "Of course it is."

He didn't sound like he was convincing himself much less her.

She curled her hands into his polo shirt, grabbing the only anchor she could find in the storm of emotions that seemed to be swirling around him. "What's wrong, hon?"

His body shuddered. Jenn couldn't tell if he was crying or had just sighed really deeply.

"I'm happy I've been cleared, but it's kind of shitty timing." He inhaled another shuddery breath. "I want to go, but I also want to stay here with you."

Jenn's stomach dipped and her nose suddenly stung. She burrowed her head into his chest and breathed in that wholly masculine scent that was simply *Matt*. "I kind of want you to stay, too, but I figured this day would come sooner or later."

He pulled away slightly. His eyes searched her face, looking for what she didn't know. "I don't want us to take a step backward, and I'm afraid that me leaving tomorrow will undo all the progress we've made."

She shook her head, even though she wasn't entirely sure her heart could take him leaving. Again. Even if this time she had a heads-up. "It won't. I can't say I've put it all behind me, because the pain of losing Tyler will always be there, but you're not the man I thought you were, or the man I'd needed you to be all these years for my peace of mind."

She wanted to smooth the lines of worried struggle that played across his face and reassure him that everything would be okay.

But you don't know if everything really will be okay.

Matt drew in a shaky breath. "Have I ever told you how wonderful you are?"

She gave him a half smile. "No, but if you want to start now I'm down with that."

"You really are wonderful, Jennifer McDonnell." His gaze swept over her face. Indecision still haunted his eyes, but she could also see the steely determination that had made him one of the best pitchers in history. "If I get on that plane tomorrow, I want—no, I need—to know that when this season's over you won't have changed your mind and gone back to hating me. I don't think I could take that."

She brought her hand around to his cheek, smoothing the worry while getting seriously turned on by the rasp of whiskers against her fingertips. "I won't change my mind. I promise."

Matt looked down at Jenn, desire and confusion churning in his gut right alongside bittersweet happiness. He was beyond glad to get back to baseball, but for the first time in his life he felt like there was more for him than pitching a perfect game or winning a championship.

There was Jenn.

This woman his brain whispered. *She's more than all of those things combined.*

But dammit, he'd set goals for himself, and he wasn't going to quit on his team.

It wasn't just about him. It was about the team. The fans. And yeah, his legacy if he was being completely honest with himself.

"I won't change my mind. I promise." Her whisper wound through his mind, brightening up the dark spaces that still existed despite the inroads he'd made.

"This isn't our last night together." He hoped if he told himself that over and over that it would be true.

She shook her head and said, "No, it's not," but he could see the doubt in her eyes.

It killed him.

With a groan he crashed his lips against hers, needing the anchor of her body, of her lips and tongue and teeth to keep him from drifting away in his sea of doubt. With a moan she opened to him, kissing him back with a passion that nearly took his breath away.

He started to back her up against the door, but then his brain clicked on and told him to slow it down.

Even though every cell in his body was screaming to hurry hurry hurry, to claim her for his *now dammit*, he slowed the pace and then pulled away.

He pushed an errant curl off of her forehead. "Please don't tell me to stop."

She met his gaze with her own, and even though he could see the wheels churning in that head of hers, he also saw her own desire and need in the green depths.

"Take me to bed, Matt," she said before grabbing his hand and leading him down the hallway to her bedroom.

Jenn led Matt to her bedroom on wobbly knees, nerves and desire a crazy mish mash inside of her body. She turned on the bedside lamp before turning back into him, needing to feel the solid heat of his body.

It calmed as much as it aroused.

"Are you sure about this?" He asked, his hand flexing on her shorts-clad hip.

Her heart tumbled just a little bit more. How had she convinced herself all this time that he was an asshole? He wasn't. At least, not now.

She swallowed past the lump of nerves in her throat. "I'm sure."

Before he could respond, she lifted her head and pressed her lips to his, loving his sensitivity but knowing that the more they talked the more nervous she was going to get.

Silly to be nervous considering he's already seen you naked once.

Yeah, but that was ten years ago.

And you weren't in love with him.

Jenn tried to silence her thoughts as their tongues tangled together, slowly caressing each other. The heat from Matt's hand burned into her hip, while his other had crept up to the back of her neck and cupped her there.

She moaned and wiggled closer to him, pressing her breasts against his chest. Her nipples tightened into hard nubs behind her t-shirt, and she was suddenly glad she was small breasted enough to not have to wear a bra all the time. She wrapped her arms around his neck and rubbed against him, the friction shooting an arrow of desire from her nipples straight to between her legs.

Matt's hand tightened on her hip and she stepped backward until the backs of her knees met the edge of the mattress. She broke the kiss long enough to pull his shirt off, and then her own.

God, he was glorious.

Her hands roamed the ridges and bumps of his pecs and abs, spreading through the dusting of hair on his chest before wrapping around his biceps.

Had a more beautiful man ever existed?

She reached for the button of his slacks, suddenly needing to see him naked. She wanted—no needed—to explore, to trace his skin and memorize every detail.

"Slow down. There's no rush."

Her fingers fumbled with his fly. "I know. I just…" she swallowed "…I just need to see you naked."

He kissed her hard and fast. "You're killing me, sweetheart."

"Same here."

She finally managed to work the zipper down. Matt toed his shoes off, then reversed their positions so he was sitting on the bed. He hooked his index finger into the waistband of her shorts and said, "Come here."

He pulled her towards him—not that she would have resisted—and pressed small, open-mouthed kisses against her skin. Her belly button. Hips. Abdomen. Sternum. The tattoo on the underside of her breast. He caught a nipple in his mouth, sucking hard before nipping at it then moving on to the next one. Heat pooled in Jenn's belly and below, making her squirm.

Matt unbuttoned and unzipped her shorts, slid them down her legs along with her panties. She stepped out of them, kicking them somewhere behind her. He kissed her stomach just below her belly button, tracing the skin with his tongue.

Her hand curved behind his head and held him there.

He chuckled before grabbing the back of her thighs and bringing her closer. He laid back on the bed. She climbed onto the mattress beside him, but before she could settle in he grabbed her around her hips, picked her up and positioned her so that she was directly over his head.

"Matt, I don't think…" he forced her hips down and swiped her pussy with his tongue. Whatever she'd been about to say fled her mind.

His tongue caressed her folds, dipping inside of her before moving back up to her clit. He kissed her intimately, his tongue mimicking one of the French kisses he was so good at. Slow, sweet caresses followed by little nips. She gripped the quilt on either side of his head, her hips moving against his mouth of their own volition.

His hands gripped her hips. Her ass. And then he was there, a finger inside of her. He moved it in time with his mouth, curling and pressing into her most sensitive spot and all of Jenn's thoughts scattered with the orgasm that suddenly shuddered through her.

She gasped, her muscles tightening around his finger as his mouth sucked her clit. The quilt bunched up in her grasp, her fingers tightening around it almost to the point of pain.

Slowly, she came back down to earth as Matt sweetly kissed her right in the middle of her pubic hair. Carefully, she moved so that she was lying beside him, staring up at the ceiling as her heart rate returned to somewhere near normal.

"Do you have any idea how hot it is when you ride my face like that?"

And just like that, she was ready to go again.

"Is it?"

He propped himself up on an elbow and traced her nipple with an index finger. "Oh, yeah."

Desire sluiced through her body. "How about we get the rest of those clothes off of you?"

His grin was devastating.

"I think that sounds like a fantastic idea." He stood up and quickly divested himself of his slacks, boxers and socks. He bent at the waist and popped back up with a foil packet in his hand.

"Prepared this time, huh?" she teased.

He climbed back on to the bed, his dick jutting out and bobbing with every movement. "That doesn't bother you, does it?"

She shook her head, fascinated with the sight. "Not at all. If you weren't, I was."

Thanks, Mom.

He set the condom on the bed next to her head before hovering over her. "Good, because I never want to hurt you like that again."

Before she could respond his lips were on hers, coaxing her mouth open. She could taste herself on his lips and tongue, causing more wet heat to pool between her legs.

Her hands explored his body, the hard muscles that bunched with every small movement.

He should totally pose for ESPN Magazine's *body issue.*

She felt him reach for the condom, barely heard the ripping of foil she was so focused on feeling as much of his body as she could. His weight settled over her and she drew up her knees, opening herself fully.

Without breaking their kiss he pressed into her, taking his time, allowing her body to adjust to him. Even if it hadn't been a while since she'd last been with anyone, Matt was big, but God, he felt good.

She tilted her hips up, needing all of him. He slowly slid home, seating himself completely.

He broke their kiss and whispered. "You okay?"

She nodded.

He flexed his hips, slowly withdrawing before pushing back in.

Her eyes drifted shut, his words as he'd climbed back into bed haunting her, even as the ridge of the head of his penis dragged against her inner walls.

Slow.

Slow.

So. Freaking. Slow.

She tightened around him. Gasped his name.

"Matt."

Just as slowly, he pushed back inside until he was seated to the hilt.

Oh, God.

Jenn grasped his biceps, could feel them bulging and flexing under her fingers as he slowly slid his cock in and out. In and out. In. And. Out.

It was everything.

This feeling burning in her chest. The tension gathering in her muscles. The slow drag of his body against and inside of hers.

It.

Was.

Everything.

Oh, God.

What was she doing?

She shouldn't be doing this. Having sex with Matt.

Making love with Matt.

He'd torn her world in two the last time this had happened.

That couldn't happen again.

But God, oh God, no one had ever felt so. Fucking. Right.

Matt suddenly shifted the position of their bodies, so that they were both sitting and facing each other.

The movement jerked her back to the here and now.

To Matt. And the fact that he was still inside her.

"How the hell did you do that?"

He winked at her. "Yoga."

She snorted. "I've never learned that in any of the yoga

classes I've attended."

His hands wrapped around her lower back, and he rolled his hips against hers, making her gasp. "Maybe you should take some yoga classes with me."

She rolled her hips against his, loving how every time she did she could feel him deep inside, rubbing against all her most sensitive places. Matt dropped his head and sucked a nipple into his mouth, torturing the tip with his tongue.

Oh, God. The man was magic.

He released her nipple with a pop and kissed the side of her neck. "Stay with me, Jenn."

How did he know?

He ground against her again. "I can hear you thinking from over here. Just turn it off. Let go. I've got you."

That's what she was afraid of.

But then he spread her legs just a little wider, pushing himself deeper inside, and all thoughts other than "oh, my, God" scattered on a ragged gasp.

He chuckled. Damn him.

But the tension was building again, and she could feel her body racing towards orgasm. Matt worked a hand in between them, rolled his thumb over her clit and commanded, "Look at me, sweetheart. Stay with me."

She opened her eyes and met his gaze with hers. Their faces were merely inches from each other, and somehow this position was more intimate than anything she'd ever experienced. He rolled his hips against hers again, and it was almost like he was touching her soul.

She wanted to climb inside of him. Own him as completely as he owned her.

His hazel eyes had darkened to an olive green, and his jaw was clenched in concentration.

This man.

This handsome, driven, intelligent, athletic god wanted

her. Was inside of her.

And God, she wanted him. All of him.

"It's okay. Let go. I'm here." His voice was a whisper that sounded like every prayer her soul had ever uttered.

She broke, her muscles spasming around him as tears burned at her eyes. She wanted to look away, but couldn't, was caught in the web of his gaze. She saw the moment he came, the way his eyes glazed over and his jaw clenched, felt his body grow taught against hers as he thrust into her one last time.

His fingers dug into her lower back. Hers dug into the back of his neck.

Her heart was racing. Racing. Racing.

Thumpthumpthump.

Thumpthumpthump

Matt kissed her cheek and whispered, "Don't cry, gorgeous."

"I'm not crying."

He raised an eyebrow. Wait, why were her cheeks wet? *Well, that's embarrassing.*

He lifted a hand and gently wiped away her tears. "It's never been like this for me, either." His voice was barely a whisper.

She squeezed her eyes shut and buried her face into his neck. She could still feel him inside of her, somehow still hard. His hands rubbed her back and her breath caught.

Why had she spent so much time hating him when if she'd just womaned up she could have been loving him instead?

Matt breathed in the scent of sex and Jenn's shampoo, the combination causing his heart to stutter and his dick to twitch. Granted, it didn't help that he was still inside of her and every now and then her pussy would clench around him.

He wanted to believe that meant she didn't want him to leave. In any way, shape or form.

Unfortunately, he needed to dispose of the condom before they had a mess on their hands.

With another kiss to her curls, he said, "I need to clean up real quick."

"Oh, yeah," Jenn said before pulling away and carefully untangling their bodies.

She scooted up to the head of the bed, and he felt bereft without her near.

Mentally shaking himself, he kissed her again before getting off the bed and walking to the bathroom where he quickly disposed of the condom and cleaned up. When he returned to the bedroom, she was under the covers but watching him, her gaze wary and lonely.

The sight was like a swift kick to the heart.

He climbed under the quilt, laid on his side and pulled her tight against him. She turned so that her back was to his front in the spoon position. His cock instantly grew hard and Jenn chuckled. "Is that a bat in your pocket or are you just happy to see me?"

He laughed and rolled her over. "You are so freaking goofy sometimes."

She grinned. "It's one of my more adorable traits."

"I think everything about you is adorable," he said before kissing her and showing her just how adorable he thought she was.

CHAPTER TWENTY-THREE

@ESPN: Sources confirm @MattRobertsTX has been cleared to play. Returns to AAA today.

@Deadspin: Party's over! Matt Roberts to report to Wranglers' AAA club today.

@BleacherReport: Matt Roberts reports to Wranglers' AAA today, cleared to play. Mystery woman reportedly not pleased.

"WHERE THE HELL DO they get this shit?" Matt muttered to himself as he perused Twitter while the private plane taxied down the runway of the executive airport the Wranglers used to transport players between the big club and their AAA affiliate just outside of Oklahoma City.

The plane slowly came to a stop and Matt pocketed his phone before unbuckling his seat belt and standing to grab his carry-on. The doors opened and Matt walked down the stairs and waited for his luggage as a golf cart motored towards them. He did a double-take when he realized Darrin was driving it.

His agent brought the small vehicle to a stop and climbed out to greet him. They shook hands and bumped shoulders before Darrin stood back, looking like a fucking

GQ model in his custom slate gray suit.

"Dude, it's the middle of August. You've got to be burning up."

Darrin smiled, but his clear green eyes were serious as they looked at Matt. "I'm fine. The question here is how are you?"

Matt shrugged, getting the feeling Darrin wasn't talking about his head. "I'm fine. The doctor cleared me yesterday and management apparently wanted me here ASAP so I could start my rehab stint."

"I know all of that. I mean how are you really? You gonna be able to get back out there considering what happened the last time?"

He was more worried about his heart than his head, but he wasn't about to admit that to Darrin. Or anyone, really. "Absolutely. This is probably my last chance at a championship."

Darrin nodded.

"What are you doing here anyway? Don't you have other clients to pester?"

Darrin snorted. "It's a two-fold sort of thing. You're my friend first and my client second, so I wanted to make sure you really were okay. I was already on my way here when Chase and Owen called me earlier to tell me about that letter they received from the Devils River Conservation Association. They figured I should know about it, too, since it looks like this could become a pretty big legal battle."

Matt raised an eyebrow. "What letter?"

"You don't know?"

"Know what?"

"Oh, hell. I'll fill you in on the way to the car and then over to the ballpark," Darrin said as Matt's luggage was wheeled around to him.

He grabbed the suitcase handle and readjusted the strap of his laptop bag on his shoulder before walking it over to the golf cart and loading it up. Darrin slid behind the wheel and Matt sat on the passenger side. As they drove away from the plane, Matt asked, "Okay, so what's going on?"

"I can't believe your brother didn't tell you."

"He's been a little preoccupied the past few days. So what's up?"

Darrin shook his head. "Preoccupied?"

"It's a really long story. Let's get to this letter thing first."

"Fair enough. Apparently Chase and Owen were out at the ranch late last week and Daniel had a letter for them that had been mailed directly to the ranch rather than our P.O. Box. At any rate, the gist of it is that some guy's trying to convince the state of Texas that it would be a great idea to pump water from the Edwards-Trinity Aquifer in Val Verde County all the way to San Antonio and other parts of the state."

Matt shook his head. "Why would anyone think that's a good idea?"

Darrin made the money sign with his fingers. "It's all about money. San Antonio's water situation isn't looking good these days, and this guy with some place called the West Texas Water Company is trying to sell them on the idea of cheap water from the Aquifer to help fulfill demand."

"But that's like robbing Peter to pay Paul. If you pump water from the Aquifer, that's just going to drain the Devils River since it's fed from ground water. Not to mention the impact on Lake Amistad—which is low as it is—and San Felipe Springs in Del Rio, all of which flow into the Rio Grande." He'd seen just how low Amistad was while he was at home. It was depressing.

"Yup. And taking the water out of the ecosystem in Val Verde County would also dramatically decrease the amount of water available further down the Rio Grande in towns like McAllen and Laredo."

They reached Darrin's Mercedes and they pulled into the parking space beside it before drawing to a stop. He cut the engine and they both climbed out. Matt grabbed his bags as Darrin pulled a set of keys out of his pants pockets and hit a button on the key fob. The trunk popped open, and Matt tossed his suitcase and laptop inside before slamming it closed.

Once they were inside the car and pulling out of the airport's parking lot, Matt picked up where they'd left off. "So why did we get a letter from this conservation group?"

"Ends up it's a group of other landowners and some conservationists and environmentalists who are trying to preserve the purity of the Devils River. They're lobbying the state to knock out this guy's proposal and consider alternative methods that wouldn't be as harmful to the environment or to the water supply of Val Verde County."

"Sounds like it could get messy."

"It could, yes, especially since the Devils Ranch borders the Devils River Natural Area."

"I had completely forgotten about that."

While their ranch was about 1,900 acres, the Natural Area was a 37,000-acre state park. It had originally only been 20,000 acres, but Texas Parks and Wildlife had purchased an adjoining 17,000 acre ranch a few years back. The Devils Ranch bordered the state park on one side, which was one of the reasons why they'd won their auction bid—everyone else wanted to put up high fencing, which was not allowed by the state. Matt, Chase, Owen and Darrin had been fine with that, and had actually seen the idea of not having fencing on that side as a boon to the hunting ranch they hoped to open up—having an easy path for various and sundry wildlife was not only good for the ecosystem, but also for business.

Matt pulled himself out of his thoughts as they pulled

up to the ballpark. Darrin parked close to the front office and turned off the car.

"You doing okay?" he asked.

Matt shrugged. "As okay as I can be."

It had helped to think about something else for a few minutes.

"Nervous at all?"

"I would be lying if I said I wasn't, but I'm excited, too."

And missing Jenn, don't forget that part.

Matt shook his head. "Let's do this thing."

"What do you mean you're not going to let me pitch?"

Reed Thornhill and Wallace Carter, the manager of the Wranglers' AAA team, sat calmly at the conference room table. Darrin had his agent face on. Meanwhile, Matt was pacing like a caged tiger.

"Matt, we can't risk it. You had brain surgery two months ago. If we bring you back now the media and fans are going to question our motives and whether we have your health in mind or are just grasping at a pennant race," Reed said.

"But I've been cleared!"

Reed slowly inhaled. "We all know that, Matt, but the media's already all over this story. I'm surprised we don't have ESPN camped out in the parking lot with video cameras."

"Give them time," he muttered.

"We have to handle this properly, not only in the eyes of the media and our fans, but also for your future health."

"Reed, I wouldn't be here if I didn't think I could play. I feel fine. Hell, I feel great." Other than feeling like a piece of him was missing, that is.

Focus, Roberts, focus.

"I don't doubt that. And I completely trust Dr. Cushon when he says you're ready. I've seen the CT scans. They admittedly look great. But the fact remains you suffered a very traumatic injury on the mound that resulted in brain surgery. The Wranglers don't take that lightly."

Matt rubbed a hand over his face. "So you brought me up here to what? Parade me in front of the media and the minor league guys to act as some kind of cheerleader? Fuck that."

Reed and Wallace glanced at each other before Wallace cleared his throat and said, "Actually, Matt, we were hoping you would be willing to stick around and possibly start learning the ropes."

"Learnings what ropes?"

"Matt, what do you see yourself doing once your contract's up?"

"I still have two years. I haven't thought about it much." Until recently. For some reason, though, he wasn't willing to talk to them about that.

Darrin pinched the bridge of his nose and shook his head, but didn't say anything.

"You're smarter than that. You know better, and you know how fleeting this game can be."

He swallowed past the lump in his throat. "So what are you trying to say, Reed?"

Reed glanced towards Darrin, who was once more the alert agent rather than the disbelieving friend. "What I'm trying to say is that I—we—think that you could be a great coach. You know the game. Hell, you love the game. You're great with the rookies and the younger players, and people respond to you. You're a born leader, Matt, a born leader with a ton of baseball knowledge and in-game experience that would translate extremely well to a coaching position."

"So let me get this straight—you brought me up here not to let me play again, but to try to coerce me into retiring before my contract's up so I can do something I'm not even sure I would enjoy? Got it."

"The thing is, Matt, there are only two years left on your contract. Considering your injury, and the fact that three of our pitchers are entering free agency in the off-season, we need to find a way to bring in another ace."

"Wait. So you want me to coach so you can bring in my replacement?" He couldn't believe it. He'd been with the Wranglers organization his entire career—which was unheard of these days— and had even taken less money just so he could remain with the team. He'd been nothing but loyal, and this was what he got for that loyalty?

Screw that.

Knowing he was on the edge of saying a lot of things he could never take back, Matt opened the conference room door and hastily made his way outside. Sweltering heat greeted him.

In the distance he could hear the sounds of bats hitting baseballs, accompanied by the occasional smack of a ball into a leather glove.

God, he'd missed those sounds.

There was a picnic table under the shade of a large oak tree on the side of the building, and Matt made his way over and sat on the table, looking out at the street in front of him. Cars whizzed by, occasionally drowning out the sounds of the ballpark behind him.

Meanwhile, he felt like he was stuck, caught between two completely different worlds.

One was the one he'd known for over ten years, the world he loved and had been lucky enough to make a career out of. The other was one he'd also known for years, almost his entire life, really, but that was still somehow new to him.

On one hand, there was baseball. On the other, there was Jenn.

Both of them held his heart in their hands.

The hell of it was that without the implied threat of shipping him off somewhere else, Matt would have seriously considered the offer to coach within the Wranglers organization. Considering he still wasn't completely sure what he wanted to do once he retired, it was a start, an offer. It was a way to remain involved with the game—and the organization—he loved long after he'd stepped off the mound.

The implied threat, however, made him want to hop on the next plane back to Del Rio and walk away from baseball and straight into Jenn's arms.

Considering leaving her this morning had been one of the hardest things he'd ever done, the thought was tempting.

He wasn't a quitter, though, so high-tailing it back to Texas wasn't an option he was willing to choose at this point.

Matt heard footsteps behind him, and then Reed appeared beside him, looking uncomfortable.

"Listen, Matt, that didn't come out like it should have."

"I'm not sure there were too many other ways for that to come out, Reed."

The other man sighed. "The thing is, we want to keep you in this organization. The fans love you, and everyone who works for the Wranglers respects you."

"It sure doesn't feel like you respect me much right now, Reed."

He sat on the table next to Matt. "I probably respect you more than anyone I've ever known. You do things the right way. You're a student of the game. You treat it seriously. You take care of yourself. You give back. You have so much more to offer than a nasty breaking ball—which the team does appreciate, by the way—and I would just hate to see you throw that future away by coming back too early and getting injured again."

"You do realize that ninety-nine point nine out of every one hundred pitches doesn't directly hit the pitcher, right? What happened to me was pretty rare, statistically speaking."

"We know that. The problem is that the media and your average fan doesn't know that, especially considering the number of high-profile pitchers who have been hit by comebackers over the past few years."

"And they're all pitching again."

"They're also much younger than you are."

"Jesus, Reed, you make me sound like I'm ancient."

"In baseball years you are ancient."

Reed spoke the truth, but Matt still didn't like to hear it. "Be that as it may, we have a real shot of winning the World Series this year. After how close we were last year, I don't want to let the team down."

"The only way you would let the team down is by coming back too soon and getting hurt again."

Matt shook his head. "Whereas to me, I'm letting the team down by not playing. I've been cleared. Hell, I'll even wear one of those dorky looking protective padded caps if it'll make you feel better."

"Those have to be custom fitted."

"I'm sure we could get a rush order."

Reed snorted. "If we had more time I would feel a lot more comfortable letting you pitch again."

"We don't have time, though, Reed. You and I both know the minor league season ends in three weeks and then the conference playoffs begin. We have time to get me three, maybe four rehab starts before then."

"I should have known you would make this difficult."

Matt brushed his comment aside. "Just give me a

chance to prove I'm okay, Reed. Give me a few starts in the minors, see how I'm pitching and if I'm mentally solid out on the mound. Even if you and the team decide my stuff isn't there, at the very least I'll be able to be in the dugout for the end of the season and the playoffs and provide some of that leadership you say you respect so much."

"I don't know, Matt. It's too risky."

"It's not like you don't have an insurance policy on me."

"It's not about the money."

"Bullshit. It's always about the money."

"Not this time, not when player safety is involved."

Cars flew by in front of him. "Just one chance, Reed, that's all I'm asking."

"And what happens after that one chance?"

Matt grinned, knowing if he hadn't managed to completely sway Reed he was damned close. "You give me another."

CHAPTER TWENTY-FOUR

"LADIES AND GENTLEMEN, DO we have a treat for you this beautiful Friday night. On the mound for your Oklahoma City Twisters is Wranglers Ace Matt Roberts in his first rehab start since being hit by a line drive just over two months ago and undergoing brain surgery. Stay tuned, because this promises to be a game you don't want to miss."

Jenn bit her thumbnail as she listened to the Twisters' feed via the minor league baseball app she'd downloaded on her phone.

Matt had called her late Tuesday night and told her about the ambush at the Oklahoma City offices, and how he'd managed to convince Reed Thornhill to let him pitch again. Jenn wasn't surprised that Matt had successfully argued his case—the man could be incredibly convincing when he wanted to be—but the thought of him out on the mound again had nerves dancing in her belly.

He'd assured her that he was going to wear a special hat to help protect his head, but she had her doubts regarding its effectiveness, especially considering from everything she'd read most players refused to wear them because they were uncomfortable. Google searches had also shown her photos, though, and she had a feeling most of those players simply didn't want to look un-cool.

They'd talked and texted throughout the week when they'd had a chance—he'd been busy throwing bullpen sessions and taking in scouting reports, and she'd been busy with in-service since classes began next Monday.

"And we're back as the Twisters defense takes the field here in the top of the first inning. Carl, tell us about the Raptors' offense."

"Well, Jack, the Sacramento Raptors' offense has been one of the best in the minors over the past month, posting a team batting average of .398 with twelve homeruns, twenty-six RBIs and twelve stolen bases on thirteen attempts. Their lead-off hitter, Eric Cole, has reached base safely in twenty consecutive games, the longest running streak in the minors right now, and their clean-up hitter, Enrique Palomas, has a batting average of .423 over the past month."

"Sounds like the Twisters have their work cut out for them tonight. Your Twisters lineup looks like this: Arturo Blanco in center and leading off, Will Bowen is your shortstop and number two hitter in the lineup. First baseman Hank Adams batting third with left fielder Ed Young in the clean-up spot. In the five-hole is third baseman Ernesto Salvador and batting sixth is right fielder Michael O'Brien. DHing tonight is Jackson McCoy, followed by catcher Adrian Soto at eighth in the order. Batting last is second baseman Thomas Everett, who Twisters fans will notice has dropped down in the batting order over the past week or so."

"Yeah, Everett's had some problems seeing the ball the past couple of weeks and Twisters manager Wallace Carter felt dropping him down in the batting order might help take some pressure off the youngster."

"Right you are, Carl. And on the mound we have Matt Roberts in his first rehab start with the Twisters since that horrific line drive to the head just over two months ago."

"Honestly, Jack, I'm surprised he's back so soon, especially considering how long it's taken other pitchers to come back after suffering similar injuries."

"Well, you have to think that the Wranglers organization is being very cautious with Roberts' rehab stints and that he'll be on a short leash. You'll also notice he's wearing one of the padded caps that was approved by MLB a few years ago. Even though they've been available for a while, players have mostly opted not to wear them, citing discomfort and heat as their primary reasons."

"Well, there's also the fact that they don't look very cool."

"I would hope players are taking their health more seriously than how their uniform looks, but when you're dealing with a lot of young guys, mostly between the ages of eighteen and twenty-five, you do have to wonder if looks don't play a part in the decision to wear or not wear the protective gear."

"Ah, the folly of youth."

"And the umpiring crew has signaled the game's ready to begin. Adrian Soto jogs towards home plate as Eric Cole steps into the batter's box. Roberts shakes off a few signals before approving one, winds up for the pitch and oh, just outside for ball one."

"Jack, that fastball was clocked at ninety-six miles per hour."

"It sure appears that Roberts' velocity hasn't been affected any. Roberts approves the pitch selection, winds up and wow, that was a nasty twelve to six breaking ball. In there for a strike."

"All Cole could do is stand there and take it."

"Cole signals for time and steps out of the batter's box, adjusts his gloves and his helmet before stepping back up to the plate. The thirty-five-year-old veteran right-hander fires a fastball right down the middle for strike two."

"So far Roberts is looking very comfortable out on the mound."

"Roberts approves the signal from Soto, winds up and gets Cole with a slider just inside the strike zone. Cole can't believe it and walks away shaking his head as Raptors first baseman Mario Gonzales makes his way to the plate. Gonzales gets ready and takes the first pitch for a strike."

"Jack, that looked to me like another slider, low and on the outer edge of the plate."

"I do believe you're right, Carl. And Gonzales takes ball one. Man that was barely outside of the strike zone. Here's pitch number three of the at-bat, a fastball down the middle fouled off by Gonzales. Roberts sets, nods to Soto, and Gonzales makes solid contact and holy mackerel sends it flying right back to Roberts, who ducks then easily reaches up and snags it for out number two of the inning!"

"Jack, I imagine everyone in the Wranglers front office saw that just then and felt a brief moment of panic."

"Carl, I imagine everyone here at the ballpark and everyone listening on the radio almost had a heart attack when they heard the way that ball came off the bat, and then the gasp from the crowd. Roberts, however, made a heck of a play to grab that as it flew past him, and smiled as he climbed back up on the hill."

Jenn's heart was racing. Could she listen to any more of this? She looked down at her thumbnail. Crap. She'd bitten it and three of her other nails on that hand off. Oh, God, this was driving her crazy.

She couldn't not listen, though, so she left the game on as she tried to do other things, like finalize lesson plans, dust the mini blinds and finally read a book. After browsing through the new releases she finally settled on re-reading an historical romance she'd read a while back and had completely fallen in love with. The hero was a mathematical genius who did the accounting for a gaming hell in London, and the heroine was a geeky science and mathematical genius in her own right—a bluestocking in Regency terms—who decided to explore the darker side of London before settling down to married life. It was fun, sexy, and made her cry just a little bit.

In other words, it was the perfect thing to get her mind off of the baseball game she couldn't seem to turn off.

As she flipped through virtual pages on her e-reader, she listened to the game with half an ear and her stomach in her throat. She was in the middle of chapter four when they pulled Matt in the top of the fifth inning. He'd given up two hits on forty-six pitches, striking out six batters and showing full command of all of his pitches. Pretty damned good, considering he hadn't even picked up a baseball in over two months.

She listened to the applause as he left the field, and reached for her phone. She turned the radio feed off—she loved baseball, but her nerves were shot right now—and then texted Matt.

Great game tonight.

He wouldn't see it until much later, but she wanted to let him know she'd been listening and supported whatever decision he made, even if most of those decisions ended with her in Del Rio and him somewhere else.

Great game tonight.

Matt read Jenn's text and smiled, barely resisting the urge to call her right then and there. He still needed to shower and get changed, then address the media.

Unfortunately, that meant it was probably at least another hour before he would be able to call her.

Matt: Thanks. I'll call you when I'm done here. Might be late.

Jenn: That's okay. Call when you can.
Miss you.
Matt: Miss you, too.

He'd just put his phone up when Thomas Everett, the Twisters' second baseman threw his helmet into the locker beside his, muttering to himself as he tore off his gloves and then cleats.

Matt looked around the locker room. Everyone else was ignoring Thomas' little temper tantrum. He sighed and said, "Everyone has bad nights, Everett."

The twenty-four year-old stopped in the middle of removing his socks and looked up at Matt. "Sure. But I've been having a bad night for the past three weeks. If this shit keeps up I won't even be in the starting lineup in another week."

Matt sat on the bench that ran in front of the lockers and casually untied his cleats. "Defensively you're doing great. That catch you made tonight in the top of the seventh?" Matt shook his head. "That was amazing, man."

"There's a 'but' in there."

Matt bit back a grin. "But offensively, when you get up to the plate, you're thinking too hard and you're pressing. We pitchers love guys like you—super talented guys who are in a funk. Y'all overthink, then you press and you start swinging too early or too late. You hack at everything, even garbage balls in the dirt. It makes for an easy out."

Thomas slumped and dropped his socks to the floor. "I know, and I don't know how to fix it."

"You never went through a hitting slump in college?"

Thomas was a Stanford graduate who'd been a first-round pick out of high school but had chosen to go to college instead of heading directly into the minor league system. As a senior two years ago he'd been chosen by the Wranglers in the third round and had quickly worked his way up through the minor league system until he was now just one step away from playing with the big boys.

Matt had a feeling the pressure of trying to make it up to the main ball club on the forty-man September roster, or at least get an invitation to spring training next year, had a lot to do with the kid's current slump.

"I had one in college." Thomas shook his head. "Of course, the guys all told me all I needed was a slump buster, so they went to some local bars trolling for a chick to bring back to me."

Matt rolled his eyes at the long-standing idea that sleeping with a, ah, plus-size woman would magically cure all hitting woes. "So what happened?"

"I'd decided to stay in—I had mid-terms coming up and had an academic scholarship to uphold—and around midnight I heard banging on my front door and drunken giggling. I opened the door and two of the guys pushed this chick into my room, slammed the door and ran off. She was actually kind of cute, but definitely more on the, shall we say voluptuous side, and obviously drunk off her ass. I asked her where her phone was and she couldn't find it, then she ran back outside and started puking over the railing outside. Next thing I know she's basically passed the fuck out on my doorstep, so I carried her back inside, put her on the couch, called my teammates and chewed their asses out. When I woke up the next morning she was gone."

"I think that's the most fucked up slump buster story I've ever heard." And he'd heard some doozies.

"I know, right? Weirdly, though, our next game I hit two home runs and had five RBIs, so I guess it worked. Kind of."

"I'm not finding a drunk woman and taking her back to your apartment."

Thomas shook his head. "Thank God. That was embarrassing and awful, not to mention kind of demeaning towards her. But that still doesn't tell me how to get out of this slump I'm in now."

"So the theory is that a slump buster works because sex gets you to relax, right?"

"Right."

"In your case, you didn't get laid, but something made you stop thinking so much at the plate. The key is figuring out what that was and try to replicate it."

Matt peeled his socks off while Thomas sat on the bench beside him, silent but at least calmer now. "Man, I have no freaking clue."

Matt stood and clapped the second baseman on the shoulder. "Here's the great thing—you don't have to get it figured out today, or even tomorrow or the next day. Everyone in the Wranglers' organization believes in you. All hitters—even the great ones—go through slumps. All it takes is one good at-bat to get you out of it."

Matt grabbed his bag out of his locker and headed towards the exit, but was stopped by Thomas yelling at him, "You're not as big of a jerk as I figured you would be."

Matt smiled and shook his head. That seemed to be a common sentiment here lately.

CHAPTER TWENTY-FIVE

MATT MANAGED TO GET three more starts in with the Twisters before the minor league season ended on September
second. All had been good starts, with management finally
letting him pitch a full game in his final start on Sunday.
The final game of the Twisters' season had been the next
day, and the minor league club had unfortunately been one
win shy of making it to the conference playoffs.

In the three weeks since he'd last seen Jenn they'd
talked every single day, usually at night after a game or in
the evenings once she'd gotten home from school if he'd
had a day game. His brother had also gotten his head out
of his ass, groveled appropriately to Jo and they'd gotten
engaged just last weekend.

He'd made sure to send an anonymous bouquet to Jo's
school, just to make Chase jealous and piss him off.

No, it wasn't the most mature thing, but it had been
pretty funny to hear Chase rant about some anonymous
douche who'd sent his fiancée flowers until Matt had finally
come clean and told him the anonymous sender had been
him. Chase hadn't been as amused as Matt had been, but
Jenn and Jo had gotten a good laugh out of it at least.

Today, though, Matt found himself in the dugout in

Oakland, the smell of sewage combined with sweaty men pungent in his nostrils. God, he hated Oakland's stadium. It was notorious for having sewage backups during heavy rain events, and unfortunately there had been some flooding just two days prior. While the sewage backup had at least been taken care of, the scent still lingered in the air.

They were a month away from the post-season and were up four games over Oakland and leading their division. He hadn't been put back into the rotation yet, and when he'd tried to ask Toby about it earlier today he'd been brushed off.

He leaned against the railing of the dugout, the sound of his teammates' chatter like a faint buzz in the background. Vaguely, he realized they were in the seventh inning when the PA announcer told everyone it was time to stretch, but his mind was elsewhere.

He missed Jenn. Even more, though, he missed the joy he used to feel every time he took the mound or, hell, every time he heard the Star Spangled Banner before every game. While his four minor league starts had been great on paper, the spark he used to feel hadn't been there.

"So have you heard from Matt?" Jo asked Jenn over the phone a few days later.

Jenn lowered the volume on the TV broadcast of the Wranglers' pre-game and sighed. "Yeah. We talk pretty much every day."

"That's a good thing, right?"

"Yeah, I guess." She toyed with the hem of her shorts.

"Okay, what's going on?"

Jenn shrugged, even though Jo couldn't see the action. "I don't know. That's the problem. We talk constantly. He'll send me random text messages and photos from wherever he is. He's sent me flowers every week since he's been gone. We have these really deep conversations sometimes about the future, about life in general, but I still don't know exactly what's happening with us."

Jo chuckled. "It sounds like you have a boyfriend."

"On paper, yes."

"Jenn, Matt cares about you. I'm pretty sure he's totally gone over you. Have you told him how you feel?"

She cringed. "Hell, no! For one, there's still a tiny bit of fear there that he'll break my heart again. For another, he's got enough on his plate to worry about; he doesn't need me freaking out and pressing him for a declaration he isn't ready to give."

"I really don't think he's going to break your heart again."

"How do you know that, though? He didn't even mean to the first time, but it still happened. And now? Jesus. If I took everything I felt ten years ago and multiplied it by a million that still wouldn't fully encompass everything I feel now."

"As someone who was recently there, don't keep holding your feelings in. Tell him. My guess is he's either scared to say the words first or he hasn't quite labeled his feelings yet, even though they're there. He's a smart guy, but he's still a dude. They need a little help sometimes."

Jenn's palms grew sweaty at the thought of opening up like that to him. "I don't know if I can yet, Jo."

"Well, what's it going to take?"

She sighed. "I don't know."

"So do you plan on ever putting me back into the rotation?" Matt asked after finally managing to corner Toby three days later in his office.

The Wranglers manager looked up at Matt and then back to his computer screen. "As a matter of fact, yes. Dombrowski started feeling some shoulder tightness this morning during his bullpen session, so I'm starting you on Friday against the Astros. You okay with that?"

Relief washed through Matt. "I'm great with that. Thanks, Toby."

"You've worked hard to get back here, Matt. You've earned it."

Matt nodded and turned to leave. He was almost to the door when Toby said, "Oh, by the way, could you close the door real quick? I have something else I wanted to talk to you about."

Matt closed the door, curiosity mingling with nerves. "What's up?"

"I hear you were offered the opportunity to start coaching with the Twisters once you decide to retire."

His laugh was more of a bark than an actual laugh. "I don't know that you could say I was offered anything. Reed pretty much tried to threaten me—it was either give up playing and coach or trade me."

Toby shrugged. "He was just testing you, trying to make sure you still had your head in the game after all the reports that had started coming out, and then that YouTube video. At any rate, all threats aside, what did you think about the offer?"

Matt shrugged then crossed his arms over his chest. "I think it could be a good one when I'm ready to retire, but I have some other things I need to consider, some people I need to talk to, before making any decisions. Why?"

"Just curious. Word is Thomas Everett hasn't been able to stop talking about you, said you really helped him get his head on straight those last couple weeks of the season."

"I just talked to the kid."

"Matt, he'd had one hit in twenty-five at-bats prior to

whatever you said to him. You did more than talk to him."

"No, seriously. All I did was talk to him. I mean, I tried to help him get out of his head a little bit, but it's not like I gave him technical pointers on hitting or anything. Besides, didn't the kid graduate from Stanford with something like a 3.8 GPA? With brains like that, you'll figure things out sooner or later."

His manager smiled. "That's the thing, though. You knew Everett was smart—you even knew he'd graduated from Stanford, which most guys in the majors could care less about when it comes to the guys down in the minors— and you apparently knew just what to say to him to help him step out of his own way. That's the sign of a great coach—someone who knows how to motivate his players as individuals rather than using the same method for everyone."

Matt ran a finger under his collar, uncomfortable with the praise. "That's just common sense. We all respond differently to different methods of teaching."

"Exactly. Anyway. I just wanted you to think about it, and to know that whatever you decide I'm behind you one hundred percent."

"Thanks, skipper," Matt said before turning, opening the door and walking out of Toby's office.

Not quite ready to think about his conversation with Toby, he pulled out his phone and texted Jenn.

> Matt: I'm starting Friday night. Home game versus the Astros. Let me fly you up here?

He re-pocketed his phone, not expecting a quick response since it was the middle of the school day for Jenn. His phone vibrated almost immediately, though.

> Jenn: Sure. Need to get a substitute.
>
> Matt: Can't wait to see you. I'll email you flight details.

Friday afternoon Jenn arrived in Dallas after her first ever flight on a private plane. A tall, elegantly dressed man with mocha skin and clear green eyes greeted her as she stepped onto the tarmac.

"You must be Jenn," he said, holding out a hand. "I'm Darrin Mann, Matt's agent."

She took his outstretched hand in hers and shook. "Hi, Darrin. Nice to meet you."

He didn't look anything like what she'd thought. When she thought of sports agents she thought of Jerry Maguire or fat, balding men with nicotine stains on their teeth. Darrin was probably closer to Jerry Maguire than fat and balding, but his sheer beauty combined with his expertly-tailored and highly fashionable suit made him look more like a runway model than a fierce negotiator.

Something about the sharpness in his eyes, though, made her think that in Darrin's good looks were most definitely deceiving.

He ushered her to a waiting golf cart, and they then made their way to the parking lot and a pristine, newer model Mercedes Benz that probably cost four times as much as her Edge. She swallowed before placing her carry-on in the trunk, making sure not to scratch the paint job or leave so much as a fingerprint smudge on the black paint.

Darrin silently held the passenger side door open for her, and she climbed in. So far he hadn't said more than a few words to her, and she couldn't figure out what he was thinking.

He probably thinks you're a country bumpkin gold-digger.

Darrin opened the driver's side door and slid in.

As they pulled out of the small airport's parking lot he said, "Matt's already at the ballpark. Practice starts early, and he ended up in an impromptu meeting with management this morning, otherwise he would have been here to pick you up."

Jenn looked out the window. "Thanks for the heads up. Everything okay?"

Darrin was silent for a moment before saying, "Yeah, I think so. It's been a crazy month for him."

She turned and looked at him. "He's kept me fairly up to date on everything going on, but I have the feeling he's purposely glossed over some of the rougher patches."

A small smile curved his lips. "Knowing Matt, most likely. You know he's crazy about you, right?"

Jenn raised an eyebrow. "I know he likes me and is attracted to me, but I don't know about crazy about me."

Darrin snorted. "Please. He's never been like this over a woman, and I've known him for most of his professional career."

Not knowing how to respond to that, Jenn turned her head and stared out the windshield. "So where are we headed?"

"Matt's arranged for you to get a tour of the ballpark and meet some of the other WAGS, who you'll most likely end up sitting with during the game. Most of them are great women, but there are a couple you might want to watch out for."

"WAGS?"

"Oh, sorry. Wives and Girlfriends."

"Ah, that makes sense." Kind of. Did this mean she was his girlfriend?

God, I feel like a kid asking myself such stupid questions.

They chatted about unimportant things the rest of the way to the ballpark. Jenn found out Darrin had actually grown up in Beaumont and had graduated from the University of Texas with a Master's in Sports Management. He'd played basketball and football in junior high and high school, and while he'd loved the sports he hadn't been quite good enough to play at a collegiate level.

Thirty minutes after landing in Dallas she found herself standing along the first base foul line as a lot of well-built men took batting practice and fielding practice. A couple of the younger guys were shirtless, and even though they were just this side of jailbait she couldn't not appreciate the sight.

She didn't see Matt anywhere, and tried not to worry.

After a brief tour of the field, the dugout and the currently empty locker room her tour guide, Laura, took her up to the suites where she'd be watching the game. A couple of women were already there, a middle-aged one dressed to the nines and the younger wearing blue jeans and a Wranglers t-shirt, which made Jenn feel slightly better about her choice of skinny jeans and a tank top she'd made from one of Matt's old World Series t-shirts after seeing a tutorial on Pinterest.

She liked to think it still smelled like him.

The two women stopped talking as Jenn and Laura approached their seats, both of them smiling warmly at her. The brunette in the Wranglers t-shirt reached out and grabbed Jenn's hand. "You must be Matt's girlfriend, Jenn."

"I…" dammit, everyone but her seemed to think she was his girlfriend, but she wasn't about to let her insecurities show to a couple of strangers, "…yes, I'm Jenn."

"I'm Melissa, Adam Peterson's wife. It's so great to meet you. And this is Chelsea, Toby's wife."

Adam was the Wranglers' shortstop, and Toby was, well, Toby. Everyone knew who he was. Jenn exchanged handshakes and smiles with the other two women, and Laura said, "Now that you're all settled in, I'll leave y'all to get to know each other. These two can show you the ropes, I'm sure."

Uncomfortable silence settled over them as Jenn searched for something to say.

"So how long have you and Matt known each other?" Melissa finally asked.

Jenn fidgeted. "Since we were kids, actually."

Melissa and Chelsea shared a look, and Jenn sighed inwardly.

Melissa smiled. "Well, from what I've heard he's totally in to you. You're a teacher, right?"

Jenn nodded. "Seventh grade English."

"I used to be a teacher. High school biology," said Chelsea.

"Used to be? What made you quit?" Jenn asked, fearing she already knew the answer.

The older woman shrugged and smiled. "I met a man and fell in love. I tried for a few years after we got married, but it was just too hard with him being gone all the time and us being newlyweds. For a while I wondered if it was worth it, being married to a guy who at that time was a player. There was so much uncertainty—would he get traded? What if he got hurt? But I loved him, and I was never one to take marriage lightly, so I stepped back from the ledge and decided my relationship with my husband was more important than any silly fears I was holding on to. I quit teaching and went on the road almost full time with the team, even tutored some of the players' children for a while. Once Toby retired and became a coach things got a little easier, but there's instability there, too. Baseball can be a cruel mistress if you let it, but if you fight for what's important, she loses a lot of her hold."

Melissa gaped at the other woman, while Jenn tried not to squirm.

"You never told me any of that!"

Chelsea shrugged. "That's partially because you and Adam were high school sweethearts and had planned for all this to happen." She swept her hand towards the suites and the field below them before looking Jenn dead in the eye. "Not all of us have the luxury of planning, of preparation. Sometimes love just smacks us right upside the head and we have to make some really hard decisions."

Jenn searched for something to say. "So, um, I take it Matt's mentioned me?"

Chelsea laughed. "He does more than mention you, Jenn. I've known Matt for years and I've never seen him so happy. It's like he's a different man these past couple of weeks."

Well that was interesting.

"Girl, that man is head over heels in love with you," Melissa said. "But more importantly, how much do you know about the WAGS?"

"Nothing."

Melissa and Chelsea sat and Jenn followed. "Then here's what you need to know."

CHAPTER TWENTY-SIX

IN A GAME EERILY similar to the one in San Antonio ten years earlier, the Wranglers beat the Astros 10-1. Matt had pitched six scoreless innings before being pulled more for precautionary reasons than pitch count reasons. He felt good afterwards, high from the win and excited to see Jenn.

He impatiently sat through post-game media interviews, answering all questions directed towards him but unable to keep from glancing at the time every few minutes. Finally, he was free and made his way to the locker room to pick up his bag before heading out to meet Jenn. He found her standing just outside of Toby's office with Chelsea and Melissa, and was surprised to see how relaxed the three of them seemed to be with one another. Granted, Chelsea and Melissa were fantastic women and he was glad Jenn had met them and was getting along with them, but he hadn't dared to hope the three of them could become what appeared to be such fast friends.

Jenn's back was to him as he approached their little group, but Melissa looked up and smiled at him as he approached. "Good game tonight, Matt."

Jenn's body tensed briefly before she turned and faced him. Wariness and hope mingled in her gaze. What had put that look there? Before he could say anything, though, she smiled and threw her arms around his neck.

"I've missed you," she murmured into his ear.

He dropped his bag and hugged her back, whispering in her ear, "I've missed you, too," before claiming her mouth with his own and showing her just how much he'd missed her. Like every time with Jenn, he went from half-mast to hard in less than a second, and nearly groaned at the lust that pounded through his blood.

"Dude, get a room," Adam's voice teased from behind him.

Matt broke the kiss and tucked Jenn under his arm before rolling his eyes at the young shortstop. "Like you have any room to talk. Wasn't it just last week I walked in on y'all in one of the locker room showers?"

Melissa blushed as her husband reached her side.

"Hey, the curtain was closed," Adam said.

Matt snorted. "That's beside the point. Anyway. I am going to take this lovely lady home and catch up. See y'all tomorrow."

He bent and grabbed his bag, his other hand holding Jenn's. He led her out of the building to the sound of Adam's catcalls, and Matt chuckled. Once they were in the parking lot and walking towards his pickup, he asked Jenn, "Did you bring a bag or anything?"

"Yeah. Darrin took it back to your place after he dropped me off here, that way I didn't have to worry about it."

He nodded as they reached his truck. He hit the unlock button on the key fob, opened the back door of the crew cab and threw the bag in before closing the door and pulling Jenn in for a tight hug. "God, I've missed you."

Her hands fisted in the back of his dress shirt. "I've missed you, too."

He kissed the top of her head. "You hungry at all?"

She shook her head. "Once they pulled you out of the game I kind of gorged myself on nachos and hot dogs. You know, ballpark food."

"Why after they pulled me out of the game?"

She snorted. "Because I was too nervous while you were in it to eat a single thing. Even water was making me feel nauseated."

He cupped her chin in one of his hands, lifting it so that their gazes met and held. "I am so sorry if I've made you worry."

He could tell she wanted to look away, but forced herself to maintain eye contact. "Matt, I've worried every day since you left, every time you've gotten up on the mound. I know what happened a few months ago was a freak accident sort of thing, but it obviously happens every now and then, and I don't know if I could handle you dying or being in a vegetative state."

Whereas just months ago Jenn's fear would have angered him and made him feel like he was being pushed into making a decision he didn't want to make, tonight it made him feel relief. Knowing she worried about him was a weird balm to his soul; it meant she cared. Really cared. It also meant the conversation he'd had with management this morning had been the right one.

They reached his condo in Uptown about thirty minutes after leaving the ballpark, and as he opened the front door he tried to see the place through Jenn's eyes. It was nice, sure, but it was also kind of cold. In the three years he'd owned it he'd never bothered to make it a home; instead, it was just a place where he slept and occasionally brought women.

He set his bag on the floor beside the front door, shut it

and locked it behind them. Jenn chafed her hands over her bare arms.

"You cold?"

"Kind of. What do you have your thermostat at, forty?"

He laughed as they walked into the living room. "Seventy. I'm usually really hot when I get back from a game, so I like to have it cool in here."

"Makes sense."

She stood in the middle of his living room, her eyes darting from here to there. He stepped towards her and took her hands in his own. "Why are you so nervous?"

She inhaled a shaky breath. "I don't know. I mean, I kind of do, but I don't. If that makes any sense."

A curl had escaped her ponytail and he tucked it behind her ear. "I'm glad you could make it."

"Me, too."

"You know I don't expect sex, right?"

She actually snorted at that. "Please. You think I came all the way up here to not get laid? I'm going for the full service experience here, buddy."

He chuckled. "Well, in that case…"

He wrapped his hands around her hips and pulled her to him before claiming her mouth with his own. If the kiss outside Toby's office had been "hi," this kiss was *hello.* He teased her tongue with his own, loving the feel of her fingers tangling in the hair he'd allowed to grow back over the past month.

Wordlessly, he led her back to his bedroom where he slowly, reverently removed her clothes until she stood bathed in moonlight filtering through the window, her nipples hard and goosebumps covering her flesh. She trembled a little, and Matt quickly removed his own clothes before leading her to the king size platform bed in the middle of the room.

As he lay her down, he showered kisses over her body,

loving the feel of her under his hands and mouth.

She sighed, a small, breathy sound that had his cock straining, so hard it almost hurt. Her hands drifted up and down his arms, his back, cupping his ass before sliding around and exploring his abs before trailing lower. She fisted his cock, stroking it as their mouths met in a hot, open kiss that had turned from slow and sweet to fast and dirty in an instant.

He played with her nipples, rolling each one between his fingers and pinching lightly, making her gasp against his mouth. Her hand around his cock tightened.

Matt reached for the nightstand and blindly searched for a condom. He found one, pulled it out and ripped the foil packet. "God, Jenn, I need to be inside of you."

"Hurry, Matt. Please." Her quiet begging almost undid him.

He quickly rolled the condom on, settled between Jenn's thighs and slid home.

Home.

As his hips pumped in and out, he reached up, found her hands and grabbed them, holding them tight above her head. She surged up and kissed him, nipping at his bottom lip before licking it and kissing him fully.

He groaned into her mouth and let one of her hands go so he could touch her. He worked a hand between them, moving his thumb in circles over her clit. She moaned and tightened her legs around him. He slammed in to her, high and deep, hitting that place inside of her that she liked, and her pussy tightened around his dick.

"Come for me, baby." He slammed into her again.

Jenn tightened her hold on his hand and grabbed the comforter with the other. His name on her lips was a curse, a prayer, a command, as she climaxed, her inner muscles milking his own orgasm from him. With a groan, Matt felt his own release.

As their breathing slowed he shifted so that he was propped on his elbows, keeping at least a little bit of his weight off of her. Jenn's eyes were closed, her cheeks flushed and her hair wild on the mattress. He could just make out the pulse beating in her throat, and fought to get his own pulse under control.

The longer he looked at her, the longer he stayed there suspended while still inside of her, though, his pulse quickened until his heart was almost hammering out of his ribs.

This woman.

God, this woman was everything to him.

More than baseball.

More than another championship.

More than the World Series ring and the NCAA championship rings.

More than the accolades, the awards, the MVPs and the records.

Looking down at Jenn, at her beautiful face so relaxed post-sex, Matt finally felt the pieces fall into place. The pieces he hadn't even realized he'd been looking for, but had been missing in his life.

"I'm retiring."

Jenn's eyelids flew open at Matt's quiet, casual announcement. She could still feel him inside of her—let's face it, physically and emotionally—and she vaguely realized that now was a bit of an odd time to make that sort of an announcement.

Matt, though, had always done things his own way.

"You're retiring?"

He nodded, looking much more at peace than she'd figured he would when he made that decision. "After the end of the season. It's time, and while my stuff's still as good as it was, my heart isn't in it anymore."

She rubbed her thumb over his chin, along his jawline. "What changed?"

"It stopped being fun a while ago, which I never told anybody. When I got hurt and it forced me to step away from the field, I had to face the fact that in chasing a dream I'd neglected a lot of other areas of my life."

"Like family," she said quietly, knowing that while the rift between Matt and Chase had definitely lessened over the past few months it would still take some time before that relationship was truly whole.

"Like family," Matt reiterated. "And like love, too."

Her thumb stilled on his jaw as her gaze flew up to his. She swallowed, but couldn't seem to form words. She blinked, licked her lips and finally squeaked out, "Love?"

His expression was serious as he looked down at her. "Yes, love."

Her heart beating like a hummingbird on crack, she managed to ask, "What about love?"

"You don't realize it, do you?" he asked as he traced the lines of her face with an index finger.

"Realize what?"

"How could you not know I love you?"

Her stomach dipped and her pulse kicked up another notch. "You love me?"

"More than anything." He kissed her slowly, sweetly before continuing. "I love you more than baseball, Jenn. More than records and awards and championship rings. I've loved you for ten years, and I've spent all this time running from it because you didn't fit into my plans. But I'm tired of fighting it, I'm tired of living half a life and coming home to a cold, empty condo every night. I love you more than I ever knew was possible, and I think you love me, too."

Jenn's nose and eyes stung, and she rapidly blinked

away tears. "You love me more than baseball?"

"More than baseball."

She wrapped her arms around his neck and brought his weight fully down onto hers, unable to hold back the tears any longer. She'd loved him for so long, had felt so much heartache and so much joy because of him that hearing his words was like a balm to her soul.

"I love you, Matt," she said as he pulled away to watch her. He wiped away tears and she smiled. "They're happy tears. I promise. It's just that no one's ever made me feel the way you do—happy, sad, complete heartache and utter joy. I'm so sorry I wasted so much time being a bitch towards you and blaming you for so many things, including the loss of Tyler."

He opened his mouth to speak, and she held two fingers against his lips, keeping him quiet. "No, I need to say this. I did blame you for the loss of Tyler. It didn't seem fair that you were out playing a game while I was miserable and heartbroken, having to bury our baby. A baby you knew nothing about, because of me. I was an idiot—no, I was a total fuckwhit—and I'm sorry."

She moved her fingers and let him speak. "Jenn, you don't have to apologize. We both made mistakes, but the past is the past. I don't know that we were ready for each other ten years ago, or would have even made it for the long haul ten years ago. Fate played a certain hand here, I'm sure, but what matters now is that we've put all the past stuff behind us and have a future to look forward to. Together. Hopefully."

She nodded, her heart flip flopping in her chest and her body and soul feeling freer, lighter than it had in years. "You really love me more than baseball?"

"Absolutely."

"That must mean you love me a whole, whole lot."

His grin was wicked. "If you don't believe me, I'll show you."

And with the same determination he'd had had every time he stepped onto the pitcher's mound, he proceeded to show her just how much he really did love her.

It was definitely more than baseball.

EPILOGUE

"WE'RE HERE IN THE bottom of the ninth of Game Seven of the World Series. The Giants are down to their last batter and the Wranglers currently hold a one-nothing lead over San Francisco."

"This has definitely been a pitcher's duel, Craig, with hits hard to come by for either team."

"Roger that, Nathan. This has definitely been a hard-fought battle that is indeed coming down to the wire. Meanwhile, Wranglers ace Matt Roberts is still in this game, refusing to hand the ball over to pitching coach Troy Matherson or the skipper, Toby Prince."

"Well you can't blame him, Craig. Roberts has pitched lights out this game and is only at a hundred and one pitch-es. We've certainly seen him go deeper pitch count-wise before."

"Plus, Nathan, there's all the speculation that this will be Roberts' last game and that the veteran right hander will retire after this season."

"Absolutely, Craig."

"And it appears the Giants have substituted Fox as a pinch hitter here. Fox steps up to the batter's box. Roberts goes into the windup. Fires a fastball down the middle for strike one."

"That thing was clocked at ninety-eight miles per hour, Craig."

"Roberts has certainly been on top of his game tonight, Nathan. I can't recall him ever pitching this well. Fox steps back into the box. Roberts winds up. Curveball just outside for ball one. He shakes off a couple of pitches to catcher Miguel Rodrigo, finds one he likes. Sets. Goes back to the curveball for strike two."

"That was a nasty pitch, Craig."

"Indeed it was. Fox calls for time, steps out of the batter's box and back in. Roberts sets, nods to Rodrigo. Winds up and oh my, Fox smokes a ball towards left field. This could be trouble for the rookie Carpenter. He's back to the warning track and oh my goodness makes a leaping catch to win the game! Wranglers win! Wranglers win! The hometown crowd just erupted in celebration."

"Man, this stadium is rocking right now, Craig. What a sight to see."

"No kidding, Nathan. Not only did they just see their team win a World Series Championship, but they also just witnessed a Game Seven perfect game. The last time a perfect game was thrown in the World Series was by Don Larsen in 1956…"

Matt stood on the makeshift stage that had been erected in the middle of the infield after the game. He was sticky from the champagne that had been sprayed liberally around the locker room immediately following the Wranglers win, but he had a hard time caring. Diane Johnson, the on-field reporter, stood beside him and signaled they were ready to go.

"Matt, I know you must be feeling all kinds of emotions right now, but tell us what was going through your mind on that last out." She pointed the microphone towards him.

"Oh, sh—crap."

The crowd in front of the stage, and his teammates gathered around him laughed. "What's it like, knowing you're the first person since 1956 to pitch a perfect game in the World Series?"

Matt shook his head and fought back tears as emotion overtook him. He found Jenn down in the crowd, wearing that old shirt of his that she'd turned into a tank top, tears streaking her face as she beamed up at him and said, "It's a hell of a way to go out, that's for sure."

"Does that mean the rumors are true? You're retiring?"

Matt smiled at the cameras. "It just means it's a hell of a way to go out. And tonight's not about me. There were eight other guys on that field with me who provided amazing defense in a couple of sticky situations." Matt looked around. "Carpenter, where are you? Get over here."

Carpenter grinned as he shoved through bodies to get to the front of the stage. Matt clapped him on the shoulder and said into the microphone, "This guy right here? We might not be standing here if Carp hadn't made one of the best catches I've seen in years. I didn't even know you could jump that high, man."

Carp blushed before turning on every ounce of southern charm he had. "Aww, shucks. That was nothin'. I've jumped higher tryin' to get away from a freshly castrated bull on my daddy's farm."

The crowd laughed, their attention drawn to the likeable rookie, and Matt casually sidled away until he was able to jump off the stage and head towards Jenn. She jumped into his arms, wrapping her legs around his waist and showering him with kisses.

"You threw a perfect game, Matt! A perfect game! In the World freaking Series!"

He laughed. "I know, baby, I know."

"Why do I seem more excited about this than you do?"

He shrugged. "It's just a game. Like I said, it's a great way to go out, and one day I'll probably look back on this and think, 'holy shit, I actually did that,' but right now? The only thing I really want to do is get you home, naked and on top of me."

She kissed him then, long and deep and Matt felt a peace he'd once thought would be impossible to achieve. When she broke the kiss, she nuzzled his ear and whispered, "Would now be a bad time to tell you I'm pregnant?"

He drew his head back and looked at her, searching her face for any signs of worry or stress. Instead, she simply looked happy, and was actually kind of glowing. "Are you serious?"

"As a heart attack."

He grinned. "Now that's what I call a perfect game."

She smacked him on his left shoulder but couldn't hide her smile. "Oh, and I totally forgot to tell you, but my parents are going to be on that *Doomsday Preppers* show. You okay with the possible media backlash?"

He laughed, a deep belly laugh that made their bodies shake and brought tears to his eyes. "For you? I'm okay with just about anything. I love you, Jenn."

"More than baseball?"

He looked around at the confetti that still lazily flew through the air, the crush of fans around them and his still-celebrating teammates and said, "More than a Game Seven win in the World Series."

"Wow. That's a lot."

"Damn straight it is."

She kissed him again, and the cheering, the interviews on the PA system and the catcalls from nearby fans all faded into the background until all he was aware of was Jenn wrapped around him, carrying his child and showing him more love than he sometimes knew what to do with.

It was so much better than baseball.

ACKNOWLEDGEMENTS

First, I want to say "thank you" to you—the reader—for taking the time out of your busy day to read this book. I hope you enjoyed Matt and Jenn's story as much as I enjoyed writing it. These were two characters who ended up surprising me (Matt, especially) in all the best ways.

Second, I have to acknowledge my husband and his never-ending support. I wrote the bulk of this book in the first two months after he received a kidney transplant, partially as a means to escape our somewhat uncertain reality, partially as a way to process many of the emotions I'd been feeling since we'd found out how sick he was in June of 2014, and mostly because his illness has made us both realize that we can't keep putting off living and reaching for our dreams. You never know which day will be your last, and "some day" may never come. Those were lessons that I suddenly understood, and which drove me to keep pushing on.

Third is another "thank you" to everyone who's purchased Between the Seams (Chase and Jo's story), found me on Facebook, emailed me, commented on my blog, reviewed the book, etc. Y'all have no idea how much it means to me to know that there are people out there who really, truly enjoyed that book and were looking forward to this one.

Fourth: thank you, to my beta readers for the fantastic feedback and general cheering section as soon as you finished this book. Your input is invaluable.

Fifth: thank you to all of the great radio baseball announcers I've listened to over the years. You don't know it, but you totally shaped my announcers in this book. Craig Way (aka The Voice of the Texas Longhorns) is one of the best in the business, and his "prodigious clout" call is one of my all-time favorites. I'm spoiled to have great radio guys for the Round Rock Express and Texas Rangers. Mike Capps with the Express is a minor-league gift, and makes listening to AAA baseball incredibly enjoyable. For the Rangers, Matt Hicks and MLB Hall-of-Famer Eric Nadel bring the game to life. Y'all have no idea how enjoyable you make those long drives between Austin and the ranch during baseball season.

Last but not least I want to give a shout-out to the indie writing community. The world of publishing is changing by leaps and bounds, and there are so many indie writers out there who are willing to share their knowledge with us newbies. Thanks to all of you for sharing your sales data, your marketing strategies, your general advice and virtual hugs when needed. Most people think we writers are a bit anti-social (and, yes, we admittedly can be), but there are so many thriving, supportive, friendly writing communities out there that it's sometimes hard to believe the stereotype.

Cheers!

Aubrey

P.S. Love what you read? Share the love and leave a review and/or rating so other readers can find books to read!

BASEBALL AND OTHER LESSONS PLAY-LIST

Flashback Scenes:

Maroon 5 – "She Will Be Loved"
Evanescence – "Going Under"
Breaking Benjamin – "So Cold"
Kelly Clarkson – "Behind These Hazel Eyes"
Matchbox20 – "Hand Me Down"
Linkin Park – "My December"
Sarah MacLachlan – "Fallen"
Liz Phair – "Why Can't I?"
Dashboard Confessional – "Vindicated"
Michelle Branch – "Are You Happy Now?"
Jann Arden – "Insensitive"
Evanescence – "My Immortal"

Present Day:

Jenn:
Pistol Annies – "Hush Hush"
Coldplay – "Paradise"
Easton Corbin – "Clockwork"
The Civil Wars – "The One That Got Away"
Kacey Musgraves – "Merry Go Round"
Sara Bareilles – "Gravity"
Demi Lovato – "Heart Attack"
Jon McLaughlin – "Beautiful Disaster"
Taylor Swift – "Style"
Heart – "Alone"

Matt:

The Lumineers – "Stubborn Love"
Mumford and Sons – "Little Lion Man"
Ed Sheeran – "Kiss Me"
Neon Trees – "Sleeping With a Friend"
Mike Ryan – "Dancing All Around It"
Matt Nathanson – "Car Crash"
Matt Nathanson f. Sugarland – "Run"
Matt Nathanson – "I Saw"
Ed Sheeran – "Small Bump"
Wade Bowen – "Trouble"
John Mayer – "Heartbreak Warfare"

EXCERPT: BETWEEN THE SEAMS

What happens when life throws you a curveball?

Chase Roberts is the quintessential Good Guy. Attractive, athletic, intelligent and successful, the former college baseball star and one-time major league prospect is the kind of guy any woman would love to take home to Mama. Except there's one small problem: Chase has never really gotten over his former best friend—and first love—Jolene "Jo" Westwood, who broke his heart as a teen. Now, all grown up with two thriving businesses, Chase has enough to worry about.

Jo Westwood just wants to come home to Del Rio, Texas, help nurse her grandmother back to health and go back to her calm--okay, boring and lonely--life in Austin once the summer's over. Unfortunately (fortunately?), her best-laid plans come to a screaming halt the moment she accidentally bumps into her former best friend--and first love--Chase Roberts in the feminine hygiene aisle. The cute boy she once knew has become a HOT man. A hot man who seemingly hates her. Great.

As the long, hot summer drags on, Chase and Jo find themselves spending more and more time together, resurrecting not-so dead feelings and putting the past behind them. Unfortunately, summer only lasts so long, and even love may not be able to survive long-held secrets that threaten to tear them apart.

CHAPTER ONE

"Yo, Chase, did you hear a word of what I just said?"

Chase Roberts snapped out of his reverie and glanced over at Owen Daniels, his best friend, business partner and occasional pain in the ass. "Sure."

Owen snorted. "No, you didn't."

A pretty blonde entered the building across the street, and Chase fought the overwhelming urge to follow her. "Did you see the blonde across the street just now?" He asked instead.

Owen opened the driver's side door of his car. "I thought you'd sworn off women? Called them all second-hand groupies or something like that."

Chase looked at the building—Mitchell's Drug Store—one more time before climbing into the passenger seat of the low-slung Mustang. "I didn't say they were all second-hand groupies. There just happen to be more than I would like."

"Must be tough, being chased by hot, scantily-clad women all the time."

Owen pulled away from the curb and Chase fought the urge to turn and watch to see if the blonde came out of the drug store.

"It is when the only reason they're chasing after me is because of my brother." Chase's brother, Matt, was Mr. Baseball. The long-time ace for the Texas Wranglers, Matt was well-loved in their hometown of Del Rio, Texas. So well-loved the high school baseball fields now bore his name. Without a sponsorship. So well-loved that he had his own menu item at Francine's Diner. So well-loved that there was a freaking Matt Roberts Day, complete with a downtown parade. In November. After the World Series and before Winter Ball started. Hell, his brother had been given keys to the damned city.

As much as Chase loved his brother, he got tired of the groupies who decided that if they couldn't have Matt they would just settle for Chase. After one too many stories posted about him on internet message boards and questionable websites, Chase had decided about a year ago that maybe a female hiatus was in order.

Besides, he had a business to run, and even with his last name he still wanted to project the image of responsible, trustworthy businessman—not wannabe playboy.

"Boo-freaking-hoo."

Chase ignored Owen's sarcasm. "Anyway. Did you happen to see her?"

"Who? The curvy blonde going into Mitchell's?"

"Yes. That one. Apparently you did."

Owen shrugged. "She looked like she had a nice ass."

"She looked familiar."

Owen turned into the parking lot of Roberts Ventures, LLC, and swung into the space next to Chase's pickup. "Previous one-night stand?"

Chase snorted. "No. Definitely not one of those." Hell, Chase could count on one hand the number of one-night stands he'd had over his entire lifetime. His brother's groupies just made it sound like he was, well, a player.

They got out of Owen's Mustang and entered the building. Chase's executive assistant and all-around office goddess looked up and smiled at Chase. As soon as Kimberly's gaze landed on Owen, her smile quickly turned to a frown.

Chase didn't know why Kim didn't like Owen, and no amount of gentle prying had managed to get the information out of her. "Good morning, Kim."

"Mornin', Chase. We got the Sutton contract in, and

Frank Wimbly called earlier, said he found a spot out by the lake that he would like to take a look at."

Chase nodded. "Thanks. I'll take a look at the Sutton contract and give Frank a call back."

He made his way to his office, shaking his head as the sound of Kim scolding Owen could be heard from down the hall.

Never a dull moment he thought as he got back to work.

Jolene Westwood was usually pretty hard to embarrass. As a high school guidance counselor, she'd heard—and discussed—some of the most embarrassing things human beings experienced. From high school crushes to missed periods to kids grappling with their sexuality, she thought she'd heard—and seen—it all.

But embarrassment was much easier to deal with when it wasn't your own, and unfortunately she was currently knee-deep in it on this lovely evening.

She'd just been standing there, in front of the pads, tampons and Monistat cream y lined the back wall of the Del Rio Walmart, debating small pack versus value pack, when she accidentally backed up into someone.

A solid someone who radiated warmth and *man*.

Slowly, she turned around, her hands still paused mid-air, holding the bright yellow and blue boxes up like some sort of offering.

Or maybe as a big fat red light.

No pun intended.

Her gaze wandered up from the box of Crest toothpaste in one hand to the center of what was definitely a polo-clad male chest and up to a jaw shadowed with dark stubble. Firm lips. Slightly crooked nose. Brown eyes that made her think of warm, cinnamony Mexican chocolate. Dark eye-brows. Dark brown, almost black hair that curled out from under a blue YETI coolers ball cap.

Jo swallowed a gasp—or, more realistically, a long-ing-filled sigh—and took a quick step back.

Chase Roberts.

Childhood best friend.

Teenage crush.

The boy she'd long ago said goodbye to.

Her stomach flip-flopped as she slowly lowered her hands and her gaze. Mentally drank him in.

Six-one.

Two hundred pounds.

1.87 ERA.

At least, those had been his college stats. If anything, he looked like he might have gained a couple of inches, and whatever he weighed, it sure looked like it was pure mus-cle.

Realizing she was staring like an idiot, she mentally shook herself and somehow found her voice. "I am so sor-ry, Chase. I didn't see you behind me."

Stupid, Jolene. Of course you couldn't see him behind you, it isn't like you have eyes in the back of your head.

His melted chocolate gaze traveled up and down her body before settling on her face. "I'm sorry, you seem to have me at a disadvantage—you know my name, but I don't know yours."

Jo smiled, even though she was cringing on the in-side, and she fought back the sense of disappointment his words evoked. They'd been friends for years and he didn't remember her? Hell, her mother had tried to end his par-ents' marriage, until the truth finally came out years later that Chandra Sommers had never slept with Bo Roberts. Ends up Sarah Roberts had known that for far longer than Jo had—Chandra was more than happy to let her daughter believe the worst. And he didn't remember her?

Serves you right, for ending things the way you did.

Her voice tinged with the disappointment she apparently couldn't hide, Jo responded. "Sorry. I've changed some since the last time we saw each other. Jolene Westwood."

Chase's brows drew together over those hot chocolate eyes. "I feel awful, but I don't remember a Jolene Westwo—wait a second. Jo? Jo Sommers?"

Jo could feel her cheeks warming and knew she was probably beet red by now. Could this be any more awkward? "Sorry. I changed my name a few years back, after my parents died."

"Westwood is your grandma's name, right?"

Jolene nodded and swallowed. "Yeah."

Lame, Jolene, lame.

Chase stood before her, a brown-eyed god with a 92 mile per hour fastball and a nasty curveball, looking for all the world like a pitcher who couldn't understand a single one of the signals the catcher was sending him.

Jo. Jo Sommers. His childhood friend and teenage crush. The captain of the cheerleading squad and smartest girl in the room (and hell, their class).

He'd known it was her as soon as she'd turned around and allowed that sea glass gaze to travel up his body oh so slowly. He'd never be able to forget those eyes—they'd haunted him for so long they were a permanent part of his psyche at this point.

She may have changed a little bit—her blonde hair was softer, longer and wavier than he remembered, and she'd gained some curves since he'd last seen her when they were in college, but he sure as hell would never be able to forget her.

So why was he playing stupid now?

She'd fueled more than one of his teenage fantasies, even after she'd suddenly stopped talking to him their freshman year of high school. As a teen he wondered if it had to do with the health issues—and eventual scarring—he'd had as a kid and young teen. Had she been embarrassed to be around him?

As an adult, he realized there could have been other reasons, but even a cocky teenage athlete can be felled by one simple brush off from the prettiest girl in school.

"So, uh, what brings you back to town?"

Smooth, Roberts, real smooth.

Worry briefly turned those sea glass eyes stormy, but the expression was gone so fast he wondered if he'd imagined it.

"Gran had a hip replaced. She refused to go to a rehab facility, and pretty much ordered me to come take care of her." A small grin played at the corners of Jo's generous mouth, and for a brief second Chase was reminded of the girl she used to be. The one who'd been his playmate and confidante.

"How's she doing?"

Jo waved her hand, and then blushed as she looked at the box she still held.

"I'm really not trying to accost you with tampons, I swear."

Chase barely managed to choke back the laughter that threatened to escape. "Well, at least they're not used."

Jesus, Roberts, that was awful.

Her blush deepened, and the chuckle that had been threatening to escape somehow managed to rumble out. Jo shook her head, smiled, and tossed the box into her cart. "I'm glad to see you still have a sophomoric sense of humor, Chase."

"At times, yes." Unfortunately.

Their gazes met, held, and then a slow smile bloomed

over Jo's face before she, too, was laughing. "How about we try this again?" She held out her hand. "Hey, Chase! Nice to see you again."

Chase wrapped his hand around hers, and he swore he felt tingles shoot up his arm. "Jo, it's good to see you, too."

Unsettled, he dropped her hand and stepped back. A look of confusion flitted across her pretty face before she once again replaced it with an odd, too-placid-to-be-real smile.

Had she felt it, too?

"Well, uh, I better get going." She gestured to her cart, which held a small amount of groceries and toiletries. "Gran's waiting for me to get back so I can cook supper. Can't let her starve."

Chase took another step back, feeling the need to put some amount of distance between them. He flexed his hand, still feeling slight tingles in his fingertips. "No, can't let her starve."

Jo began to push her cart away, and before he could take the words back he blurted out, "We should do lunch some time. Or supper. Catch up. For old time's sake."

God, he sounded like an effing idiot. Catch up for old time's sake? Yeah, because *that* sounded like a brilliant idea.

An expression Chase couldn't identify clouded Jo's eyes before it, too, was gone almost as quickly as it came. "Um, sure." She nodded her head once, her wavy blonde hair falling over one shoulder. "We'll have to do that."

Chase nodded in ascent and shoved his hands into his pockets. Jo shot him one last glance before turning from him. Chase allowed himself to enjoy the view as she walked away.

Couldn't not appreciate it, really, as it was a damned fine view. The same damned fine view he'd seen just this morning walking into Mitchell's Drug Store.

"Jolene, is that you?"

Jo set down her grocery bags and blew a strand of hair out of her eyes. "Yes, Gran, it's me."

"Good, that rehab woman just left and I'm starving."

Jo rolled her eyes. "I think that rehab woman has a name."

"Yes, the Devil's Harlot!" Gran shouted back from the living room.

Jo sighed and yelled back. "She's not a harlot, Gran." Who even used the word "harlot" anymore? "She works for Val Verde Regional Medical Center. Last I checked, Satan wasn't on their payroll."

Gran harrumphed from the living room. Jo finished putting up the groceries and walked into the living room. "Did she make you do something new today?"

Her grandmother sat in a big, somewhat comfortable chair. She waved a hand in the air dismissively. "Just a new exercise. Nothing too bad."

"Then why the name-calling, Gran?"

Gran gestured towards the flat screen TV mounted on the wall across from her. "She was lusting after that Roberts boy. Acting like a cat in heat."

"Roberts boy? Chase? Why was Chase on TV?" Jo's mind went back to the embarrassing scene in Walmart, and realized it was a good thing Gran couldn't read *her* thoughts. Chase Roberts all grown up was definitely worth lusting after.

Gran waved the remote. "No, not the sick one, bless his heart. The older one."

Sick? Was Gran referring to Chase's childhood illness, or did he only look like the picture of health? Hot, hot health.

"And we're back at the top of the eighth inning, and Wranglers ace Matt Roberts is back out on the mound."

Jo looked at the television and saw Chase's older brother, Matt, readying the mound for another inning. The camera zoomed in on his face, and Jo had to admit that he was definitely attractive. Always had been. Problem was, he'd always known it, too.

While Chase had been popular and well-liked in his own right, Matt had always had that "it" factor that just drew people to him. Throw in obnoxiously good looks and talent that had scouts looking at him as a freshman, and you had a combination that was hard for any girl to resist.

"The PT was openly lusting after Matt in front of you?"

Gran pursed her lips. "The shameless hussy wouldn't shut up about him. Went on and on about how 'hot' he is. Cat in heat, I tell you!"

Jo loved her Gran, she truly did, and while Jo was by no means remotely promiscuous, her grandmother's old-fashioned views sometimes came across as a little, well, old-fashioned.

"Well, Gran, in all fairness he's not an unattractive man."

"Don't you start acting like a hussy too, Jolene!"

Jo sighed. "Gran, just because a woman thinks a man is attractive, that doesn't make her a hussy. Come on, you thought Pawpaw was handsome before you married him, didn't you?"

Gran's eyes misted over and a small smile tugged at her lips. "Oh, your Pawpaw was so handsome in his dress blues. He had the most beautiful eyes—that's where you get yours, you know—and the sweetest smile. Curly black hair. Such a fine figure the first time I saw him. I knew right then I was going to marry him."

Jo smiled. "You just proved my point, Gran."

The older woman shrugged and absently massaged her hip. "Always been too smart for you own damned good."

Jo leaned over and kissed her grandmother's wrinkled cheek. "And you know you wouldn't have it any other way, young woman."

Gran couldn't hide her smile. "Don't go getting a big head, young lady. Now what's for supper?"

Later that night, feeling restless and crampy and borderline maudlin, Jo climbed out of the full size bed in the room that had been her's as a teen and pulled a box from the top shelf of the closet. She set it on the floor, brushed the dust off and opened it.

Inside were high school mementos.

Her Homecoming mum from her senior year, the bells still shiny but missing a glittery letter from her name. A set of royal blue and white pom poms. The corsage Billy Walther gave her for senior prom, the roses dried and in a protective plastic case, the lilac elastic band's color still as vivid as the day he'd slid it on to her wrist. There were other pieces of flotsam and jetsam, memories of years gone by.

A newspaper article talking about how she'd made valedictorian. The notecards from her graduation speech. An old report card. Her acceptance letter to Baylor. Notes she and her best friend Jenn McDonnel had passed during algebra.

At the bottom of the box lay her senior memory book and four yearbooks. She withdrew all of them and returned to the bed, leaving the other items on the floor where she'd left them.

She wasn't sure what had her feeling nostalgic. Maybe it was being back here in Del Rio, sleeping in the same room she'd slept in as a teen far too often when things went downhill at home. Maybe it was seeing Chase tonight. Or maybe Aunt Flo was just a mean bitch who made her do crazy things.

She opened the memory book, smiling at the memories and the thoughts of an eighteen-year-old girl hell-bent on changing the world. Or at least her little corner of it.

10 Years From Now I...
Will be Oprah's go-to psychologist on all of her shows
Will own my own practice
Will be married with two kids—boy and girl—to a gorgeous man who owns his own business, makes a lot of money and will never cheat on me
Will be a great mom who never cheats on her husband or abandons her kids
Will be living somewhere super cool, like New York City or Chicago or San Francisco
Will be making a six-figure salary with no debt, a nice house and driving a BMW
Will no longer feel the need to be perfect
Will know what love really is
Will be a member of the Junior League
Will be gearing up to run for office

Funny how the only one of those things that had happened was number seven.

Jo brushed away a lone tear that rolled down her cheek, hating herself for feeling maudlin but realizing that if she was there was probably a good reason for it.

She hadn't gone on to become Oprah's therapist, and instead of opening her own practice had decided to help out high school kids. God knew as a high school counselor she certainly wasn't making a six-figure salary, her student loan debt was mind-boggling and her dreams of owning a shiny new BMW had been replaced with the reality of driving a Ford Fusion. Mr. Right still hadn't come along, and at thirty-two she was beginning to wonder if he ever would. The only guy she'd loved as an adult had been shipped off to Afghanistan, and he'd ended things before leaving the States. And she certainly wasn't a member of the Junior League or planning on running for office any time soon. As for her current town…well, she sure hadn't pictured herself back in Del Rio taking care of her grandmother, but she supposed her adopted town of Austin was pretty cool. At least that's what people and dozens of weekly Top Ten lists always told her.

Jo continued to flip through the memory book, smiling at the photos and random pieces of high school life she'd glued to the pages. Towards the back, folded up and tucked underneath a photo of her, Jenn and Chase, was a lined piece of notebook paper, which she unfolded.

Dear Chase,

I'm sorry.

I'm sorry I haven't been talking to you much. I think I've hurt your feelings. I never meant to do that.

But I can't. I can't talk to you knowing that my mom has a thing for your dad. It's weird and gross and makes me embarrassed and ashamed.

My dad doesn't care who she sleeps with. I think the whole town knows that by now. He probably doesn't care if I sleep with someone, either.

But I'm not my mom. And I can't be around you because I'm too embarrassed and hurt and afraid you'll hate me.

You're my best friend. You, Jenn and me. We're the Three Amigos. I don't want to hurt you.

I'm so sorry.

Love,

Jo

She folded the paper back up and placed it in the book again, tucked neatly under the photo of her, Jenn and Chase. They'd been going into the ninth grade, the best of friends since elementary school. Until that awful day when Jo had overheard her mom on the phone with Chase's dad. The things her mom had said had made her hot with embarrassment and shame, and even though she didn't think Chase's dad would ever cheat on his wife, Jo still felt awful and as if it was somehow her fault. If she and Chase hadn't been such good friends, her mom might not have ever met his dad. So she'd done what seemed best to a fourteen-year-old girl—she'd distanced herself from her best friend even though it had killed her.

She'd written the note to him to try to explain, but in the end had chickened out. She couldn't. She was too embarrassed and ashamed and didn't want Chase to think she was like her mom.

Instead, she'd folded the note and tucked it into her diary. That night, after eating supper with her parents and being told not to eat so much—that "thinness is perfection!"—by the woman everyone thought of as The Easy Mom, was the first time Jo made herself throw up.

Want to keep reading? Purchase *Between the Seams* now, available at the following retailers:

Amazon
Barnes & Noble
Kobo
iBooks

WANT TO TRY SOMETHING DIFFERENT FROM AUBREY?

Big Girls Need Love Too: A Novel

Are best friends always meant for each other?

After years of believing, Molly Sampson is beginning to have some doubts. Despite the fact that she's waited on her best friend Benjamin Davis for years, he's dating a woman who might as well be the definition of "perfect."

Fed up, Molly makes a New Year's resolution to fall out of love with Benjamin. Along the way she goes on some horrendous dates, quits her job, and meets Joe Connolly—a cute coworker she can't help but be drawn to.

When Benjamin and Abby break up, Molly's forced to make the toughest decision of her life—keep waiting for Benjamin, or take a leap of faith with Joe.

CHAPTER ONE

Molly Sampson mentally catalogued her flaws. She'd become more than aware of them after being her older sister's maid of honor a few months ago.

Five foot four inches. Forty-eight. Forty. Fifty-two.

Her measurements also served as the numbers to the combination lock she used when she went to the gym. She looked at them as a motivational tool.

Despite having a gym membership, she didn't know what number corresponded with her weight, since she only stepped on a scale when she had a doctor's appointment. She'd done her best to erase the memory of that particular measurement from her mind.

So really, why was she sitting here in Clicks—a smoky pool hall a mile away from her apartment—knowing good and well her best friend Benjamin intended to hook her up with some unknown guy? Especially when the population of their hometown of Waco, Texas consisted of spoiled, rich Baylor brats, men who were already married or single dads who barely managed to pay their child support—if they paid it at all.

What were you thinking, asking Benjamin to set you up on a bunch of blind dates? Molly took a sip of her Pineapple and Parrot Bay. *Oh, yeah, it was that whole trying new things, meeting new people, attempting to date resolution you made.*

She rolled her eyes. Whatever had possessed her to make a New Year's resolution like that—hell, to make one at all for the first time in her twenty-six years of life—was beyond her. But she'd only made the resolution a few days before, and she didn't like to renege on a promise, even if it was a silly one made in the early hours of January first to no one but herself.

She sneezed. Man, she knew this had been a bad idea. Not only was the cigarette smoke aggravating her allergies, but she had to have been temporarily insane to agree to meet a guy in a bar of all places. Could she get any more cliché? How romantic could neon Lone Star beer signs and Corona advertisements be anyway? Although she did have to admit that the grass-skirt wearing Spanky the Monkey— the pool hall's mascot who hung from the ceiling in the bar area—did add a certain amount of class to the establishment.

"Earth to Molly. Did you hear a word I just said?"

Her head snapped up at the sound of Benjamin's voice. He stood across the table from her, holding one of the bar's famous Big Ass Beers in his hand, with an impatient expression on his bearded face. Man, she must've really zoned out, because Benjamin rarely got impatient.

"Sorry, hon. I was thinking."

"Stop doing that."

"But thinking is good."

"Not when you're mentally cataloguing every single flaw you think you have."

She tucked a strand of dark auburn hair behind her ear. "What makes you think I was doing that?"

He raised a brown eyebrow.

"Okay, you're right. Get out of my head."

The problem with being best friends with someone you've known since junior high was that they also knew all of the things you obsessed over.

"Moll, you know I love you, but sometimes you just think way too damned much."

"I know. I know. It's just…" she paused, trying to find the right words. "I haven't been on a date in three years. I haven't kissed someone in almost two. And it's been so long since I last had sex that I'm pretty sure I've forgotten how to do it. So right now I kind of feel like I'm jumping into the deep end of the pool and all I know how to do is doggie paddle."

He took a swig of his beer before responding. "At least you know how to doggie paddle. And I know it's a big step, Molly. But don't you think it's time to get back out here in the world and try to meet someone? You're great. Any guy would be lucky to have you."

I don't want just "any guy," though. I want you.

And that was the one thing her best friend didn't know about her—that her other New Year's resolution had been to fall out of love.

ABOUT THE AUTHOR

Aubrey has been reading and writing since she was about two and a half and has been an avid romance reader since she read her first romance novel in the 6th grade. She wrote her first novel in high school. It was an ~~awful~~ imaginative historical romance that involved a cross-country trip via covered wagon, and maybe some Indians. She thinks it's still on a floppy disk somewhere (DOS computer, y'all), but can't be too sure. These days, she writes contemporary romance with a lot of humor and sass and characters that have issues.

She graduated from Seton Hill University's Writing Popular Fiction program with a Master of Arts in 2008. When she's not writing, she can be found with her husband and their two dogs at home in Austin, on their ranch in west Texas, watching a football or baseball game, or with her nose stuck in a (usually virtual) book.

Connect with Aubrey:

Website: http://aubreygross.com

You can also find me on Facebook, Instagram, and Goodreads. And while you're at my website, be sure to subscribe to my newsletter for updates on new releases!

Publisher's note: This is a work of fiction. Names, characters, places, and incidents are a product of the author's imagination. Locales and public names are sometimes used for atmospheric purposes. Any resemblance to actual people, living or dead, or to businesses, companies, events, institutions, or locales is completely coincidental.

Book layout © 2015 Indie Book Design
Book cover © 2015 by Indie Book Design

Baseball and Other Lessons/Aubrey Gross -- 2nd ed.

Epub Edition June 2015 ISBN: 978-0-9962821-2-3

Print Edition ISBN: 978-0-9962821-3-0